continued . . .

Titles by Gerry Bartlett

REAL VAMPIRES HAVE CURVES
REAL VAMPIRES LIVE LARGE
REAL VAMPIRES GET LUCKY

Real Vampires Get Lucky

GERRY BARTLETT

Good luck!
Gerry Bartlett

B
BERKLEY BOOKS, NEW YORK

THE BERKLEY PUBLISHING GROUP
Published by the Penguin Group
Penguin Group (USA) Inc.
375 Hudson Street, New York, New York 10014, USA
Penguin Group (Canada), 90 Eglinton Avenue East, Suite 700, Toronto, Ontario M4P 2Y3, Canada
(a division of Pearson Penguin Canada Inc.)
Penguin Books Ltd., 80 Strand, London WC2R 0RL, England
Penguin Group Ireland, 25 St. Stephen's Green, Dublin 2, Ireland (a division of Penguin Books Ltd.)
Penguin Group (Australia), 250 Camberwell Road, Camberwell, Victoria 3124, Australia
(a division of Pearson Australia Group Pty. Ltd.)
Penguin Books India Pvt. Ltd., 11 Community Centre, Panchsheel Park, New Delhi—110 017, India
Penguin Group (NZ), 67 Apollo Drive, Rosedale, North Shore 0632, New Zealand
(a division of Pearson New Zealand Ltd.)
Penguin Books (South Africa) (Pty.) Ltd., 24 Sturdee Avenue, Rosebank, Johannesburg 2196,
South Africa

Penguin Books Ltd., Registered Offices: 80 Strand, London WC2R 0RL, England

This is an original publication of The Berkley Publishing Group.

First edition: June 2008

Library of Congress Cataloging-in-Publication Data

Bartlett, Gerry.
    Real vampires get lucky / Gerry Bartlett.—1st ed.
        p.   cm.
    ISBN 978-0-425-22154-9
    1. Saint Clair, Glory (Fictitious character)—Fiction.   2. Vampires—Fiction.   3. Children of gangsters—Fiction.   I. Title.

    PS3602.A83945R425 2007
    813'.6—dc22   2008008227

PRINTED IN THE UNITED STATES OF AMERICA

10 9 8 7 6 5 4 3 2 1

This book is dedicated to
Donna Maloy,
a great writer and a great friend.

One

"I smell blood." The yummy scent hit me like a whiff of Coco at the perfume counter.

"You're dreamin', Blondie. Quit thinkin' with your fangs and grab those bags of Christmas lights." Valdez hummed "Deck the Halls" while he hopped out of my aging Suburban.

"I'm serious, Valdez. Blood." I sniffed the air again. "Take a whiff. B positive. Lots of it."

Valdez stuck his nose in the air, his tail brushing my leg. *"You're right. Get in the car and lock yourself in. I'm gonna investigate."* He was suddenly all business, his growl making even my nerves twitch.

Valdez looks like a dog, but he's my bodyguard, a shapeshifter with a little something extra I've never quite figured out. Trust me, we've been together long enough for him to know I wasn't going to just sit in the car checking my manicure. I grabbed Valdez's collar.

"Wait a sec, Terminator. You took an arrow in the hip back here. Remember? Be careful."

He jerked away from me, almost knocking me on my

butt. Valdez in protector mode is just about unstoppable. *"Flesh wound. But that doesn't mean this isn't still a prime spot for an ambush."* He nodded toward the security lights at the back of the building. Out again. *"Next time park on the street."*

"Shut up, Valdez. Someone's bleeding out." I crept around the car and toward the Dumpster a few feet away. I know blood and this was fresh, from someone close who was still alive.

"Hey, you creeps! We've called the cops. If you think you can attack us, you're S.O.L.," Valdez shouted. He speaks in my mind, but anyone within range can hear him too. *"My boss has a big gun."*

We both stopped and listened. No running footsteps. A good sign. Because of course I didn't have a big gun. I'm vampire, for crying out loud. I've got *skills*. But, wait, I did hear something. Gurgling. Someone gasping their last breath. I hurried around the Dumpster.

A woman lay on her back, her throat torn open. "A vampire did this."

"You sure?" Valdez wasn't even looking at her. He was too busy scanning the area in case whoever had done this was still around.

"Yeah, I'm sure. I've seen this type of wound more times than I can count." And it never got any easier. I shot up an arrow prayer for the victim's soul. Shocked a vampire prays? Get over it. Not all vamps are demons from hell. But whoever had done this had a roasting pan with their name on it waiting for them. "Check out her neck, Valdez."

"I'm not checking out squat. I'm in defense mode. That asshole could come back, you know."

I inhaled. Except for the previously mentioned blood smell, there was just a tinge of another vampire in the air. "Whoever did this is long gone." I shook my head. What kind of out-of-control vampire had found it necessary to kill like this? Did we have another rogue killing people here in

Austin for sport? And her attacker obviously had a screw loose, letting perfectly fine B positive leak all over the concrete instead of draining the lady dry. Why? I'd think about that later.

"Save her, Blondie. Can't you see she's still breathing?" Valdez had finally focused on her. *"Heal her like you healed me. I'm gonna take a better look around."*

He was right. The lady wasn't dead yet, but she was a breath or two away from it. I wished . . . Heal her. Okay, I could sure as hell try. I stepped around a pool of blood, wrapped my hands around her throat and "saw" the mangled flesh become whole again. Remember those skills? The edges slowly sealed under my fingers until the wound finally quit seeping. But it would take more than a little hands-on healing to keep this woman alive. I breathed in the cold night air. There was something familiar . . .

Valdez trotted up to check out the woman again. *"All clear. You're right. Whoever did this took off."* He nosed her long dark hair aside. *"Throat looks good."*

"She's lost too much blood, Valdez. Calling 911 would do nothing except get the police here to investigate." The paranormal community in Austin keeps a low profile. Cops are always a last resort. I pulled out my cell phone anyway. It was her best shot at survival.

"Wait. This scene already looks suspicious since the wound's healed and there's all this blood. I say she's too far gone for paramedics to save. What're ya gonna do about it?" He gave me a long look.

"I'm sorry, but I guess we got here too late." I wasn't about to admit that I'd already realized there was only one way to keep this woman from dying.

"Don't be cute with me. You know what you have to do if you don't want her permanently dead. Turn her, Blondie. Make her vampire."

"No freakin' way." I edged back and almost stepped on the woman's fabulous Hermès Birkin bag. Someone had dumped the contents, emptied a nice Gucci wallet and then tossed it all aside a few feet away from the blood. Stupid thief. Unless this woman carried around bags of diamonds or cash, the purse itself was probably worth more than whatever had been inside.

"Yes freakin' way. I've hung around you long enough to recognize that the lady had great and expensive taste. Like that purse near your feet. You gonna just let her die?"

I jerked my gaze away from the woman's barely moving chest. It *was* an awesome bag, but there was something even more interesting lying next to it.

"Check this out." I picked up a knife covered in blood. One sniff and I knew this lady had gotten her own licks in. Definitely vamp blood on the blade. I looked at the woman with new respect. Great taste and she knew how to use a weapon. I really *didn't* want her to die. I grabbed a pack of tissues and wiped off my hands.

"Seriously, Glory. You gonna do something or just stand around and watch her give up the ghost?"

"I don't turn mortals into vampires. Never have. Never will." I'd had a few hundred years of regrets about my own change and I'd vowed never to make that decision for anyone. The very thought made me want to run like hell. Forget I'd ever seen—

"I get it. Turning somebody vampire is a big deal. But I know you, Glory. You're not cold enough to just walk away." Valdez paced around the woman, sniffing at her brown leather Bottega Veneta boots tucked into skinny jeans. *"If you can't do it, call Flo. She'll do it. And, damn it, hurry."*

"Flo. Good idea." I flipped open my cell and hit speed dial. My roommate, Florence da Vinci, was probably right upstairs in the apartment we shared. She could zap down here and . . . Voice mail.

"Try Blade."

Jeremy Blade. My sometime lover, friend and the hunky Highlander who'd made me vampire way back in the day when my brain had been fogged by lust. Speed dial actually got him.

"Jerry, oh God, Jerry, I need your help." I really felt bad about the woman. She couldn't even moan, but I could hear her heart slowing, barely beating. Then there was just the whisper of her breath, a death rattle. I patted her on the shoulder. "Hang on, honey. Help is on the way." Or I sure as hell hoped so.

"Gloriana. What's the matter? Are you hurt?"

"Not hurt, but freaking out. I found a woman. She's dying, bleeding out because a vampire . . . Never mind the details. Can you come to the alley behind my shop? Like five minutes ago?"

"I'm in Louisiana, sweetheart. Closing on the sale of my casino here." Jerry sighed. "You want to save her, you've got to turn her, Gloriana."

"You know I don't—" I cringed when I heard the woman gasp what had to be her last breath. Valdez just looked at me, like I was a spineless coward if I didn't take care of this. Oh, crap. Turning somebody vampire . . . I mean, can you blame me? We're talking a permanent condition with, trust me, *lots* of complications. I'd never wanted to be responsible for someone else. And—

"Gloriana, keep hesitating and you won't have to do this."

"Okay, okay. Damn it, Jerry, tell me what to do."

"Good girl. Now drain her first. Completely. To the point of death."

"Not a problem. She's about there now." I pulled my winter white pencil skirt up to my thighs before I stepped gingerly into the huge pool of blood under the woman's body and squatted beside her. Yeah, yeah, I know. But the skirt was vintage Chanel and if you've ever tried to get blood out of wool, you get it.

"Make sure, Glory. Can you use her neck?"

"Don't think so. I healed her, but it's too soon to mess

with it. You should see the really wicked knife next to her body. This lady didn't go down easy."

"Whoever did this could come back. Forget the woman. Get the hell out of there."

Okay, a minute ago I'd have jumped on an excuse like that. But there was the old "Glory's a helpless female" tone in Jerry's voice and, sorry, but I'm *not* helpless.

"The alley's clear. Valdez is on guard duty. I started this, so I'll damn well finish it. I'll try her wrist." I held the phone with one hand and tuned out Jerry's rant about my wrong-headedness. I picked up the woman's wrist. It was cool, limp, lifeless. Maybe I was too late.

Now I felt really bad. If Flo or Jerry had found the body, this lady would be upstairs by now, ready for her vampire initiation. I ran my tongue over my fangs. They'd been ready for action since the first whiff of fresh blood. I bit into a sad excuse for a vein. Pitifully little action, then zilch. Her skin felt cold and I pulled back. "She's drained dry, Jerry, now what?"

"Force her to drink from you. Cut your wrist and put it to her lips. You should have learned this long ago, Gloriana."

"I don't think so. I wish I wasn't learning it now." I snatched up the knife, slashed it across my wrist and didn't even wince—thank you very much. I held the welling cut to the lady's blue lips. Blue under Mac's Lady Danger lipstick. She did have great taste. I took a second to mourn her blood-soaked suede coat with the lynx collar. That coat would have brought big bucks in my shop, Vintage Vamp's Emporium, which was steps away from us, on the ground floor of my apartment building.

Maybe you're wondering how I could be so . . . detached while squatting in a pool of blood with a dying woman dangling from my wrist. Hey, I've had four hundred plus years on this planet. I could tell you stories . . . Never mind. At least I'd just done all I could do to save her. And if she didn't

make it? Then I wouldn't have brought a new vampire into
the world, which was a good thing actually.

"Jerry, she's not drinking." Not breathing either. Detached? Who the hell was I kidding? I couldn't just let another human *die*. Yep, *another* human. I may be an immortal
with a liquid diet, but I'll never accept the fact that I'm not
human too, damn it.

Unfortunately, I'd made a big deal out of never wanting
to turn anyone. So now it was amateur hour. Jeez, sometimes I can be so *clueless*. I should have at least learned the
basics of this thing. In case of emergency. Like now.

"What else can I do?" I blinked back tears and told myself I'd have the meltdown later. The woman's neck was
looking good. But with all that blood loss, she was knocking on Heaven's door and the Almighty was just about to
roll out the welcome mat. Damn it, I *had* to save her.

"Force her, Glory. Pry open her lips and drip your blood
down her throat. Once she swallows even a bit, she'll start to
revive." Jerry's calm voice settled me down a little. Hell, of
course he was calm. He wasn't here hip deep in blood with
the Grim Reaper staring over his shoulder.

But I knew from experience that vamp blood is powerful
stuff. I laid the phone in a dry spot on the concrete and went
to work. "Come on, honey. This is delicious high-octane vampire blood. One sip and your motor will be purring again."
I glanced at Valdez. He'd pawed through the contents of her
purse and stared down at a New York driver's license.
"What's her name, Valdez? Maybe she'll respond to that."

He snorted and looked at me, his dark eyes gleaming in
his furry face. *"You're not going to believe it, Glory. Her name's
Lucky."*

Two

"Quit playing, I'm serious." Had she swallowed yet? I stroked her throat, desperate to coax down a drop.

"So am I. See for yourself." He nosed it over to me and I glanced at it.

Lucky Carver. Hmm. I'd taken her for midthirties, max, but the DMV put her at close to fifty.

"Come on, Lucky. Live up to your name. Drink and you'll be good as new. No, better." Hey, the truth. Well, in a lot of ways. I pulled open her coat. High quality red cashmere sweater. Her whole outfit cost more than a year's worth of Fangtastic, my blood substitute of choice lately. The woman obviously had her priorities.

"I don't think she's gonna make it." Valdez pushed a tube of mascara across the concrete.

"I started this, I'll damn well finish it." I glanced at my cell phone, sure Jerry could hear me. He probably expected me to wimp out on this turning thing. He knew how against the whole concept I'd been for the last, oh, four centuries. Well, I'd fooled him recently when I'd finally developed some of my vamp powers. If I could pull this off, he'd be blown away. And blowing Jerry (hey, you know what I mean) is one of the things that keeps me going and going and . . .

"Lucky, you've got to drink or you'll miss the shoe sale at Nordstrom's. Boots half price." Aha! Her throat worked against my fingertips. Obviously I'd found the key to her will to live. A sigh, then another swallow until Lucky suddenly latched on to my wrist with both hands, sucking like my blood was liquid Godiva.

"Whoa, lady. Leave me enough to get upstairs, will you?" I pried my wrist from her grip and saw her cheeks had turned pink. Heartbeat had picked up, breathing too. Her eyelids fluttered, then I was staring down into hazel eyes with pretty flecks of gold, tattooed eyeliner setting off long dark lashes.

I could tell the moment the lady snapped to the reality of lying on cold concrete in a pool of her own blood with a dog and a blond, blue-eyed twentysomething hottie (me, of course) staring down at her. I grinned, pretty jazzed that I'd brought her back from the brink. Next thing I knew Lucky had a knife at my throat.

"Hey, I just saved your sorry butt." I used my vamp speed to jump out of reach. "How about a little gratitude, Lucky?"

"I saw your fangs. Listen, you blood-sucking bitch, you shoulda finished what you started because I'll see you staked out at high noon for this." She tried to sit up, then fell back.

"*I* didn't tear open your throat, lady. Did you hear me? I *saved* you."

Lucky closed her eyes and gripped her knife. I could practically see the wheels turning when her eyes popped open again. "How do you know my name?"

I kicked her driver's license toward her. "I can read. You know, you look really good for a woman your age."

Lucky gasped and tears filled her eyes. "You. Saw. My.

Age?" She snatched up the license and stuffed it into her bra. "You tell anyone, anyone, and it'll be high noon on an anthill with a honey facial, vampire."

"Leave her here, Glory. Let her see who does what when the sun comes up." Valdez pressed against my leg and growled. *"You should be kissing Glory's feet, lady. You were on a slippery slope toward the hereafter when we found you."*

Lucky's mouth dropped open. "What kind of paranormal freak show is this? A vampire with a talking dog for a sidekick?" She finally managed to sit up. "Who did this?" She looked at the pool of blood, then down at her ruined coat. "You say you didn't—"

"No, I didn't. But some vampire did." My wrist was already healing, so I picked up her purse and stroked the supple tan leather. "I'd say it was a clueless guy. No self-respecting female vamp would leave this treasure lying inches from blood spatter."

"You're right about that." Lucky looked around. "Where's Brittany?"

"Who?" I watched the woman slip her knife into her boot.

A knife in her boot. And the other knife still on the concrete next to her.

I brushed it with my foot. "This yours too?"

"Yeah. A lot of good it did me." She grabbed it, made a face, then wiped it on her coat. "I'd like to know where the hell Brittany is."

Brittany. Oookay. The name conjured up an image of a pop star with toothpick arms and lips that absorbed a gallon of lip gloss a week.

"We found you alone, bleeding out. Maybe your bud Brittany went somewhere to check her, um, lipstick. Unless *she's* vampire and decided to off her BFF."

"She's not my friend, she's my bodyguard. And a shifter not a vampire." Lucky bit her lip. "I trusted her. I didn't think— Aw shit." She rubbed her forehead, and a tear trickled down her cheek.

"I'm taking another look around. Just in case . . ." Valdez took off down the alley.

"You say a vampire tried to take me out? Guess I should have been carrying a stake in my other boot."

I shuddered and put a hand over my heart. The word "stake" does that to me. "You don't seem surprised by the fact that vampires and dogs with special gifts"—I looked over to where Valdez circled another parked car—"even exist. And you have a shape-shifter for a bodyguard. Who or what are *you*?" I sniffed but all I smelled was that delicious blood congealing on the concrete.

"Human and don't you forget it." She had her knife out again. "My family's done business with vampires, shifters and weres for decades." She narrowed her gaze. "Give me my purse."

"Would it kill you to say 'please'?" I dangled the bag over a puddle. Not that I'd ever desecrate a work of art like that, but, as a threat, it worked like a charm.

"I'm . . . sorry." She glanced down at her ruined coat, then ran a hand over her throat, obviously surprised when it came away without fresh blood on it. "I'm still out of it, I guess. I don't remember a thing about the attack. One minute Brit and I are here talking about a call I got. Then . . ." She sighed and plucked that pack of tissues out of the mess. She went to work on cleaning her bloodstained hands. "You healed me?" She checked me out like I'd never have the goods to do such a thing. "Or did you have help?" Now she examined Valdez, who'd trotted up to stand next to me.

"I did it. Just one of my many talents." No way was I giving the V-man credit for this. Even if he *had* saved my life more than once. His gig as my bodyguard was payback to Jerry for something neither of them would discuss.

It had been too long since my own change to remember how a brand-new vampire felt, and the lady had taken a pretty hard hit what with the ripped open throat and all. So her hands were shaking when she tossed the dirty tissues aside.

"My coat is ruined. I've been attacked by one vampire and another one knows how old I am." She sighed and rubbed her forehead. "I feel like shit and obviously look like it too."

I took pity and dropped her purse in her lap. "Hey, you're alive." Sort of.

"Uh, Glory. Blade's still on the phone." Valdez never took his eyes off Lucky when she picked up her knife again. She carefully wiped it on a tissue and closed it with a snap.

"Jerry!" I grabbed the phone. "Did you hear? I did it! I saved her life."

"Damn it, Glory. What took you so long?"

"Well, excuse me, but I was busy, what with the blood and the explanations." I watched Lucky rummage through her purse. Looking for another weapon? Valdez growled a warning and showed some teeth. I gave him an ear rub.

"She's awake? How does she look?"

"Pretty good, considering. Valdez and I are finished. We were just about to leave Miss Gratitude here and head upstairs."

"Finished?" Jerry chuckled. "Honey, you've barely started. Take your new vampire upstairs with you. You know how this works."

"Fortunately, since this is a new gig for me, no, I don't." I had a queasy feeling that I really didn't want to hear this.

"You made her, now you've got to show her the ropes."

Lucky reached for her wallet and picked up her scattered credit cards. When she had all her cards in a row, she muttered about a missing gold card then looked at me like maybe *I'd* taken it.

"Ropes?" Now I was pissed. "The only rope I want to show this ungrateful bitch is a noose for her scrawny neck." I picked up a tube of Mac's Russian Red and stuck it in my coat pocket.

"She's your responsibility, sweetheart. Sorry, but you owe it to her to take her on."

"This is why I never turned anyone before." Jerry had done this for me. But we'd been heavy duty lovers back in the day. We'd needed to stay together, for the hot sex if nothing else.

"It doesn't have to be forever, Gloriana, just until she can deal with her new situation on her own."

Hmm. So why did Jerry still insist on keeping tabs on me with the whole bodyguard bit? Could it be love? He said so, but then eternity loomed, and to be tied to the same sixteenth-century male . . .

"Glory, you're not going to just leave her there, are you?"

"Okay, okay. I know what I have to do." Sort of. "Call me, Jerry, when you get back to town." I hung up and put my hand on Valdez's collar when he growled again. Lucky struggled to her feet, cursing when she slipped in her own blood and stained her boots. I resisted the urge to give her a hand, sure she'd just slap it away.

She started collecting her scattered treasures. An antique hand mirror had survived without a crack. A BlackBerry and enough cosmetics to open a stall at a flea market were tossed into her bag. She stared at her cell phone for a minute, obviously still confused despite her tough talk.

"Is there anyone you want to call? Like a husband? That family of yours? Cops?" I was obviously going to be stuck with the woman. It couldn't hurt to make nice. Her fingers were bare, but that didn't mean the vamp who'd torn out her throat hadn't lifted a few baubles as a souvenir, including a wedding ring. "Anything missing besides your credit card?"

She reached up and felt her earlobes. "Damn it, those were my favorite two carat studs." She looked at my David Yurman knockoffs and sniffed, "No husband this decade. I'm definitely not calling my family. And no cops. I'll get my stuff back, *my* way." She wobbled on her high-heeled boots.

"I feel weird. What exactly did you do to me?" Her eyes rolled and I grabbed her before she hit the ground. Out cold.

I pulled her coat off and tossed it next to the door to collect later. Then I slung her over my shoulder and stuck her purse and my own sad-looking handbag on my other shoulder. I punched in the security code on the keypad beside the back door to my apartment building.

"Valdez, drag that coat inside, then pick up the bags of Christmas lights in your teeth and let's get upstairs. This woman's pretty small, but her purse weighs a ton." Small like in a size six to my ten, okay, twelve. I could feel muscular legs as I held on to her. She was in shape. Nice way to be stuck forever. Not like I'd been on the big V-day with my weakness for roast beef and lemon tarts.

Valdez dragged the coat across the threshold, then grabbed the plastic bags and trotted inside while I held open the door. He headed up the stairs first, like he usually did, to make sure the coast was clear. I have a few enemies and seemed to be making more by the day, despite the fact that I'm really a very nice person. I have lots of friends too. Which is one reason I'm determined to stay in Austin and make a go of my vintage-clothing store. The paranormal community here is great, for the most part.

I glanced over my shoulder at Lucky's pale face. Maybe somebody with a grudge had followed her here from New York. What was she doing in Texas anyway? And in the alley behind my store? It wasn't exactly on the Austin highlights tour.

A woof from Valdez and I headed up. I had lots of questions and, until Lucky woke up and lost the attitude, I wasn't getting any answers. I have vamp strength and could have carried Lucky for miles and not broken a sweat. But, damn it, her bloody boot was bumping against my vintage wool yellow and white houndstooth swing coat. I prayed a dry cleaner could get the blood out. Stupid. I should have shucked the coat, locked it in the car, then picked her up.

Cursing my lack of planning, I juggled my load to unlock the dead bolt. I flung open the apartment door and dumped Lucky—okay, I was gentle—on the couch while Valdez dragged in the bags of Christmas lights. Forget decking the halls tonight. I headed to the kitchen and a bottle of A-positive Fangtastic. Smelling Lucky's blood and the tiny sip I'd taken had given me a raging thirst. I stood over her and swigged straight from the bottle. Whoa. I leaned down and sniffed. Oh, God. Lucky smelled a lot like me. How creepy was that? I dragged off my coat, moaned at the sight of a smear across the sleeve and looked at the clock.

A few minutes until dawn. No wonder my thoughts were scattered and I was barely able to keep my eyes open. I pulled Lucky's boots off, checking out the size (too small for me, but perfect for my roomie), then hustled downstairs for her coat. I dropped it in a plastic garbage bag and set it by the door. I did know a good dry cleaner. I wasn't going to give up on a designer label without a fight.

Lucky was going to sleep like the dead until sunset anyway, but I tried to make her comfortable, even tossing a throw over her. Then I headed for my own bed. Valdez waited outside my closed door while I undressed and put on a comfy nightgown. When I let him in, he settled on the foot of my bed for guard duty during the vulnerable daylight hours.

I closed my eyes. Lucky. She had a hell of a surprise coming when she woke. And I'd have to give her the gory details about her new life or death or whatever. I jumped up, ran back to her side and dug into her purse until I found her knife, then pulled the other one from a clever scabbard stitched into the side of her right boot. I stuck both knives on a shelf behind a book, *How to Dress Ten Pounds Thinner*, then fell into bed again.

Lucky had sure lived up to her name tonight. If I hadn't come along when I did . . . But would she be grateful now that she was one of the undead?

Me, I wasn't feeling so lucky. My roommate hadn't come home before dawn. This wasn't unusual, but she hadn't left a message on the answering machine. We'd agreed to check in with each other after some near misses for both of us. Believe it or not, there are some people who don't appreciate our fashion sense and sparkling personalities. So we keep tabs on each other.

I hoped Flo was okay. I hoped *I* was okay. Responsible for a new vampire. Crap.

Three

Screams, no, make that shrieks, jerked me from a sound sleep. I nudged Valdez with my foot.

"Sounds like our guest just woke up."

"And she's freaking out." Valdez yawned and jumped off the bed. *"Want me to check on her?"*

"My vampire, my problem. But thanks. I wonder how much she remembers about last night." I rolled out of bed and reached for the red robe I'd tossed on a chair the night before.

"Careful, Blondie. Sounds like she's about to blow. I'll be ready to move in if she acts ungrateful." Valdez stepped back when I opened the door. Jeez. I winced as the noise ramped up another octave.

"Hey, hey, calm down." I stalked into the living room. I don't know what I expected. Maybe that she'd seen the empty Fangtastic bottle with a half inch of what looked an awful lot like blood (because it was, of course, though a synthetic variety). Or that she'd woken up in a strange place and her favorite boots weren't on her feet.

Oh, no. Instead, Lucky, who wasn't feeling so fortunate, stared into the silver hand mirror she'd had tucked into her purse.

"What's wrong with me? Why can't I . . . see myself?" She looked up, her eyes swimming in tears. "And where am I?"

"Take a breath. Try to relax. You're in my apartment. I'll answer all your questions in a minute." I snatched up the mirror, took a second to admire the delicately engraved C on the back that told me this must be a family heirloom, then set it on the coffee table and headed for the kitchen. I'm not too good without my evening jolt of Fangtastic. And I definitely needed something before I dealt with all the upcoming drama.

"Where are you going?" Lucky leaped up and grabbed my arm. She swayed then seemed to rally, her French-manicured fingernails digging in.

"The kitchen. For a bottle of breakfast. You probably need one too." I pushed down an uncharitable thought that my stash of the expensive stuff wasn't going to last long with a houseguest scarfing it down. Would it be tacky to ask for a donation? I eyed her fabulous Birkin bag. If she'd give me that beauty, I'd happily keep her swimming in Fangtastic.

"A liquid breakfast? Are you an alcoholic or something? I usually have stone cut oatmeal, skim milk with a few blueberries for the antioxidants, of course, and coffee, black."

"Of course. Gee, let me write down your order." I looked at her nails doing a number on my vintage quilted robe. At least she'd gone in for a blunt tip or I'd have a hole in the nylon.

She took the hint and released me. "Sorry." She ran a hand through her hair.

"It's okay. You're confused. Sit." Now I could see she had subtle highlights—brown, mahogany, a touch of copper. That cut and color must have cost her a fortune. New York. A fortune and a half.

"I'm feeling weird and I can't remember how I got"—she swept a glance around my admittedly shabby digs—"here. Who the hell are you anyway?"

I sighed, bit back a chorus of "Why me?"s and guided her back to the couch. "Gloriana St. Clair. Call me Glory. I brought you here last night. This is my apartment. It's right upstairs from where I found you."

"Last night? You . . . *found* me?" Lucky dug into her purse and pulled out her BlackBerry. Her hands shook as she punched through it. "Yeah, right. I'm in Austin. Texas."

I checked the ticking kitty clock I'd brought home just because Valdez hated it. I had about thirty minutes before I was supposed to take over from the day help in my shop. I needed to throw myself into something fabulous and get downstairs. That is, if I could figure out what to do with Lucky.

Uh. Oh.

Lucky had picked up her mirror again, hyperventilating between eye rubs. She sobbed and leaped off the couch again.

"Tell me why—" She gasped and her eyes rolled.

Swell. Out like a light. I hoped this wasn't going to become a habit. Swooning is so nineteenth century. I dragged her back to the couch, then headed for the kitchen again. Ah. Fangtastic. I took the first swallow of the night and sighed, grateful for the surge of energy. Then I sat across from Lucky and watched her stir to life again.

"Feeling any better?"

Lucky stared up at the ceiling. "I feel like shit." She turned her head, watched me take another swallow and wrinkled her nose. "What the hell are you drinking? It looks like—"

"Blood?" I smiled and saw her eyes widen. Oh, yeah. My fangs were out. "It is. I'm vampire, Lucky. You told me last night you were down with that. Which is cool." And strange. But I kept that to myself.

"I . . . I don't remember." She sat up, really pale and still very shaky. "But I know some vampires. Clients. I sure don't pal around with them. They give me the creeps, always staring at my neck like I stare at a chilled bottle of Grey Goose." She bit her lip. "Sorry. I didn't mean . . ." She put her hand to her throat. "Thanks for letting me crash on your couch."

"This isn't a slumber party, Lucky. Last night you were bleeding out. There was only one way to save you." Boy, did I hate this. My next words would change her world forever. And I do mean *forever*.

She jumped when Valdez sat down next to her feet and looked up with a doggy grin.

"It was great. Blondie was a hero, otherwise you'd be dead meat, sister."

"I was bleeding out?" She frowned at Valdez, not at all surprised by a talking dog. Interesting.

"I'd say someone wanted you dead, Lucky."

She stared at me. "But I'm not. You . . ."

"I healed your wound and brought you upstairs." Okay, so I left out a major detail. Lucky would figure things out soon enough.

"Wow. Thanks." Lucky shook her head. "God, I have got to slow down. I mean, what was I thinking? Meeting a client at three in the morning in an alley in Austin freaking Texas?" She put her head in her hands. "I feel strange." She opened her eyes. "You have any Valium on you?"

"Drugs won't cure what ails you." I gave Valdez a look that sent him ambling to the door. He stopped for a sniff at Lucky's really cute boots and pretended to be thinking about taking a whiz on them.

Lucky screamed an obscenity and lunged. When she'd settled on the couch again, she clutched the boots to her chest.

"Shape-shifter?" She gave Valdez a hard look when he grinned. "My client last night was a shifter. A damned female were-cat. But she knew my rules. I don't do business with animals. A shifter who wants to deal with me does it in person, if you know what I mean." She examined her boots for damage. "Damn it, there's blood on the toe. Whoever the hell did this is gonna pay." She glared at me, but her paper-white face and trembling lips ruined the effect. She looked like she was about to faint again.

"Yeah, whoever did this *should* pay. But please remember that I'm not the bad guy." Female were-cat. It couldn't be— Lucky looked like she was about to crash again. I jumped up and grabbed another bottle of Fangtastic out of the fridge. Maybe I should nuke it. Most vampires like it hot, but I spent a long time in Vegas. So I developed a taste for it cold. Whatever. I twisted off the top and handed it to Lucky.

"Drink. This will make you feel better. Stronger physically anyway."

Lucky put the boots next to her and sniffed the bottle. "Did someone *die* for this?"

"Gee, I don't think so." I saw her horrified look and took pity. "It's a synthetic. I order it on the Internet. I can't afford the really exotic blood types, but A positive isn't too bad."

Lucky put the bottle on the table with a thump. "Yeah, I'm *positive* I can't drink this shit. I'm queasy." She pressed a shaky hand to her flat (don't you hate her?) stomach. "Come on, Gladys. The shifter here must eat. Don't you at least have a few crackers?"

"Glory." I polished off my own Fangtastic and sat across from her again. Time for a reality check. I picked up the hand mirror and aimed it at her face. "Remember how you couldn't see yourself a few minutes ago? Sorry, hon. News flash. There was only one way to save you last night. I had to turn you. You are now a gen-u-ine vampire."

Here came the meltdown. Ear-piercing shrieks, then sobs and wails. I felt her pain, even had to blink back a tear or two of my own. Hey, I'd *chosen* the vamp thing and still had a bucket full of regrets. Finally, she sniffled and groped inside her boot.

"Looking for your knives?"

"Where are they? Give them to me." She teared up when I shook my head, then slumped and grabbed the mirror. "Nobody home. Damn it to hell! How will I do my hair, my *makeup*?" She cried noisy sobs into her boots.

"I'm sorry, Lucky. Really." I handed her the bottle of Fangtastic again. "Drink. I know it's not black coffee, but you'll get the same kick. And it looks like you need it."

"I need *something*." She sniffled, then ventured a sip. She took another swallow, then another until the bottle was half-empty. A ladylike burp behind her hand and she was looking better. "Not exactly the Kona blend I prefer, uh, preferred." She sobbed again. "This can't be happening. No coffee, or, or chocolate!" She looked wildly around the room, like maybe somebody would jump out of the bedroom and shout "April Fool." No such luck.

"You just drank what passes for blood around here. Run your tongue over your teeth."

"Oh, my God! Fangs! But I paid a fortune for bonding." She poked a finger in her mouth and winced. "Last week I had my teeth whitened. Laser." She snarled tentatively and I could see she did have some pretty choppers.

"The fangs only come out when you're around blood or get really, uh, excited." Like when you want to kill someone, or at least take them down a pint. Or when you're aroused. But I was so not going there. "And good news. You're stuck now, for, uh, eternity with freshly whitened teeth." I looked her over. "I'd kill for your figure."

Her eyes bugged. "Have you? Killed, I mean?"

I took a moment to soul search. There'd been a few acts of self-defense back in the day and then there'd been some really desperate times, before the synthetic came along. Hey, when you're crazed by bloodlust . . . Nope. My dirty laundry was staying in my personal hamper.

"I'm civilized, Lucky. Not dangerous unless you get between me and the last pair of half-price Jimmy Choos in my size."

She actually managed a tiny smile. "My nerves are a little ragged or I wouldn't ask such a personal question." The smile disappeared. "We all have our little secrets. And a vampire . . ." She shrugged. "You do what you've got to do to stay alive, I guess."

Now I was alarmed. Had I given the big V to a serial killer? "You mentioned a bodyguard last night. What's that about? That purse is worth a fortune, but going around with a bodyguard seems a little extreme."

"Brittany. She should be here. And not just to guard my purse. She's not allowed to leave my side when I'm on assignment."

"Assignment?"

"Never mind. She obviously cut and run instead of defending me from whoever did this." Lucky stroked her throat. "I'll make her regret it. I'll rip out *her* throat. She'll be my first, er, victim."

There was no mistaking the look in Lucky's eyes now. Scary. And trust me, I've seen some really badass people in my day. "Chill out, Lucky. There will be no throat ripping. The vampires in Austin don't appreciate anything that draws attention to us."

"So I'll take her out somewhere else." Lucky pulled a nail file out of her bag and went to work on her manicure. "Jeez, look at this. I bet I fought like hell. Check out the damage to these tips."

"You obviously didn't go down easily. You even had a bloody knife next to you." I was definitely going to watch her carefully. Just because I admired Lucky's taste in accessories didn't mean she wasn't bad news.

"Ha! I hope I put a serious hurt on that throat-ripping bastard." She looked at me with narrowed eyes. "Are we going hunting later? Surely we don't just drink this stuff out of a bottle."

"Damn right we do. No hunting humans."

"Aw, come on, girlfriend. You gonna tell me you never" —she winked—"take a sip of the real thing?"

I'd like to deny it, but even I'm not immune to the lure of a hot body with good quality AB negative pulsing through it. I managed to shrug, like it was no big deal. "Hey, of course you can go to the source occasionally. But it's dangerous. You could get caught, and you don't want to be outed as a vampire. Trust me on that. If you're discreet and wipe out the mortal's memory afterward . . ." Oh, great. Lucky was touching her tongue to her fangs like she couldn't wait to give them a test drive.

I grabbed her arm and shook it. "Don't even think about going out on your own. Give me time to clue you in."

"I'm an adult, Gina. Just tell me the essentials, I'm sure I can figure out the rest." There went the tongue to the fangs again.

"Start by figuring out my name. It's Gloriana, Glory to my friends, and it remains to be seen if you're going to qualify."

Lucky gave me a hard look. "You don't have to be a bitch about it."

"Just remember that you're a newbie in this world. You don't make a move without me. Until I think you're ready, we're going to be joined at the hip." Maybe I was being a little harsh. Lucky was probably still in shock. Waking up as a vampire would do that to you. I put my hand on her shoulder and gave it a warning squeeze. "Give me time to teach you what you need to know."

"Just give me the short version. I've got . . . commitments."

"Forget them. This is the first day of the rest of your life."

She tried to shrug off my hand, but I wasn't letting go until she took me seriously.

"Ow! Lighten up, would you?" She smiled. "You don't want to make me mad, sweetheart. I work out five days a week with Umberto, my trainer. He's a Nazi bitch, but he keeps me in shape. And then there's the kickboxing and running. I'm up to six miles a day." She looked me over then ran her hands down her slim thighs. "No offense, but I'm sure I could kick your ass."

Valdez woofed and grinned at me. Oh, yeah, he was all about a little girl-on-girl wrestling. All we needed were bikinis and mud, and we'd be a guy's fantasy come true.

"Trust me. I'm tougher than I look." My jaw ached from grinding my teeth. No wonder she'd been attacked in an alley. Miss Congeniality she wasn't. I fought a serious urge to toss her skinny ass across the room, just to prove I could. I may look soft, curvy and about as dangerous as a plus-size lingerie model, but I *am* strong. Four hundred years of stored power strong. It would have been nice if I'd paid more attention to my body before I'd taken my own vampire turn. But back in the early sixteen hundreds women didn't run *anywhere*.

Lucky sniffed and went back to filing her nails, obviously unconvinced she couldn't take me, but smart enough to re-alize she wasn't exactly recovered from her near-death experience.

"I can hook you up with some good exercise videos. There really is hope for those thighs." Lucky picked up her bottle of Fangtastic and took another swallow.

"You are too kind." Had I saved her just so I could kill her? I counted to ten, then thirty. "No, no hope for these." I sat down and plucked at the robe that I'd thought disguised my figure flaws. "When you're turned vampire, you're stuck. Not just with the nice, white teeth, but with the body you have now. Neither of us will gain or lose an ounce or an inch. *Ever*." I reared back when Lucky launched herself at me and pressed me to her perky breasts.

"Thank you, oh, my God, thank you. I can't wait to tell Umberto to take his crunches and slam dunk them up his skinny—"

"Discretion, Lucky. But I'm sure it's tempting. I'd hate working out like that." The closest I'd come to a crunch had been a really nasty encounter with a Big Grab of Cheetos.

"Everyone hates working out." She sat back and actually smiled. "But Umberto doesn't get all the credit. I've got my plastic surgeon on speed dial. Doctor Rodrigo is a genius. Tummy tuck, face and brow lift. And you should see my breasts." She gave me a wink, clearly in a good mood now. "Well, maybe not."

"I'm sure they're awesome." Lucky was living up to her name in the body department. Then she rubbed her forehead.

"Oh, hell. The Botox just wore off. I'd scheduled another round next week." She gave me a hard look. "You're not kidding about this, are you? I mean, it's almost too good to be true."

"It's true. I could work out to a thousand DVDs and run from New York to L.A. and back and not lose a single pound. The healing vamp sleep always puts me right back to how I was on day one of my vampire life."

She dug out her mirror again, then made a face. "There's no loophole, is there? For this mirror thing? What if I look into a pool of water?"

"Sorry, Lucky, you have to take the bad with the good. Now you're immortal. Forever, uh, young." I wasn't about to bring up that birthday I'd seen on her license or we'd definitely end up bitch slapping each other. "Only thing that can take you out is a stake in the heart." I remembered a near miss I'd had recently. "When you're asleep you're really vulnerable. That's why I live in a building with great security and double dead bolts on the door."

"And a bodyguard, one who has the balls to stick it out, is a good idea too," Lucky added, glancing at Valdez and obviously comparing him to the missing Brittany.

"Valdez always sticks and has the scars to prove it." I looked at him too.

"Finally. Some appreciation." Valdez smiled and wagged his tail.

I glanced at the clock again. I had to call downstairs and let them know I was running late. "You'd also die if someone cut off your head."

"He'd have to catch me first." Lucky welled up, blinking rapidly. "Oh, hell. I took precautions and thought I was safe before. I just don't know how anyone could have pulled this off." She wiped her eyes then tucked her mirror into her purse and dropped it on the floor by her feet.

"That's something we need to think hard about. Whoever attacked you may want to finish the job when they find out you lived after all."

"Because you saved my life." Lucky managed a watery smile. "I'm sorry if I've sounded less than grateful. I am. I owe you. Big. And I always repay my debts."

I took a moment to ponder just how a lady who could afford a Birkin bag could repay me. There was that massive Visa bill for one thing. And I could really use a wardrobe update. Hey, I'd wrought what amounted to a miracle, bringing a mortal back from the edge of death. A reward wouldn't be out of line. Especially since Lucky promised to be a major pain in my oversized butt.

"The way somebody tore open your throat, you were pretty close to dead when we found you." No harm in laying it on.

"You sure a vampire did it?"

"I smelled vampire. So one had been around. Is Brittany . . . ?"

"Shifter with a little demon thrown in. I can't, couldn't, have a bodyguard who checked out during daylight hours." Lucky glanced at Valdez again like maybe she was thinking of trying to hire him away from me.

Valdez obviously read her mind. *"I'm on the last of a contract with Glory, then I'm giving up the bodyguard biz."* He yawned. *"Long hours. Stress. Takes it out of you."*

"That's what Brittany says." Lucky shook her head. "I can't believe she flaked out on me. I bet we find Brit's body . . . somewhere." She swallowed. "Damned bloodthirsty bastard."

"Not really. He or she let you bleed instead of draining you. But maybe when I drove in, I scared him off before he could finish you."

Lucky stroked her throat. "I . . . I healed." She shuddered. "Scar?"

"Not even a pink spot. You slept off the injury. A vamp perk." I leaned closer and tried to read her mind. Not my favorite habit, but handy. All I got was a jumble of "Oh shits" and "Oh wows." No surprise there. "Who'd you meet, Lucky? Any idea who did this? You have any enemies?"

"Dozens, vampire. Quit staring a hole in me. You want me to add you to the list?" Lucky glared, a knife suddenly in her right hand. Where had that one come from?

Valdez was suddenly between us, every one of his impressive canines on full display. *"Chill, lady, or you're going to find yourself with a hurt that even Glory won't be able to fix. Understand?"*

"Excuse me?" I jumped up and dragged Valdez back by his collar. Which would have been impossible if he hadn't decided Lucky was suitably warned off. "I can handle this."

"Okay, okay. I guess I overreacted. You sure you don't have any Valium?" Lucky sighed and tucked her knife back into the sleeve of her red sweater. "I can't believe I almost forgot about this one."

Clever. And scary. I guess I should have done a body search. Not that a knife wound would do more than slow me down a little. "Valium doesn't work on vampires. I get that you're confused. What's with the knives?"

"I like knives. Goes with the name. Carver. Get it?"

"Sure. My boyfriend's called Jeremy Blade. He's into knives too." I'd never understood it either. I mean, why bother? Not when a mortal is no match for a vampire anyway. And against another immortal? Well, good luck with that. My response has always been to run like hell.

"You're not taking this one away from me. I need *some* defense."

"Not from me. I'm on your side, remember?"

"So you say." She fiddled with her sleeve until you'd never know there was a six-inch blade in there.

"Yes, so I say." I stood up, definitely tired of this conversation. "I've got to go to work."

"You're not leaving me. Alone?" Lucky actually fluttered her eyelashes.

"I've got a business to run, Lucky. You weren't exactly in my night planner."

"No, seriously. I'm freaking out. Maybe the shifter I met in that alley set me up." She pulled out her BlackBerry again. "She said she lives near here. That's why we met where we did." She looked up again. "You sure you didn't see Brittany? No sign of a struggle or a . . . body?"

"Nope. Valdez had a good look around." I liked the idea that this had been a personal grudge. Bad news for Lucky, but better than thinking an out-of-control vamp was ripping open random throats for sport. The last thing we needed was Austin in a vampire-hunting frenzy. I went through one of those in the early eighties in Tucson. Call me chicken, but I'd packed up and moved on in the middle of the night. Didn't even throw a farewell party. I still miss some of my mortal friends I left behind there.

"That shifter paid me what she owed me. No problem. But—" Lucky dug in her purse again. "Well, hell, that cash is gone."

"Your purse was tossed aside. Last night you claimed a credit card was missing. And your diamond earrings."

"I can't remember . . ." Lucky groped in her bra and pulled out her driver's license. She narrowed her gaze on me again.

"Stop it. I saw your birthday. My lips are sealed. And I didn't steal your gold card either." I felt Valdez bump against my leg. "If I was a thief, I'd have left you for dead and strolled away with a Birkin bag to add to my purse collection."

"Right. I owe you. I said I get that." Lucky slipped her license back into her wallet, then swallowed and looked sick again. "You sure my throat didn't look like a cat clawed it open?"

"Nope. Definitely vampire. And you put up quite a fight. If a cat was involved, I'd have seen at least a few claw marks on you. I'm guessing the vampire worked alone. As for your bodyguard . . ." I glanced at Valdez. "Maybe she got scared off. If she went back to the alley later, all she'd find is a pool of blood."

"I wish I could remember something. There are a lot of vampires who'd like to see me out of the picture."

"What kind of business do you run anyway?" I thought I'd already figured it out, but I wanted to hear her say it. This sophisticated lady with a penchant for top-drawer duds was—

"Loans. I make personal loans for clients who don't have access to traditional resources."

A loan shark. "Charge some pretty stiff interest, do you?" I'd been tempted to deal with these people myself. Back when I'd developed a little gambling problem. Valdez bumped me again. Okay, a serious gambling problem. Hey, I'd lived in Las Vegas. But I'd done the whole GA thing and had been clean for over five years. Of course that was like a nanosecond when you're talking eternity.

"Quit giving me that look, like *I* was the bloodsucker." Lucky looked down into her boot.

"If you've got any more weapons, I didn't find them." I ignored the dirty look she gave me. "I'm not stupid, Lucky. I had to bring a stranger upstairs, to save her life, but I thought I'd disarmed you. If you keep giving me attitude, you can just head out and let your money-lending family take care of you. I'm sure one of their vamp clients would help you get used to your new status. Especially if taking you on could work off some debt."

"Hey, *now* who's got attitude? We provide a service. My family's been dealing honorably with the paranormal community for decades. My grandfather started the business and my father took over from him. I'm just a . . ." She looked down at her hands twisting in her lap. "An enforcer—I collect from delinquent accounts." She looked up, chin high. "I have an almost one hundred percent success rate too."

"Wow, impressive." I'd saved a damned loan shark. No, make that an *enforcer* for a loan shark. That explained the knives anyway. And the bodyguard. I had to admit she was right about one thing. When you live a nontraditional life, getting traditional financing can be a bitch.

She looked me dead in the eye. "I'm not ashamed of what I do. Someday I'll head the company."

"Good for you. But after last night, you won't be able to keep regular daytime office hours. Of course if you're used to doing business in alleys at three in the morning, maybe that won't be a problem. I'd double the guard though."

"I'll never see daylight again?" Some of the starch went out of Lucky and she collapsed. "No food. No reflection. You didn't save me, damn it, you ruined my life."

"Sorry about that. Next time I see a dying mortal, I'll just walk on by. Valdez and I never did get to put up the Christmas lights." I dug my cell phone out of my purse. "I'm supposed to indoctrinate you, so to speak. Help you get used to the life. But if we've got a personality conflict . . ."

"Hey! You can't just send me out there alone!" Lucky's eyes filled and she sniffed. "You did this to me, you *have* to help me figure things out."

"This is exactly why I never turned anyone before." I sighed and called the shop. "I hope my day help can stay late, because bringing you up to speed will take a while." The long list of "don'ts" ran through my mind. Don't go out in daylight. Don't try to eat. I could tell her horror stories about me and Cheetos. Don't bite humans unless you wipe out their memory. Hmm. I could wipe *Lucky's* memory and . . . Naw. I knew my duty. Unfortunately.

"Looks like we're going to be stuck with her for a while." Valdez had read my mind, of course. I rubbed his silky ears.

"Yep, she's got a lot to learn." The phone in the shop was ringing. And ringing. When nobody answered after ten rings, I jumped up and headed for the bathroom. Either they were really busy down there or something was wrong.

"Trouble?" Valdez stopped by the bathroom door.

I stopped and looked back at Lucky. She'd finished her Fangtastic and was busy trying to rub out the bloodstain on her boot.

"Yeah, trouble."

Four

"Come on, Lucky. Decide. Either come down with me or stay up here. Take a shower. Raid my roommate's closet." Did I have a death wish? *Nobody* raided Flo's closet. And she still hadn't come home, something I'd worry about later. "She's about your size. And she has great shoes." Hey, I was desperate.

Lucky sat slumped on the couch. In the same position she'd been in when I'd hit the shower. I *was* desperate to get downstairs and check on things. I'd called twice more and still no answer.

"Go. I'll stay here." She picked up her purse and pulled out her cell phone and flipped it open. "Oh, God."

"What?"

"My father's called six times. I didn't check in. If I don't report by . . ." She glanced at her wrist. "Shit. My Rolex is gone. Doesn't matter anyway. I've got to call right now or Daddy will send his goons to check on me."

"Goons?" I didn't have time for this. But if an invasion was imminent . . .

Lucky wasn't listening to me. She'd obviously hit speed dial.

"Dad, it's me. I'm, uh, okay." She put a shaking hand over her eyes and sobbed, then handed me the phone.

Oh, swell. I cleared my throat. "Hello?"

"Who the hell is this? Why's my baby girl crying?"

"I'm Gloriana St. Clair, uh, Lucky's new friend." I tried to hand the phone back to Lucky but she slapped it away.

"Listen, lady, put Luciana back on. Now."

"She's a little upset, sir." Hey, this guy sounded like a "sir." "She had a near miss last night."

"Near miss? What the hell does that mean?"

"I'll let her tell you." I dropped the phone in Lucky's lap and ran into my room to get my shoes and purse. I could hear Lucky talking and crying. By the time I got back to the living room, she was sniffling and held out the phone again.

"Daddy wants to talk to you."

"I don't have time. I've got—"

"Goons on your doorstep?" Lucky stuck the phone in my hand. "Talk to him. He's, uh, grateful."

A grateful loan shark. Okay, I guess I could spare a moment. "Hello, this is Gloriana."

"You got any idea who tried to take my girl out?"

Hmm. Cut to the chase, why don't you? "No, we didn't see anyone. And Lucky's bodyguard is missing. Maybe—"

"Don't make sense. Brittany's been with us for years."

"Well, sir . . ."

"Call me Carl. You did good, little lady. Sure, having a vampire daughter ain't my notion of a swell time, but we'll figure it out. I want to repay you. Anything you want." The man coughed. "Within reason, of course. Just tell Lucky what you want."

"That's very kind of you." I saw Lucky pull a tissue out of her purse and wipe her eyes. "There is one thing Lucky has . . ."

"Put her on. I'll make sure she gives it to you. And, little lady?"

"Yes?" I couldn't stop grinning. Maybe saving someone would actually pay off.

"You spread the word. There's a million cash for whoever finds the asshole who tried to take my little girl out."

"A million. Dollars?" Visions of financial freedom made the room spin.

"You bet. Put Luciana back on the phone. And thanks."

"You're welcome." I handed the phone to Lucky.

"Glory, we've got to go." Valdez dropped his leash at my feet. *"I've got to go."*

"One more minute."

Lucky snapped her phone shut, her face pale again. "He said to give you whatever you want. As a reward." She saw my gaze move to the object of my desire. "No! Please! You have no idea how many months I waited to get this. I had to bribe the salesclerk." She snatched up her purse and clutched it to her chest.

"Sorry, Lucky. But immortality comes with a price." I stalked to the kitchen and pulled out a plastic garbage sack. "Here, you can use this for your stuff." I dropped it next to her. "Have it ready for me when I come back." I almost skipped to the door, Valdez on my heels. My own Birkin bag. Sweet.

"Can't I just write you a check?" Lucky pulled out a leather checkbook.

"Nope. Taking cash for turning you vampire would seem kind of, umm, sleazy. But I'll accept a token of your gratitude."

I ignored Lucky's grumbling as I walked to the door. "Come straight down to the shop when you're dressed. No wandering off."

"Maybe I should take a look around. Whoever attacked me thinks I'm dead. And Brittany's missing." Lucky had a speculative look I didn't like. "Got a stake handy?"

I grabbed her hand and squeezed hard enough to make her look at me.

"What? Ouch, you've got a grip like a linebacker." She jerked her hand free. "And trust me, I've been gripped by more than a few."

Trust her? Not on your life. Especially not with a stake. I looked into Lucky's eyes and put the whammy to work. "Listen to me, Lucky. You are to come straight downstairs. My shop is right outside the door." I told her the code to get the door open.

"You are not to tell anyone you're a vampire until we've had time to go over the ground rules. Nod your head if you understand what I'm saying." She nodded, obviously unable to do anything else. God, I love the whammy. Maybe I'd hold off teaching her that particular vamp trick. I released her and told her to snap out of it.

"I'll change and come downstairs. You say I can raid your roommate's closet?"

"For now. When you come down, maybe we can find you a few things to wear in the shop. Unless you brought luggage."

"No, I was flying in and flying out. There's a makeup bag in my rental car downstairs. I don't suppose . . ."

"Use my makeup for now. I've got to go."

Lucky got up and sighed. "I don't know how the hell I'm supposed to do makeup without a mirror." She wrinkled her nose when she spied the blood-soaked coat I'd stuffed into a plastic garbage bag the night before. "Why don't you dump that thing on your way out?"

"Let's give a dry cleaner a shot at it first."

She shuddered. "I'll never wear it again. Toss it."

I picked up the bag and carried it to the door. If I could get it clean, it was perfect to sell in the shop. Oh, hell, the shop. What was going on down there?

"Fine." I opened the door. "Valdez stays with me. I'm worried about what might be going on down at the store."

"Go. I can take care of myself." Lucky headed down the hall toward Flo's room.

I bit my tongue before I made a snarky comment. Take care of herself? I don't think so. If I hadn't stumbled across her, she'd be in the morgue downtown right now. My cell rang when I was halfway down the stairs. Caller ID told me Jerry was checking up on me.

"Hi, Jerry."

"Gloriana, what happened last night with the person you found?"

"She's now a vampire, thanks to me." I dropped the bag with Lucky's coat, punched in the security code and pulled open the outside door. "And I'm stuck with her. She's a very complicated person." I waited inside while Valdez darted to the park across the empty street and took care of business.

"Obviously she has enemies, unless you think the attack was random."

"Doubt it. She's a loan shark. Here to collect a debt. I figure someone owed her more than they could pay and decided to settle things permanently."

"This doesn't sound like someone you need to be involved with."

"Too late. I'm involved up to my eyebrows." Which could stand plucking. Lucky's had been perfect. Sure, our bodies never change, but our hair, nails and brows still grow. Fast if we've been drinking a lot of high-octane blood. And don't get me started on my legs.

I picked up the bag with her coat again. "Listen, Jerry. I've got to go. No one's answering in the shop and I've got to check on things."

"I'll be home tomorrow night. Be careful, Gloriana."

"Thanks for the concern. See you tomorrow." I snapped the phone shut and stepped outside, stopping to clip on Valdez's leash. Hmm. Shop lights on. I could see people inside, several gathered in front of the vampire mural Flo had painted on one wall. I know, but my roomie's not into subtle.

She's studied *under*, if you get my drift, a lot of famous artists. So the mural was cool.

I pushed open the shop door and looked around for the hired help. Lacy, the were-kitty, was one of them. A student, Melissa, was another. I knew I was late, but at least one of them should have greeted me when I came in. Customer Relations 101.

"I'm the owner here. What's going on?" I tied the bag closed and dropped it by the door. No need to start a freak-out over a bloodstained coat.

"She's hurt, but she won't let us call the paramedics." A brunette in faded jeans ran up to me. "She says someone attacked her right here in the shop."

"Who's hurt?" I surged forward, Valdez at my side. Lacy sat in one of the overstuffed armchairs a friend had consigned. She was pale as a ghost and I could see a bloody bandage wrapped around her neck.

"My God! What happened?" I looked around. No sign of Melissa. Had she taken off before or after Lacy had been attacked? After and she was so fired.

"I'm okay, Glory. Just after Melissa left, I was in the shop alone. Someone"—she looked significantly at the small crowd of interested mortals—"came in and put a, um, knife to my throat. I guess he wanted to rob us, but two more customers came in just then and the guy panicked and took off."

"That was us!" A blond college-student type, her boyfriend hugging her like he'd never let her go, seemed thrilled to have been so close to death.

"Let's close the shop." I turned and smiled at the group. "Sorry, folks, but obviously Lacy needs medical attention. Come back in about an hour and say, 'I helped Lacy,' and I'll give you twenty-five percent off anything in the store."

"Good deal." College girl dragged her boyfriend to the door. "We can get a snack at Mugs and Muffins next door, sweetie. Check our e-mail on your laptop." She patted him on his stuffed backpack. "We'll be back."

"I told Barbie she didn't need to be hangin' out in a place called Vamps with a vampire painting on the wall." A middle-aged man in jeans, a plaid shirt and a sleeveless down vest elbowed his friend, who was dressed in similar fashion. Like they'd interrupted a hunting trip to check us out. "You see where she was hurt? Neck wound, Earl."

"Don't mean nothin', Leroy. And you can't tell a teenager where to shop, how to dress or who to date. She'll just start sneakin' around. I figure she'll get over the black lipstick soon enough if you leave her be." Earl hitched up his pants. "Lady wants us to leave. Coffee sounds good. Got to admit though, that painting's pretty creepy."

"Told ya." Leroy and Earl headed out the door.

They weren't the first worried parents to check us out. Usually we passed with flying colors. Too bad they'd picked tonight to drop by.

Finally I turned the lock and got a good look at Lacy. She was pale and getting paler. I reached for the makeshift bandage.

"Not here. Let's go in the back." She got to her feet. Lacy wobbled and made a face. Once we were both in the back room, I helped her to a chair.

"What did he look like, kitty girl? Did you at least scratch his eyes out?" Valdez was right beside me.

"He was butt ugly. And he caught me by surprise. I got in a few good swipes, but I never thought another vamp would come right here in the shop and attack one of us when a customer could have shown up at any time." Lacy put her hand to her throat.

"Ugly and dumb as dirt if he thought he could get away with this." Valdez sniffed. *"Security cameras, Glory. We need them in here. I'm talkin' to Blade about them when he gets back. What do you bet this guy was lookin' for you? It's your shop."*

"Valdez, I don't want to make this all about me." I grabbed Lacy's arm when she swayed. "Go watch the front door. Lacy's hurt. Save this for later. And leave Blade out of this for now—until we know more."

"Just doin' my job," he muttered as he turned tail and walked stiff legged back to the door.

"Think, Lacy. Did you recognize this vampire? Ever see him before?"

"Someone from the EVs, I think. I didn't get to go to their headquarters with you guys, but Derek took pictures with his camera phone. I think this man was in one of them and not on our side."

EVs. Energy Vampires. The leader had wanted to drain my energy for his top-selling drug. Would you believe it? Vampire Viagra. But I'd managed to get the best of him, and I thought we'd called a truce. He'd promised . . . I pulled off the bandage. Fang marks.

"Oh, God, Lacy. I'm so sorry."

"Why? You're not responsible for every vampire in Austin. And I figure the EVs are wild cards anyway. Hey, I'm okay. I did fight the bastard." She shuddered and touched her throat. "He was so damned strong!"

"It comes with the territory." I grabbed a cloth, wet it and dabbed at the wound. "It's stopped bleeding."

"I know. I wrapped it so the customers couldn't see the marks. We get enough vamp-wannabes because of our name and the mural."

"Damn it. Maybe this *is* all about me. I'm really, really sorry. At least let me heal you." I put my hand on her throat and thought healing thoughts. Cool, huh? Just like with Lucky, I felt the wounds close under my fingertips.

The back door crashed open, and I do mean crashed. With double dead bolts?

"Get your hands off my daughter, vampire!"

I jumped back from Lacy like my hands were on fire. "Hey, I'm healing her." Okay, so I was a wimp, but if you've never seen a mama were-cat with a mad on, don't judge me.

Valdez landed in front of me on legs that were spring-loaded. *"There's nothin' that tastes nastier than were-kitty, but, lady, you come one step closer to Glory and I'll take a chunk out of your hide that even a designer suit won't disguise."*

The woman, who stood a good six feet tall not counting her four-inch heels, merely sniffed. "And why did she need healing in the first place?"

I took a second to admire her shoes, this season's Dolce & Gabbana pumps, before I realized she was stalking me. Valdez growled and Lacy edged toward the door. I grabbed Lacy's arm.

"Oh, no, you don't. You're not leaving me here with your mother." Not that we'd been introduced, but even if she hadn't screamed "daughter," I could smell were-cat on the lady. And then there was the fact that she had Lacy's red hair and creamy skin. Who knew Lacy even had a mother nearby? She'd begged me for a job here. Was always short of funds. And, while she usually had a boyfriend, I'd never known her to entertain family.

"Mother, please leave. I'm okay. Glory would never hurt me. She's my friend and boss." Lacy gave me a look that said let her go before her mother decided to take on Valdez to defend her. I dropped her arm and put a foot between us.

"Listen to Lacy, I'd never hurt her." Mom-cat just gave me a look like she'd be a fool to believe a vampire.

"Another vampire attacked me. And I'd like to know how the hell you knew about it anyway? It only happened twenty minutes ago." Lacy was braver than I was, actually stepping around Valdez and going toe-to-toe with her simmering mother.

"Darling . . ." Mom-cat gave me a look that had *me* edging toward the door. "I had this *feeling*. You know how I am about my kittens, especially you, my little one. And I could smell vampire a block away."

"I'm not a kitten, Mother. And it's not like we're pack animals. I'm an adult. I have a life. And you can see I'm fine." Lacy was a few inches shorter than her mom, but she matched her stare for stare.

Both were impressive, slim hipped, toned and athletic. The way they were making eye contact, I expected hissing and clawing any minute.

"Ms. Devereau?" I held out my hand, maybe not my brightest move. Valdez sure didn't think so. He practically knocked me back, but I stopped him with a look. "I'm Gloriana St. Clair. I can't tell you how much I rely on Lacy. She's a wonderful asset here."

My reward was a snarl. "Sheila Lyons. Devereau is her father's name, which I have never taken."

"Here we go again." Lacy sent me an apologetic look, then grabbed her mother's arm. "Come on upstairs. You can check me out for any lingering ill effects from the attack. Let me describe the vampire who came after me. I've even got a friend who can e-mail a picture to show you. Maybe you can help me hunt the attacker down."

Ah. Lacy definitely knew how to handle her mother. That lady was practically vibrating with the urge to take charge of a vamp hunt. I watched them go, then turned to smile at Valdez, who was still snarling.

"Guess we showed her what's what around here." Valdez sat and scratched behind his ear. *"Glad I didn't have to bite her. Were-cats taste like shit. Bet I could have taken her if it came to a smackdown."*

"My money's always on you, puppy. Thanks." I took over the ear scratching. "Just remember that some were-kitties are okay. Especially Lacy."

"Yeah. Had to admire how she stood up to that mother of hers." Valdez sighed as I went to work on his other ear.

"And I need her to cover days here. But after this, I wouldn't be surprised if she quit." I looked around the shop.

Merchandise had been tossed around in the apparent panic over discovering my bleeding clerk.

I shut the back door and shoved a table in front of it since the dead bolts were now history. Then I unlocked the front door and posted Valdez next to it in case the attacker decided to make another try. I picked up a vintage cane and wished I had time to whittle it into a point. I'd never staked another vampire, but anyone pushing into my shop with murder on his mind definitely had it coming.

Customers and the evening rush kept me busy for the next several hours, so it was after midnight when I finally realized Lucky hadn't come downstairs. Damn.

I picked up my cell phone. The home phone rang until the answering machine picked up. "Lucky! If you're there, please pick up. I'm worried about you."

A breathless Lucky answered the phone. "I'm fine. You have company. Or I guess I should say *we* have company. I was on my way downstairs when he was coming up. He says he's a friend of yours."

"Who's with you, Lucky?" I smiled through my dread as another customer came through the door. Had the vampire who'd attacked Lacy somehow managed to get past our security and up the stairs? And how had he convinced her to stay? My whammy should have made her hell-bent on getting to the shop.

"Your roommate's brother. Damian?" Lucky said something away from the receiver. "I told him I have to come downstairs, but he said you'd be busy. So he's helping me understand my new, uh, role. As vampire."

Oh, great. Nothing like a love 'em and leave 'em vampire to initiate Lucky into her new world. Damian was plenty powerful enough to override one of my whammies and he'd be more than willing to give Lucky a demonstration of the perks of vampire sex. Hmm. He did know his way around a bedroom, not to mention a woman's body. I pushed down any residual sizzle and decided to give in to the inevitable.

"Careful, Lucky. He's not a commitment kind of guy. And you're vulnerable right now. After the shock you've had."

"Yeah. I *am* in shock, what with my near-death experience. Damian is helping me feel, um, better." Lucky giggled. Oh, boy. I was not walking in on Casanova and Lucky doing the bedroom bossa nova.

"Put Damian on the phone."

"Gloriana." Damian had a way of rolling his Rs . . . "I am so proud of you. You made a new vampire!"

"Yeah, well, I didn't have much choice."

"Yes, you did, *cara*. You could have left her to die. Which would have been such a waste of a beautiful woman."

I heard Lucky giggle again. Gag me. A customer stopped in front of me, a question in her eyes. "I've got to go. I'll be home just before sunrise. Don't be there. Go home to your own coffin, Damian." I hung up.

"Coffin?" The customer was bug-eyed.

"What? Oh, no. *Coffee.* A friend. And he always drinks the last of the decaf."

"Men." She rolled her eyes. "What do you have to go with this dress?"

Ah, business. Something I could definitely handle. I helped the lady accessorize her fifties cocktail dress and put my worries about my new protégée on the back burner. So Lucky got her heart broken. It probably wouldn't be the first time or the last. I rang up a nice sale and picked up my cell phone again. Thoughts of what Lucky and Damian might be up to made me want to talk to Jerry. But I got voice mail. Damn it. There were other men I could call, but the new self-sufficient me didn't need a man. I did try Flo though. It had been a long forty-eight hours since I'd heard from her. Another voice mail. I was striking out on all fronts.

"Glory, are you all right?" Diana Marchand, the vampire who owns Mugs and Muffins, that business next door where I'd sent everyone earlier, rushed in an hour before dawn.

"Sure, why wouldn't I be?"

Diana sat on a chair next to where I tried to bring order to my selection of vintage shawls. No customers at the moment, but the night shift should be letting out soon and we'd have a mini rush.

"Oh, I don't know. Maybe because all my customers could talk about was your clerk getting attacked in here earlier this evening. What happened?"

"Lacy's okay." I threw down a red velvet shawl that I really wanted to keep for myself—perfect for Christmas. "But I need to keep a stake behind the counter. A damned rogue vampire attacked her. Probably one of the EVs. At least I could heal the wound for her."

"A vampire?" Diana grabbed my arm. "Did you know one of my employees found a pool of blood in our alley this morning? No victim though. Hector refuses to go to the Dumpster anymore. Do you know anything about that blood?"

"Unfortunately." I looked up toward my apartment. "I now have a new houseguest because of it."

Diana jumped up. "What?"

I sat in the vacated chair and pulled off one of my boots to rub my aching foot. If customers came in, they could just enjoy my Christmas tree socks.

"I found a woman bleeding out back there. Vampire attacked her." I sighed as I got the second boot off.

"Did she say who did it? Maybe it was the same one who came in here tonight."

"No, she was just about gone when I found her." Okay here goes. I grabbed Diana's arm. "Would you believe it? I turned her vampire!"

"No way!" Diana knew me well enough to know my views on doing this kind of thing. I blended with mortals, didn't drink from them and sure didn't make a mortal into a vampire. This was like announcing that Sarah Jessica Parker had decided to give up her Manolo Blahniks.

"Yes! All by myself." I saw Valdez raise his head at his post by the front door. "Well, almost. Blade told me what to do over the phone."

"And she came through all right?" Diana was clearly impressed.

"It was touch and go at first. But she made it through the day. I left her upstairs."

"By herself? The first twenty-four hours are critical. Maybe I should go check on her for you." Diana started for the door.

"Don't bother. Damian's with her. Teaching her God knows what."

Diana fell back into her chair. "Damian!"

"I know." I patted her hand. We were both veterans of the Damian not-a-fan club. "But she's pretty savvy about men. She'll be okay."

"What about this attack? What's a vampire doing hunting in our alley?" Diana was really pale, but then it was close to dawn.

"She doesn't remember anything about the attack but, get this, she's a loan shark—her family loans to paranormals." Just then the doorbell tinkled and two customers walked in, clearly hospital workers fresh off a night shift. "Well, back to work. Stop by sometime and meet her."

I smiled and stood, walking over to drop my boots behind the counter. "My new guest's name is"—big grin—"Lucky Carver."

Diana headed for the door. "Sounds like she *was* Lucky you found her, Glory. See you later." She was out the door before Valdez even got his usual head pat. I waited on customers, happy to see my day help arrive a few minutes later.

By the time I dragged myself upstairs, I had less than fifteen minutes until sunrise and I felt it. I opened the door to a scene right out of my worst nightmares.

Five

Damian was on the couch teaching Lucky how to find a vein. At least he was still above the waist, but, knowing Damian, the always interesting inner thigh was on his agenda.

"Hello?"

Lucky looked up, her cheeks pink, her fangs wet with Damian's blood. "Oh, hi, Glenda. Damian was just showing me—"

"Glory." Nice. She got Damian's name right but couldn't remember who *made* her? I should just hand her over to Casanova. But he'd break her heart and then I'd still have to deal with her, only with the screwed-up notions of vamp behavior that Damian was no doubt eager to teach her. Mind control was his favorite.

"Good-bye, Damian. Thanks for helping out, but Lucky and I don't need you."

"Speak for yourself, sister." Lucky snuggled against Damian, clearly all for joining the dark side. "You just took off and left me here. I was about to make a horrible mistake."

"What?" I gave Damian a stern look when he chuckled.

"I almost put on Florence's favorite boots. Damian says his sister would rip out my throat if she caught me in them."

"It's true. You know how Florence is about her shoes." Damian was still grinning and even I had to admit he was sex on a stick, especially with that devil lurking in his dark eyes.

"And how would you know what her favorite boots look like?" I stalked to the kitchen and grabbed a cold Fangtastic. After I twisted off the top and took a swallow, I stormed back to the living room. "Well?"

Damian laughed. "They're *all* her favorites. Lucky would be better off wearing her own soiled boots until the rest of her luggage gets here."

"Luggage?" Flo and I already had every closet and drawer stuffed.

"Surely you realize, Gloriana, that Lucky will have to stay in town for a while, to learn what she needs to survive as vampire." Damian smiled down at her.

"I should get a hotel room." Lucky frowned. "But when would the maid clean? If I'm, like, asleep all day."

"A hotel room is out of the question. I have spare rooms. You can stay with me, Lucky." Damian had on an earnest look now, like he was doing this out of the goodness of his so-called heart.

"Really?" Lucky was all over the idea. "I haven't sent for anything yet, but obviously I've got a lot to learn. And I'll have to get used to"—Lucky licked her lips—"all this."

Oh, but it was tempting. Then Damian's hand landed on Lucky's thigh. Could I really leave her in his way too skilled hands?

Lucky glanced at me then eased away from Damian. "Thanks, Damian, but maybe I should stay here. With Gloria. I have a feeling there's some girl talk involved."

I smiled my approval. Lucky was pretty quick on the uptake. One scowl from me and a heavy hand on her thigh and she'd figured Damian out.

"Whatever you wish, *cara*." Damian picked up Lucky's wrist and rubbed her vein.

"I'm getting worried about Flo. She usually reports in. And she isn't exactly having a lucky streak where boyfriends are concerned."

"Oh, I forgot to tell you. Florence called before Damian got here and left a message on the answering machine. I didn't pick up because I didn't know if you'd want me answering your phone." Lucky sighed when Damian ran his finger up to the crook of her elbow. "Uh, anyway, she said she's staying with Richard tonight. I guess you know who she was talking about."

"Sure, I know Richard." And I'd had an almost fling with him. But I'd always suspected he still had feelings for Flo and their affair was back on in a big way.

"My sister and her lovers." Damian winked at me. "Do you have trouble keeping track, Gloriana?"

"Flo's safe with Richard, that's all I care about. So, Lucky, you can sleep in Flo's bed." I got up, walked to the door and flung it open. "Damian, thanks for dropping by. Head out before the sun catches you." I stood next to the door, Valdez, teeth bared, by my side. He doesn't particularly like Damian either.

Lucky stood and smoothed her skirt, short and tight and obviously from Flo's closet. "Bye, Damian, thanks for everything." Lucky linked arms with him and walked him to the door.

"My pleasure, *cara*." Damian smiled. "Gloriana, you are so busy with your store. If you wish for me to tutor Lucky . . ."

"I can handle it." I faked a smile, then slammed the door and locked it as soon as Damian was in the hall. "Lucky, be careful of that one. He's not above teaching just what he thinks will help him score."

"I can hear you, Gloriana. You wound me." Damian laughed and I finally heard him walk down the stairs.

I made a face. "Vampire hearing. Not that I care how much

I 'wound' him, but keep that in mind. You want to keep a secret, don't even whisper it when a vampire is around unless you want him or her to know it too."

"Supersonic hearing. Cool. And don't worry, Glory. I wasn't born yesterday." Lucky wrinkled her nose. "Unfortunately. You look like you're about twenty-three."

"Four hundred plus, but I was twenty-four when I was made vampire." Young, by today's standards, but back in the day twenty-four had been practically ancient.

"Awesome. Sometime, when I'm not so dead tired, I'd like to hear about how things were back then. And what you've been doing all these years. To have survived so long, you must be pretty clever." She smiled, then sat down and peeled off her boots. "I've known many men like Damian, guys who're sure they're doing you a huge favor by coming on to you. But a vampire lover . . . Damian said it can be amazing."

I took a moment to reflect. "Yep, with the right vampire. But vamp men are *men*, first, last and always. Some know which of your buttons to push and some just want you to push theirs, if you know what I mean."

"Do I ever." Lucky sighed and picked up an overnight bag Damian must have brought up from her car. "At least Damian didn't seem put off by my age. He looks on the sunny side of thirty, while I . . ." Lucky grimaced. "Well, you know."

"Damian's so ancient he probably helped discover fire. He's gone through thousands of women." At least I hadn't been one of them, but not because he hadn't tried. "He even claims to be the original Casanova."

"Hmm. Now you've got me interested." Lucky yawned, a real jaw breaker. "I'm exhausted. Is it like this every night right before dawn?"

"Yep. Once the sun comes up, you'll be out until it goes down again."

"So many hours, wasted." Lucky's shoulders sagged. "I'm used to running on about four hours' sleep a night. Sleeping all day is ridiculous."

"You don't have a choice, Lucky. That's the way it works. The sleep heals any major hurts you might get when you're awake, if that makes you feel better. You'll get used to it." I nodded toward the kitchen. "You want a drink before you bed down?"

"I guess you mean that fake blood. I'd kill for a latte, but Damian told me it would just make me queasy now." Lucky sighed. "I drank from him, Glory." She licked her lips. "I didn't think I'd like it, but he was so sweet about it. And the taste! The fake stuff is seriously flat after that."

"Sweet, generous Damian. You're the new vamp in town. Not that you're not sexy or whatever, but, Lucky, he'll try to seduce you because that's his knee-jerk reaction to any attractive female." I finished my drink and made a face because Lucky had hit the mark. Fake versus the real deal? And from an ancient vampire like Damian . . . "Bed time."

"I called my neighbor who's looking after my cat. I just wonder . . ." Lucky's shoulders slumped. "This"—she gestured toward her throat—"is so damned complicated."

"You'd better plan to stay here at least long enough to learn what's what. And not from Casanova Sabatini either. I promise I'll sit down with you and we'll figure things out."

Lucky laughed but it was a bitter sound. "Figure things out? Honey, I've got forever to do that." She headed down the hall.

"Oh, Lucky."

"Yes?"

"I brought you something from the shop." I held out a gently used leather hobo.

"You're kidding." She grabbed the strap and looked inside. "It's a knockoff."

"Oh, well." I followed her down the hall. Oh, yeah. There was my reward, empty and ready to go.

"You won't change your mind? I'll pay you—"

I held up a hand. "Nope. Taking money for saving your

life would be tacky. But this"—I stroked the Birkin bag's supple leather and smiled—"this is, um, appropriate."

"Aw, Glory, have a heart. A thousand bucks."

I just smiled and strolled toward my bedroom, Lucky right behind me. I tossed Lucky a pink gown. Lucky looked it over and wrinkled her custom-made nose. "Take this. Flo sleeps raw."

"Nylon? You are determined to punish me, aren't you? I like silk teddies."

"Sorry, Lucky, but you were saved by an ordinary working woman who just happens to be vampire." I smiled. "I have a few silk teddies, but I save them for special occasions that don't include sleeping. And I'm not punishing you, though you have complicated the hell out of my life. By the time you hit the sheets, you'll be dead to the world and what you're wearing won't matter."

"Dead?"

I heard Lucky's plaintive wail as I headed for the bathroom. Maybe I should have stopped to explain, but what was the point? Roll out the coffin, vampires are as good as dead during daylight hours. I heard some thumps that sounded like Lucky's boots hitting the wall in Flo's bedroom.

Valdez hopped on the foot of the bed and gave me a sympathetic look. *"Relax, Blondie. You did the right thing. Lucky owes you, not vice versa."*

"Thank you. But maybe I should have locked up all the knives in the kitchen. If she wakes up first and isn't all that happy—" I couldn't finish the thought; the sun was coming up and with it oblivion.

I woke up with a start. Just after sunset. Sometimes it's like that. Other times it takes me a while to get moving. Lucky. I nudged Valdez off the bed and got up. I was coming out of the bathroom when Lucky grabbed my arm.

"Is . . . Was Damian really Casanova?"

I laughed and pried off her fingers. "Maybe, maybe not. But nobody's better than Damian at fantasy." I headed for the kitchen, Lucky on my heels. "Sleep well?"

"No dreams, which is a bummer. But I woke up thinking about Damian and, um, sinking my teeth into him. Is that sick or what?" Lucky staggered to the couch and collapsed, my pink nightgown a tent around her.

"Perfectly normal. Feeding is erotic with the right guy."

"Are you and Damian, uh, involved?" Lucky wiggled her bare toes, which were painted scarlet.

"No way, no how." I handed her a Fangtastic and sat across from her. "I warned you, Lucky. Damian is bad news."

She sagged back against the cushions. "Of course he is. I have a history of falling for the wrong guy. But forget him. For now." She took a swallow and groaned. "This is disgusting. Is there only one kind of fake blood? There's got to be something better than this."

"Sure there is. But the rare ones are expensive. This is a fairly common blood type." I have a thing for AB negative, but it's not in my budget. "And there are other brands."

"Hey, I'll kick in if you want to order something better. It's the least I can do while I'm staying here." Lucky gave me a searching look. "But why don't you just drink from, what do you call them, uh, mortals? I don't mean kill or anything, but Damian says you can drink enough to satisfy the urge and not leave a person on the verge of death."

Damian says. Like he was her go-to guy for everything vampire. "Listen, Lucky. Damian is a very ancient vampire. He has tricks that you've yet to learn. You can't just go around drinking from mortals. You want to start a vampire-hunting frenzy?"

"No, but Damian said you can fix it so they don't remember what happened. Even erase the fang marks. You're going to teach me all that, right?"

I sighed and sat down across from her. So much for keeping

the whammy a secret. "Yes, I'll teach you all that." And what a pain this was going to be. Hey, I'm a woman with a business to run, friends to shop with and a lover to keep happy. And with a million dollars on the line, I was going to do my damnedest to track down a killer wannabe in my spare time.

"Get dressed and we'll go out. I'll show you around the shop, explain some things."

"Great!" Lucky jumped up and headed for Flo's bedroom.

I just hoped I could control her once she got some skills under her belt. I got dressed and transferred my stuff into my new purse, doing a quick strut around the living room for Valdez.

"It's a purse. What's the biggie? Except that it costs a lot and obviously Lucky didn't want to give it up." Valdez lounged next to the door. *"That alone makes it a sweet deal."*

"They're hard to come by. And not just expensive. Very expensive." My phone beeped. Text message. I flipped open the phone and sat on the couch. "I NO WHAT U R." I looked up, but Valdez was busy chewing on the end of his tail. I took a shaky breath. Wrong number. Obviously. Then I realized there was a video attached. Oh, shit. There I was, kneeling in a pool of blood, biting Lucky's wrist. How? Who? Valdez was in the picture, peering over my shoulder. Quality wasn't great, but it was definitely me.

"I NO WHAT U R." The phone beeped again. My stomach cramped, and I headed to the kitchen for a Fangtastic before I checked the new message. How had this messenger gotten my number? I saw my laptop on the breakfast table. Duh. The information was everywhere. I gulped my drink, then sat again. New message.

"I NO WHAT U R, VAMPIRE. TO KEEP UR SECRET, PAY $500. LEAVE BEHIND DUMPSTER IN ALLEY BEHIND UR STORE. 2NITE."

Money. Blackmail.

"Glory? You okay? You look a little freaked." Valdez walked up, and I snapped the phone shut.

"Just a text that I'm over my cell minutes this month. I'm going to have a hell of a bill." I wasn't about to share the text. Not yet anyway. Text message. Fairly small payoff. One of the teenage Goth types who hung around my shop had probably wandered into the alley while Valdez and I had been focused on Lucky and had taken the video with a cell phone. I'd play along for now. Even scrounge up five hundred bucks and follow instructions. A vampire against a kid with black lipstick and spiked hair? What a laugh. All I had to do was catch him or her picking up the cash, and the whammy would take care of this situation. That thought did a lot to calm me down.

I made a quick call to check on things in the shop. A locksmith had been in and repaired the back-door dead bolts. Lacy wanted me to deduct the cost from her pay. Tempting, but I didn't take her up on it. Hey, she'd been attacked while working for me. Vampire attacks behind my shop and inside it. Could Lucky's killer be the same one who'd tried to take out Lacy?

I didn't have to go in to work tonight, but now I had to get down there and pull out some cash, somehow get to the Dumpster without Valdez seeing the envelope . . . This was complicated as hell. But if any Goth types were stupid enough to aim a cell phone at me for *Vampire at Play, Part Two*, I could wrap this up in short order.

When Lucky met me in the living room dressed head to toe in one of Flo's outfits, I had a new reason for my frown lines. My roomie is a kind and generous person, but when someone pours what I now realized were size-eight hips into her favorite size-six jeans . . .

Both of us jumped when the hall door opened. Flo and her date, Richard Mainwaring. Lucky took a second to check out Flo then took a minute or more to stare at Richard. He was definitely stare-worthy with his white blond hair and startling blue eyes. Tonight he was especially yummy in a blue sweater that had the look of cashmere. Not that I was lusting for anything more than the sweater. Or having a flashback to a night when he and I had almost . . .

"Those had better not be my new Prada peep toes on your feet." Flo turned to me, her dark eyes, so much like her brother's, flashing. "Who is this shoe-stealing skank?" Her nostrils quivered. "And why does she smell like you, Glory?"

Lucky sat down, reverently plucked off the shoes and placed them in Flo's outstretched hands. "You must be Florence. God, you have the most incredible shoe collection I've ever seen. I would never harm such an exquisite pair of pumps, but I just had to try them on. We wear the same size!" Lucky said this like she'd just discovered her long-lost twin.

"Who the hell are you?" Flo examined the shoes carefully.

"This is Lucky Carver, Flo. A temporary houseguest."

"Silly name," Flo sniffed, but I could see the compliment to her shoes had cooled her off considerably. "A houseguest? If I didn't know better . . ." She focused a narrow-eyed gaze on me. "Did you turn this woman *vampire*?" She sounded incredulous.

Hey, I'd made no secret of my reluctance to do the deed. "I had to. Valdez and I found her bleeding out behind the shop."

"You shoulda seen our Glory, Flo. She saved Lucky's"—Valdez's snort was the doggy equivalent of a laugh—*"life."* He bumped against Flo's leg until she handed the shoes off to Richard and gave the dog an ear rub.

"Behind the shop! Who did this?" Flo looked from me to Lucky and back again.

"Good question." Richard set the shoes on the coffee table.

"By the time I got there, Lucky was near death with no sign of her attacker. She had a bodyguard who's still missing."

"Maybe the bodyguard did it." Flo picked up her shoes

again. "You should get another one. You wear another woman's shoes without permission, Lucky, and *anything* can happen."

Lucky put her hands on her hips. "Glory told me—"

"It was an emergency. Come on, Flo. This is serious. If the bodyguard did it, she had help. She's a shape-shifter. This was definitely the work of a vampire. I healed Lucky's throat, then, uh, you know."

"I'm proud of you, Gloriana. How did you know what to do?"

I basked for a moment in Richard's look of approval. "I got Blade on my cell. He talked me through it." I moved closer to Lucky and inhaled. "Does she really smell like me? I can't tell. I thought so at first, but now . . ."

"Slightly." Richard smiled and put his hand on my shoulder. "Because she is so recently made. The similarity will fade in time."

Hmm. Richard sounded like an expert on the subject. I wondered how many mortals he'd "saved" since the Crusades. Yep, he's really ancient.

Flo looked at his hand on my shoulder. "Where is Jeremiah?" She'd said the magic word. Richard frowned and stepped away from me.

"Jerry's in Louisiana, but he'll be home soon." I bit back a sigh. I guess Jerry and I are considered a "couple" if only because we'd been on and off for over four hundred years and he'd "made" me just like I'd made Lucky. But, while we connected in bed like nobody's business, out of bed we'd always had our issues. That first flush of lust and love had settled into familiarity territory.

"Are Jerry, Jeremiah and Blade all the same guy? Or does Glory have several guys on the hook?" Lucky's admiring glance made it clear she had no problem with that.

"All the same handsome man." Flo tossed her hair and stared at Lucky. "Tell me your real name. This Lucky is not it."

"Luciana Carvarelli. Sue me, but I got tired of the whole Mafia princess thing."

Whoa! Mafia?

Lucky laughed. "Kidding. Papa's a tough bastard, but not into kissing anyone's ring."

Florence said something in Italian and Lucky answered in the same language. Next thing I knew they were headed down the hall toward Flo's bedroom, both talking a mile a minute complete with hand gestures.

"They're going to find some shoes for Lucky to wear. Apparently Lucky's good boots were ruined by a huge bloodstain." Richard grinned and sat on the couch, patting the seat beside him. "This could take a while. Tell me more about finding Lucky. We need to figure out who tried to kill her." He'd lost his smile and wasn't that a shame?

But I'm not the airhead I sometimes pretend to be. If whoever tried to kill Lucky really wanted her dead, he or she'd be damned mad that Lucky had survived and not too happy with the vamp who'd saved her either. But I get pretty brave when there's a million dollars at stake. Hmm. Richard could be a help. The former priest believes in justice in a big way. And nobody's better than he is at finding rogue vampires—those out of whack freaks who think taking out mortals is their right.

I sat beside him. No need to bring up a reward just yet. "Lucky told me she'd met with a were-cat earlier, but claims that meeting was uneventful." I had to smile. To someone not in the paranormal world, a were-cat meet would seem anything but ordinary.

"She give you a name?" Richard had actually whipped out a notebook from his jeans pocket. He grabbed a pen from the coffee table.

"No, but I have my suspicions. You have to wonder why they met in *our* alley." I gestured toward Lucky's large tote bag, which was now mine, mine, mine. "Lucky's cash was missing and one of her credit cards, but they didn't take all of them. So I don't think it was a typical robbery. They did pick up a pair of diamond studs and a Rolex though."

Richard made a note. "That bag looks expensive." He smiled. "I guess I've gone shopping with Florence one too many times, but I've gotten to know a designer bag when I see one."

"You're right." I smiled back. "It costs the earth and whoever attacked her left it." I leaned closer. "Lucky's surprisingly cool with our world. Her family runs a loan business for paranormals. She calls herself an 'enforcer.'"

Richard frowned. "Someone is damned careless to send a mortal female out to collect from paranormals."

"It's an unusual family."

"But an ambush in your alley. Damn it, she *is* lucky you happened along when you did."

"I was tempted to let her die." I said this in a small voice, like I was making confession to the former priest. "Now I've created another vampire." I grabbed Richard's arm. "I'm responsible for her, Richard. Forever."

"Now you know how I feel about you, Gloriana." The hall door had opened and closed silently, and Blade, hunky in worn jeans and an untucked white shirt, stood just inside. He nodded at Richard, then at Valdez, who'd hopped up when Jerry had appeared.

"Responsible." I left my hand on Richard's strong arm and smiled tightly. "Like a stone around your neck."

"Gloriana, I have always loved you and you know it." Jerry pulled me up and into his arms. "If you would consent, we could let Father Richard here marry us right now."

"I hardly think words spoken by a defrocked priest would be binding, Jerry." I resisted the urge to lean into him. I do love Jeremiah Campbell the third. And I'd be taking on a cushy lifestyle as Mrs. Jerry. He's amassed a nice fortune along the way. But I like my independence and, call me a slut, variety too.

Then I took a deep breath. Oh, God, but he smelled

delicious and familiar and like the home I'd left behind centuries ago. I slid my arms around his waist.

"I'm sorry, Jerry. That wasn't very nice of me." I cleared my throat and looked up at him. "While I am honored by your proposal, I must regretfully decline."

Valdez growled and flopped down in front of the door. *"You wouldn't know a good deal if it bit you on the ass, Glory. Take Blade up on his offer. Then I could get on with my life."*

His life as something other than my guard dog. He was the latest in a long, long line of guard dogs Blade had insisted I keep with me. That old responsibility thing.

"Not selfish, are you, pup?" I had felt Jerry stiffen at my refusal. I stepped back from him before he could push me away.

"No more selfish than you are." Valdez gave Jerry a sympathetic chuff. *"Give it up, man. Any woman who flipped me off like that would be a speck in my rearview mirror."*

"I wasn't flipping him off, damn it." I felt tears fill my eyes. But I hadn't exactly been tactful either. Jerry's jaw was tight and he didn't say a word. Richard wisely kept his mouth shut too. I felt like scum. Nothing like rejecting Jerry in front of an audience. Even worse. In front of a man he respected. Well, hell.

Six

"I love you, Jerry. I do. But marriage should be permanent and I'm not—" Before I could do more than squeak, Jerry had me up in his arms. He carried me into my bedroom and dumped me on my bed, then closed the door with a look. Blade's got powers on top of powers. I tried to catch my breath. No luck when he landed on top of me.

"Such a sharp tongue. I can think of better uses for it than flailing my ego." Jerry stared down at me, all intense male and sex.

I could feel him hard between my thighs. "I just said I didn't want to marry you. But if there's any other way I can be of service . . ." I slid my arms around his waist, then slipped one hand inside his jeans. Firm back *and* front.

"You're a woman of many . . . talents, Gloriana." Jerry grinned, and I did kiss his smiling mouth, tasting him, almost able to forget that everyone in the next room had supersonic hearing. "Since you've wounded my pride yet again, I won't object if you want to kiss and make it better."

I pulled back and looked at him. "Where exactly is your pride anyway?" As if I really had to ask. Men.

"A little lower than that."

I sent Jerry a mental message. *"We can't—"*

"Can't we?" Jerry nibbled his way to my neck, sucking until I wanted to beg him to drink from me.

"Only if we're very quiet . . ." I worked my hand around to his zipper, the sound of it as loud as machine-gun fire. But with his fingers up my skirt and inside my panties, I could care less.

"You're never quiet. Which is just one reason I love you. You scream your pleasure."

"Is that a problem?"

"Not at all, scream away."

I wrapped my legs around him as he drove home. *"Oh, yes. Right. There."* He moved and I sank my fangs into his neck to keep from shrieking. Thank God my bed doesn't squeak but the headboard hit the wall and . . .

"The floor. Now."

Jerry slid us off the bed and onto the worn wood. He rolled me on top of him. I pulled back and licked my lips. I sat on my "throne" and just absorbed the moment and him. His blood surging through me, lighting me from the inside out. The love shining in his eyes, warming me from head to heart. And then there was his cock filling me until I couldn't bear one more second without moving over him. We found our rhythm, just as we always did. I offered my own neck but he shook his head.

"This is all for you, lass. You'll be sorry I'm not tied to you."

Sorry? Probably. But I couldn't think about it when I was soaring toward the pleasure of all pleasures. I bit my lips until I could taste my own blood, but swallowed my scream when I came. I felt the heat of Jerry's release inside me and sighed as I collapsed on top of him. He shoved up my sweater and made quick work of my bra.

"No more," I whispered, okay, whimpered.

"Yes, more. I'm not through punishing you for hurting me."

Oh, God, he was hardening inside me again while he explored my breasts and pulled first one nipple, then the other into his mouth.

"I'm sorry."

Jerry dragged a sharp fang across my breast until he drew blood. Just a drop, but enough to make him growl with pleasure and lick it clean. He knew he wasn't hurting me, just exciting both of us.

"I'm not giving up on us, Gloriana."

I kissed him, more thrilled than I should be by his stubborn possessiveness. I was in the moment, looking neither forward nor back as I rode him until we both fell into each other's arms, too satisfied to do much more than grin at each other.

"Satyr."

"Slut."

Oh, but I loved his smile. I couldn't take offense. When he's right, he's right.

"What must they be thinking?" I spoke out loud as I slipped off of Jerry and tossed my panties into the closet. I could tell by feel that my hair was a mess and grabbed a brush from the dresser.

"Didn't you hear the TV go on? They're trying not to think. Valdez must have picked the station."

Sure enough, I could hear the roar of NASCAR now that I tuned in to the reality in the next room. I helped Jerry to his feet and rescued his shirt from atop the lamp shade where it had landed during round number two.

I drew on some lipstick before pausing in front of the bedroom door. Jerry squeezed my shoulder and I turned to finger comb his tousled hair.

"You're not embarrassed, are you?"

"Not if we're okay now." I leaned against him for a

moment. I probably *should* be embarrassed. Cheeks flushed, whisker burn on my breasts visible because I had on a low-cut top as usual. Hey, I've got assets and I know how to use them.

"We're okay. But next time you reject me, try not to do it in front of an audience." He kissed me again, but didn't smile when he was done.

I touched his hard jaw and looked into his dark eyes. "That was really horrible of me. It won't happen again. I promise. Just don't put me on the spot. Please?"

"Some women would consider a proposal better than being put on a spot." Jerry opened the bedroom door.

The volume on the TV was high enough to make the walls shake. Jerry kept his arm around me as we walked back into the living room. Richard looked up, his face solemn. Yep, Jerry hadn't been the only one I'd managed to insult.

"Uh, Richard. Sorry about that defrocked priest slam. Totally out of line." I tried a smile.

Richard just stared at me, like Jerry was welcome to me, warts and all. Jerry had no trouble reading that message. His hand moved toward his back where I knew he kept a knife stashed.

"Flo and Lucky still in Flo's room?" I grabbed Jerry's arm and looked longingly down the hall. Maybe I should just scoot down there and leave the men to their brooding silences and threatening gestures.

Richard nodded. "They're having quite a chat. Seems your guest has no clothes, but came with all manner of knives. Blade, Gloriana had to disarm her. Twice."

"What the hell do you mean? Knives?" Jerry's arm dropped away from my shoulder.

"She's into self-defense, Jerry. Smart in her line of work." I gave up all thoughts of escape. I settled into a chair, grabbed the remote and turned off the TV.

"Hey, they were only three laps from the finish." Valdez looked from me to Jerry and settled with a chuff next to the door.

"But forget me. I just work here." I heard him muttering about enduring my noisy bedroom antics, but a look from Jerry shut him up.

"Perhaps you should have let this woman die, Gloriana. She sounds dangerous." Jerry sat in a chair across from Richard.

"I *am* dangerous to people who attack me." Lucky, Flo right behind her, came down the hall. She wore a pair of boots I knew Flo had just bought a month ago. Gee, the women had really bonded. "You must be Jerry. Thanks for helping Glory save my life." She held out her hand. "I hope you know I'd never harm her."

Jerry and Richard, both old-school gentlemen, had jumped to their feet when Lucky spoke. Now Jerry smiled and raised her hand to his lips. "As long as you mean that, then it was my pleasure to be of some assistance."

"Hey, *I* did the deed, you know."

"Of course, Glory." Lucky had at least remembered my name this time, but she looked a little bemused, like she'd fallen under Jerry's spell or something.

"I hear you like to use knives." Jerry gestured and Lucky sat in the chair he'd vacated.

I saw her grab at her sleeve then shoot me a dirty look. I just smiled at her. Valdez had stolen her extra knife after she and I had crashed. He'd tossed it under my bed, then sacked out himself. When I had a chance, I was going to stash it with her other knives.

Lucky smiled back, then hit Jerry with what she probably thought was a sultry look. "Nothing like a sharp . . . blade to rev my engines."

Flo and Valdez snorted in unison while Lucky looked up at Jerry through those long, dark lashes.

I wondered what kind of mascara she used, then snapped out of it and sent her a mental message to cool it. She looked startled, obviously not used to mental messages, especially ones that promised serious damage to her boots while she slept. I patted Valdez to make my point. Lucky caught on fast, because she ventured a mental message of her own. Hmm. Lucky had a potty mouth.

Bitch. I snarled and proved I'd picked up a rather interesting vocabulary myself over the years. If she kept coming on to my boyfriend she could see how long it took her to pry her precious boots out of her ass. Jerry just grinned, like seeing me jealous did a lot for his "wounded" ego.

"If you want to wear any of my things, Lucky, you'd better find your own boyfriends." Flo sat next to Richard on the couch and put a proprietary hand on his muscular thigh.

"No worries." Lucky held up her hands in surrender, but she was still obviously checking Jerry out.

"Glory, did you order more Fangtastic? We're almost out." Flo glanced at Lucky. "With a guest here, it will go fast. Unless we go out—"

"Maybe I'll order that new brand. I got an e-mail with a coupon for it. Will was raving about it the other day." William Kilpatrick had been an auxiliary guard dog for me recently. But constant shifting into his more human vampire form had made keeping him on impossible. Sue me. A guard dog is one thing, but when you can picture him as a hunky male, things get a little too freaky. Jerry had paid him off, but Will was still in town, looking for more work.

"Will? That's not Will Kilpatrick, is it?" Lucky tore her gaze from Blade's biceps and actually focused on me.

"Why do you want to know?" This couldn't be good. I knew Will had a thing for gambling. We had that in common. But while I'd kicked my habit with a twelve-step program, Will never even admitted he *had* a problem.

"He's one of the clients I came to Austin to find." Lucky jumped up. "You think he could have attacked me? With a debt the size of his, I figure he's suspect number one."

"Will wouldn't—" I wasn't sure what exactly to tell Lucky. The look in her eyes said slash now, ask questions later. Pain in the butt or not, I liked Will. And I had to sympathize on the gambling issue. It's a sickness. Valdez pushed his head under my hand. I smiled down at him. He's gotten really good at sensing my moods, and right now I was seriously conflicted.

"So it *is* him. Do you know where to find him?"

"He's probably across the hall, with Lacy. She's his newest lover." Flo obviously didn't care if Will got ripped a new one. He'd ignored her in favor of hitting on Lacy. Of course Flo hadn't exactly been herself when Will had come to town. Will and I aren't the only vampires with addictions.

"Lacy Devereau?" Lucky was on her feet. "She's the were-cat I met last night." She picked up her purse, realized it was now mine and dropped it with a thump. "Damn it, Glory, where did you put my knives?"

"You think Lacy set you up for Will?" I was nose to nose with Lucky now. "Lacy wouldn't do that. She works for me. She's not a killer. In fact, a vampire attacked her in the shop last night. A customer scared him off or she'd be victim number two." Hmm. Lacy was an immortal. Could she be drained dry? Or turned vampire? I had no idea and didn't want to find out.

"Did she recognize her attacker?" Jerry was on his feet, his hand on my arm. "Could he have been after you, Gloriana?"

"I don't know. Lacy said she thought he was an EV. Apparently Derek's been showing off the pictures he took out at their compound." I covered Jerry's hand with mine and squeezed. "Simon swore—"

"That he wouldn't hurt you or your friends. Not that he wouldn't try to drive you out of business."

"He would too, Glory." Flo was on my other side. "That bastard." She turned to Lucky. "Simon Destiny calls himself King of the Energy Vampires. Pah! He's nothing but a demon's servant." Flo straightened her shoulders. "We should go out there again. I've heard the demon he serves is terrified of spiders. We get a bunch of tarantulas and—"

"Whoa, Spidey. I, for one, don't want to anger a demon.

But I've got to be able to run my business without my clerks being scared off, or worse."

"Kings? Demons? I don't know who or what the hell you're talking about and I don't care." Lucky looked like she was ready to kickbox someone to hell and back. "I bet Will attacked me. You have any idea how much he owes my family?" Lucky charged into the kitchen. I heard drawers slamming and knew exactly what she was doing. Sure enough, she came out with a wicked-looking steak knife in each hand.

"I'm impressed that you're obviously ambidextrous, but you're not going to need those here." I used a vamp move to snatch them out of her hands.

"Son of a . . ." Lucky looked around the room but nobody offered to help. We all knew and liked Lacy. And as for Will? His sister had been married to Jerry's best friend. Jerry had known the Kilpatricks forever. It would take proof out the wazoo before he'd lift a finger against Will.

"If you'll calm down and promise to behave, I'll call Lacy and Will over here and we'll find out the truth." I stared into Lucky's eyes until she stalked over to a chair and sat down.

Valdez snorted and she gave him the evil eye.

"Are you laughing at me, dog breath?" She crossed her legs and pretended to aim a kick in his direction. "I'm the one who almost died. And the last person I saw before the attack might be right across the hall. If that bitch set me up . . ."

"You're wrong." I threw open the door and walked across the hall to knock on Lacy's door. First though, I sent a mental message to Richard and Jerry to stop Lucky if she lunged in Lacy's direction.

"Hi, Glory. What's up?" Lacy was dressed in skinny jeans and a tank top. You'd never know to look at her that she's were-cat. Not that I should think in stereotypes of course. I mean, look at *me*. I sure don't fit in with the pale, thin and brooding vampires you see in the movies. Instead I look, um, healthy. Like I never missed a meal, or a snack or . . . you get the picture.

"How are you doing, Lacy? Is your mother still here?"

"No, thank God. I convinced her I'm okay, but she's on the warpath. At least she didn't run into Will last night. You heard how she feels about vampires. If she knew I was letting one sleep over . . ."

"Is Will here?"

"Sure, you need him for something?"

"Can you both come over to my place for a minute? It's important." I kept Lacy from seeing inside my apartment. If she had set up Lucky . . . No, I couldn't think that. She was my good friend as well as an employee who would be hell to replace. I pay a decent commission, but clerking in a vintage-clothing store isn't exactly the fast track to big bucks. Employee turnover is a bitch.

"Sure, give us a minute and we'll be right over." Lacy looked back over her shoulder. "Will's putting a roast in the oven."

Yep, Will cooks, even trained in Paris at the Cordon Bleu, night classes. He's a born vampire, not "made" like me or Lucky. Born vamps can eat and drink and even procreate if the planets are aligned or something. They also consider themselves superior to us made types. And for good reason. I sniffed and smelled garlic. No, it's not a vamp repellant like some legends claim. It just smelled delicious. Which is pure torture to a noneating vampire like me.

"What's up, Glory?" Lacy smiled tentatively. "You need to hire Will again?" She lowered her voice. "Which would be great. He really needs the money."

"We'll discuss things when you both get over here."

"Fine." Lacy turned and I hustled back into my own place.

"They're coming." Lucky and Jerry had settled at the

kitchen table with a couple of bottles of Fangtastic. How cozy. "No one is going off half-cocked. Right, Lucky?"

Lucky looked up from her study of a knife that had probably come out of Jerry's ankle holster. "Blade says you can find out the truth with some kind of mind control. Prove Will and Lacy didn't conspire to take me out and I'll drop it." She handed the knife back to Jerry.

I'll be damned if she didn't brush her fingertips across his wrist. And he smiled, like he wouldn't mind letting those fingers take a tour of his more interesting places. I thought about giving Lucky a new do—something short and spicy because I'd ripped half her expensive hair out by the roots. Then Jerry winked at me. Maybe I'd jerk his lovely locks out too. Though, damn him, he'd probably still look good enough to . . . never mind.

The hall door opened.

"Allow me." Richard was in front of Will before I could say "Wait for me, Batman." Flo did the same thing to Lacy. We'd caught them off guard. Because they hadn't had time to block or look away. Instead they were both under the whammy, staring slack jawed and vacant eyed and at our mercy.

"You guys make quite a tag team." Lucky walked over to where Will and Lacy stood like zombies. Well, not exactly like zombies, because, trust me, once you've seen and *smelled* a real one you'll never— Okay, I needed to focus.

Lucky waved her hand in front of their eyes. "Un-freakin'-believable. Now what happens?"

"Now I ask them questions and they *have* to tell the truth. No choice. This is what I call the whammy." I gently shoved Richard and Flo aside and got in Will's face. "Will, did you try to kill Lucky Carver night before last?"

He got a puzzled look on his face. "Who? I didn't try to kill anyone. I shape-shifted into cat form and Lacy and I got it on that way. Man, was the fur flying!"

I put my fingers over his lips. Too much information and the visual had veered into yuck territory.

"Lacy, did you meet Lucky Carver in our alley?"

"Yes, I owed her family money. I paid her off, including all that damned interest, then hooked up with Will." She smiled. "He is the most incredible—"

Now I had to cover *her* lips. "Did you see anyone else when you were meeting with Lucky? A vampire in the alley?"

"Didn't see one. Smelled one, but figured I wasn't the only client Lucky was meeting. Her bodyguard was there, a badass shifter who kept giving me the evil eye. Me, I couldn't wait to get out of there. Will had promised—"

"Okay, I get it. Now shut up." I turned to Lucky, who was breathing down my neck.

"That was incredible. You've got to teach me how to do that." She turned to Jerry. "Or maybe *you* could."

"It's easier with mortals. Weres and vamps can block you if they know what you're trying to do. That's why we ambushed them. And you've got to make eye contact." Jerry looked at Richard. "I suppose it's possible the same vampire who attacked Lucky went after Lacy the next night. Maybe he or she thought Lacy saw something."

"What about my bodyguard though?" Lucky bit her lip. "Brittany *can* be a badass. That's why I hired her. I can't believe she'd let anyone past her, unless . . ." Lucky sidled closer to Jerry. "Maybe that vampire put her into one of these trances." She gestured at Will and Lacy. "But where is she now? How long can one of these hold?"

"It's too much of a coincidence to be different attackers. I suppose an EV could owe Lucky's family money too." I hoped this was all about Lucky. It would be too freaky if she'd been attacked just because she'd happened to be in the alley behind my shop.

"I can give you the names of the clients I'm trying to

track down here." Lucky dug her PDA out of her purse.
"You got a computer and printer? I could e-mail the list to
you and you could see if you recognize any names. I don't
know if any of them belong to this EV thing or not."

"Do it, Lucky." I rattled off my e-mail address, then
glanced at Will and Lacy, took pity and snapped them out
of it.

"What the hell just happened?" Will stared at Lucky.
"And who's this?"

"That's the loan, uh, officer I met the other night, Will.
Lucky Carver. She represents the Carvarellis."

"Oops. Well, got to jet. Dinner in the oven." Will
headed for the door.

"Not so fast, Kilpatrick." Lucky blocked his path and
poked Will in his broad chest. She was nothing if not gutsy.
"You owe us money. I'm here to collect."

Will snarled, his fangs suddenly enormous. "I'd like to
see you try."

"If you owe a debt, you pay it, Kilpatrick." Jerry was suddenly between Will and Lucky. "And back off. Ms. Carver is
under my protection."

"She's my responsibility, Jerry. Not yours." Now I was
getting pissed. He'd known Lucky for five minutes and now
she was under *his* protection? Lucky was *my* vampire, thank
you very much.

Will still looked like he was either going to bolt or do
something stupid. "Will, calm down." I put my hand on his
arm. "Did you try to rip out this woman's throat last
night?" I pointed to Lucky.

"Hell, no!" Will was as close to the door as he could get.
Obviously he'd counted and knew the odds against him
weren't good. "I've never seen her before in my life."

He reached for the knob and I slapped the door. "You're
not going anywhere. Yet." I glanced at Jerry. "You want to
ask him the same question? Since now Lucky's under *your*
protection?"

"Are you two going to fight over me?" Lucky grinned and glanced at Flo and Richard. "You guys want in on this?"

"Forget him. Where did you get this incredible purse?" Flo picked it up and looked inside, obviously not the least bit interested in Will's problems. "I want one. Does it come in red?"

"Sure. There's a waiting list, but—" Lucky gave me a dirty look. "It's Glory's now. Because I'm *so* grateful that she saved me."

"Nice." Flo grinned at me. "I may need to borrow—"

"Sure. Whatever." I'd just about had it with the whole bunch of them. "Lucky, go ahead and send the e-mail with your client list to me." I held up a hand when I could see both Richard and Jerry ready to object. "I'll forward it to both of you. And to Freddy since he's been in Austin a lot longer than any of us. Maybe he'll recognize a name that we wouldn't." Frederick von Repsdorf, his partner and his mother were part of my extended family. Not actual relatives, but the closest I'd come in a long time. They were one of the reasons I'd moved to Austin. That and a lust for some cowboy action.

I looked around the room. Not a Stetson or pair of boots in sight. When had my life gone so wrong?

Seven

"You're really going after whoever attacked me? My family could—" Lucky scanned the crowd.

"We need to handle this ourselves. Anybody could have found you in that alley. The vampire who left you for dead didn't give a damn about what that might mean for the vampires who live here." I saw Richard and Jerry nod. Flo was busy checking out the compartments in the Birkin bag.

"If you do find whoever did this . . ." Lucky stroked her throat. "Well, kill the son of a bitch. My family will be happy to compensate—"

"Really, Lucky. First things first. We need more information." No way was I letting Will get his paws on my shot at financial freedom. Besides, he'd probably piss it away at the nearest casino.

"Speak for yourself." Will put on a sympathetic look. "How much will they pay?"

Lucky frowned at him. "You're a deadbeat, Kilpatrick. Find the right vampire and we'll talk. But you're still on my short list of suspects. And get this. Killing me won't cancel a debt. It will only make things worse." A cell phone rang—a blast of "SexyBack."

Lucky picked up her phone from the coffee table. She frowned and shut it off.

"This 'family' business sounds interesting." Jerry glanced at me.

I deliberately stepped in front of Lacy and Will, who were edging toward the door.

"We keep good records and have stiff penalties for non-payment." Lucky said this like we were supposed to be impressed. Yeah, right. How reassuring to know a loan shark was well organized.

"For one thing, the Carvarellis have collateral. At least for large loans. Something very special to the debtors. You'd forfeit it. Right?" Lacy kept her hand on Will's arm. "I had a cousin who lost his family's vacation home in Vail. Boy, was his mom pissed." Lacy made a face. She and I had both had an up close and personal with a pissed mom-cat.

Lucky smiled at her. "Everyone knows the Carvarellis always get their money, one way or another."

"That's why, even though my loan was pretty small, I was determined to pay it off. But Will—"

"Darlin', say no more. Really." Will patted her hand. "Ms. Carver, I may have lost my temper there for a minute, but I fully intend to pay back every damned dime I owe your family."

Lucky shrugged and picked up her BlackBerry again. "So you say. Talk's cheap, Kilpatrick. That token you gave my father will be forfeited in thirty days. And then the serious shit hits the fan."

"I wondered—" I glanced at Jerry. "Seems like loaning to paranormals is a lose-lose proposition. What if they don't really care about their collateral. What's to keep a borrower from disappearing on you? Flying the coop, so to speak?" And, yeah, I meant that literally.

"We have paranormal enforcers on the payroll too. Trust

me, you don't want any of them after you." Lucky flicked
her gaze over Will. "You need a reminder of what might
happen, Kilpatrick?"

"They send in the clowns." Will muttered it. Broadway
show tune? His serious face said otherwise.

"What do you mean?" I turned to Lucky but it was Jerry
who spoke up.

"Clown Demons. A man in Scotland refused to pay. And
they came after him. Those buggers are no joke."

"Clown Demons." I tried and failed to keep a straight
face. "What do they do, laugh you to death?"

"Dying would be a relief after the ten thousandth bad
knock knock joke." Jerry grinned and I figured he was kidding.

"Truth. Honest." Lucky finished punching in a text and
shut off her PDA. "They hound you. Embarrass you because
they never leave your side." Lucky looked at Will and shook
her head. "Keep smiling, buddy boy. By the time the clowns
get through with you, no woman will ever look at you
again. And your friends will avoid you. And when the practical jokes start, you'll wish you were dead."

"All right. I get it. Pay up." Will frowned, then looked at
Jerry. "I don't suppose you've got more work for me."

"Not as *my* bodyguard." I was sure about that. Will popping in and out of dog body had been tough to take. Especially since his vampire body, which he'd insisted needed to
be naked, was centerfold material. And with Blade paying
him . . . Well, let's just say I don't need that kind of frus-
tration.

"Mayhap I'd like to see you with a couple of clowns."
Jerry's accent deepened and he moved closer to Lucky. "Tell
me, lass, what has the man given as token?" He gave Will a
hard look. "I think I know, but I hope to hell I'm wrong."

"It's a ring. A family heirloom." Lucky smiled and focused on Jerry. "Love the Scottish accent. From the Highlands?"

"Aye." Jerry wasn't smiling. "The ring. Would it be sportin' the Kilpatrick family crest, by chance?"

"I can explain—" Will paled and eased toward the door.

"You risked your family's honor for a gaming debt?" Jerry moved in on Will. "You know what it would do to your father if he found out you gave that ring to a bunch of soulless moneylenders?"

"Hey, it's an honest profession. We do a service." Lucky seemed to realize this was not the time to start a debate on the merits of loan sharking when Jerry didn't even spare her a glance.

"I'll not let you disgrace your family, Billy boy. How much do you owe?" Jerry had a fistful of shirt and Will up against the door.

"Quarter of a mil, give or take." Will was smart enough not to try to fight him off. Or to smile.

"A quarter of a *million*?" Wow. I thought *I* had problems when I maxed out three Visa cards.

Jerry dropped Will and stepped back. He turned to Lucky. "I want to buy the ring. Not discharge this worm's debt, just take the collateral out of your hands. Send in your clowns."

"Hmm. That's kind of irregular. I'd have to call my father." Lucky glanced at Will. "I'll get back to you on that."

"I'll do any kind of work, Blade, if you'll front me the money. Even do the dog thing again." Will had the nerve to smile at me. "Come on, Glory. We got on well enough. You made anyone mad lately?"

"Of course. She brought Lucky back from death and made her vampire. I figure whoever wanted Lucky dead will be mighty pissed." Valdez had obviously been a silent observer long enough.

"There you go. Sounds like we need to double your guard." Will exchanged looks with Valdez. Probably sending him a silent mental message that he'd cook for the pup, if Will came back as my guard again. Valdez will do anything for a good meal. Even accept another dog into the family.

"Well, gee, you don't have to sound so damned happy about it." I sent Valdez my own mental message that there'd be generic dog food all around if Will came back.

"But maybe I won't have to work after all." Will moved closer to Lucky. "Your family know you're vampire now? How's the old man going to take the news?" He nodded toward Lucky's cell phone. "What's it worth to you to be the one who tells him? Or would you rather I break the news?"

"Daddy knows and he's thrilled. Now the company will live on forever." Lucky smiled at Blade. "I'm going to make damned sure my father takes Blade's offer. Then I send in the clowns to work on you, Kilpatrick. Or would you like me to call *your* father for you? Maybe he'll bail you out. I'm sure he'd like to have his ring back."

"It's not his ring, it's mine. He gave it to me centuries ago." Will looked like a sullen child. "How the hell am I supposed to come up with that kind of cash so soon?"

"Try Prince Igor of Transylvania. He's always had a soft spot for a sob story." Jerry leaned against the door, his arms across his chest.

"I've gone to that particular well too many times. He said he'd have to tell my parents next time. For my own good. What a crock."

"Prince Igor of Transylvania? For real? He's a vampire?" Lucky tapped into her BlackBerry. "I don't have him in my records."

"You wouldn't. He's old money. But he's always doing fund-raisers, for his many charities." Flo frowned at Will. "You should be ashamed asking Igor for money. He is kind and helps many deserving people who are down on their luck. But a gambler. Pah! You should suffer the penalty for stupidity."

I kept my mouth shut, glad I'd never spilled my guts to Flo about my own gambling problem.

"According to my records, Kilpatrick, you've had this debt for over a year. You think we don't realize you've been dodging us? I don't care where you get the money, just pay up." Lucky sat and leaned down to pull off a boot and rub her foot. "Flo, these boots are cute, but they hurt like hell."

"I know, Luciana, why do you think I passed them on to you?" Flo laughed and shook her head. "Richard, I want to go out. I've had enough of William's issues. And I'm, um, thirsty. I want a little more than a bottle of Fangtastic." She looked at Lucky. "Come with us. I'll give you a lesson in being vampire. We're very careful. The mortals never know they've been touched."

"No way!" I grabbed Lucky when she shoved on the boot and hopped to her feet. "You and I are going shopping." I checked out my clock. "Well, the mall's closed, but you can come down to the shop. Meet Derek, who's working tonight, and see if there's something down there you'd like to wear." I glanced down at her feet. "I've got a pair of barely worn Prada pumps in your size."

Lucky looked torn. Shopping? Or taking her new fangs out for a test drive? She sighed and glanced at Flo. "Rain check? I need something of my own to wear and Prada . . ."

"Say no more, girlfriend. We do it another night." Flo pulled Richard toward the door. "Jeremiah, quit frowning at William and let us out. He's a big boy and made his own mess. Now he must deal with it." Flo tugged on Richard's hand. "Come, lover, I'm sure Glory will e-mail you those names. As soon as we've fed, we'll go by your place and see if we recognize any of them."

I had to give Flo credit. She knew her man. Richard never had been fond of the synthetic stuff. He followed her with barely a nod of good-bye to the rest of us. I stalked into the bedroom and grabbed my laptop. My printer was in a corner next to the TV. I plugged it in and got busy checking my e-mail. In moments I had the list in front of me. I figure my eyes widened because suddenly Jerry was right behind my left shoulder.

"Who is it? Do you see a name you know?"

Lucky hovered nearby. "There are a dozen names there, but not all of them are known to be in the Austin area. Kilpatrick's on there and I'm not ruling him out." Lucky got a fierce look. "We always collect a debt. Papa's got enforcers all over the world. Just let anyone try to take out cousin Alfonso in Thailand. Or Maria in Paris." She suddenly welled up and collapsed on the sofa. "They wouldn't have ended up bleeding out in an alley. I am such a failure."

"Now, Lucky." I liked my new vampire much better in kick-butt mode. "You were ambushed. Your bodyguard flaked out." I looked around and realized Will and Lacy had taken advantage of the distraction and left. I hoped he didn't decide to run and take Lacy with him.

"I thought my bodyguard was my friend. How could she leave me there to die?" A fat tear streaked down Lucky's cheek.

"Maybe she didn't leave voluntarily."

"Then we have to find her." Lucky looked up, her eyes wet and her nose pink. Waterproof mascara. I was definitely checking out the brand.

"Gloriana, give me the list. Who's on it?"

I thrust it at Jerry. "You'll see. I recognize at least one name. Greg Kaplan. The creep who almost got me drained by the Energy Vampires."

Lucky got up and headed for the door. "I need to get out of here. I want to look for Brittany."

Jerry glanced up from the list. "Gloriana, you're not—"

"I'm going with her. We'll be in the shop if you need us." I ignored Jerry's grumble. "Work on that list." I walked up to him and slid my arms around his waist. "If you're still here when we get back . . ." I pulled down his head and whispered an interesting proposition in his ear.

"I'll be here." He snugged me closer and gave me a long and satisfying kiss. "Be careful, lass. Valdez, stay close."

"You got it, boss." Valdez dropped his leash at my feet.

"We'll *all* be careful." I held on to the leash, but didn't bother to clip it on. It was just for show anyway. I pulled Lucky out the door. She stopped at the top of the stairs.

"You guys seem pretty tight." She glanced back at my apartment.

"Tight. Loose. Jerry made me. Just like I made you, Lucky. So we feel bound to each other."

"Excuse me?" Lucky ran down the stairs. "I'm not *bound* to you. I'm my own woman. And now that I'm vampire . . ." She concentrated, then grinned. Her new fangs were a dazzling white. "I figure I don't need anyone or anything." She tried to open the outside door, then looked down at the keypad. "Except maybe the code to get out of here."

"In a minute." I put my hand on Valdez's head. I could tell he was bursting to spout off to Lucky about how *not* ready she was to take on the world. "I'll just say this one more time. There's a lot you don't know yet. About your powers or lack of. About the predators out there who live to take a vampire fang as a trophy." Now *that* erased her megawatt smile. "And about how to keep safe and below the mortal radar. It's all about survival, Miss Not-So-Lucky. I've managed to stick around for over four hundred years so maybe, just maybe, I know a thing or two about it. Ya think?"

I waited a beat or two. Finally she looked sheepish and nodded. "Okay, okay, I get it." She glanced up the stairs again. "Besides." Here came the grin again. "No way am I risking my new life before I've had a chance to try a vampire lover."

"That's as good a reason as any. So listen and learn." I reached over and punched in the code. "Trust me, Lucky. There's nothing like sex with a vampire male, especially an ancient one. Mortals never quite, um, measure up after you've had a vampire ring your bell."

"Do I have to hear this?" Valdez was through the door as soon as I pulled it open. *"Wait here. I'm checking out the area."*

Lucky tried to head out after him and I stopped her with an arm across the door. "Wait. Let Valdez do his thing."

"You take orders from your *dog*?" Lucky tried unsuccessfully to shove my arm out of the way.

"Just like you listened to your bodyguard. You did listen to her, didn't you?"

"Yeah, yeah, point taken." Lucky sighed. "Brit was really careful. She didn't want me to meet in the alley at all. We had a big fight about it. And now—"

"And now we try to find her." I heard Valdez shout the all clear in my mind. "Let's go."

"We should walk around the block if you want to check out the alley. If we go through the shop, you'll be stuck." Valdez nodded toward the large shop windows.

I could see a few customers looking through racks of clothes and Derek helping a woman pick out a porcelain figurine. I itched to go in and see the day's totals and maybe boost a sale or two in the clothing department. But Lucky was already halfway down the block. I made sure no one was looking, then put on a burst of vamp speed to catch up with her.

"You should have good night vision now, Lucky. Check it out." We turned the corner, and I noticed the security lights at the end of the alley were still out.

"Wow, you're right. It's like I've got headlights."

Valdez trotted a few feet ahead of us, head down, tail up.

"I—" Something hit me right between my shoulder blades and I went down hard. "What the—" Snarls, curses, some mine, some Valdez's, none Lucky's, flew as I rolled and got ready to kick some ass. I gasped when a stake pricked my chest through my black sweater set.

"Nobody move or this bitch dies."

"I'm not moving." Not even to drag some cold night air into my lungs.

"Brittany!" Lucky appeared next to the woman who was poking me with what felt like a giant spear. "Stop! This is Glory. She saved me."

"She stole your purse." Poke. Poke. "I saw her carrying it." Poke. Brittany, six feet of womanly curves and flowing blond hair, seemed to be gathering steam for the death strike. "Run, Lucky. Grab your purse and take off while I finish this bitch."

Lucky, ungrateful bitch herself, was obviously thinking this one over.

"Tell her the truth, Lucky."

"Okay, okay. She saved my life, Brit. I *gave* her the purse. In gratitude. I'd be dead if she hadn't found me bleeding out in the alley. Honest. Let her go."

An astonished Brittany glanced over her shoulder. "Are you kidding me? You gave up your Birkin bag? *Willingly?*"

I saw my chance. I hadn't watched ESPN wrestling with Valdez just for the muscular male bodies, writhing in next to nothing. I used my legs in a scissor kick to throw Brittany off balance as I grabbed her wrist and squeezed. I jumped up and tossed the stake halfway down the block, ready to finish her.

"Ow! Son of a—" Brittany was flat on her face, Valdez on her like a dog-skin rug. "Oof. Get off me." She raised her head and sniffed. "Rafael?"

"Who wants to know?" Valdez put a paw on her injured wrist and she yelped.

"Rafe, baby, it's me, Beth." She had tears in her big blue eyes.

Valdez leaned down and dragged his nose through her really gorgeous blond mane. *"Holy shit."* He leaped off her, knocking me on my butt.

"Hey!" I stomped on her injured wrist again when it looked like she was going to get up. She screamed and stopped struggling.

"Stop! It's Brittany!"

"Stop! It's Beth!"

I kept my foot where it was and faced the chorus. "I don't care if it's Santa Claus. She just tried to stake me." I could see Valdez was thinking about a head butt. "Don't even. I'm not letting her up until I get some explanations." Lucky made some threatening gestures with her generic hobo bag. "Lucky, you should be with me on this. Where the hell was your 'bodyguard' when you were almost killed?"

"Yeah, Brittany, where were you? A vampire, not this one, tore open my throat and left me for dead."

"I . . . I don't remember. One minute I was checking out this alley . . ." She looked at Lucky, then me. "Then I woke up in the rental car this morning. I've been looking for you ever since."

"Where's your cell phone? You could have tried calling me." Lucky looked like she wanted to believe this story, but, like me, she saw there were holes in it you could heave hobo bags through.

"I lost it. My purse, my ID, even the keys to the rental. I found my stuff this afternoon in the Dumpster, but the battery in my cell phone was dead."

I moved my foot ever so slightly and Brittany gasped. "I think you broke my wrist."

"Doubt it. But you ever aim a stake at me again . . ." I frowned down at her. I've had way too many close calls lately. And I couldn't forget how I'd found Lucky alone and bleeding out in this alley.

Brittany reached for Valdez with her good arm. "Rafael, baby. I'd never betray a client. You know that."

"Quit torturing her, Glory. Let's hear her out." Valdez stopped short of actually vouching for her. He put a paw in the middle of her chest when she tried to get up. *"Stay put, Beth, until we hear the rest of your story."*

"There *is* no rest. I woke up in the backseat of the rental car, realized Lucky was missing and started searching. I saw the blood in the alley, but when I couldn't find her, I hoped someone had saved her." She had a watery smile for Lucky. "Or that Lucky had saved herself and used one of her knives to get away."

"I used a knife. But I'm no match for a vampire. Or at least I wasn't." Lucky actually patted me on the shoulder.

"Ah, gratitude." I wasn't sure what to believe and I still had a sore spot where the stake had pricked me. I looked down and checked out my sweater. Yep, a tiny hole and a bloodstain, but black is pretty forgiving so hopefully no one else would notice.

"What do you mean?" Brittany tried to get up again, and this time Valdez moved out of her way.

I stepped back, determined to keep my eyes on her. She had legs a mile long and wore her designer jeans tight and her cable knit sweater loose. The stake had come from somewhere. She probably had a damned arsenal tucked in her waistband.

"Hand over your weapons, Brittany." I held out my hand.

"You want to leave me defenseless?" Brittany said it to me, but glanced at Valdez.

"I don't think you're ever defenseless, lady." Valdez nodded. *"Give."*

Brittany sighed, but handed me a gun she'd had tucked into her waistband. I dropped it in my purse. I've never been big on guns. They aren't much help when you make a vampire mad.

"You're not going to believe what happened, Brit. Glory came along and saved me. She had to make me vampire or I would have bled to death." Lucky showed off her new fangs.

"Oh, my God. Your father is going to have me killed for this." Brittany was pale and held her injured wrist against her chest.

"I've talked to him. Neither one of us thought you could have done this to me. And Daddy's actually decided it's pretty cool to have a vampire in the family. Now the company will go on forever." Lucky reached out and touched Brittany's arm, then looked at me.

"Do you think I can heal her, Glory? Like you did me?"

"You sure you want to? I know you two were buds, Lucky, but I haven't heard anything yet that convinces me she wasn't in on the plot to take you out."

"Hey, I told you—"

"Oh, hush, Brittany. I believe you, but Glory doesn't know you like I do. Give me your arm. Vampires can do this healing thing. I want to practice on you." Lucky grabbed Brittany's wrist and I heard the bodyguard's hiss of pain.

"Fine. You can try. But it takes a lot of power to heal someone, Lucky. You're awfully new." I shut my mouth when Brittany eeked and big, fat tears ran down her porcelain cheeks. Valdez—no, make that Rafael, baby—stayed by my side but his eyes never left Brittany aka Beth.

Valdez has always kept his past a secret. He knows everything about me, except my weight of course. *No one* knows that. But I know next to nothing about him. If he and Brittany, sorry, but I was calling her that, had hooked up, then he must be pretty hot in his human form. Because Amazon bitch or not, she was gorgeous. I'd always suspected, okay, fantasized that Valdez was actually a stud muffin under all that Labradoodle fur.

Not that I have *feelings* for him. Eww. We're friends; that's all. Oh, and we have that guard, guardee relationship. He makes me feel safe. Which is nice. Okay?

Lucky had been concentrating with pursed lips and closed eyes. Her grip was obviously pretty tight if Brittany's face was anything to go by.

"Lucky, you can let go of me now. It feels better, honest." Brittany gently pried Lucky's fingers off her wrist, then tentatively moved her injured hand. "Damn, girl, you did it." She flung her arms around Lucky and gave her a hug. "I'm so glad you're alive!"

"Maybe we should go upstairs for this reunion." Valdez

glanced at me. I got his message. He wanted Blade around for backup. In case his old pal Beth was a wild card and decided to pull out another stake.

"Wait a minute." I held up my hand. "Lucky, didn't Damian go down to your car and get your overnight bag last night?"

"Yes, yes he did." Lucky stepped away from Brittany. "You weren't in the car then, Brit. Damian would have seen you."

"I don't know where the hell I was. Or how much time passed before I woke up. What day, er, night is it anyway?" Brittany looked at Valdez, like maybe she hoped he would help her out here. Nope, he just stared at her, his teeth glinting in the moonlight.

"It's been forty-eight hours since Lucky was found back here. Two days, two nights." I jingled my keys, wishing I stashed knives on my body like Lucky and Blade did. Maybe a key in the eye . . . I could tell the shifter was strong. Maybe too much for me alone. I glanced at Valdez and saw he was ready to attack if it came to that. "You couldn't have been sleeping in the car during the day; we have regular foot patrols in this neighborhood. The cops would have seen you and pulled you out."

"I . . . I don't know where I've been. I . . ." Brittany reached out to Lucky. "I can't remember . . ."

"Convenient." I almost jumped back when Lucky and Valdez stared at me. "What? Are you just going to buy this story? And will you sleep well tomorrow during the day, Lucky, with this, this deserter guarding you?"

"I swear . . ." Brittany bit her lip and looked around, like maybe she'd find some kind of evidence to back her up. "I'd die for Lucky. It's what we do, right, Rafe?"

"It's what I do. You, babe, I'm not so sure about. Last time we were together, you ran. I was left with a torn shoulder that was a bitch to heal."

"I had a reason. I had to save—"

"Enough. Brittany probably had the whammy put on her. Like you did those two upstairs. Like you do to mortals. You said you could wipe out their memories. Someone did that to Brit." Lucky linked arms with her bodyguard and pulled her toward the street. "Let's go to Glory's shop. I need clothes. Brittany, you need clothes too. Then we'll call Daddy. He'll arrange to have stuff sent for us."

"You think Daddy Carvarelli will just accept this lame excuse?" I followed, but I wasn't entirely happy about it. No way was I turning my back on Brittany. Not until I had some kind of proof she wasn't in on the attack.

"He never thought Brit could have done it. He and Brittany go back a long, long way. She was his bodyguard when he was just a teenager. He liked having a hot blond woman with him all the time." Lucky stopped in front of my shop. "Look, Brit, Vintage Vamp's Emporium, isn't that cute?"

"Yeah, cute." Brit tentatively put her hand on Valdez's shoulder. "You. You believe me, don't you, Rafe? I'd never flake out on a client. And I didn't have a choice when I left you, before."

"Save it for later, chica. Let's go inside. And keep in mind there are mortals all around us. Time to show off your defense." Valdez nodded his head and I pulled open the door. *"And your loyalty."*

Yep, there were mortals in the shop and, other than my salesclerk, Derek, at least one vampire. Friend or foe? I didn't recognize him. And he was showing signs of aggressive behavior. Fisted hands, stiff shoulders and muscles on top of muscles.

Damn, were we going to have another showdown? I couldn't say I was sorry; I was still flying on adrenaline and here was a chance for Brittany to show whose side she was on.

Eight

"Hey, Glory, just in time." Derek was busy ringing up a sale and there were two other women waiting to pay. "I could use some help. Got to love the Christmas rush."

"Sure." I turned to Lucky and Brittany. "Stay." I smiled when the customers gasped. "My dog, of course. Valdez, stay." I gestured to the front door and Valdez ambled over and sat down. Looking at him, you'd think he was just a well-trained, cute-as-a-button Labradoodle. And you'd be wrong. If either Brittany or Lucky tried to leave, they'd be wearing his teeth marks on their butts. Valdez sent me a mental message.

"Glory, that other vampire looks familiar. Keep your eye on him."

I checked him out. Not your typical hunk-type vamp. This one looked like he'd fallen on hard times and he could use a shave and a bath. Lucky and Brittany gave him a wide berth on their way to the sweater section.

I helped complete sales, breathed a sigh of relief over the day's totals, then pulled out $485 in cash and stuck it in an envelope. Damned credit-card customers. Of course I couldn't afford not to accept credit, even debit cards, but it made the cash on hand pretty skimpy. I spotted some coupons my neighboring business had left for free coffee at Mugs and Muffins. I stuffed five of those in and licked the flap, sealing the envelope.

Lucky headed into a dressing room with an armload of black. I popped into her mind and realized she was thinking of going Goth. Hey, she was a vampire now. Queen of the Freakin' Damned. Obviously she'd be in there some time while she perfected her new look.

"Derek, I'm going out to the car. I left some bags and price tags I bought the other night out there."

"Yeah, sure." Derek grinned when Valdez jumped up and followed me. "Guess you should walk the dog while you're out." My clerk knew Valdez would never let me go without him anyway.

I threw the new dead bolts and glanced outside. The lights were working and Valdez bounded out, head high as he sniffed for trouble.

"Make it quick, Blondie. I feel like this is Death Alley back here. Too much has happened."

I shivered. "No kidding." I pulled my car keys out and made a big deal of opening the back of the Suburban. I did have a bag of stuff I could bring in. I grabbed it, slammed the rear door closed, then froze.

"Did you hear that?"

Valdez whipped around and stared at me. *"What?"*

"I think I heard someone moving near the back door of our shop."

"Stay here, Blondie. I'll check it out."

I watched him hustle to the doorway, then I tiptoed over to the Dumpster and jammed the envelope under one corner. With vamp speed, I was back where Valdez had left me by the time he came trotting back.

"Nothing there. Probably just a rat."

"Gross. Let's get inside." I glanced back at the envelope, but it was just a bit of white paper, blending in with the trash around it. I hoped it satisfied the creep trying to ruin my life here. I thought about telling Valdez about it, hiding in the car and trying to catch the blackmailer, but a mortal could wait until daylight to pick up the cash. Damn it. I sniffed the air. No one else nearby. If anyone was waiting for the money, he wasn't here now.

We headed back inside and dumped the tags and bags I'd brought in on a shelf in the back room. I was headed to the counter when the dirty vamp approached me. Valdez didn't waste a second putting himself between me and the new guy.

"May I help you find something?" I could see the guy's hands were empty.

"Are you Gloriana St. Clair?"

"Yes, who wants to know?" Sure, I sounded surly. But I've had some bad encounters in the shop and this guy had hard eyes, though I had to admit they were a gorgeous blue.

"I'm Etienne Delacroix. We have a mutual friend."

"Who?" French name. I've had a few French lovers in the past. The distant past. But this guy hadn't been one of them.

"Gregory Kaplan."

Valdez growled and I grabbed a pencil, the only pointy wooden object close at hand.

"Greg is not my friend."

Etienne grinned. "Excellent. This was a test, you see. I hate that bastard. I would like to see him wearing a pencil through his black heart."

I looked around, but the only mortal in the shop at the moment had stepped into a dressing room.

"Maybe I've got a test for *you*." I leaned in and put on my fiercest face. Valdez bared his teeth and made a sound so menacing Brittany came running from the other side of the shop.

"What's up?" She took a whiff, wrinkled her nose, then leaned close to Etienne. "You giving my friend here a hard time?"

She had dangerous down to an art form. Etienne paled and made a grab for the pencil, knocking my arm aside. Big mistake. Valdez chomped down on the man's dirty jeans and obviously got some leg too. Etienne yelped.

"I mean you no harm. I swear it on my mother's life." Still, he'd managed to get the pencil and held it like a dagger.

Brittany apparently wasn't worried about death by graphite. She sneered. "Unless your mother's also on a liquid diet, she probably kicked the bucket centuries ago. Now if you want to swear on your *own* life . . ." She whipped a stake out from under her baggy sweater. Obviously Brittany packed a spare. When would I learn to do a body search?

"Whoa, Brit, those things make me nervous now." Lucky dumped an armload of clothes on the counter and checked out Etienne. "There a problem here?" She showed off her new fangs, then looked at Valdez, who still had Etienne's leg between his teeth. "Hey, V-man, great defense."

Valdez wagged his tail, but didn't let go.

"This guy says he knows Greg Kaplan." Brittany obviously wasn't thrilled that Valdez was getting all the credit here.

"You know where to find him? I'm looking for him." Lucky dug in her bag and pulled out her BlackBerry. "He owes my family a ton of money. Play your cards right and there might be a finder's fee in it for you."

"I could use it." Etienne jerked when Valdez pulled on his leg and he finally dropped the pencil. "Please, I would like to help you. Maybe we can work together. He owes me too. And I heard him talking about Miss St. Clair. I wanted to warn her. He is not a man she should have dealings with."

"What the hell do you know about me and Greg?" Greg

had lured me out to the Energy Vampire stronghold like I was the catch of the day.

"Oh, my God! That dog is biting—" My mortal customer screeched, dropping two sweaters and a pair of hundred dollar Levi's "red line" jeans and her credit card on her way to the door.

"Stop her." I gestured to Lucky. "Here's how. Look into her eyes and tell her to stop. This will try out your whammy. If it works, she won't be able to move. Hurry!"

"Cool." Lucky bounded across the room, threw herself in front of the door and locked eyes with the woman. "You are *not* going to move." She clapped her hands when the lady stopped in her tracks. Lucky grinned at me, then hit her with the whammy again. "Pick up the things you want to buy and pay for them at the register. Nod if you hear me."

Sure enough, the woman nodded and bent to collect her finds.

"Valdez, let go of Etienne. Brittany, take this guy in the back and out of sight while I ring up this sale. I want some answers and Derek will help you if this guy tries to cut and run before I can get back there."

"As if I need help." Brittany waited for Valdez to release him before she grabbed Etienne's arm.

"Gack!" Valdez spit out bloody blue cotton. *"What the hell you been drinkin, man?"*

"Homeless winos and stray dogs," Etienne snarled. "This violence wasn't necessary, Miss St. Clair." He reached toward me. "I mean you no harm."

"Touch her and die." Valdez growled, showing all his teeth. Etienne shouted a few obviously choice words in French, then spoiled the effect by limping with as much haste as he could manage into the back room.

Lucky was practically dancing with excitement. "Forget him. The whammy is so cool. I mean, I could tell her anything, right? And she'd do it? Like you did with Will and Lacy earlier?"

"In theory. It helps if you know a name." I really didn't want this to turn into a sideshow, but the whammy is excellent defense. If Lucky was going to start acting like Vampira, then she'd need practice erasing memories.

Lucky grabbed the woman's chin and forced her to make eye contact again. "Tell me your name."

"Janice."

Lucky grinned. "Janice, quack like a duck."

"Quack."

I was *not* going to laugh. Even though Janice looked more urban chic than waterfowl. "Enough, Lucky. I've got a business to run. Tell her to pay for her purchases. That she'll remember she loves this store and wants to come back often and bring her friends. Then say, 'Snap out of it.'"

"I love this. The possibilities are endless." Lucky glanced at the back room. "Why didn't you do that to Etienne? I could tell he was upsetting you."

"He's a vampire and obviously on guard. You can't just whammy anyone you want. Mortals, sure. Paranormals, only if they're weak or distracted and you sneak up on them, like we did with Will and Lacy earlier." I heard a crash and ran toward the noise.

"Everything okay in there?"

Brittany opened the door a crack. "Etienne had a little accident. No worries. Take care of your customer."

I turned to see Janice duck-walking around the hat rack, quacking the "Star Spangled Banner."

"Cool it, Lucky! More customers could come in. You hurt my business and I'll catch you unawares someday and make you do something really cute, but with a wider audience." I hummed the theme from *Jaws*.

"Aw, gee. You're no fun." Lucky looked disappointed but did the necessary. Finally, Janice left, her package in her hands and a smile on her face as she promised to come back soon.

A couple of college students pushed inside. Since there'd been no more noises from the back, I put on my smile. "Hi, there. Let me know if I can help you find anything."

"We want to see the— Oh, awesome!" They headed straight to the vampire mural Flo had painted on one wall. Art students. I could hear them analyze the technique and compare it to the original Edvard Munch pieces it was based on.

When one of them pulled out a cell phone and started snapping pictures, I shuddered. Had they looked at me strangely when they came in? One of them was texting, and I ran to see if I had any new messages.

I had two. The first was from a friend in Las Vegas, and I sagged in relief. The second made my stomach hurt again. I was about to start ripping out art-student throats when I realized this text had come in an hour ago and I had just forgotten to check.

First the video. I ran it twice, hating the way it zoomed in on my face as I pulled back from Lucky's wrist, fangs dripping blood. No doubt about it. Glory was a vampire.

"IF U DON'T WANT 2 C THIS ON TV, PAY $500. I SAW U, VAMPIRE."

I leaned against the counter and slapped the phone shut. So the blackmailer hadn't picked up the money yet. Would five hundred dollars be enough, or was it just a down payment? I was afraid I already knew the answer to that. It wouldn't even pay for the flat-screen HDTV Valdez wanted for Christmas. And wouldn't the video look a treat on that?

I put my head in my hands. If I were still in Vegas, I could take my dog and disappear into the night, leaving the blackmailer holding an empty envelope. But I was established here, a member of the vampire community. I didn't want to leave. If I stayed and was outed as a vamp though, every vampire in Austin would be at risk. Blade, Flo, Damian; people with deep roots in the community might have to move on.

Damn it, I'd hate to leave, and I sure as hell didn't want to ruin things for all the people I'd grown to love here.

"Glory, can you come here?" Brittany stuck her head out the door of the back room again. "Valdez, Lucky and I will cover the front."

"Lucky stays with me. You want to tell me about that crash?" I whispered as I grabbed Lucky's arm. She had a gleam in her eyes that promised art students on duck parade if I didn't keep her with me.

"Etienne gave Derek some upsetting news. I guess Derek's partner, Freddy, is related to an Energy Vampire."

"Yes, I know that, so does Derek. So what got Derek worked up?" I love Freddy, love Freddy's mother, who had had the bad taste and worse luck to have made a child with Simon Destiny, the king of the EVs. Pathetic, isn't it? A cult of vampires with a freakin' monarchy. But don't let the cheesy title fool you. They are dangerous as hell, and I'm on their shit list big-time. Neither Freddy nor his mother wanted anything to do with Daddy Dearest.

"Etienne swears he saw Freddy out there. At the EV compound. That there was a big father and son reunion. Back-slapping. Like that. Derek told Etienne to shut up with a right to the jaw. But you can ask him about it yourself." Brittany shoved me into the back room and slammed the door before Valdez could get inside.

"That woman is . . ."

"Bossy?" Etienne dabbed his bloody lip with a paper towel. In true vampire fashion, his leg had stopped bleeding, but his dirty pants were shredded below the knee.

"She's just tough. Bodyguards have to be."

I ignored Lucky's comment. It didn't take mind reading to see that Derek was ready to take another swing at Etienne. He paced the small room, his hands fisted.

"Derek, what Brittany said, about Freddy . . ."

"I don't believe this guy." He grabbed Etienne's shirt and shook him. "You got any proof?"

"Of course. I've been around a long time, my friend. Many vampires lie to stay alive. As do I." He reached into his pants pocket, and I thought Derek was going to go ballistic.

"Wait." I grabbed Derek's arm. "What are you going for, Etienne?" I doubted it was a weapon or this guy would have pulled it when Valdez had made him the taste du jour.

"My cell phone. I have pictures." Etienne waited until Derek stepped back. "I didn't know you were friendly with these people. I was just telling Brittany about the EVs and who I met out there. She's helping Lucky track down people who owe money, she said. If I can earn some fees by helping her, I will." Etienne flipped open his phone and punched in some commands. "Then this one goes crazy. Calling me a liar." He licked his lip and seemed to relish the taste of his own blood. "Hitting me."

"Freddy hates his father. He would never go out there willingly. Maybe Simon threatened CiCi if he didn't come." Derek sounded like he was trying to convince himself. Freddy was very close to his mother, but why would he sneak out there without telling his partner? The guys had been together for decades.

"Here, see for yourself." Etienne handed me the phone, but Derek snatched it out of my hands. He groaned then scrolled through some more pictures.

"I can't believe it. Why would he do this?" Derek handed me the phone, his lips trembling.

I saw for myself Freddy and Simon sharing a smile over some book they were reading. The EV torture manual? Then Greg Kaplan was in the picture. He was obviously out of favor with the king, relegated to sitting on the floor while the great one preached from a pulpit. Even more disturbing was our dear friend Freddy by his father's side. I felt sick to my stomach, and my hand shook as I held the phone for a moment.

"Nice phone." I looked him over. "Kind of surprising really."

"One of the few things I managed to keep." Etienne reached for it.

"Not so fast." I put it behind me. "You ever text?"

He looked genuinely confused and shook his head. "What kind of test? I swear I am just telling what I saw."

I probed his mind, but he was blocking me. No surprise there. I scrolled through the menu but got zip, not even any stored phone numbers. What did I expect? A video marked "Vampire Blackmail"? Of course I'm not exactly a technological whiz kid, and I couldn't tell the rest of the gang in the back room what I was looking for.

"I know why Greg hates me, Etienne, but what do you have against him?"

"He lured me out to that EV place. If you've been there, you know it looks like a temple. Gold dome. A holy place. I was excited. Promises were made in exchange for money." Etienne stared at his phone, and I finally handed it over.

"So did you go for the Vampire Viagra?" I glanced at Derek. He'd calmed down enough to pay attention to the conversation.

"Vampire Viagra?" Lucky was wide-eyed. "I thought vampire men were all super studs."

"We are." Etienne winked at her. "Of course I have no need for their drugs. And make no mistake, their Vampire Viagra is not for the same purpose as for mortals. Men *and* women vampires seek it out because it enhances pleasure. I tried it. What about you, Glory?"

Nothing like being put on the spot and, if I pleaded the Fifth, I didn't doubt Lucky would hound me until I told her anyway.

"I had it slipped into my Fangtastic. It's powerful stuff, but I didn't like the loss of control. It's like you're on sex hyperdrive. For hours."

"Ooo." Lucky apparently found nothing wrong with that.

"For myself, I prefer to take my time." Etienne managed to look very knowledgeable.

"Ahh." Lucky swung her focus to him.

"But there is something else the EVs have there. This special room." Etienne got a faraway look in his eyes. "It's like being in the sun again. I have always missed it. The sunlight. Seven hundred and fifty-two years and I haven't felt the sun on my face." He actually got a little teary. "Until I sat in that room."

Wow. I won't lie and say sunlight wouldn't do it for me. Even night owls in mortal life eventually develop a craving for the normalcy of being out during the day. Forget the Vampire Viagra, the EVs' main moneymaker. I'd accidentally tried it and didn't like it one damned bit. Well, maybe a little damned bit. Anyway, sunlight. Hmm. To loll around on a topless beach with Blade . . .

"How do they do it? Sun lamps?" I almost hoped that was it. Cheesy imitation sunlight. No big deal.

"No, they have a demon who makes it possible for them to manufacture all their special products. This one allows a vampire to stay awake during the day and, as long as he's in this room they have, the sun can't hurt him"—he smiled at Lucky—"or her. It's magical."

"Interesting." Lucky moved closer to Etienne. "I hate to waste my days."

"Forget it, lovely lady." Etienne smiled sadly. "It costs too much. I had to give them my power for visits to that room. They drained me until I can no longer read minds or shape-shift. I can barely heal myself." He walked over to the large table next to the wall. "Look." He tried to pick up one end, but, even with his muscles bulging and his face red with strain, he only managed to lift it a few inches.

"I don't believe you." Derek walked over to the table. "Oh, gosh, so damned heavy." He casually picked it up with one hand. "And I sure don't believe Freddy is really tight with his father. He must have gone out there to spy for us." He dropped the table with a thump. "He loves you, Glory. We consider you part of our family and he knows they're going to want revenge for what you pulled out there recently. You humiliated Simon. And we want the Energy Vampires out of Austin. Maybe Freddy's pretending—"

"Sure. Got to be it. I love you guys too. But I wouldn't want Freddy to risk his life for me. We need to find out why he went out there, Derek." I prayed that was it. Freddy's been a true friend for centuries. Funny how I suddenly had all kinds of doubts about that though. But in all the years I'd known Freddy and his mother, they'd never shared the tiny little fact that his father is the numero uno servant of a demon until less than a month ago.

"I'm going home, Glory. I've got to find out what's going on with Freddy. You can handle the shop now, right? Until Lacy comes in?"

"Sure, Derek, got it covered." I glanced at Etienne. He'd collapsed in the room's only chair. Lucky was busy lifting that table, laughing when she got it a foot off the ground with only two fingers. "And don't worry about Etienne. If he's as powerless as he says, Brittany and I can handle him."

"Fine. I'm outta here." Derek threw the dead bolt on the back door and left.

I quickly locked the door behind him. I heard the tinkle of the bells on the front door, and this wasn't the first hint that the store was filling with shoppers.

"Etienne, I'm not leaving you here by yourself. Come into the shop with Lucky and me." I got a whiff of him. "Did the EVs steal your luggage too?"

"I had to leave everything behind and sneak away. I could tell that I would soon be too weak to be of any use to them if I kept giving them my power." Etienne got up and ran water in the sink. He began washing his face and hands. "I have no money for a room somewhere. I paid it all to Greg Kaplan for the chance to see the sunlight room one more time. Then . . ." He took a shuddering breath. "Then he didn't let me near it." He grabbed a wad of paper towels and rubbed his face dry.

"No surprise there. Greg is a manipulative liar." I won't go into what he did to me during the sixties in New York, but I hate the SOB.

"The worst thing is trying to find a safe place to sleep during the day. I finally had to crawl into a storm sewer." He looked at Lucky, his dark eyes sad. "I'm sorry you are seeing me this way, my dear. Weak. Filthy. Unshaven. Less than a man."

Lucky melted and put her hand on his arm. "Hey, you don't look so bad. Maybe we can help you find somewhere to stay." She smiled at me. "Glory lives right upstairs. We're pretty crowded in her little apartment, but—"

"But nothing. Slow down. Let me think." I didn't like the fact that I actually felt sorry for the guy. Hey, I know what it's like to crave something you can't have. I'd risked all kinds of pain and suffering just to eat a bag of Cheetos. And, in some ways, it had been worth it. The lure of sunlight was major. No wonder Etienne looked so haggard. He'd given a hell of a lot of his power away. I shuddered. I'd come way too close to losing my own power recently.

"I don't get the whole fascination with sunlight anyway." Lucky started sifting through a stack of vintage shirts and tossed one to Etienne. "Everyone knows it causes skin cancer, not to mention premature aging. I gave up tanning years ago."

"Miss St. Clair?" Etienne held the shirt out to me. "Do you wish for me to leave?"

"No. I mean, let me think for a minute." I set the shirt on the table.

"Come on, Glory. How can we throw a fellow vampire out without any resources?" Lucky obviously liked the cleaned-up version of Etienne pretty well, especially when he stripped off his dirty shirt and began washing more thoroughly.

Hmm. He might *feel* weak, but he didn't look it. And a few days in the sun had given him a nice golden glow.

"We can at least get Etienne some clothes. I'll pay, of course." Obviously Lucky was already getting into the "all vampires should stick together" thing. Which wasn't a bad idea. I should encourage this.

"Fine. Buy him some clothes. I'll let you have them at cost. But I've got to get back to the shop." I opened the door and almost shrieked. A customer was waiting to pay and Brittany was doing her best to swipe a credit card through the slot in my paper shredder. "We'll work something out." I almost vaulted over the counter, visions of MasterCard confetti making my head swim.

Two hours later all I'd worked out was that I needed more help for the holiday rush. Brittany was a fast learner, but she did take her bodyguard job seriously. Every time someone opened the front door, she was on high alert. She almost knocked down one poor man who brushed too close to Lucky in his search for a tuxedo. She kept a close eye on Etienne too, which was a big help as far as I was concerned.

Valdez watched Brittany like she was the last rib eye in the meat counter. Lust? Or didn't he trust her? I couldn't wait to get Brit alone to ask her about the human Valdez, or Rafael as she called him. Sue me, but when you've been with someone twenty-four seven for almost five years, you get curious. Blade makes him stay in dog form. Apparently the dog—shifter—whatever, would lose a significant bonus if he shifted while on duty with me. Since he was just a few months from the end of said contract, I figured it would take a serious something for him to blow it now.

It was close to dawn when Lacy came in to take over. Now I had to deal with the issues I'd put on the back burner. Where were Lucky and Brittany staying? What if Flo needed her own bed? And then there was Etienne. Did I trust him enough to invite him upstairs? Who's to say Simon hadn't sent him to us to try to drive a wedge between

Derek and Freddy? He'd played innocent, but could he have been lurking in my alley with that high-tech phone of his?

And speaking of that alley . . . I'd made another excuse to go out to my car and had checked to see that the envelope was gone. So the blackmailer could possibly be another vamp. At least he or she hadn't waited for daylight.

Back inside, Lacy and Brittany were ignoring each other while my clerk totaled the night's sales and began to set up the register for a new day. I had to admit sales were good, but even a thousand dollars would put a serious hurt on my budget. No way was I going to keep paying blackmail. I'd seen enough TV dramas to know blackmailers are never satisfied. I had to set a trap. Catch the person. And I needed help. Unfortunately. Knowing that asking for help would lead to endless lectures, I stalled by heading to the back room. There was a small bathroom and a closet with a dead bolt that could hold a vampire during the day. It sure as hell beat a storm sewer. I'd slept in a lot worse myself during some rough patches.

"Glory, honey. There's a ruckus out in the shop." One of my resident ghosts, Harvey Nutt, materialized in front of me. He and his wife like to take care of me. Previous tenants hadn't been as cool with visits from the afterlife as I am.

"I'd say it's more of a hooty-toot than a ruckus. But I bet someone throws a chair before all is said and done." Emmie Lou, Harvey's wife, sat on the table, her red cowboy boots swinging in time to the tune she was humming.

"Would you quit that infernal noise?" Harvey paced around the small room.

"What? Our song?" Emmie's eyes twinkled.

"Elvis's 'Hound Dog' ain't our song." Harvey stomped his foot.

"Harvey's flat eaten up with guilt. He knows he killed me."

Backed over her with his pickup. Totally an accident to

hear him tell it. Apparently the two are stuck here in this store in a kind of limbo until they kiss and make up. Two decades later and there is still more yelling than kissie face.

I left the two arguing to check on the ruckus. Sure enough, Brittany and Lacy were toe-to-toe. Their body language shouted, "Die, bitch."

"Hey, what's going on?" I took my life in my hands and stepped between them.

"She was the last client we met before the attack." Brittany looked like she wanted to push me out of the way but thought better of it when Valdez bumped against her and growled. "Back off, Rafe. I won't touch your precious Gloriana."

"You bet your sweet ass you won't." Valdez sat on her foot. *"I can take you, Beth. In any form, anytime and anyplace."*

"I did not set up Lucky." Lacy slammed the cash drawer shut. "I paid off my loan and left. End of story."

"Not for Lucky, kitty girl." Brittany shimmered, and I thought she was going to shape-shift right in front of us.

"Relax, both of you." I put a hand on Brittany's shoulder and felt a tingle, like an electrical charge. "Brittany, do I have to keep reminding you that this is a place of business? If a mortal saw you change . . ." I turned to Lacy and braced myself in case the back door crashed open again. "Your mother's not going to come calling, is she?"

"She'd better not. I threatened to shave my head if she did. In our world, that's about as 'in your face' as it gets."

"I'm sorry if what happened here is causing problems for you and your mother." I was just happy Lacy hadn't already quit.

"Mom and I are always at each other's throats. Don't worry about it." Lacy frowned at Brittany. "But I don't like being accused of something I didn't do."

"Then let me get these people out of here. You set for the day? Is it okay if we leave now?"

"Yes, please go and take all of your new 'friends' with you." Lacy made a face. "Sorry, boss, that didn't come out right. I hope you believe me. I'll say it one more time. I didn't attack Lucky. And for all we know the same vampire who tried to kill her was the one who left his fang marks on *my* throat the next night."

"Wait a minute. There might be a way to find out who that was." I left Valdez between the two women and headed for the dressing rooms where Etienne sat reading a magazine. Lucky must have found some scissors and trimmed his beard. He looked less like Grizzly Adams and more like one of the Three Musketeers now in a clean black shirt and black slacks. Interesting. I think he'd also helped himself to a bottle of the Fangtastic I kept in a fridge in the back room because he seemed to have a lot more energy when he threw down *Road and Track* and jumped to his feet.

"Lucky is changing her look, she says. Obviously she's a very new vampire." He grinned, all charm and surprisingly handsome. "Wait till you see."

"Yeah, she's been a vampire for about five minutes thanks to me." I frowned. I don't know if I'd ever get used to this concept of being the responsible party. "Etienne, give me your cell phone."

"You will return it, won't you? I told you, it's one of the few things I've managed to hold on to. Fortunately, I paid for a lot of time in advance. Once it's cut off . . ." He pulled it out of his pocket and handed it over. "Something will turn up, it always does."

Ah, the mantra of the immortal. I gave him a sympathetic shoulder pat. "I'm sure it will. And of course I'll give it back to you. I just want to show one of those pictures to my clerk. I'll send copies of all of these to my own phone for backup." I turned when the curtain on the dressing room swished open. "Lucky! That's quite a look."

"What do you think?" Lucky did a saunter around the dressing area, carefully arranging a black shawl over her shoulders. Her long black skirt swished around her ankles, and she flashed her fangs. "Do I look like a real vampire now?"

"Why don't you say that a little louder? I don't think they heard you next door at Mugs and Muffins." I noticed Lucky had decided to go for the Prada pumps even though the cute little red bow on the black suede kind of ruined the effect she was going for.

"I know you and your friends don't dress vampire. But I kind of groove on the whole dangerous female thing. Like that vampire in the mural on your wall." Lucky growled and flashed fang.

"We don't look vampire because there's no such thing as a stereotypical vampire. We come in all shapes, sizes and ages." I didn't know whether to be happy or sad that there were no mortal customers in the store at five thirty in the morning. My shop is open twenty-four hours a day, five days a week, closed Sundays and Mondays. Hey, it's a novelty and fits into the Sixth Street lifestyle in Austin. We're surrounded by clubs, stuck between a twenty-four-hour coffee shop and a tattoo parlor. The Tatt-ler had just opened last week, and Blade had gone in actually hoping to buy a London newspaper. Imagine his surprise when they'd offered him a discount on a nice snarling tiger for his upper thigh. Cute female tattoo artist. I hate her.

Anyway, I work most of the night shifts myself. My vampire customers love the fact that we're open when they need us to be. But even they weren't here right now. Just me and my gaggle of "friends." It was like a paranormal sitcom, currently without the laugh track.

"Look, Lucky. I'm tired. I really don't want to go into this right now. Trust me, it's a security issue. We blend with the crowd so that misguided fools who think we're all demons from hell won't come after us with pointy stakes."

"Yeah, yeah, I get that. But Etienne's promised to take me hunting." Lucky smiled and linked arms with him. "If I'm going to be stuck this way, I'm going to do a hell of a lot more than drink fake blood from a bottle."

"Not tonight you're not." Not ever if I had anything to say about it. And I should, shouldn't I? I mean, I'd *made* this fang-flashing vamp. If she accidentally killed someone, I'd be responsible, indirectly anyway. And what was it with Lucky and men anyway? First Damian, then Blade, now it was on to Etienne. She was determined to hook up with a vampire. I wondered if she was this fast and loose before her transformation. To be honest, I'd been the one to fill her head with the whole "vampire lovers can't be beat" idea. Naturally she was eager to test that theory herself.

Etienne though, we didn't know jack about him. I gave him a stern look.

"Yes, Miss Gloriana? You wish me to leave?"

Etienne, at least, seemed to have figured out who was calling the shots here. I gave him a grateful smile.

"Of course not. It's almost dawn. I'm prepared to offer you a safe place to sleep. In the closet in the back room. But only if you respect my wishes regarding Lucky."

"You can't just shove a man into a closet." Lucky grabbed Etienne's arm. "Or order me around."

"I don't mind, Lucky. Really. I'm grateful to be out of the weather. Thank you, Gloriana. You are very kind." Etienne patted Lucky's hand. "Tomorrow night. We feed together. Patience, *ma petite*. You have forever to learn what you need to know."

I gritted my teeth. "Whatever. Lucky, you and Brittany can double up in Flo's room. Just pray she's staying at Richard's again tonight."

I tuned out Lucky's whining and decided it was more urgent to see if Lacy recognized Greg Kaplan from the photos in the phone. Back at the register, I scrolled through them until I came to the one with Greg in the picture.

"Here, Lacy. Check out the guy sitting on the ground. Is he the one who attacked you?"

Lacy grabbed the phone and her eyes widened. "No. But I see the guy. The one at what looks like a pulpit. That guy standing next to Freddy, Derek's partner. Oh my gosh, he's the one who tried to take me out."

Nine

"You've got to be kidding me." I sat down hard. Oops. Next time I'd check to see if there was a chair behind me.

"Glory, are you okay?" Lacy hovered. Valdez and Brittany exchanged looks like they were trying not to laugh their asses off. Etienne and Lucky hadn't bothered to join the party, thank God. They were still next to the dressing rooms, Etienne serving as Lucky's "mirror" as she tried on black shawls. At least my inventory didn't include black lipstick and nail polish. Though the local Goths who liked to hang out at my shop had been pressing me to carry it.

I waved away Lacy's concern. "I'm fine. I just can't believe Simon Destiny himself came down from on high to attack you."

"*I believe it.*" Valdez settled next to me on the floor. "*You really pissed him off out at the compound. He promised to leave you and your friends alone, but I bet he figured your business was fair game.*"

"What's going on here? Gloriana, are you all right?"

I looked up to see Jerry frowning down at me. I'd been so busy worrying that Simon might use his demon's magical powers to come after someone during the day I hadn't even heard the door open.

"I'm fine. Just tired. We were getting ready to come upstairs."

Jerry looked around. His eyes narrowed when he saw Brittany. "Who's this?"

"Lucky's long lost bodyguard. Valdez knows her."

"And vouches for her?"

"Didn't say that." Valdez earned a hate-filled glare from Brittany. *"But I doubt she took out Lucky. What's her motive?"*

"Exactly!" Lucky came up with Etienne in tow. "Brit's been with the family for years. She's like a sister to me. Right, Brit?"

"Sure." Brittany nudged Valdez with her foot when he did a doggy version of a chuckle.

I figure bodyguards *never* feel exactly like family members. There's the whole paycheck thing. Not to mention the enormous life or death responsibility.

"And this is?" Jerry pulled me to my feet and put a proprietary arm around me while he gave Etienne the once-over. It felt pretty good to be claimed. I leaned against him.

"Etienne Delacroix." Etienne stuck out his hand. "You must be Jeremy Blade, Gloriana's friend. Lucky was just telling me something about the vampires she's met since she had her, um, accident."

"It wasn't an accident. It was an attack. And anyone we don't know to be innocent is automatically a suspect." Jerry didn't shake hands. Instead he reached for one of the knives I knew he had hidden in his waistband as if he'd like nothing better than to whittle some truth out of the new guy.

"You have doubts about me, monsieur? Read my mind. Put me under what your Gloriana so charmingly calls the whammy. You will see that I have spent the past weeks and my last dollars at the Energy Vampire headquarters trying to buy a little sunshine." Etienne laughed bitterly. "More fool I. Go ahead. Take your best shot. I've nothing to hide."

"You think I won't?" Jerry grabbed Etienne's arm and seemed disappointed when the man didn't put up a struggle.

"He's drained dry, Jerry. He gave up his power to the EVs." I gave Etienne a sympathetic look; I'd had a near miss with that kind of thing myself. "I told him he could sleep in the back room for today."

"Lacy, how do you feel about that?" Jerry didn't release Etienne yet.

"I figure he'll be dead to the world. No biggie."

"Lock him in anyway, Lacy." I smiled at Etienne. He just shrugged and smiled back.

"What about the rest of you?" Jerry wasn't smiling.

"They're coming upstairs. I figure Brittany and Lucky can double up in Flo's room."

"Florence came home. She and Richard had a fight. She's reorganizing her shoes." Jerry finally let go of Etienne.

"Oh. That's terrible." Not the fight. Flo loves a good fight. And apparently excels at the kiss-and-make-up stage. No, the terrible part was the thought of another shoe inventory. Picture centuries worth of shoes. Which *must* be dealt with properly. Sometimes alphabetically, sometimes by color. Oh, and then there are the seasons. And of course every shoe must be stuffed with archival tissue and carefully inspected for damage. Once there had been a nasty scuff on one of her treasured Ferragamos. Trust me, you don't want to be around during one of Flo's shoe inventories.

"Come home with me, Gloriana. Lucky and Brittany can take your room. Valdez, you stay with them upstairs to keep an eye on things."

"Wait a minute, boss." Valdez knew exactly what he was in for.

"Maybe we should get a hotel room." Lucky had already picked up on a vibe here. She glanced at Brittany.

"No time. It's less than an hour until sunrise, Lucky. You've got to start paying attention to these things, hon, or you'll get caught in a bind." Brittany looked down at Valdez.

"Maybe Rafe can give me some pointers on my new gig, bodyguard to a vampire. That is, if you're sure your father hasn't fired my ass."

"No, I told you, he doesn't think you had anything to do with the attack. He'll be glad you're still alive. When we get upstairs I'd better call him and let him know we found you and tell him what happened."

"Fine. Better head out then." I was more than happy to take off with Jerry. Usually I balk at letting him order my life, but this plan suited me perfectly. I couldn't wait to leave this menagerie behind and soon did exactly that.

"Thank you for rescuing me." I lay back in the leather seat of Jerry's Mercedes convertible and just relaxed for the first time in what seemed like days. Blade drove with the easy confidence that he did everything. Actually it was *my* Mercedes. But I'm pretty stubborn about accepting expensive gifts from Jerry. Now if he'd bought me my own red Birkin bag . . .

"I'm sure Florence will handle things if any of them cause problems. Or interfere with the shoe inventory." Jerry grinned at me. "I wish it wasn't so close to dawn. You're looking very sexy tonight, Gloriana."

"Thank you." Sexy? I looked down. What had I thrown on a lifetime ago anyway? Oh, yes, the black cashmere twin set that now had a stake hole in the chest. Damn Brittany. At least the V-neck dipped low and the leather pants were formfitting. Too much butt, but Jerry didn't seem to mind.

"But I know we need to talk." Jerry had that look, like he was ready to launch into all the reasons why I would be so much better off with his "protection."

"Yeah, sure." I was so not in the mood to do the whole "what's best for Glory" thing tonight. And I had a surefire way to distract my man. I reached over and rubbed his hard thigh, then explored a little further. Umm.

"What the hell are you doing?" He didn't make a move to stop me though when I slid down his zipper and slipped my hand inside to stroke his hot length.

"Communicating. This"—I slipped my fingers down to cup his sacs—"is just a friendly gesture to show I'm willing to listen."

"Yes, I'd say that's friendly." Jerry had to clear his throat. He'd put the top down on the convertible because we both loved the cold night air.

"Now what were you saying?" I circled his cock and moved my hand in a rhythm that almost lifted him off his seat.

"I—" Jerry gasped as I bent to take him into my mouth.

"Woman, it's a good thing these streets are deserted. You could get us both arrested for public lewdness."

I wasn't worried. Wouldn't be the first time I'd whammied a cop into forgetting one of my, ahem, indiscretions. I sent Jerry a mental message to keep his eyes on the road and to let me do all the work here. His hand slipped into my hair, first gently then tighter as I drew on him and nipped him with my fangs. We raced up hills and down, and the movement made the pressure of my mouth against him even more interesting. Suddenly the car stopped, and I was thrown over the seat to land on my back.

"You wanted to tell me something?" I grinned up at him.

"I want you naked. Now."

Jerry loomed over me. Oh, my. I love it when he gets all ferocious and insatiable. But I also love those damned tight leather pants, and he obviously wanted them off. He growled and went after them with his teeth. I jerked his head up with a handful of his hair.

"Don't. You. Dare."

"Hurry, then." His eyes were dark with hunger, his fangs glinting in the moonlight.

I raised my butt and tried to wiggle them down. I was just about to tell him to shred the damned things when I finally managed to jerk one leg free.

"Took you long enough." He paused, braced above me and tantalizingly close to the gate to Heaven. "Maybe I've changed my mind."

I grabbed his ass. "Get in here, mister." I took a shaky breath. "Please."

"Now that's more like it." Jerry grinned and plunged into me.

"Oh, my God!" I knew I'd been worked up, but this was really something. I felt the cold leather of the seat on my behind, the chilly air on my breasts because the sweater set had vanished. Jerry's lips ravaged my neck just before he sucked so hard I blew apart in one enormous orgasm. He stroked, raising my hips to meet his. I wrapped my legs around him and tried to hold on, but was so limp I felt like I'd never hold anything again. When he came, I felt the rush of heat deep inside me, surprised by an answering spasm of my own. Wow.

"Where are we?" I asked when I finally managed to catch my breath. Jerry's head lay on my breast. Nice.

"My driveway."

"Oh." I looked up at the night sky. Was that a faint pink in the east? In my bones I knew it had to be. I figured I should be really uncomfortable scrunched up in the tiny backseat of a Mercedes convertible with a two-hundred-pound-plus male on top of me. Instead I felt boneless and content and wished I could watch the sunrise this way, just once. Tears pricked my eyelids and I sighed.

"Guess we'd better get inside."

"Guess so." Even Jerry's voice sounded rough. Emotion? Nah. Probably predawn exhaustion.

"I can't move."

"Neither can I."

"What if we just put the top up and sleep here all day?"

"Dangerous. Sunlight could come in the windows."

"You should have pulled into the garage."

"I didn't want to take the time to use the garage-door opener."

"How many centuries have we been doing this?" I grinned at Jerry and shoved, trying to sit up. He finally climbed off me and over the front seat.

"More than I can count at the moment."

I heard him zip up as I pulled off my leather pants and panties and picked them up along with my sweater set. Naked as God made me except for my black suede ankle boots, I climbed out of the car and followed him to the back door, waiting for him to unlock it.

"We're hopeless." I leaned up to kiss the smile on his handsome face.

"I'm not complaining." He swung me up into his arms and threw open the back door.

"Surprise!"

"Ma!"

Oh, sweet God in Heaven, just take me now. Yes, it was Angus Jeremiah Campbell III's mother. The bitch of Castle Campbell. The one woman in the world who hated me more than life itself. Oh, wait a minute, there are two women who hate me that much. The other one was standing by her side. Mara Kilpatrick MacTavish. They both stared at my bare bum like it was a grotesque, "too awful for a Barnum and Bailey Circus" sideshow. And come to think of it . . . I struggled to get down, but Jerry's arms tightened around me. All I could do was put my purse over the offending body part. Thank God I carry a tote.

"Jerry, put me down."

"I don't think so." He smiled at his mother. Nodded to Mara. "This visit is unexpected."

I grasped for a pleasantry. Hey, I felt like I owed it to the ladies. They weren't shrieking and covering their eyes in horror. You had to admire that kind of self-control.

"Is Randolph with you, Lady Campbell?" Pray God the little bugger had fallen into the Atlantic during the flight over. Okay, don't tar and feather me yet. We have a history and I'd have the scars to prove it if it weren't for my healing vamp sleep.

"Of course. And here he is now."

Jerry's mum has always had a cat. Kind of like a witch's

familiar. I think that's why my bodyguards have always been dogs. Whatever Mag loves, I . . . don't. Anyway, Mag's cat is an immortal shifter so the cat can look however the mistress wishes, and what she wishes is unusual to say the least.

I admit when I saw this season's Randolph, I flinched and almost felt sorry for him. "Um, dare I ask the breed?"

"Dare I ask your breed or should I say breeding?" the creature who looked like an escapee from the movie *Alien* said in a whispery voice. He jumped up into Mag's arms. "Oh, why bother? Scratch my ear, Mother."

"He's a sphynx." Mag ran her finger along one of his long pointy ears. "This breed doesn't shed, you see."

"How convenient for your wardrobe." I really didn't want to have this conversation while naked in Jerry's arms. I turned my attention to Mara, who had just slipped Jerry's cell phone charger into her pocket. Oh, didn't I tell you? Mara's got this little problem. She's got sticky fingers. I never leave my purse where she can get to it. Speaking of . . . A tote can only cover so much. I gave Jerry an elbow.

Jerry got the hint. "Excuse us, ladies. We'll see you at sunset." And with that, Jerry strode around the two open-mouthed females, through the kitchen and den and up the stairs. By the time he'd reached the sanctuary of his bedroom I was shaking. Hysterical laughter. Yep. I was never one given to tears of self-pity. Well, not much anyway.

"Oh, God, Jerry. Did you see your mother's face when we walked in like that?"

"Unfortunately." He dropped me on the bed, closed and locked his bedroom door with a look and began tossing off his clothes. "I'm worn to the bone, lass. Climb into bed. I would hold you."

Now you didn't think I'd argue with that, did you? I threw my clothes on the floor, jerked off the boots and crawled in, burrowing under the covers and into the safety of his strong arms. With a sigh, I relaxed completely for the first time in what seemed like years. Sure, I had his mother to look forward to when we woke. And Lucky. Not to mention psycho Simon out for revenge. And then there was the promise of a cool million if I could nab Lucky's attacker. Which would come in handy if I didn't figure out who my texting tormentor was soon. Okay, so maybe I wasn't so relaxed. Then Jerry started kissing a path down my shoulder while his hands stroked my hips. Hmm.

"Tell me that's not your mother standing over us."

"Wish I could." Jerry rolled over and sat up, the blanket falling to his waist. "Ma, you're invading my privacy."

"It's sunset, Jeremiah. I didn't come all this distance just to sit around and wait for you to"—disdainful sniff—"shag your mistress."

"By God!" Jerry jumped out of bed, heedless of his nakedness, and manhandled his startled mother out of the room before slamming the door in her face. "I'll not have it. Do ye hear me, woman! Ye will respect Gloriana, or ye can fly yer ass right back to Castle Campbell this night!" He slapped the door with his palm for emphasis.

I threw the covers over my hot face. Oh, God. This was so not happening. I knew his mother hated me. Hell, she'd tried to stake me once, centuries ago, just to get me out of Jerry's life. I'd never told him that and desperately threw up a block so he couldn't read my thoughts now. I heard him muttering obscenities, then the bed sagged next to me.

"Gloriana, sweeting." He tugged the cover down so he could see my face.

"Shag?" I had to laugh.

Jerry grinned. "Da's put a satellite dish in at the castle."

"Wow. Sheep, scenery and satellite. Maybe I should give Castle Campbell another shot." I rubbed his whiskery cheek. "Seems your mother has given us our marching orders. What do you say?"

Jerry's eyes darkened as he kissed my palm. "I say

there's no better way to start a night than by shagging my mistress."

A scandalously long while later I lay in his arms, breathless and boneless again. That man has no end to his repertoire.

"Don't worry about your mother, Jerry. I'm used to her attitude."

"You shouldn't have to get used to it. I'll not allow her to treat you with disrespect."

"Aw, Jerry, I know how she feels." I cupped his chin in my palm. His dark beard was rough, but his lips were hot when he kissed my fingertips. "She *is* your mother. I've got things to do. Let me drive home. Deal with my guests. You can deal with yours."

"I won't let her run you off. At least stay for a while." Jerry smiled. "I know you're proud of how strong you've become. Ma respects strength."

"Well, Ma will never see me as anything more than a whore." I sat up, still naked and more whore than I liked to admit. Okay, here came that inferiority complex I'd spent centuries trying to rid myself of. But, face it, Jerry's family includes lairds with castles and servants and family crests. My family had been honest working-class folks.

I love the way such class distinctions have blurred in the centuries since we'd met, especially in America, but Mag Campbell is old guard. She's class; I'm classless. And that'll never change for her.

With dread sitting like a stone in my stomach, I pulled on last night's clothes and followed Jerry downstairs. If you want to understand how different my world is from the mortal world, picture this: a mortal mum comes to visit, you'd smell the bacon cooking, the biscuits in the oven, and sit down to a fine meal on the table for what is essentially breakfast. (Hey, I watch TV. Loved *Ozzie and Harriet* and *Leave It To Beaver*.)

In the vampire world, especially back in the old days, a fine meal might have been a fresh young lad or lass ready to be drunk from, then sent on his or her way with a bit of coin in hand and nary a memory of having a vein pierced. Sigh. Some of the old ways were pretty fine.

"Finally." Mara sat at the dining-room table with a bottle of Fangtastic, one of the exotic types, in front of her. She'd poured the liquid into a crystal goblet. Mag was obviously sulking but she also had a goblet at her elbow. A pair of silver candlesticks usually sat in the middle of the dining-room table. I'd tell Jerry to have his housekeeper check Mara's room for them while his guest slept during the day.

"Ladies." Jerry held out a chair for me. I did my best to slide into it gracefully, but leather pants just don't slide. Finally I was seated. Jerry came back from the kitchen with two bottles of Fangtastic. He usually nuked his, but hadn't wasted time with it. He did get out two glasses from the china cabinet against the wall though and poured out the drinks before he sat next to me.

His mother sniffed and nodded toward me. "This is *her* doing. Drinking bottled swill when Mara says there is a college full of young people nearby. I fear she is making you less of a man with her peculiarities."

Well, nothing like a direct attack. The Campbells were obviously still old-school. I'd always made my preference for synthetics plain.

You could have struck a match off Jerry's hard jaw. "I don't believe you meant to question my manhood, did you, Mother? Not when you intend to enjoy my hospitality."

Hmm. That set Mag in her place.

"Of course not. I've always been proud of you, Jeremiah. You are a worthy heir to your father." Mag made a show of taking a sip of the offending brew, then pressed a napkin to her pursed lips. "I simply can't survive on this, this disgusting—"

"I take your point, Ma. But I drink what I please. And I've already told you what I expect in regard to Gloriana, have I not? If you wish to go hunting later, I'm sure Mara will be glad to take you. I know you understand how to be discreet. I expect to be staying in Austin for a while yet." He put his hand over mine and smiled into my eyes. I was about to add a kiss to cap off the performance when Mara spoke up.

"You'll come with us, won't you, Jeremiah?" Mara leaned across the table, trying for a cleavage shot.

"I have business to tend to. You can manage without me." Jerry did glance at her, but he didn't seem too mesmerized.

We sat in silence for a moment. Mara smiled at Jerry, frowned at me and reached for Mag's hand to give it a comforting pat. Randolph jumped up on the table and leaned against his mistress while giving me a baleful look.

I cleared my throat. So I was outnumbered. I could afford to at least pretend to be civil. "So, Mag, are you here for the holidays?"

"Obviously. That and Jeremiah's birthday."

"Oh, right." Jerry's birthday. New Year's Eve. How could I have forgotten? And if you don't think he's a typical Capricorn, you don't know your sun signs. Stubborn. Controlling. Dynamic.

"So you'll be staying for several weeks?" Jerry didn't sound thrilled.

"Is that a problem, Jeremiah? I haven't seen you in three years. And Mara told me you had a nice home here." Mag looked around the spacious dining room. "Which I see you do. Obviously you have room to spare."

"Of course. Stay as long as you like." Jerry picked up my hand. "As long as you understand my wishes are to be considered."

"Naturally. But when you hear my news, perhaps you'll decide your wishes must be *re*considered."

"News?" Why did the word suddenly sound ominous? I gripped Jerry's fingers. Mara was practically dancing in her seat with excitement. This did not bode well. Mara happy usually meant me not so much. The witch would like nothing better than to have Jerry for herself. Forget the fact that she'd been married to his best friend for centuries.

"Mara has something to tell you."

"This is a family matter. After Gloriana leaves." Mara looked significantly at the door.

"Gloriana *is* family. Tell us, Mara. Is it something to do with Westwood? Did you track him down?" Jerry leaned forward.

"No. He left Switzerland and vanished." Mara got a hard look.

She and Jerry were both desperate to track down the vampire hunter who'd killed Mara's husband. Yet, despite her genuine grief, Mara seemed to have already set her sights on hubby number two, her husband's best friend.

"I haven't given up on finding him, but when I stopped at Castle Campbell and talked to Mag, I decided the time was right to share *this* news."

"All right, already." It was all I could do not to jump up and shake it out of her. I hate this kind of "worm it out of me" stuff. "Spill, Mara."

"My daughter, Jeremiah. The daughter Mac and I raised as ours?" Mara got up and walked around the table. She stood behind Mag and put her hand on her shoulder as if the older woman was her support. "Lily's *your* daughter. Not Mac's. I never told him. Never told *anyone*. But she's yours."

Oookay. Talk about your charged silences. Jerry sat still as a stone. Mag sniffed, tears running down her cheeks. I bit the inside of my cheek to keep from shouting, "Lying bitch!" And Mara glowed, like she was sure this would get her the man she'd always wanted.

"Why should I believe you?" Jerry said it quietly, but he might as well have shouted. Mara gasped and turned pale, and Mag gripped Mara's hand and gave me a dirty look. Hello? What did I have to do with this?

"Do you remember what Lily looks like?" Mag decided to take over the debate. "She's the spit of ye, boy. I saw it years ago, but thought it the dreams of an old woman. Ye never gave me a grandchild. Which I was glad of with the kind of women ye choose to consort with." A nod to me in case Jerry missed the inference.

"Every other child in the county looks like a Campbell, Ma. That means naught. My brothers were lusty lads before they were turned."

Implying that he was not? I knew for a fact he was anything but lacking in the activity department, but once a man's turned vampire his swimmers apparently quit fertilizing eggs. By the time I'd met him in London he'd been vampire for ages. I was bursting with questions but determined to keep my mouth shut. I sipped my Fangtastic to keep said mouth occupied.

"I never lay with any Campbell but you, Jeremiah. I didn't. Only you. When Lily came, I knew for sure who sired her. Remember, Mac was fair. And I have red hair, like my mum."

And green eyes, the lying bitch. Creamy skin. The whole Irish beauty package. The Kilpatrick had brought home an Irish bride to the dismay of the Scottish countryside, but he was his clan's leader so they'd had no choice but to welcome her. They'd produced beautiful children though. God, I hated her. I took another sip.

I wanted Jerry to deny he'd ever slept with Mara but he didn't. Ho. So there *had* been some action in that department before he'd been turned vampire. Now who was the slut? But of course Mag didn't cast any stones at Mara. Mara's family came from wealth and the aristocracy. Apparently her hurried marriage to Mac hadn't raised any brows and, when a dark-haired babe had popped out, no one dared suggest Mac hadn't sired the babe.

Jerry still just sat there. I could see him thinking and thinking and counting and thinking some more.

I didn't say it, but if Jerry was the responsible party, why hadn't Mara's father come after him with a shotgun and a priest? I looked up to find three pairs of eyes—one green, two dark brown—staring holes in me. Damned mind-reading vampires.

"Well? Why didn't the Kilpatrick make Jerry marry you, Mara? Or weren't you . . . sure?" I didn't smirk, but, boy, it was tough to keep my face appropriately solemn.

"You don't understand, Gloriana." Mara sniffled and managed a tear. "Mac and I were promised. Da had a lot of pride—"

"And a parcel of land as I recall that had already been bespoken." Mag shook her head. "Men and their dealings. It's all about the land. Young MacTavish and Jeremiah knew naught of this. Mara was forced to marry to satisfy her father's wishes."

"And I loved Mac." Mara produced a snowy hanky from her abundant cleavage. What century was she living in? "Jeremiah and I . . . It was a mistake. Too much May wine and moonlight."

"I don't even remember it."

We all stared at Jerry. Finally. I was beginning to wonder if he'd ever weigh in on the subject. And a heavy subject it was. Mara's a born vampire. Her daughter Lily would be a born vampire too. I'd never met her. By the time I'd made it to Castle Campbell, she'd left the neighborhood for greener pastures. Can't say I blamed her. Unless you were into staring at admittedly incredible scenery or herding sheep, the Scottish Highlands, pre–satellite dish, were a giant snooze. Especially if you were a lowly Londoner, born and bred.

"Where *is* Lily?"

This question earned me hate-filled looks from Mag and Mara. Randolph just raised a long gray leg and licked it.

"Well? Answer Gloriana. Where is she?" Jerry got up and paced the length of the room. He drained his glass and stalked into the kitchen, returning with another bottle of Fangtastic, which he opened and drank deeply from, abandoning any pretense of refinement.

Had he accepted this nonsense? Just on their word? I got up and rubbed his shoulders, reminding all and sundry who'd spent the day in his bed. Right, Mara?

"We don't know where she is, Jeremiah." Mag cleared her throat. "Perhaps you can help us find her. I know you have friends with resources. Lily doesn't even know Mac is dead. But it might ease her hurt to know her real father is still alive."

"Ease her hurt?" Jerry turned, his hands fisted. "Mac was her real father in every way that counts. As I recall it was her *real* mother who drove her to run away to live on her own. Mac doted on her."

"Yes, he did." Mara wiped at her eyes. Ha, feigned tears if I've ever seen them. "My daughter is willful. She and I . . . we didn't always agree on how she should behave."

I really wanted to say something here, but knew better. Knew enough this time to block my thoughts too. "I'm going. This *is* a family matter." I wrapped my arms around Jerry's lean waist and hugged him hard. "Give me the car keys, and I'll drive myself home. Call me later, okay?"

"Sure." Jerry walked me to the door. "You can stay if you wish, but I don't blame you for wanting to get out of here. Think I could go with you?"

I smiled and hugged him again. "Your mother would probably tackle you before you made it to the car." Mag har-rumphed from the dining room—that vamp hearing—and I knew I was right. "But if you need me . . ." *Please say no.*

"No, this is my mess to deal with." He turned to look back at his mother and Mara. "But I'm not altogether con-vinced this isn't a scheme they've cooked up to suit their own purposes."

The women in question didn't bother to deny it, just sent more go-to-hell looks my way. Neither his mother nor Mara said good-bye, though I heard Mag say something about how selfish I was to take Jerry's car. I knew he had more than one extra car but didn't bother to clear that up. Randolph did walk over to stand by the door, spying for Mag, no doubt.

"Thanks for understanding, Gloriana."

"If this is true, it's good news. You have a child!"

"You haven't met Lily. She's not exactly an angel. I just thank God I never slept with her, but half the men around Castle Campbell did."

Whoa. For once I was speechless. I hugged him again and climbed into the Mercedes. We'd never bothered to put the top up and the seats were icy. I started the motor and cranked up the heat.

"Gloriana." Jerry leaned down and kissed me long and slow. "Be careful tonight. There are too many dangerous people out there. Feel under the seat."

I reached under it and felt a wooden handle. A nice baseball bat. When I pulled it out, I could see that it had a point on one end.

" 'Be prepared.' If you'd just been born a few centuries later, Jerry, you'd have been a hell of a Boy Scout."

"There's also a gun in the glove box." Jerry kissed me again, then glanced back at the house. "This is damned complicated and will take some time to sort out. I don't know—"

"Take the time you need. I understand." And I did. But I can't say I didn't resent the fact that he'd be bonding with Mara over a daughter while I had the new vampire from hell to deal with. Well, as long as he kept his mother away from me, I could handle anything. I put the car in gear and backed out of the driveway.

At the street, I stopped and put the top up. It was starting to snow. Wouldn't it be cool if we had a white Christmas? This was almost unheard of in Austin. I took it as a sign that everything was going to turn out all right. Though how was anyone's guess.

Ten

I'd driven about a block when my cell phone rang. Of course it wasn't where it was *supposed* to be. I fumbled through my purse and finally had to pull over to find it. At least I didn't have a new text message.

"Hello."

"Glory, this is Lucky. Valdez insisted I call you."

Valdez has a problem with cell phones. Paws can't punch in numbers because, believe me, he's tried. And then there's the whole mental telepathy thing. Not a lot of range.

"What's the matter? Are you all right?"

"We're fine. But Flo and I need to go shoe shopping and he doesn't want us to leave. Says we've got to have your 'permission.' Like we're prisoners or something. If I put you on the phone to him, will you tell him to let us go?"

Oh, it was tempting. Lucky could go out, her killer could take another shot, succeed this time and I'd be off the hook. But she was taking my best friend along. I put the car in gear and headed out again.

"He's just doing his job, Lucky. Or have you forgotten what happened a few nights ago?"

"No, I haven't forgotten. But we can't just sit around here. I'm going stir-crazy. And Brittany thinks she can take care of us."

"She's done great so far." This was going nowhere. "Let me speak to Flo."

"Glory, you won't believe it. Luciana and I were going through my winter boot collection and discovered I have no cordovan leather midheel pointed-toe thigh-high boots." Flo said something in rapid Italian over her shoulder. "And Nordstrom's is having a sale. We must go."

"Flo, *you* can go, but Lucky's in danger. Someone tried to kill her. They could try again."

"You don't think I can protect her?" More rapid Italian. I suck at languages. Though I can say "shit" in about six of them. I was ready to throw one in when Brittany came on the line.

"I've got their backs, Glory. You might as well let me take them to the mall. Trust me, no one stops Lucky when she's on a quest."

"Are you serious? Don't you think your track record speaks for itself?" I heard Brittany suck in her breath. "Put Florence back on the phone. Now."

"I'm sorry, Glory. I was thinking with my shoes and not my head. I love you, you know I do. You are my best friend, always. But Luciana . . . She really appreciates a good shoe inventory. She *understands*." Flo sighed. "Do you know she carries pictures with her in that little berry machine in her purse?"

"Her BlackBerry?"

"Yes, that's it! Or maybe it's in her phone. Whatever. She has pictures of every shoe she owns. Can you believe it?"

No, actually I couldn't. I love a good accessory as much as the next woman, but this was bordering on the psychotically obsessive. Which was no surprise actually.

"I'm glad you've bonded, Flo. So wouldn't it be a shame if you got her killed while boot shopping?"

Florence was muttering in Italian again. "You're right. And I'm not about to trust this Brittany who left Lucky bleeding in our alley. What if I call Richard? If I apologize for a tiny little insult I made to his manhood, he will come over."

"You didn't! What on earth did you say to him?"

Flo laughed. "If I tell you, I really will have to break up with him and he has a way with his, um, never mind. I call, I grovel, I make promises . . . He will come and take us to the mall. Watch Lucky and Brittany and me, of course. What do you think?"

An evening of peace and quiet? Flo really is my nearest and dearest friend. Too bad I'd still have to go down to the shop. Where Etienne waited. And Derek. What had he found out about Freddy's trip to the EV stronghold? I felt a headache coming on and realized I hadn't finished my Fang-tastic.

"Fine. If Richard will come, then you can all go. I'd hate for you to have a deficient boot collection."

"Great. And maybe we'll bring you a little surprise." Flo said something to Lucky again in Italian. I was getting really sick of feeling like the only one who didn't know the secret code here.

"Put the phone up to Valdez's ear. I want him to meet me down in the shop. You can drop him off down there. But, Flo, promise you'll bring Lucky straight home after the mall closes. No side trips to practice her fang action."

All I heard was a doggy chuff that meant Valdez was on the line.

"Valdez, I may be insane but I'm letting them go out without you or me. Meet me in the shop. I'm almost there. I'm driving Jerry's Mercedes and"—I smiled because even without telepathy I could still read his mind—"I'll park in front."

My answer was a bark that made me laugh before I broke the connection and stuck the phone back in my purse. Why was I meeting Valdez in the shop? I needed to go upstairs and shower, change clothes and put on fresh makeup before I went to work. I'd brushed my teeth and washed my face at Jerry's but not much else. I was just about to call Flo back when I looked up and saw a man standing in the street in front of the car.

I slammed on the brakes.

Greg Kaplan. When I reached under the seat for Jerry's baseball bat, Greg threw himself on the hood of the car, then rolled to the ground.

"I'm hit! Call a lawyer."

I opened the car door and jumped out, bat in hand. "Give me a break, Greg. I stopped. I did not hit you."

Another car pulled up and a man got out. "Everything okay here?" He had his cell phone out and looked at Greg on the pavement. "Need an ambulance?"

"No!" I pulled Greg to his feet. "My boyfriend was play-ing a joke on me." Oh, God, another car was stopping. Well, what did I expect at seven o'clock at night on a residential street not far from one of Austin's freeways? I thought about the whammy, but, as more cars slowed in both directions, I had to admit the crowd was more than I could handle alone.

"Greg, come on. Back me up here."

He just grinned and limped around, collecting a business card from a lawyer and another from a financial advisor in case this "incident" resulted in a big settlement.

"What happened to the baseball bat?" The first man who'd stopped just wouldn't move on.

"Yeah, honey." Greg threw an arm around me. "Tell our Good Samaritan about your special bat." He tried to wrestle it from me and we had a little tug-of-war that ended when I stomped on Greg's foot.

I laughed and showed the crowd the point. "This is what

happens when you leave your autographed Hank Aaron bat
lying on the den floor in the middle of the night. I got out
the chain saw and put a nice pencil point on this puppy."

"Oh, man." This earned Greg some sympathetic looks.
The first man muttered something about canceling his
membership to his online dating service and climbed back
into his SUV after waving everyone else off. As soon as he
drove away, I jumped in my car and slammed the door in
Greg's face. Too bad Greg wasn't giving up. He stood in my
path until I finally had to unlock the passenger door and let
him in so traffic could move around us.

I kept the bat in my lap, ready and willing to make use
of it. Greg didn't act scared, which was just plain stupid
on his part. I wouldn't hesitate to skewer him like one of
those corn dogs Emmie Lou had told me about at the Texas
State Fair.

I couldn't stop thinking about all the things I could do
with a million dollars, and I'd bet my double Ds Greg had
attacked Lucky. His name *had* been on that debtor list. Of
course, I would have to prove Greg had done it—or he
could confess. Hmm. Worth a shot.

"What do you want, Greg?"

"I figure I owe you an apology. I'm sorry I tried to get
you involved with the EVs."

"Involved? It was a little more than that. That's like
comparing a death blow to a love tap." I wasn't about to list
all his sins against me and my dog. Poor Valdez had really
had a rough time.

"Now, now. No need to overdramatize the thing.
Though you always were the little actress, weren't you?"

"You're not winning points here, Greg."

"Sorry. I'm upset. I need to get away from the EVs and
I'm looking for a job. I know you have a lot of contacts in
Austin. I was hoping you'd hook me up with something."
He actually had the nerve to wink. "Or someone."

"You've got to be kidding me. You almost got me killed.

You owe me a hell of a lot more than an apology. And the only thing I'm interested in hooking you up with is the business end of this bat."

"Hey, baby. That's a little harsh. You were never in any real danger. Besides, you were crazy about me once upon a time."

"If I ever loved you, I sure don't remember it." Don't ask. It was last century, the sixties and he was really cute in a Paul McCartney kind of way.

"Yeah, well, I had my reasons for wiping your memories back then. But this is a new century. A fresh start. And I've got some hot information for you. I figure we could work a little trade."

"I can't imagine what you could possibly know that could help me."

"Your buddy Frederick von Repsdorf has been hanging around the EV compound."

"Old news." I waved my hand. "I'm sure Freddy's got his reasons. We can't pick our parents, you know."

"How about this?" Greg moved closer. "Someone tried to take out your store clerk recently. Know who did it?"

"Yes. King weasel-face Simon Destiny." I shrugged, *still* quite the actress. "Can't you come up with anything original? I've got a houseguest, Lucky Carver, sometimes known as Carvarelli. What do you know about *her*?" Ah. That got a reaction. Greg looked like he'd been jabbed by the business end of my bat.

"There's a Carvarelli in town?"

"Yeah. And she's a new vampire." I never took my eyes off Greg. If he thought he'd killed Lucky, now was when he'd really react. But instead he just looked worried. Like the fact that she was in town was the big deal. "She doesn't have enough power yet to interest the EVs, but she might be a good customer for the Vampire Viagra. She's got plenty of money and you know how these new vampires like to experiment. Maybe I could set up a meeting for you. Do you pay commission if I get you a new customer?" Like *I'd* ever traffic in drugs. But Greg sure did.

"No! Don't even mention you know me." Greg leaned forward.

I aimed the pointy end of the bat at him and nudged him back.

"Why not? You owe her family money?"

"What if I do? So do half the vamps, weres and shifters in town. I bet you do too." He started to open the glove box, and I rapped his knuckles.

"Stay out of there. I never borrowed from anybody. I just maxed out my plastic." Dumb luck on my part. I had hung out with mortals in Vegas, where my gambling habit had gotten me in trouble. I hadn't known about the Carvarellis or I might have dug my own hole with loan sharks.

Greg snorted. "Yeah, right. They probably turned you down because you didn't have the kind of collateral they wanted." He ran his hand along the Mercedes' dashboard. "But maybe now you do."

"Forget me. Maybe you thought to get out of debt by taking out the debt collector. Did you rip out Lucky's throat the other night? In my alley?"

"I don't know what the hell you're talking about. You said she's a vampire. Obviously she healed."

"No, she didn't. I healed her and turned her vampire myself."

Greg stared at me. "No shit."

"Yeah, maybe not my smartest move."

"Are you kidding? You saved a Carvarelli. This could be your big break. Or is old man Carvarelli steamed? Did he blame you for making his daughter into a freak like us?"

"No, nothing like that. He kind of grooves on the immortality thing. But whoever tried to kill her could take another shot. Now that pisses him off. And since I made her vampire, I feel kind of responsible for Lucky."

"Damn, Glory. You never did know how to take advantage

of your opportunities. What you got is a Carvarelli eternally and I do mean *eternally* grateful to you." Greg fondled the gearshift. "Nice wheels. Lucky set you up with this? Or was it Blade? You're really doing well these days. Why can't you have a little sympathy for an old friend?"

"Maybe that old friend left Lucky for dead practically on my doorstep."

"I'm not stupid. Killing Lucky wouldn't wipe out my debt, only wipe out *me*. Old man Carvarelli would hunt me down and stake me personally if I took out his daughter." Greg shook his head, then snagged my wallet from my purse.

"Hey, put that back." I poked him with the bat. "I'm not rich. The car is a loaner, from Blade."

Greg flipped open my wallet, ignoring the blood dripping from the gouge in his side. "Thirty-three dollars and a generic Visa card. Not even Platinum. I bet it has one of those low loser limits." He tossed the wallet back inside.

"You'd be right. I screwed up my credit when I was in Vegas. Did a stint with Gamblers Anonymous."

"You and I are a lot alike, Glory. Not rich like Simon or Blade. We have to make our own way in this world. We should help each other. I could show you how to turn this Lucky thing to your advantage."

"Yeah, I'm really anxious to work with you, Greg. Especially after you tried to turn me into an EV sacrifice." I poked him again. This time he flinched. Think I should feel guilty? If he tried, he could be healed before I could reapply my lipstick.

But to impress me, he moaned with pain and held up a bloodstained hand. "God, when did you become so cruel?" Then he put his other hand on my shoulder. "Look at me, Glory. Is old man Carvarelli offering a reward for whoever tried to take out his daughter?"

Damn it, I felt Greg trying the whammy on me. It was one of his old tricks. I blinked and blinked again, but blurted out the truth before I could stop myself.

"A million dollars."

"Hot damn. Now that's what I'm talking about. Let's work together. Fifty. Fifty. You got any ideas?"

"Sure. You're suspect number one." I looked away from him before I told him anything else. Like my current social security number, my bank balance or that the limit on my Visa was actually pretty healthy at the moment.

"I'm not that stupid, Gloriana. I'm going to nose around. See what I can find out. You and that dog of yours keep an eye out for suspicious characters." Greg sounded like he was now running the show. I wasn't about to let him go around me on this and steal my reward.

"Lucky's father expects to deal with me on this reward thing. But definitely check out the EV compound. You think Simon could owe Lucky's family money?"

"No way. The EVs are rolling in it. You have any idea how much they rake in with their Vampire Viagra?" Greg got a dreamy look. "I don't mind telling you I've been tempted to put my hand in the till, but that would be suicide for sure."

"I'm not agreeing to anything, not officially, but if you come to me with something concrete that leads to figuring out who attacked Lucky, maybe I'll consider a split."

Greg grinned. "Fair enough. You *will* be hearing from me." And, in typical Greg fashion, he opened the car door, morphed into a bat and flew away.

I sighed, then realized Greg had switched off the heat. It was still snowing and clearly below freezing. And neither of us had so much as shivered. Sometimes it's pretty neat being a vampire.

Then the phone beeped. Text message. So much for peace on earth.

"U STIFFED ME. NOW UL PAY. $5000 OR C URSELF ON THE NEWS. 24 HOURS. DETAILS LATER."

What? My blackmailer didn't like the coffee at Mugs and Muffins? And details? Yeah, I needed details. Like where the hell I was supposed to get that kind of money. I ground my teeth, then threw the car into drive. I had to figure out who was behind this. If this freak kept adding zeros like they were nothing . . . Well, it was time for drastic action.

I parked and headed into the shop to find Valdez in a huddle in the back room with Etienne. Derek worked the front.

"What's up?" I looked significantly at the mortal customers browsing through the clothing racks. Christmas was just two weeks away and we were doing a brisk business in holiday dresses and red sweaters.

"Talked to Freddy." Derek stuffed a vintage beaded evening bag into a sack and thanked a customer. "No worries. He thought he could smooth things over for you with his father. I told him to forget it." Derek turned to me and leaned on the counter. "I'm afraid you're not going to like the next part."

"What?" I kept glancing at the strange pair in the back room. Anyone else would think it was a man talking to a dog. I knew it was a two-way conversation.

"I've persuaded Freddy to take CiCi and get out of town. We're all going to Paris for the holidays."

"Oh. Wow." I put my hand on Derek's arm. "Okay. Being noble here. That's great. For the best and all that. But what am I going to do without you?"

"I've got a couple of replacements all lined up." Derek frowned, finally acknowledging the odd couple behind him. "For one, Etienne says he has retail experience and he's desperate for money."

"But I'm not that desperate for help. Am I?"

"Believe it or not, Valdez finally remembers where he knows him from. They go way back. Last job they did together was in New Orleans." Derek leaned in for a whisper. "Seems his previous names included Steve Delaney. He and the V-man worked security together a time or two. And get this, they were rivals for the affections of the fair Beth, who goes by the name of Brittany these days."

"You've got to be kidding." I moved over when a customer tossed a cashmere sweater, red of course, on the counter. "Coincidence?"

"Maybe I shouldn't leave now." Derek got a worried look around the eyes, but kept a fake smile for the customer.

"No, no. You have to go. It's a good idea. I'm going to talk to Etienne myself."

Derek turned to give the customer his full attention. The guy would be hell to replace. He was a doll with the ladies. Before I could get to the back room, he'd talked this woman into adding a pearl collar to her outfit to give it the authentic retro look.

I stepped into the back room and closed the door. "You guys have something to tell me?"

"Glory, you're not going to believe who this is. I didn't recognize him at first. He's got the beard now and he used to shave his head. And then there's the phony French accent." Valdez gave a doggy shrug. *"Hell, maybe I'm losing my touch."*

I put my hand on his shoulder. "And maybe your buddy here didn't want you to recognize him. Eh?"

"What can I say? I never thought to see my old friend Rafael trotting around on all fours again and with such a hairy ass." Etienne laughed, flashing white teeth and seemingly restored to good health. "And Beth here too. What are the odds?"

"Indeed." I sat on the room's only chair. "Derek says you're angling for a job. He's leaving me shorthanded here at the holidays, but you can imagine my reluctance to trust a total stranger with the amount of cash I hope to rake in."

"Steve's not a total stranger, Glory. He's saved my life more than once." Valdez sat on the floor next to me. *"And he should know that if he does anything, anything, to hurt you or your business, he'll live or should I say, not live to regret it."*

"Man, that's putting it right out there, isn't it, Steve?" I patted Valdez's head. "You interested in clerking in my store? Pay's the pits, but I offer a nice commission on sales."

"I don't know. Doesn't really sound like what I'm looking for. I was hoping maybe Lucky might need me to help protect her and show her the vampire ropes. I've got a lot of experience along those lines, as Rafe here can tell you. Seems like you'd do better to work the store yourself and pass Lucky off to me." Etienne grinned with what I felt was a very practiced effort to charm me.

I couldn't argue with his logic, but I also didn't trust him not to . . . hell, what? Steal the reward money if he caught her killer in another attempt? Now that didn't sound very nice of me or ethical or whatever. But what if *he* was the killer? Seemed like his arrival in town—in my shop—was a little too timely.

"Why don't you just help Derek tonight and we'll play it by ear? See what Lucky says when she gets here." I looked at my watch. The mall should have closed by now. "She and her entourage should be arriving momentarily."

"Yep, I think that's Flo coming in right now." Valdez was on his feet and at the door leading into the shop. *"Let's keep Etienne's real name our little secret, Glory. You can respect his right to privacy, can't you?"*

I could respect it. Hell, I'd had dozens of names myself over the years. It's part of the survival thing. You move on, you create a new identity. I'd tried to stick with a variation of my real name and at least once a century I went back to Gloriana, which was a huge relief. Etienne was French for Stephen. Fine. Not such a stretch after all. And I was sure Valdez would clue Brittany/Beth in on their connection anyway. Oh, God, but this was getting complicated.

"Well, Gloriana? Are you going to open the door?" Etienne was close behind me, his breath warm on the back of my neck. Then his hand landed on my butt.

I whipped around and pulled out the stake I'd hidden

behind the door in the brass umbrella stand. (See? I'm learning.) I held it against Etienne's chest. "Back off, buster."

"Whoa, Glory. I told you he's okay." Valdez knew better
than to get between me and his buddy, and he obviously
hadn't seen the butt/hand contact.

"That's all right, *mon ami.*" Etienne held up both hands
and backed up a foot. "Glory is a survivor, like us. She
knows how to take care of herself. Congratulations, *mon petit
chou.* You dazzle me."

"I'm not your shoe. Or your hat or any accessory to you.
Keep your charm and your distance." I looked down at
Valdez. "How long since you've seen this guy last?"

"Fifty, maybe sixty years." Valdez's eyes gleamed with
pride. *"You're dazzling me too, kiddo. When'd you put the stake in
here?"*

"After the fire. Seemed like the time to increase our defense. I've got some others hidden around the shop." Not
nearly enough though. I really liked Blade's baseball bat
idea. I was going to see about making a few of those for myself. Definitely needed one behind the counter. I opened the
door to the shop and gestured for Etienne to precede me. No
way was he getting behind me again. Maybe I should be
flattered. Not every man likes a big butt, but I pick who
gets to touch. You know what I mean?

"If you want to continue sleeping back here, Etienne,
you're going to have to pull your weight. Go help Derek
wrap up whatever he's selling. Breakables need bubble
wrap, it's under the counter. Tell him to show you how to
run a credit card." I'd moved the shredder to the back room
after the scare with Brittany. Etienne just grinned, like he
could care less that I'd just had him at stake point.

"Glory, you must see the boots we got. And a little something for you." Flo had a Nordstrom's bag while Lucky carried two more. Brittany didn't carry anything. I guess so she
could fend off any attackers. I slid the pointy cane back into
its hiding place and walked out to meet them.

Richard followed the ladies with his usual sardonic look. I never could read his mind but it really wasn't necessary. Shopping wasn't his thing, but he would do anything for Florence. As I said, she's *really* good at the kiss-and-make-up part.

While I admired the turquoise earrings Flo had picked out for me, Etienne hurried to take Lucky's packages. And wouldn't you know he broke into rapid Italian with both Lucky and Flo? God, I hate linguists. I could see Derek struggling to help three customers at once. Forget Etienne. I had a business to run. I sent Richard a mental message to see if he could herd the crew upstairs and out of my way.

When I finally got a break from ringing up sales—love the holidays—Valdez was the only one left of the paranormal bunch.

"You mean Etienne left with the rest of them?" I said this to Derek since Valdez was being petted by a Goth who was waiting for his girlfriend to come out of the dressing room.

"Afraid so. I guess he really didn't want to work here."

"Then I'll be damned if he'll sleep here." I made sure I said that loud enough for Valdez to hear. Pals or not, I was not going to be taken advantage of. I may be little and cute. Okay, maybe not so little, but I'm no pushover.

Derek nudged me. "Those guys are back again."

I checked out the two men lurking by the vampire mural. Leroy and Earl, if I remembered correctly. "May I help you find something, gentlemen?"

"Lookin' for my daughter." The first one, dressed in a red plaid wool shirt and khakis, scanned the room. "Hangs out with one of those Goth freaks." He didn't seem to care if the man with Valdez heard him.

I forced a smile. "We're a pretty small shop. You want me to look in the dressing room for her? What's her name?"

"Becky. Forget it. I already called her name. She ain't here. Come on, Earl."

Earl tipped his Oakley cap. "Thank you, ma'am. Kid's

out past curfew. Sorry to bother you." This earned him a shove toward the door.

"Oookay." I headed to the dressing room. "If you're in there, Becky, you can come out now."

"Thanks." A flushed teenager scurried out. "Sorry. My dad. Well. Just sorry." She grabbed the Goth, who had put his hair into three neat spikes of green, yellow and purple. Those, along with his various piercings and silver dangles, made him into his own personal Mardi Gras float. Hey, I'd spent several decades in New Orleans. Let the good times roll.

"I can't believe he didn't recognize you, Neil." She tossed a black velvet skirt on the counter. "He just sees *through* my boyfriend. Forget the fact that Neil is an honor student who is a computer *genius*." She snuggled up against him as she counted out the exact change for her purchase to Derek. "Babysitting money. And Daddy is wrong. I still have fifteen minutes until I have to be home. Mom gave me extra time because I had this babysitting gig tonight and Neil picked me up." She made a face. "I love that y'all are open late. Bye now." She and Neil left after a final pat for Valdez.

"Nice kid. Jerk parent." I looked around and realized we were alone again. I still hadn't made it upstairs to the shower I was longing for.

"Oh, Glory, I forgot to tell you. A package came for you today. Will said he ordered you a little something. A peace offering. It's in the back room." Derek sat on the stool we kept behind the counter. "It's actually pretty quiet right now. Why don't you go back and see what it is? He seemed pretty excited about it. He came in right after I got here to see if it had arrived."

"He knows Jerry's really mad at him. I bet he hopes I can talk Jerry into helping him out financially. Fat chance." I gestured and Valdez came trotting up to me. "I'll take Valdez with me in case this thing explodes or something crawls out of it."

"Thanks, Blondie." Valdez rolled his eyes.

Sure enough, there was a FedEx package on the big table in the back room. Heavy, or it would have been if I'd been a mere mortal. When I saw the return address, I couldn't wait to rip it open. Bloodthirsty. From Transylvania. Oh, my God! Will had sprung for a case of AB negative, my absolute favorite of all blood types, but it was expensive. I wondered for a nanosecond how Will could afford it, but cracked open a bottle anyway.

I treated it like a fine wine. First a sniff. Mmm. The aroma. Heady. Full-bodied. Sorry if I'm grossing you out, but this is my thing. Now for the first tiny sip. Ahhh. Smooth going down. Delicious. I sat and savored the taste, trying hard not to guzzle it. I checked for an invoice and finally found a catalog. The prices were much more reasonable than I'd expected, and I remembered that I had a discount coupon upstairs on my computer. Wow. Bells tinkled and I got up to go into the shop again. Richard and Flo.

"Where are Lucky, Brittany and Etienne?"

Flo and Richard looked at each other and grinned. "Next door."

"Mugs and Muffins?" Unusual, but maybe Brittany wanted something to eat.

"Nope." Richard was merrier than I'd seen him in a long time. "The Tatt-ler."

"Why?"

Flo giggled. "Lucky wants a tattoo to go with her new Goth look."

"And no one thought to tell her . . ."

"And spoil the surprise? I like Lucky's shoes, but she is not so nice sometimes. To you. To Brittany. Maybe she needs to learn a lesson." Flo strolled over to the mural and pretended to study it. "Glory, I once 'studied' "—she gave me a wink—"with El Greco. Why don't we do a wall with a tribute to him?"

Richard growled and grabbed Flo's hand, hauling her to

the door. "I have heard quite enough about your former lovers, Florence. Artists. I'm sick of them. Did I ever tell you about the time I worked in the Vatican catacombs? I learned many secrets there. How would like for me to whisper a few in your . . . ear?"

"Ricardo, you intrigue me." Flo gave me a finger wave as she let him pull her out of the shop.

Derek grinned while he straightened a pile of vintage jeans. "Aren't you going to run over to the Tatt-ler and tell Lucky about vampires and tattoos?"

I sighed and moved to help him. "Maybe later. You know, I never did get to shower and change clothes. Things are quiet now." Maybe too quiet. No customers. Not that that was cause for alarm. We always had lulls between one and two in the morning. "Is it okay if I go upstairs and take Valdez with me?"

"Sure. What about Lucky?"

"Etienne was so eager to take her on. Let him handle her and her tattoo."

"Good news, Glory." Valdez dropped his leash at my feet, obviously ready for a walk before we went upstairs. *"I can hear them talking next door. Brittany booked them a hotel room. I guess they're going to try to handle their own security from now on. And if you're serious about kicking Steve, I mean Etienne, out, he's already talking his way into staying with them."*

"That *is* good news." I opened the door, Valdez doing his usual reconnaissance before I was allowed outside. He did his thing in the park across the street while I thought about popping into the Tatt-ler and cluing Lucky in about vampires and tattoos in case Etienne didn't. But, remember, Valdez isn't the only one with supersonic hearing.

I could see movement behind the plateglass windows and neon signs and hear Lucky talking to Brittany about which tattoo she wanted. Her father hated tattoos so she was starting with something she could keep covered. The whole vampire thing was shock enough for dear old dad this week.

She really liked the giant fiery dragon. But her butt just wasn't big enough. Now if she had a fat ass like Glory . . . Giggle. Giggle. Too bad. She'd just have to settle for the baby dragon instead.

Hmm. Have fun, Lucky. Hope that needle's dull, dull, dull.

Valdez and I headed upstairs.

Eleven

"Glory, we're going to be staying at a hotel near the Irwin Center where they have concerts. Brittany checked it out. A lot of musicians stay there and she says she can arrange for the staff to leave us alone during the day and clean at night."

"That's fine, Lucky. I'm glad you've got it all worked out." Lucky, along with her crew, had limped into the shop a few minutes after four. I'd decided that if she really wanted Etienne to be her guide to all things vampire then so be it. I did have a few concerns though and pulled Lucky into the back room and closed the door.

"Oh, great. Now that we're alone, let me show you my awesome tat."

Before I could say hell, no, Lucky had her skirt up. Her thong was skimpy enough to give me a good look at the snarling baby dragon on her left butt cheek.

"Cute. Nice butt too. Lipo?" I couldn't resist. Hey, she'd admitted she had her plastic surgeon on speed dial.

"Oh, sure. And they both hurt like hell despite all claims to the contrary." Lucky sighed.

I looked at my coveted Bloodthirsty and came to a reluctant decision. "You need to feed and I don't want you drinking from mortals."

"But that's what vampires do!" Lucky sat on the edge of the table, then hopped right back up again.

"You can drink a blood substitute like I do." I grabbed a bottle. "This is a new one. Try it, it's really very good."

"No, thanks, really." Lucky smiled. "I know you're on a budget. And you've been very generous already. Daddy's had his assistant doing research on this feeding thing. Remember, we work with paranormals, lots of them vampires. She found out what the best products are and has arranged to have some delivered to the hotel tonight."

"Wow." Which was all I could manage to say. Money talks. So do connections.

"Oh, it gets better. The good stuff is being hand carried by some of Daddy's goons. Seems he feels Brittany needs help." Lucky made a face.

"You keep talking about goons. Are these more paranormals? Like the clown demons?"

"No, just Daddy's muscle. Retired boxers, football players who've taken one too many hits to the head." Lucky grinned. "I have to admit some of them are pretty cute, just not too swift. They'll give Etienne and Brittany a break."

"You've really hired Etienne? After knowing him for about five minutes?"

"Brittany and Valdez apparently have known him for centuries. I figure they're serving as references. And Daddy's assistant checked up on him, of course. He's about as trustworthy as *they* are." Lucky put her hand on my shoulder. "I know you feel responsible for me, Glory. Because you made me and all. But, face it. You look about twelve and I've been around the block more than once."

"My looks have nothing to do with it and you know it. I'm over four hundred years old." Nice compliment though. I stored it away to savor later.

"Etienne is older than you are. Says he is anyway. And he's a good-looking guy. Can you blame me for wanting *him* to show me how to sink my teeth into vampire ways instead of you?" Lucky winked. "And I really don't let another woman order me around, ever. Not even my own mother. In an Italian family, or at least *my* Italian family, Daddy calls the shots. Mama shops, tells the servants what to serve for dinner and looks pretty when Daddy comes home. Period."

"Gee, that sounds like a laugh riot for her. I'm surprised Daddy let you work for him."

"Mama didn't give him a son. So I set out to prove I could fill the void." Lucky smiled sadly. "I've got a cousin Carlo, who still thinks he's going to get the nod when Daddy decides to retire. This immortality thing just might give me an edge if I play my cards right."

I waited for the relief I should have felt at having Lucky off my back. But if I didn't have her around, then how was I going to find her killer? I had a million reasons to want to follow up on that.

"You know, Lucky, I might be able to help you with your collections. If you could clear some more of those debts in the Austin area, that would really impress your father."

"You're right. You have that list of the people who owe us. Any of the names ring a bell?"

Greg. But I really didn't want to send Lucky out to the EV compound. Whether she wanted me to feel responsible for her or not, I wasn't about to throw her to *those* wolves.

"Glory, Lucky, you've got to come out here and see this." Even through the closed door, we could hear Valdez laughing.

"I guess we'd better go see." I was glad I didn't have to decide about Greg yet. Sure, I hated him, but he could also be useful, maybe find some of the other names on Lucky's list.

Lucky opened the door and we both stared at the two women standing behind Will Kilpatrick. Will had a harried look as he hurried up to me.

"Glory, did you get my gift?"

"Yes, thank you, Will. First bottle was absolutely delicious."

"Knock. Knock."

"Knock. Knock."

"Aren't you going to answer them, Will?" Lucky looked past Will and smiled at the blonde on his right. The brunette on his left gave the blonde an elbow when she smiled back. Apparently this was serious business.

"Knock. Knock."

"Knock. Knock."

"Who's there?" A female customer decided to answer.

Will turned and gave her a charming smile. "Sorry, darlin', but they'll only answer to me. It's a joke, you see. Sent by someone"—he looked at Lucky—"who really hates me and is punishing me."

"Knock. Knock."

"Knock. Knock."

"You really should answer, Will. If you don't, things can get pretty ugly." Lucky linked arms with Brittany and Etienne. "Then again, don't answer. Refusal-to-answer scenarios are fun to watch, if not to participate in."

"Knock. Knock."

"Knock. Knock."

The volume was increasing. The female customer covered her ears and decided she had had enough. She left the shop without buying anything.

"Okay, that does it. Will, get out and take your knockers with you." I slapped a hand over my mouth.

Etienne and Valdez laughed until they cried. Valdez actually rolled on the floor, his tail thumping the wood floor.

"Knock. Knock." Blond knocker grabbed a yellow throw pillow and bopped Will over the head in perfect time.

"Knock. Knock." Brunette knocker reached for a bronze statue, and Will caved, covering his head.

"Who's there?" he screamed from behind the counter.

"Wire." Brunette.

"Wire who?" Will was totally whipped now.

"Wire you ignoring us?" Blondie smiled sweetly.

"Oh, God." Will collapsed on the floor behind the counter.

"Knock. Knock." Brunette.

"Knock. Knock." Blonde.

"Take it outside, Will." I strode behind the counter and pulled Will to his feet. I actually felt sorry for him and led him to the back room. I handed him one of the new bottles of Bloodthirsty and tried to slip him out the back door before the two knockers could get there. But when I opened the door, there they stood in the alley, blond and brunette demons with angelic smiles this time.

"Knock. Knock."

"Knock. Knock."

"Glory, did you talk to Blade? You think he'll help me?" Will took a deep swallow of the Bloodthirsty and slammed and bolted the door. Seconds later, the girls were inside and behind him again.

"Knock. Knock."

"Knock. Knock."

"I'm sorry, Will, but Jerry's got a lot on his plate right now. His mother's in town and he's got a domestic crisis brewing. You're going to have to find the money somewhere else." I took a deep breath and then waited a beat while the demons knocked another round. I really felt bad for Will. I knew what it was like to gamble and lose control, always sure you could win back what you've lost. Now there was a glimmer of hope. The reward. If we could work together to catch Lucky's killer . . .

"Who's there?" Will had noticed the brunette reaching for a china lamp base.

I'd noticed it too. "Hey, hands off the merchandise!"

"Boo."

"Boo who?"

"Keep crying, buddy, but that won't make us stop. Pay up and we'll leave you alone."

"There's one way you might be able to get the money." This was really getting on my last nerve. Thank God I'd never heard of the Carvarellis in Vegas.

"What? I'll do anything." Will sank down on the edge of the table.

"Knock. Knock."

"Knock. Knock."

"Lucky's father is offering a reward to whoever finds out who tried to kill her. I'll split it with you if you can help me find the vampire who ripped out her throat the other night and left her for dead."

"And it's enough to cover my debt?"

"Knock. Knock."

"Knock. Knock."

"More than enough. But don't try to cut me out on this, Will. We work together. I've got a list of who in the area owes Lucky's family money. I figure that's a great suspect list."

"Yeah, you're right." Will sighed.

"Knock. Knock." Brunette was looking around for another weapon. Her eyes lit up when she saw a hall tree against the wall.

"Knock. Knock." Blondie reached for a chair.

"Who's there?"

Thank God he'd answered. But how long could Will stand this? It was already rubbing my nerves raw.

"Orange."

"Orange who?"

"Orange you sorry you tried to stiff the Carvarellis?"

"I'll slip the debtor list under Lacy's door." I couldn't wait for Will to leave.

"Don't bother."

"Knock. Knock."

"Knock. Knock."

"Why?"

"She says she can't live like this?"

"Knock. Knock."

"Knock. Knock."

"Who's freakin' there?"

"Police."

Will took a deep swallow of Bloodthirsty. "I don't blame her. Police who?"

"Police pay so we can stop telling these lame jokes."

I was not going to ask. I was not going to ask. I was not— Oh, hell. "Where are you staying, Will?"

"Knock. Knock."

"Knock. Knock."

Will dredged up a smile. "Don't worry, Glory. I wouldn't do that to you. Damian's got a room over his garage. Flo and Richard saw me having a meltdown in the alley. Flo hooked me up."

"Knock. Knock."

"Knock. Knock."

Will flipped the dead bolts and opened the door to the alley. "After you, ladies. Move out a little, Glory's not the one you're torturing." He turned to me and smiled. "E-mail that list to Damian. He'll see that I get it."

"Knock. Knock."

"Knock. Knock."

"Who the hell's there?" He stopped and looked behind him. "Bang who?" Suddenly he burst out laughing, leaning against the door frame. "Who knew they had X-rated knock knocks?" He grinned tiredly. "Damian's not on that list, is he?"

"No, I already checked for all my best buds and their families." I patted his cheek. He needed a shave, a shower and a break. "You're the only one on there I'd count as friend. Take care. I'll work on Jerry for you."

"Knock. Knock."

"Knock. Knock."

Will drained his Bloodthirsty and put the empty bottle in my hand. "Not bad, is it? Thanks, love. Next time Jerry's mum starts in on you she'll hear from me, I tell you that."

"Knock. Knock."

"Knock. Knock."

He leaned close and kissed my cheek. "I think the blond one likes me. She doesn't hit as hard as the brunette." He turned to stroll into the dark. "Who's there?"

I shut the door and turned the locks. Poor Will. At least when dawn came the clown demons would have to let him sleep. No choice. Vamps pass out wherever they happen to be. But his waking hours . . . As an incentive to pay up, this one was a killer.

In the shop things were blessedly quiet since Lucky, Etienne and Brittany had left too. Then I remembered to check my cell phone. No new message, but I reread the one I'd gotten in the car. The video again. As if I needed a reminder of being caught with my fangs down.

Twenty-four hours. Five thousand dollars. TV. Now I was pissed. Where did this freak think I was getting that kind of money? I'd already tried to answer the text, but the number was blocked. Whenever I got delivery instructions, I wanted to be ready.

"Valdez. Here, boy. Derek, I'm taking the dog in the back to feed him." I said that for the benefit of the mortal customer at the counter, where Derek, who was leaving for Paris the next night, was training his replacement, a vampire who'd filled in for us before, on our new credit-card machine.

"Sure, Glory, take your time."

"Woof!" Valdez wagged his tail and followed me to the back room. Once the door closed, he was all business. *"Dish out those chocolate-chip muffins Lacy brought from next door, then tell me what's up."*

I handed him one, almost losing a finger, then sat in a

chair and flipped open my phone. "Someone saw us in the alley the night we found Lucky. Look at this."

Valdez swallowed the last of the muffin, then leaned close. *"I'll be damned. Pretty poor quality, but it's obviously you and me and a body in a pool of blood. Look at your fangs."*

"Yeah, I'm so screwed."

Valdez rubbed his muzzle on my skirt, scattering crumbs all over the wool. *"So what's this about, Glory?"*

"Blackmail. If I don't pay this creep five thousand dollars, he'll send the video to the TV station, probably to our old friend there." I'd been interviewed on a local station after my shop had been firebombed. The reporter had done her best to make something sensational of the Vintage Vamp name, my vampire mural and my Goth clientele. I had no doubt she'd flip over the video and make it the last nail in my, ha-ha, coffin. I could just see it on the ten o'clock news.

"You can't pay a blackmailer off. He'll just keep coming back for more." Valdez paced to the back door, then turned, his head down. *"This is my fault. I let you down, Glory. No way anyone shoulda gotten close enough to take that video with me on the job."*

"We were a little busy, V. Saving a life. And this was probably taken from pretty far away with a zoom. But I'll make a deal with you." I put my hand on his shoulder. I hated to do this, but . . .

"What?"

"I won't tell Jerry about this, uh, mistake you made, and you don't tell him about the blackmail. You and I can handle this on our own." Jerry pays Valdez's salary, and the shifter reports everything to his boss.

"Now who's into blackmail?" Valdez backed away from my touch. *"Damn it, Glory. What if this creep turns out to be into more than just extortion? You get hurt and Blade'll hand me my head on a platter."*

"I can't afford to pay this, this ransom, and I won't risk . . ." I took a breath. "You think I should just leave then? Sneak off in the dead of night, and leave everything and every*one* here?" I blinked back tears. "I've done that before and it's no fun, let me tell you."

"Aw, I didn't say that. Read those texts to me. Maybe it's a teenager we can scare, then whammy into forgetting the whole thing."

"Exactly!" I wiped my eyes. "Sorry for the meltdown."

"You're entitled." Valdez gave me a gentle head butt. *"Stuff an envelope with a few bills and paper or something to make it look fat enough for five thou. Then we wait to spring the trap. I can stake out the drop spot during the day. I figure that with the security in the building, as long as I'm close, you'll be okay for one day. He's not going to let big money like that sit for long. I'll like seeing this guy's reaction when a dog takes him down. I can do a pretty mean whammy myself if I can get in his face."*

"Thanks, puppy."

"Wait! Play that video again."

"Why?" Personally, I was sick of seeing it. Not only was it proof positive that I was a vampire, but it was unflattering as hell. The camera adds at least twenty pounds, trust me on that. I played it again. Yep, that swing coat still billowed around me like a damned tent.

"Look at that angle. I swear this was taken from above us. I'd say with a powerful zoom lens and from the roof of our building."

"That means . . ."

"It's no mortal teenager we're up against, Blondie. We've got a paranormal screwing us over." Valdez sighed. *"Give me another muffin. I'm gonna need my strength if I'm goin' head-to-head with another one of us."*

"Forget it. Too dangerous." We argued about it until we were both exhausted. One thing we did agree on: any paranormal who could shape-shift could have landed on our roof and taken the video. No way did we think it was anyone who actually lived in our building. We knew our neighbors, and none of them would pull a scam like this. At least we didn't think . . .

This whole thing was wearing on me, but at least now I had someone to talk to about it. And that helped, even if we couldn't figure out how to bring this to a satisfactory conclusion.

We still hadn't received drop instructions by the time Derek carried my case of Bloodthirsty up the stairs for me right before dawn. I hugged my clerk good-bye, shed a few tears because I was really worried that Freddy was more involved with his father than we knew, then went inside to a silent apartment.

"Well, Valdez, looks like we finally have the peace and quiet we crave. Guess we'd better enjoy it while we can."

"You said it, Blondie." Valdez yawned and stretched. *"Can't say I'm too happy about the way Steve moved in on Lucky and Beth the way he did. There's something off there."*

I stopped on my way to the bathroom. "But you practically vouched for him."

"Yeah. I know I did." Valdez scratched behind one ear. *"If I didn't know better, I'd think the son of a bitch had worked some mind control on me."*

"Oh, swell. That's reassuring."

"Well, Brittany thinks she can handle anything. And Lucky has told you repeatedly she doesn't want you running her life. So I guess we just back off and see what happens." Valdez ambled into the kitchen and nosed open the pantry. *"Before you get involved in the bathroom, would you open this box of Twinkies? I'm starved."*

I did the necessary, patting him on the head on my way to brushing my teeth. No lectures now on cruelty to animals. Reminder: Valdez is not a dog. He's a shape-shifter with a little something extra. Twinkies won't hurt him. And he'd die if I gave him dog food. I threaten him with it, but I'd never follow through. I rarely shape-shift because I have this phobia about it, but if I ever did turn myself into a dog (shudder), trust me, I wouldn't suddenly crave kibble.

Once I was ready, I opened the bedroom door and invited

Valdez to jump up on the foot of my bed. He guards me through the daylight hours.

"Hey, those clown demons were really something, weren't they?" I was about thirty seconds from lights out and refused to spend my last half minute of consciousness on my blackmail woes.

Valdez seemed to get it. He laid his head next to my foot. *"Confession here. Brittany and I were clown demons together once for the Carvarellis."*

I sat up in bed. "You're kidding me."

"Knock. Knock."

"No way."

"Oh, yeah."

"Why?"

"The pay's great."

"It would have to be."

"Yeah, you think it's nerve-racking to watch?" Valdez gave a doggy laugh. *"I tell you there are hundreds of really lame knock knock jokes and I know them all."*

"Tell me one."

"You sure?"

"Shoot."

"Knock. Knock."

"Who's there?"

"Line."

"Line who?"

Sunrise.

"Quit staring at your phone, girlfriend. I'm sure Jeremiah will call later. His mother is probably dragging him around town, making him play dutiful son, no?" Flo dropped a stack of boxes on the coffee table. "This should cheer you up. I will let you sell these in your shop. Vintage Gucci. The heels are too low, and they pinch my little toes. So I let them go." She grinned and sat on the couch beside me.

"Wow! Thanks, Flo." Since my roommate was notoriously reluctant to part with her fabulous shoe collection, I tried to look suitably thrilled. But I *was* worried that Jerry hadn't called. With Mag and Mara double-teaming him, he was probably being subjected to an endless round of "Why Glory's all wrong for you." Now throw in a daughter and— My phone beeped, signaling a new text message.

"See? What did I tell you?" Flo picked up the remote control and turned on the TV. "I won't start it yet, but I think you need to see this DVD I picked up last night. It will get your, um, juices flowing for Jeremiah. Trust me on this."

"It's not Jerry calling. It's a text. Jerry doesn't text." He's not that big on technology, though he knows his way around a computer. I read the message quickly, then swallowed a lump the size of one of Flo's Guccis. I thought about showing the text to Flo. Valdez bumped me, apparently abandoning his dinner of canned spaghetti and meatballs I'd nuked for him earlier to check on me.

"From you know who?" Valdez glanced at Flo. *"We letting her in on this?"*

"Glory, look! It's a new song from our very favorite singer of all time." Flo was grinning and practically bouncing on the couch.

I shook my head and stood to take the phone into the kitchen. "Be right back, Flo. Don't start without me. Valdez needs dessert."

"What does it say?" Valdez sat in front of me.

"See for yourself." I put the phone at his nose level.

"TOMORROW NITE. LEAVE $5000 CASH IN BROWN SACK UNDER TRASH CAN NEXT TO SWING SET IN PARK ACROSS FROM UR SHOP. NO TRICKS OR TV TIME."

"Well, that's pretty specific." Valdez shook his head. *"You got five thousand bucks? Just in case?"*

"Are you kidding? I could scrounge up maybe another

three or four hundred. Do a cash advance of a thousand on my credit card, but the interest . . ." I shut the phone and jammed it into my pocket. "Maybe I could stall. Write a hot check and stuff it in there."

"Text says cash."

"You know once the video goes public, the money source dries up." I straightened my shoulders. "I say we put a hundred bucks in a sack with a note explaining the deal. An easy payment plan, or we take our chances."

Valdez smiled. *"Gutsy. And worth a shot. It's not like another paranormal would really want to go to the media."*

"Exactly! You start a vampire-hunting frenzy, and all sorts of interesting things could be exposed. And the video could have been staged. I doubt the news would show it unless the person who took it came forward to verify it."

"Now you're talking. I say you make this the last payment. Put one dollar in the sack, and dare them to come out with the video." Valdez bumped against my leg. *"Open up that box of doughnuts you bought at the store. I feel like celebrating. We are calling this sucker's bluff."*

I dropped two doughnuts in his dish and tried to feel as positive as he did. Did I dare go through with this? Could I afford not to? I sat beside Flo on the couch, glad for a chance to forget my troubles for a while.

"Okay, girlfriend. Prepare to be amazed." She grinned and hit play on the remote.

Twenty minutes later we'd both been amazed. Twice. And we were about to start a third round. Valdez had retreated to my bedroom, burying his head under my pillow.

"He's still got the hottest body I've ever seen. Sorry, Jerry." I stretched out my legs, knocking over a shoe box. "And what I could do to that body." We both sighed and closed our eyes.

Right after Flo and I had become roommates, we were walking in the mall, shoe shopping, of course, when we heard music. The song was about a forever kind of love, the one thing we'd both thought we'd found, never quite got the hang of, well, you get it. We loved the deep, sexy voice, the beat and especially the message. Anyway, we looked in the window of the music store, and there was this poster.

Oh, wow. The man seemed to be looking right at us. Tanned, toned, shirtless, of course, and wearing those kind of low-riding jeans that seem to be an inch from . . . So we were hooked. We ran inside, bought CDs, and our obsession was born. Since then we'd had a kind of race going. Whenever one of us found something new from "our guy," the other one was challenged to do the same. eBay loved us.

"Yes, he's perfect! And that song! It touches me. Right, um, here." Flo ran her hand down her stomach, heading south.

"Hey! I know what you mean." I grabbed the DVD case. "When did this come out? I thought we had all of his music."

"It was just released yesterday. Check out this poster." She unfolded it, and we both sighed again. "I saw it in the record-store window when we were walking in the mall. I nagged Richard until we went inside and bought it." Flo grinned and got up to prop the poster on the wall behind our other DVDs and CDs. "Richard's already sick of it. But not of what it does to me. Let's play it again."

"God, no."

"Shut up, Valdez." I hit play just as there was a knock on the door. "I'll get it." I danced to the door, the sexy beat of the song irresistible. "Look who's here." I opened the door on Lucky, with a glowering Brittany and a grinning Etienne in tow. Lucky had on dark glasses and a trench coat, obviously incognito. She had a large tote that she dropped on the coffee table.

"What's going on, Lucky? You look like you're out spying on someone. Or are you afraid you'll be attacked again?"

Lucky pulled off her dark glasses and collapsed on the couch. "Thanks for reminding me that I have that to worry about too. Do we have to listen to *him*?"

"Don't you like Israel Caine? Flo and I are big fans. Huge fans." I still held the remote and deliberately jacked up the volume. "Check out his new hit."

Lucky frowned and pressed a hand to her forehead. "Please. Spare me. Can't you see I'm in distress?"

I hit stop.

"Hey! I was listening to that!" Flo sat up from where she'd been lying dreamily on the couch.

"Actually you were doing a little more than listening." I'll spare you the details. "Look at Lucky, Flo. She's obviously having a makeup crisis."

"Exactly! Look at me. I tried to do it by feel, like you told me, but I could tell I made a mess of it so I washed it all off. Then I figured Brittany could do it for me if I told her what to do step-by-step."

I glanced at Brittany, standing behind Lucky. Strained smile, gesturing and doing eye rolls at Valdez, who'd come in when he'd heard the knock on the door.

"Looks like she didn't follow directions."

"No kidding. She came at me like she was a bricklayer with a trowel. Feels like I've got on a mask." Lucky put her head in her hands. "I'd give anything for a mirror that worked."

"How's the bum today?"

"I'd rather not discuss it. Concentrate on my face." Lucky got down to business. "I have everything I need right in here. Six colors of base for contours. Concealer of course. Eye shadow palette, custom matched to my eye color. Eyeliner, smudge proof. Mascara, waterproof. Eyelash curler." She turned around to give Brittany a dirty look. "I'll certainly never put one in Brit's hands again. She took out half of my lashes! Then there's the blush, powder to set it all, brow gel, tweezers—or does that hair quit growing?" She looked at me hopefully, but I had to shake my head. "Well, you get the idea. This is a big deal and I know you understand. I've never seen you without perfect makeup. You too, Flo."

Okay, as a peace offering this was a pretty good one. I smiled. "I don't think I have time to help, Lucky. I really need to go down to the shop." And I really didn't have time to run a makeup clinic.

"But I've just got to wash this off and start over." Lucky wasn't giving up.

We all turned toward the door, where Valdez was snorting. I knew he was trying not to laugh. There was a knock, and I let Richard in.

"I can't believe it. Silence. DVD player broken?" He put his arm around Flo and kissed her lips.

Florence eased away from him. "You mock me. Shall I show you it still works?" She reached for the remote.

"Florence, please! If Glory doesn't have time, will you help me with my makeup?" Lucky sniffled. "I'm desperate, and Brittany just doesn't have the knack. She made me look like a cheap hooker."

"Obviously I'm needed here." Flo put down the remote with a sigh. "Come with us, Brittany. I will show both you and Lucky how to do the makeup. Richard, when I am done, we will take the DVD with us to your place. I think you need to listen to the music." She gave a little hip wiggle. "Let it inspire you."

"You're taking the music?" I heard myself wail.

"Don't worry, Glory. I'll leave you the poster. And I bought an extra CD. You can never have too much Israel Caine." Flo gave Valdez a hard look when he made a noise. "We'll be going to his concert too. He's coming to Austin. Glory and I couldn't get tickets, Lucky, but we'll get in if we have to whammy every security guard in Irwin Center."

"Whatever floats your boat, girls. He's not for me." Lucky picked up her makeup kit. "Now can we get to work on my face?"

I shook my head. Immune to Israel Caine? Weird. I turned to Etienne as the women left the room. "Any problems coming over here?" I kept wondering if whoever had attacked Lucky would try again.

"No, but then Lucky drives fast and takes no prisoners. And she sure wouldn't go into that alley again. We've been studying that list of debtors. I guess you have too." Etienne pulled a paper out of his pocket. "I may have met one of these guys out at the EV compound."

"Well, I'm sure you realize that's no place to go with your Carvarelli goons to make a collection."

"No, of course not. I'll never go near there again." Etienne glanced toward the bathroom, where we could hear Lucky complaining about my cheap facial cleanser. "Our mutual 'friend' Gregory Kaplan is on that list."

"I talked to him. He says he didn't attack Lucky and, for once, I don't think he was lying." I smiled at Richard. "Maybe you and Etienne can discover who some of these other people are on the list. And can you get hold of Lucky's BlackBerry? She seems to keep her life in there. Was Lacy the only appointment she had that night? Seems like Lacy wouldn't owe her enough to make it worth her while to fly to Austin. But then I think she mentioned a tip she'd received about Will. *He* owed her plenty."

"Whoever attacked Lucky hasn't taken any more victims since. Austin's been pretty quiet." Richard glanced at Lucky's purse. "But I know better than to go into a woman's purse. What about you, Etienne?"

"It could cost me my job. Let's wait and ask Lucky about it after the women are through."

I glanced at the clock. "Whatever. You guys are on your own. I have *got* to go to the shop." Of course I hadn't studied anything. When had I found the time? And with the Christmas rush, I didn't think I ever would.

"Of course, Gloriana, you have to take care of your business. I'll take care of Lucky." Etienne winced when we heard Lucky berate Brittany for selecting the wrong eye shadow.

Richard headed for the computer I'd set up on the breakfast room table.

"Listen, Etienne. About Lucky. I still feel sort of responsible for her." I held up a hand when he seemed inclined to argue about it. "I know. I know. She doesn't want my help. Fine. But you have to admit she's got a lot to learn. And vampires can go one of two ways. I'm asking you, as a friend of Valdez"—I glanced at my dog and was not happy to see that he was giving Etienne the equivalent of a furry frown—"to steer Lucky toward the good side. I'd like to see her drink synthetic when possible, use discretion and keep a low profile. Vampires in Austin don't appreciate attracting hunters or undue attention, if you know what I mean."

"I know what you mean, but Lucky . . ." Etienne gave a Gallic shrug. "She's a piece of work, that one. I'll try to control her, but I've never seen a woman so determined to have her own way. Tonight she's going to want to drink from a mortal. I'll handpick the person, show her how to stop short of killing . . ." He smiled, like this was Basic Vampire 101. "I'll do my best, but she's headstrong and very . . . demanding."

"Come on, brother. You can do better than that. Mind control. Seems like you even worked that shit on me." Valdez stood and stretched, then picked his leash up from the coffee table and dropped it at my feet. *"When I'm through with this gig with Glory, you and I are going to have some face time. You hear me?"*

"Yeah, I hear you. I was desperate. You should understand." Etienne glanced toward the bedrooms again. "I'm earning my pay. Never doubt it. And I'll do what I can to make sure Glory here's not too embarrassed or damaged by Lucky's crap. But this woman's got a hell of an organization behind her. I had no idea . . ."

I smiled, glad to see Etienne was finally getting it. "Yeah. Mr. Carvarelli is a worldwide force to be reckoned with. And he's got paranormals who do nothing but his dirty work. So handle Lucky with care. Whoever bungled

the hit on Lucky is going to have to live in worse than sew-
ers to survive the fallout from this fiasco."

I headed out the door and down the stairs. At least I'd
put Etienne on notice. Lucky wanted to be her own woman.
Fine. So did I. We both had to deal with the consequences.

Twelve

Another night passed in a blur. I didn't see any of the gang again before I crashed right before dawn.

I woke up to the ringing telephone. I grabbed it and looked at the clock. If it was a vampire calling, he or she must have woken up the instant the sun reached the horizon.

"Hello."

"Gloriana, I want to bring my mother by your shop tonight. Will you be there?"

"Jerry. Sure. Why are you bringing her, uh, here?" I could see it now. The shop I was so proud of through Mag's eyes would suddenly be a tacky used-clothing shop. Less than a flea market. What I called vintage, Mag would consider suitable for the dustbin.

"I'm proud of what you've accomplished, sweetheart. I want to show off you and your store."

Sweet, deluded Jerry. He didn't have a clue how much his mother hated me. "Is Mara coming with you?" Why did I bother asking? No way was she letting Jerry out of his sight until she had him tagged and bagged.

"Yes, she'll be with us. But she knows, they both know, that you and I are 'together,' Gloriana. Mara could claim I got sixteen bairns on her in my youth and that wouldn't change what you and I have."

Well, that made me feel better. "Fine, I'll see you later then." I should have known I would have to deal with Jerry's mother eventually. I hung up and started the impossible task of figuring out what to wear. I settled on brown wool slacks and a red ('tis the season, you know) sweater set. I pinned a Christmas tree pin on the cardigan and pulled on brown suede boots.

Valdez and I made a quick trip across the street for him to do his business and to leave the sack with the dollar and the note. My hand shook as I tucked it under the trash can. I hoped we didn't regret playing hardball like this, but what choice did I have? I sure didn't have five thousand dollars. I thought I noticed a stranger lurking behind one of the trees in the small park. Valdez and I both sniffed the air, but couldn't decide if it was vampire or not.

We pushed into the shop, happy to see Lacy still there talking to our substitute clerk. Several customers were looking through the racks, and I decided I needed to start a sale to spur on actual buying and solve my cash-flow problem.

"Twenty-five percent off all dresses. Make a sign, Jasmine." I smiled when at least one customer headed for the dressing room.

"Glory, I was just telling Jasmine about my day. I had some strange visitors."

"Strange?" Strange day visitors. The words struck terror in the heart of any vampire with good sense. We are so totally, totally at risk when we're asleep.

"This guy asked all about you. I just bet he was sent by Lucky's father. He mentioned her name several times. Asked if I knew her, like that. Probably checking up on Lucky's story. He took a lot of notes. Wanted to know which apartment was yours. Of course I wasn't telling him anything."

Lacy bit her lip. "But then he went over to Mugs and Muffins. Someone over there might have said something."

Diana, the owner of the coffee shop next door, has the same problem I have, finding good help to work her day shifts. We both like to hire paranormals who understand our own weird schedules, but it's not always possible. I really like Diana, but her love life is even worse than mine. She hooked up with a man she later found out was a murderer, and has had a relationship with Flo's brother, Casanova Damian Sabatini, for years. When it's off, she swears she's going to join a convent. Ever heard of a vampire nun? Hey, anything's possible. And Flo and Damian have a sister . . .

"Do you think Lucky's father is suspicious of me? Like I might have attacked his daughter myself?" We were whispering, but I wondered if we should take this conversation to the back room. I sniffed the air. Everyone in here seemed mortal so it was unlikely they could hear us. "No, that's ridiculous. What's my motive? I never heard of Lucky Carver before that night."

"This guy didn't look mean or anything, just"—Lacy shrugged—"official. Like a bean counter."

I looked down at my fabulous purse. "Maybe old man Carvarelli's decided my Birkin bag is an inadequate reward. I've been saying cash is a tacky compensation for saving a life, but maybe I've been hasty." Especially since money had become a real issue for me lately.

"Well, I wouldn't get too worked up about it. He was a little too blatant to be"—Lacy leaned closer—"a hunter or from the IRS."

"Did I hear you say IRS?" A customer tossed a silk scarf on the counter and whipped open her purse. "Sorry to eavesdrop, but I've got radar where those three letters are concerned." She handed me a business card. "Sherry Roberts, attorney at law. I specialize in tax cases. I'll help you beat those bastards at their own game. Don't be afraid to fight, honey." She smiled and added a rope of pearls to the scarf. "You do take

charge cards, don't you? This transaction just became de-
ductible since we discussed business."

"Of course we take credit cards. I like your attitude."
And the fact that she didn't have a clue the "hunter" Lacy
referred to was the vampire variety. I smiled and picked up
her card. "How about a ten percent discount?" Not that I
would ever stay in town and fight a government entity. The
IRS ever came after me and I'd have to take on a new identity and disappear. I'd hate to leave Austin though. This had
been one of the best moves I'd made in a long, long time.
Jerry had pretty much followed me to Austin. Would he
track me down if I left?

Jasmine handled the transaction while I straightened
stock and tried to calm my nervous stomach. Jerry's mother.
Mara and her snares. This could not end well. And across
the street my blackmailer would be getting the bad news
that Glory wasn't going to play anymore. What would his
or her next move be?

Lacy stopped on her way out. "There was another man
asking about you today, Glory. Good-looking! Oh my!"
She fanned her face. "Wanted to know if you had a steady
boyfriend." She winked. "I played it cool. Said he'd have to
ask you that himself; I didn't involve myself in my boss's
love life."

And I didn't involve myself in my employees' love lives
either. So I didn't ask Lacy how she could dump Will when
he needed her most. Who am I to judge? Listening to endless knock knocks would test any relationship, and Lacy and
Will had only dated a short time before he'd moved in.
Maybe Lacy had been smart. Will had used her for a place to
stay. Neither of them had pretended to have found true love.

But what was this about a stranger asking questions? I'd
worked myself up into a minor tizzy by the time bells tinkled and I looked up to see the love of my life ushering the
hates of my life through the door. Okay, fair is fair, there
were several other hates of my life besides Mother Campbell

and Mara. Mag looked like she had raw sewage sitting on her upper lip. Mara smiled the serene smile of the contented cow. Ahh. Sometimes I can be so . . . apt.

"Welcome to Vintage Vamp's Emporium." I walked forward with all the grace I could muster. Hey, I'd played queens once upon a time. I was Elizabeth I greeting her subjects. Not that anyone here was going to curtsy, far from it.

Mag had just spotted Flo's mural. "Oh, my dear. What a sad use for a great work of art. Have you no respect for the artist?"

"Glory's roommate painted that, Ma." Jerry smiled at me. "Florence knew Edvard Munch quite well."

"A roommate, at your age." Mara laughed. "But then, you never did have any money of your own, did you, Gloriana?"

"I like the company, Mara. And, since I never married again, it has been nice to share my lodgings with a friend. Do you have any friends?" I smiled slightly.

"What an ill-bred question," Mag sniffed. "But then I could expect no less. But Florence!" Her eyes lit up. "You must mean Florence da Vinci. Is she around? You know I absolutely adore her."

"No, but I hope she'll drop by later." And she would if I could get to a phone. I'd forgotten she and Mag had once been buddies way back in the day. Apparently there'd been some wild times in Venice that Jerry's dad still got mad about whenever the subject came up.

"Ma, I think you should look around. There may be something you would like to purchase." Jerry took his mother's elbow and steered her away from me.

"Here?" Mag's eyes widened. She sat her large tote on the counter and pulled out Randolph. He shook himself, then cast a disdainful glance at Valdez. My guard dog was growling and approaching with intent to maim.

"Don't take another step." I pointed at the door. "Sorry, Mag, but I think it best if Randolph stays in his carrier."

"Oh, you do, do you?" Randolph sniffed and looked around. "And where's the furry beast's carrier, pray tell?"

"*Listen, you rat-faced—*" Valdez sat when he saw the look on my face.

"Lady Campbell is a customer. Deal with it." I wasn't about to let Mag have a reason to complain to Jerry that I hadn't been welcoming. And handing her cat back to her half-dead wouldn't exactly constitute a hello-kitty experience.

"I doubt—" Mag obviously wasn't inclined to be agreeable.

Jerry grabbed his mother's elbow again. "Ma, put the cat away and come here. Did you know Countess Cecilia von Repsdorf herself has consigned some pieces here? She has excellent taste as you'll recall." Jerry winked at me behind his mother's back.

"CiCi. Yes, I have often admired her flat in Paris. I wonder if she thought to bring in any of her porcelain figurines." Mag unceremoniously stuffed a protesting Randolph into her tote and hurried over to a corner cabinet that did contain some fine pieces.

I sighed and leaned against Jerry for a moment as soon as he came back. Mara stared at us silently then followed Mag. Jerry hugged me and kissed the top of my head. "What's going on with Lucky and the rest of your problem children?"

"Can I talk to you about Will?"

Jerry's jaw tightened and he looked at Mara. "No."

"You should see what those clown demons are putting him through. It's horrible, worse than horrible. He's going mad."

"Do you really want to discuss this in front of his sister?"

"Can you dump these two and come back later? Or come into the back room now? Please?" I kept remembering Will's haunted look. Those two fiends and their endless knock knocks.

"I'm not bailing him out. I've talked to the Carvarellis.

I'll have a chance to buy the token before it is forfeited. So I can return it to the Kilpatrick. That is all I'm willing to do."

"But the demons. Can't you pay enough to get the demons off his back temporarily?"

"And then what? He'll just go back to his old ways. It's no good, Glory. He risked something too precious this time."

"You're being awfully hard on a man your best friend loved dearly."

Jerry stared down at me. "Playing the Mac card, are you?"

I flushed, but stood my ground. "You didn't see those clown demons in action. No one deserves what they were doing to Will. Jerry, please."

"I'll think about it. For you. Not for Will. But let it go for a few days. He has to learn a lesson. Gaming is not for him. He loses. He's no good at it. You'd think he'd have figured that out by now."

"I know from experience that logic has nothing to do with it. It's a disease, Jerry."

Jerry gave me a sharp look. This was the first time I'd ever admitted to him that I'd had a gambling problem. I know Valdez had clued him in, duty and all, but my pride had never let me tell him how low I'd sunk. I'd certainly never asked him for money, though things had gotten so desperate that I'd hocked and lost a ring he'd given me years before. I still missed it.

"Glory, lass . . ."

I couldn't take the pity in his eyes. His mother was bearing down on us. "I'll talk to Will, try to get him some help if you'll promise to consider bailing him out."

Jerry hugged me close. "If he'll get help, like you did, then I'll see that the Carvarellis are paid off."

Oh, God, now I was going to cry, and Mag was waving a porcelain figurine of a reclining nude in front of me. If it hadn't cost the earth, I would have shattered it over her head.

"Gloriana! Are you listening to me? What's the matter with you?"

I took the handkerchief Jerry handed me and wiped my eyes. "Allergies. It's dusty in here, isn't it? Yes, Mag, how can I help you?"

"I swear I saw this in CiCi's Paris flat last Christmas at her reception for Prince Igor of Transylvania. Gloriana, will you give me a discount? As a member of the family?"

Oh, my God, the woman had brass. She was even trying to fake a smile, but it was a poor attempt. I felt Jerry's arm tighten around my shoulders, a not-so-subtle reminder that I should meet his mother halfway. Yeah, right. Wouldn't you love an immortal mother-in-law?

"Certainly, my lady. Jasmine, please ring this up for Lady Campbell with a ten percent discount. And of course we'll take your credit card." I smiled sweetly. "Or cash. I can't accept a check however. Not from out of the country. It's just impossible for our local bank to deal with. Austin is so provincial." I said silent apologies to my very worldly bank, but I'd be damned if I'd be *that* accommodating.

"Never mind, Ma." Jerry whipped out his credit card. "Happy Christmas."

"Thank you, Jeremiah." Mag kissed his cheek.

"Oh, Mag."

"Yes?" I could see by the look on her face that she had planned to snub me for the rest of her visit now that she'd gotten what she wanted.

"CiCi, Freddy and Derek are in Paris now. She's planning a wonderful open house for Christmas. I believe she mentioned Prince Igor will be there." I grinned at the look on Mag's face. Oh, the choice to be made. Ruin her son's life or rub shoulders with the vampire aristocracy of Europe. If vampires could have sleepless days, Mag was destined for one.

Jerry kept silent and even hid his own smile, but I didn't have to read his mind to know which way he was voting. He steered his mother to a painting of a Paris street scene. Talked Mara into a fur wrap while describing a stroll down the Champs-Elysées.

In between French references, Jerry filled me in on his search for his daughter. Apparently the last-known address for Lily had been in Tokyo, but that had been fifty years ago. He was following leads in Europe and South America but with little success. The Internet was a huge help, but vampires have always been clever about staying off the grid. They don't exactly post a MySpace page.

A group of college students pushed inside. Two girls headed for the vintage cocktail dresses while the boys stopped in front of the collectible books.

"Oh, my, what fine, healthy—" Mag's nostrils quivered as she bore down on the young men.

"Mother! You'll not—" Jerry shot me a frantic look as he grabbed his mother's arm.

"Let go, Jeremiah. Can't you see Gloriana has arranged for privacy here?" Mag nodded toward the giggling girls who were taking dresses into the curtained alcoves to try them on. Mag wrenched her arm free. "Don't make a scene, Jeremiah."

"Mag!" I started toward her, then noticed Mara tucking a white silk teddy into her coat pocket. *Put that back!* I sent Mara a sharp mental message.

Mara turned and looked at me with wide, innocent eyes. "Did you say something to me, Glory? Oh, Mag, I don't think you're supposed to do that here."

I turned to see Mag leading the two dazed male students, one of them clutching a rare, old edition of *Kidnapped* (how appropriate), toward the last empty dressing room.

"Jerry! Why didn't you stop her?" I started toward Mag, but he intercepted me next to the blouses.

"Leave it alone, Glory. She'll be done soon. And they'll not remember a thing." Jerry winced. "Mara, do you wish to buy that?"

I turned in time to see a vintage silver evening bag disappear into Mara's abundant cleavage. I grabbed her arm and hustled her toward the back room. "Listen, you shoplifting bitch. I'll have that back if I have to pick you up by the heels and shake it out of you."

"Wow! I've heard of zero tolerance for stealing, but this is ridiculous." A teenager who had the Goth look down pat hurried toward the door, hastily putting a silver bracelet on the counter as she went past it.

Valdez woofed at her in case she missed the point.

"Calm down, Glory. I was just having a bit of fun." Mara handed me the purse. "I have better than this at home anyway."

"Did Mark and Joey leave without us?" The girls had come out of their dressing rooms, obviously anxious to show off the gowns they'd tried on.

"I think they went for coffee next door. I had some coupons for free drinks." I searched the counter and came up with two more for Mugs and Muffins. "Those gowns look great on you. New Year's Eve is coming up. Why not surprise the guys?"

"Good idea." The girls hurried back into the dressing rooms, and I sagged against the counter.

"Naughty Mag." Mara twitched her hips and a charm bracelet I'd had on display near the poodle skirts fell to the floor. "I'll see if I can hurry her along. And tell her to suggest to the guys that they just had coffee."

"God, Jerry, please get them out of here. And why the hell didn't you back me up with your mother?"

"I'm sorry, Glory. But I want you two to get along. If I made a scene here . . ." He ran a hand through his hair. "Damn it, I thought that this might give you a chance to show off how successful you've become. That you and Ma might actually come to respect each other." He turned when Mag emerged from her dressing room with the two students. They were pale but seemingly none the worse for wear.

They were talking about the coffee they'd had while one of them paid for his book. They decided to go back to the coffee shop to wait for the girls and left before their girlfriends came out to pay for their dresses.

"I must say, Gloriana. There are advantages to being a shopkeeper in a town like this." Mag carefully dabbed at her lips with a hanky, her cheeks pink. "You have quite a nice setup here. Though why you bother drinking the synthetic with such a nice supply of the fresh is a puzzle to me."

I was speechless. Yes, really. Well, until Mara tried to ease toward the door, her pockets bulging.

"Ahem." I put a hand on her shoulder. "Didn't you see a few things you liked?"

Mara gave me a dirty look. "Here?"

A new customer came in, so I decided to send Mara a mental message. *"Do I have to do a strip search?"*

Mara stiffened, then pulled the teddy, a sweater, black leather gloves, a silk scarf and three hankies out of her pockets.

"Jeremiah, dear, would you be so kind as to charge these for me? Mara, let me give them to you for Christmas." Mag never looked my way, though she had to know about Mara's light fingers.

Jerry merely nodded, obviously glad to get the women out of the shop. They were almost out the door when Diana and Damian came in.

"Lady Campbell, I had no idea you were in town." Damian bowed and kissed a blushing Mag's hand. "My sister will be delighted. Hello, Mara."

Diana hit him with her elbow. "Introduce me, Damian."

"Certainly. Lady Campbell, please allow me to introduce Diana Marchand. She owns Mugs and Muffins, the charming little coffee shop next door."

"Oh, Lady Campbell, I'm so honored to meet you. Jerry's mother, of course." Diana flushed, and, gag me, curtsied.

Mag was actually pleased as she glanced at me to see if I

noticed how at least one person here knew how to accord her the proper respect. Of course Diana's respect was slightly tarnished by the fact that her Jugs, I mean Mugs and Muffins T-shirt barely contained her ample chest.

"Hi, Mara." Diana had already met Mara and knew she had her sights set on Blade. Since Diana's *my* friend, her greeting was rather cool. Mara was so busy pilfering costume jewelry she didn't even bother to look up.

"The reason we came by is that Diana and I are hosting a party at the castle." Damian's smile included everyone in the room, even my new clerk Jasmine, whom he'd met exactly once. Fortunately all the mortals had left the store. "A Winter Solstice Ball."

You've got to understand that winter solstice is huge in the vampire world. The longest night of the year. Naturally it's party time. I've been to some really great winter solstice blowouts over the years, quite a few of them with Jerry.

I'd just turned to him when Mara dropped the crystal necklace she'd decided not to steal and grabbed Jerry's arm.

"My first winter solstice without Mac!" Oh, great. Here came the hanky. "You *will* escort your mother and me to the ball, won't you, Jeremiah?"

Jerry gave me a desperate look. "I thought you and Ma might be going to Paris, Mara. And if I go to a party, I'll take Gloriana, of course."

Score! I wanted to take a victory lap around the shop. Instead I wrapped an arm around Jerry's waist. "It sounds like fun. Costumes?"

"Of course. And a band for dancing." Diana dared approach Mag. "We're calling it A Night at the Movies. Everyone should come dressed as a character from a movie they love. I think themes just add to the fun, don't you, Lady Campbell?"

"I suppose. If it's done in good taste." Mag eyed Diana's T-shirt like she was doubtful the owner of a coffee shop had a clue what good taste was.

"Oh, I'm letting Damian guide me." She smiled and put her hand on his arm. "And then there's Prince Igor of Transylvania. I've persuaded him to come for the ball by making it a fund-raiser for one of his favorite charities. He said after the party he'll go on to Paris for the Countess von Repsdorf's Christmas open house. Perhaps you can do the same." Diana sighed. "I swear the aristocracy of Europe is so special. Y'all lead such glamorous lives."

Mag smiled. "Why, my dear, it can be positively exhausting. But your little soiree sounds charming. And if Igor will be here . . ."

"He promised. I got an e-mail from him just last night." Diana grinned at me. "Did you know that he owns a company that makes synthetic blood? It's a new one. Bloodthirsty."

"I love that brand! It's even better than Fangtastic." I could see Mag's disapproval. "Those booths in back are dressing rooms, Mag. Not privacy spaces for draining my customers."

"You didn't!" Diana gasped.

"Vampires need to go to the source, not settle for nonsense like this Bloodthirsty," Mag sniffed. "I find it hard to believe Igor is involved in such an enterprise. He owns many companies, but this sounds common." Mag glanced at me, like that was about what she'd expect from a mere shopkeeper.

"Ma, I think we should go." Even Jerry had noticed Mara's interest in filling her shopping bag with extras. "Glory, would you bill me for any extra items that"—he glanced at Mara—"you know."

"Sure, Jerry. And call me later. We'll talk about costumes." I removed Mara's hand from an earring display and walked her to the door. "Perhaps we should go as Romeo and Juliet."

Mag gasped. "Really, Gloriana, don't you know that couple came to a bad end?"

Diana to the rescue. "Lady Campbell, I'm sure you have

excellent taste. What would you suggest for appropriate costumes? Damian and I have been trying to decide what to wear. Not that we're a couple. Just good friends supporting one of Prince Igor's worthy causes." She held the door for Mag, winking at me just before the door closed.

Diana lost points with Mag though, just outside. I heard Diana squeal and sounds of a scuffle. Apparently Randolph had stuck his head out of Mag's tote, and Diana thought rats had invaded the building. You can understand how the owner of a food establishment would want to rid the area of such a pest. Diana's pretty wicked with a purse and her right arm. Fortunately, Randolph's immortal, with remarkable healing powers. But Diana will have to grovel some to get back into Mag's good graces.

I breathed a sigh of relief when the Campbell party finally drove off. At least the end result didn't seem too bad. Winter Solstice Ball first, Paris next. And Jerry and I could celebrate his birthday privately. Just the way we liked it.

With visions of Mother Campbell flying like a bat out of hell (literally) across the Atlantic, I headed upstairs an hour before dawn and sacked out early. A good thing I got an extra hour's rest, because I was sure going to need it.

Thirteen

When I woke up at sunset, I knew something was off. For one thing Valdez was grinning at me from the foot of the bed. He's usually not all that cheerful after a day of guard duty. Not that I figure he's awake all day. But he likes me to *think* he's suffering on some kind of high alert from dawn to dusk.

"*She's really done it this time.*"

"Who?"

"*Lucky. Who else has been a pain in your backside since the moment we found her?*"

"What did she do?" I sat up and pushed my hair out of my eyes. That's when I realized I wasn't alone in the bed. "Holy crap! Who the hell is this?"

"*Don't know.*"

"Dead or alive?"

"*In between. I don't think he's dangerous right now or I'd have already chewed his ass.*"

And what an ass. Muscular, tanned and toned to perfection. Male, very male. This was a guy who obviously had a private beach or a pool somewhere and loved the sun. Long legs with a pair of slim feet attached that shouldn't have crawled into my bed without a wash. But back to that ass . . . And up to a trim waist, broad shoulders and a tangle of black hair worn longer than most guys I know. I couldn't see his face. He was sprawled out and turned away from me, that beautiful hair in the way. I started to just crawl over there and take a peek. Hmm. Not just yet.

"How did he get here? I know I went to bed alone." I sniffed. Definitely vampire and vaguely familiar in a creepy, gag-me sort of way. "Vampires don't sleepwalk. And he'd have fried anyway unless he came from somewhere in the building." That undead thing, you know.

"I told ya, this is Lucky's doin'. A special delivery." Valdez jumped off the bed and picked up an envelope with his teeth. He dropped it in my lap. *"Here's a love note to go with it."*

"Screw that. Lucky's not going to just dump a body in my bed and get away with it." A hot body, but that was beside the point. I tore my eyes away from those world-class buns and ripped open the envelope. Hotel stationery and, oh, clever, a few droplets of blood as decoration. I showed it to Valdez.

"Is Lucky a cliché or what?"

"Just read it, Glory." Valdez settled on the foot of the bed again. *"Her goons had him all wrapped up in some kind of special silver thermal material. Sun resistant. Said they got it at a sporting goods store. Seemed real proud that they'd thought of it. Dumb jocks."* Valdez snorted.

"Not so dumb. It worked, didn't it?" I was back to bum staring.

"Yeah, well, they brought him in. Stripped off his clothes, what there were of them, tossed them in the living room, then dumped the guy in bed with you. I gave them hell. I did. One will be walking with a limp, I promise you that. But it was two against one. No, make that three. Beth was with them. Not that she did much but wring her hands and try to talk them out of it."

"Beth, you mean Brittany." I gave Valdez a hard look. "And you two used to be together?"

"Yeah, well. Ancient history. She dumped me. But she was just following Lucky's orders this time. I didn't want to get her fired. Remember, Glory, she's a working stiff just like I am. She already made one mistake when Lucky got attacked, so she's got to be careful. She was sticking her neck out by making an effort to stop this."

"Sounds like she just made another mistake if she took off and left Lucky unguarded to come over here with the goons."

"Oh, there are more goons. Four in all. Old man Carvarelli sent a damned army to watch over his little girl." Valdez nudged the letter. *"You ever gonna read this thing?"*

"Yeah, yeah." I was steamed. "How cowardly can you get? Sending me a 'package' after I'm dead to the world." Well, naked-guy package. Maybe Lucky thought she was doing me a favor, assuming Naked Guy woke up happy to be here. I looked down at the letter again. Blood. Not a good sign.

"Okay, I'll read this out loud, and we'll both see what we're up against. 'Dear Glory.'" At least she was finally consistently remembering my name. "'I'm sure you'll recognize Israel Caine.'" I looked up at Valdez. We both jumped to the other side of the bed. I grabbed that dark hair and pulled it aside. "Holy shit, it really *is* him."

"Flo's going to go ape wild."

"*I'm* going to go ape wild." I sighed, then sighed again. Now that I had a clue, I noticed his trademark tattoos, a star of David on his right bicep, a Celtic cross on his left. Not only was I hooked on his music, but I'd read about the world-famous rock star in a fanzine. Israeli mother, father who was Jewish too but had emigrated to Ireland and started passing himself off as Irish. Parents always at odds with each other. His dad had been a singer himself, out on tour when baby Ray (his nickname) had been born in Dublin.

Mom had gotten even with Dad by hanging the name on

him and having a rabbi on hand with the whole circumcision thing before Daddy was even told the baby'd been born. Messy divorce followed. At least that's what the magazine claimed. I fought the urge to smooth the tangle of hair, imagining the little boy in the middle of parental wars.

Israel Caine, Ray to his friends. The guy was every woman's fantasy. Including mine. He sang sexy love songs like he was singing just to you, making love to you with his music. Flo and I were absolutely addicted. When we'd heard he was giving a concert here in Austin, we'd gone nuts. That concert was—oh, shit—tonight!

"Okay, I can handle this. Israel Caine is in my bed. Fine. He'll wake up, run out of here, and I'll never see him again. Where's my camera phone? We should get a picture of this."

"Yeah. Strip off and we can pretend you did the big nasty with him. Torment Flo with it when she gets home." Valdez jumped off the bed, then on again. He was almost as excited as I was. I figure he's a fan too, despite all his whining when we play the CDs over and over.

Okay, I'm one sick puppy because I actually considered it, posing, pretending we'd— I froze, then fell over, burying my nose in Ray's silky hair.

"Glory, cut the crap and read the letter."

"No, Valdez, you don't get it." Oh, God, this was a disaster. No, worse. I put my hand on Ray's back, tears in my eyes. Lucky had a lot to answer for. Israel Caine was an institution, for God's sake, worshiped by millions of women, especially when he sang a slow love song. Even men loved his hard-hitting rock and strong, masculine vibe.

"Would you tell me what the hell you're talking about?"

I took a steadying breath and almost sobbed. "Israel Caine, the star of my fantasies when I can't get there any other way—" Valdez woofed. "Okay, I'll get to the point. Israel's now a freakin' vampire."

Valdez stuck his nose in Ray's face to take his own whiff.

"Damn Lucky Carver. She's really done it this time. And stuck us with him. Read the letter. I want to know why."

I pushed myself up and wiped my eyes. "Yeah, me too." I grabbed a tissue and blew my nose. Israel still hadn't moved. I touched his cheek. Cool but probably just normal new-vampire temperature. He was bound to wake up soon and then all hell would break loose. I couldn't even begin to imagine it. I crawled back to my side of the bed and picked up the letter.

" 'Israel and I had an affair years ago. I thought we were in love and I really helped his career. I was older than he was and had a lot of connections in the music biz. He was only eighteen and just getting started." I looked at Valdez. "Poor Ray. Good-looking kid, and Lucky 'helped' him right into her bed. Forget the fact that he had talent."

"Hey, stuff like that happens. The kid was probably grateful at the time. Lucky's a good-lookin' woman. Read on."

I gave Valdez an eye roll and went back to the letter. " 'As soon as he had his first hit song, he dumped me. I never forgot it. I promised myself I would get even some day.' "

Valdez was up and pacing. *"Even? Okay. So sex him one more time then dump his ass. Slash his tires. Even a little sugar in his gas tank. But turning him vampire? Jeez, Glory. Lucky's a nutjob."*

"Not arguing. Think about it. Lucky's probably had dozens of lovers since then. What's the big deal?" I couldn't take my eyes off Israel. So unfair. Then Valdez nudged me with his nose. "Okay. I'll keep reading. 'Last night I had my chance. When I saw him in the lobby of our hotel, he was surrounded by his usual groupies, who are barely legal. Ray pretended he didn't see me. Bastard.' "

"Hell, I wouldn't want to see that bitch again either." Valdez sniffed Ray again. *"This is Steve's work."*

"Of course it is. Lucky wouldn't know how to turn anyone vampire. Listen. 'Etienne read my mind and saw how hurt I was. He said he'd help me teach Ray a lesson. We went to Ray's suite an hour before dawn, used the whammy to get in and took care of Ray for good. Obviously I didn't want to kill him. Too easy.'" I took a shaky breath. She'd actually thought about *killing* Ray? What she'd done was bad enough, but to end his life . . . Well, okay, she'd done that too. Boy, she'd been smart to send a letter, because if I could get my hands on her now, she'd be dead meat. I don't care how many bodyguards or goons she had around her.

"Man, obviously you really don't want to make Lucky Carver mad."

"You don't want to make *me* mad, either, puppy. Lucky's not getting away with this." I blinked until I could focus again. "'Ray loves the sun. He spends all his free time on his boat or his private island in the Bahamas. With Etienne helping me, I made sure Ray will never see the sun again. Too bad Etienne tells me that his tan won't fade.'" Poor Ray. I ran my fingers through Ray's hair again with silent apologies to Blade. Hey, I'm only human, sort of. And Ray lit my fire in a different way. With music. When I'm with Blade sometimes Ray's songs are in the background, helping me get my groove on. It's just, I don't know, different. And Lucky had ruined it, for millions of women.

"Is that all, Glory?"

"I wish. Here's the clincher. 'Since you seem to want to help mentor new vampires, Glory, here's your chance to do it for Ray. Even at eighteen Ray was a wonderful lover. I taught him everything he knows. Enjoy, with my compliments, Lucky.'" I dropped the letter and lay back to stare at the ceiling.

"Well if that isn't a hell of a note, I mean letter." Valdez sighed and put his head on his paws. *"Somehow I don't think Ray here is going to like his new life or lack of."*

"No kidding." I sat up and just looked at Ray again. I couldn't freakin' believe it. A fantasy man in my bed. But how on God's earth was he going to, er, function as one of the primo rock stars of this and the previous century as a *vampire*?

"Hey, darlin'. Where'd you come from?"

Oh, God. His startlingly blue eyes were open. Blood-shot, but open. He'd managed to turn his head, but I could tell the effort had cost him. Obviously he'd partied hard before Lucky and Etienne had found him and taken him out. I swallowed and faked a smile.

"Hi, Ray." I pulled up the sheet, because I'd be damned if I wanted his first sight of me to be in my worn flannel Snoopy jammies. Hey, I hadn't been expecting company.

"Sorry, darlin', but I don't remember your name." He gave me a half smile, grimacing as if his head hurt, which I'm sure it did. "Where are we?" He narrowed his gaze. "This isn't my hotel room."

Guess not, with the shabby not-so-chic décor (not intentional, just all I could afford) and pink floral sheets (sue me, but I like them).

"No, this is my place. I'm Glory St. Clair."

Valdez jumped off the bed and trotted around so that Ray could see him. He stuck his nose across my tummy and had the good sense to act doggylike for the moment, merely wagging his tail.

"Your hound?" Ray stretched out his hand, which was shaking, by the way. "Doesn't bite, does he?" Valdez gave his fingers a sloppy lick until I pushed him away.

"Not unless you mean me harm." I opted for a coy look, trying desperately not to revert to slathering fan. It wasn't easy. What would Ray do if *I* gave his fingers a sloppy lick? "You don't, do you? Mean me harm?"

Oh, wow, I got one of those patented Caine bad-boy smiles. "Only if that does it for you, sweetheart."

Melt, melt. I cleared my throat. "I have a bit of news for you, Ray. Something rather earth-shattering." Oh, God, my British roots were showing. Happens sometimes when I'm really stressed. Kind of like Blade's Scottish thing.

Blade. What would he think if he walked in right now and found a naked rock star in my bed? I glanced at Valdez.

We weren't going to tell Blade anything about the naked part, were we? Valdez just wagged his tail, happy to have something on me.

"Could this news wait? I've got a hell of a hangover. Don't suppose you've got some Scotch around here. Or coffee. Even aspirin. Something to take the edge off?" Ray closed his eyes. Damn shame that. And sagged back on the bed.

Oh. Front view. Oh. I jumped out of bed, Snoopy jammies and all, and just stared. And stared some more. Shameless gawking. Dark hair. Not so much on his chest. Niiiice chest. Dark nipples. Happy morning erection, even though it was evening, despite hangover or reaction from dying and being brought back undead. The other side of those long, long legs. Oh, ew, oh. He had a piercing. There. A silver ring with what must be a half-carat, or more, diamond. Interesting plaything. I swallowed and ran to the bathroom, stopping at my closet to pick up a nice silk robe, navy with lace trim.

I brushed my teeth, my hair, dumped the jammies and threw on the robe. Thought about lipstick but figured that would be overkill. I stopped in the kitchen to toss down some Twinkies for Valdez and grab some Bloodthirsty for myself and Ray. Oh, boy, did I have some explaining to do.

I searched the living room for Ray's clothes. Are you kidding me? Apparently all he'd arrived in were silk boxers and a black T-shirt. Not that I was complaining, but he'd need more than that if he was ever leaving my apartment. Hmm. Israel Caine, Gloriana St. Clair's sex slave. Has a nice ring to it, don't you think?

Of course there was that concert scheduled to begin in about three hours. I knew because Flo and I had talked about going but couldn't get tickets. Not that that would stop us. We'd figured we'd put the whammy to work, slipping in near the stage somehow right before Israel came on. I glanced at the clock. Oh, God, Ray was in no shape to sing tonight, not without some major rejuvenation. And Flo should be home soon to get ready to go. At least it was Sunday night and the shop was closed, but . . . Ray.

Damn but Lucky had done it this time. I walked into the bedroom, but Ray wasn't there. Instead I heard the shower running. Boy, the visuals just kept on coming. Never let it be said that I didn't make the most of my opportunities. So I was reclining on the bed in what I hoped was a seductive pose, my robe falling open just so and sipping my Bloodthirsty when I heard an ominous thud.

"Uh-oh." I ran into the bathroom, glad he hadn't locked the door, and found Ray passed out in the tub, the water rapidly turning from lukewarm to cool. I shut it off and hauled him out of there. At least my recent experience with Lucky had shown me what to expect and I didn't panic. She'd passed out several times at first and had been weak and disoriented until I'd talked her into drinking some Fangtastic.

He was heavy, but I toweled him off and, thanks to my vamp superpowers, managed to lay him gently on the bed. I only copped two or three accidental feels while I tried to make him comfortable. Then I forced a sip of Bloodthirsty down his throat.

His eyes fluttered open as he swallowed and coughed. "What is this? Bloody Mary?"

"No, that was last year's brand." Then I realized he was probably talking about a tomato-juice cocktail, not my old favorite blood substitute. Before I could stop him, he grabbed the bottle and took a deep swallow, then shuddered and collapsed back on the bed.

"Something's wrong with it. Tastes funny. I don't do drugs, darlin'. If you're trying to hook me with somethin', forget it." He was talking with his hand over his eyes. Now he uncovered them again. "And you never turned on any lights, but I can see you just fine. What's up with that?" He grabbed my hand and squeezed.

"Nothing. Relax."

"God damn it. If you drugged me, I'll see you in jail no matter how pretty you are."

Valdez was growling and showing teeth because Ray still gripped my hand hard enough that it would have hurt if I'd been a regular human female.

Inside I was singing, "Israel Caine thinks I'm pretty!" But I merely said, "I didn't drug you. I don't do drugs either. Does the name Lucky Carver ring a bell?"

"Luciana Carvarelli," Ray whispered. He actually looked over his shoulder.

"One and the same."

"What's she got to do with anything? I swear I haven't seen or spoken to the woman in almost twenty years."

"But she saw you. Last night. And you knew each other once." I picked up Lucky's letter. "She says here you dumped her as soon as you had your first hit song."

"That was a hell of a long time ago. I was just a kid." Ray ran his hand through his wet hair. He was really pale and I took pity. I jumped up and grabbed some more towels and a blanket out of the bathroom closet.

"Here." I watched him towel dry his hair, then run another towel down his chest and, um, yeah, farther south. He wrapped the blanket around himself, ending the peep show.

"I feel like shit. You sure you didn't drug me? Did Lucky?"

"No, she did something more permanent." I passed him the bottle of Bloodthirsty again. "I know this tastes funky, but it'll make you feel better."

Valdez settled on the foot of the bed again, ready to jump in if Ray took the news badly. I took a second to curse Lucky for dumping this in my lap. Then another second to absorb the thrill of being so close to the sexiest man alive according to more than one poll. Oops, make that the sexiest man *formerly* alive.

Ray took a few tentative sips, then finally a swallow. "What's wrong with my teeth?" He stuck his finger in his mouth. "Shit! Did Lucky break my teeth? That woman must have the memory of an elephant."

"No. There's something else happening with your teeth." There was no delicate way to put this. I took a steadying gulp of my own Bloodthirsty and felt the slide of my fangs before giving him a bright smile. "Your teeth aren't broken, Ray. You've got fangs now, like mine."

Ray quit poking in his mouth and stared, those incredibly beautiful baby blues suddenly wide and watery. "No freakin' way."

" 'Fraid so. Lucky really got even with you for dumping her. She turned you vampire."

Fourteen

"I'm not hearing this."

"Really. Lucky's a vampire now too. Someone tried to kill her, and to save her I made her vampire."

"Cut the crap, you freak. Let me out of here." Ray practically fell out of bed and was halfway to the door before Valdez leaped in front of him.

"Stop right there. You ain't goin' anywhere." Valdez gave Ray a body check that landed the singer flat on his ass. Ray just sat there, his blanket falling to the floor while he looked ready to puke his guts out.

Can't say I liked the "freak" tag. But I walked up to Ray and put a sympathetic hand on his shoulder anyway, cutting him slack because of the shock factor. He crab walked to the other side of the bed and grabbed a book I'd left on the nightstand.

"Stay the hell away from me!" He tossed *The Secret* at my head.

Hey, I had a secret for him. I caught it in midair,

enjoying his look of astonishment. "Valdez, I think you scared Ray."

"Aw, you think the badass rock star is freaked out by a talking dog?"

Ray put his hands over his ears. "This is a bad acid trip. You say Lucky did this to me? Well, make it go away. Or maybe I'll sleep it off." He crawled back into bed, giving me another nice look at his backside before he pulled the sheet over his head. "And dogs don't talk."

I sat on the bed beside him and pulled the sheet down until I could see his face. "Sorry, Ray. My dog *does* talk. And apparently when you do someone like Lucky Carver dirty, you pay for it, even if it takes her twenty years to even the score."

Ray sat up straight. "I didn't do a damn thing to Lucky. I thought I loved her. I would've married her if . . . things hadn't happened."

"Funny. Lucky says you dumped her on her cute little ass."

"Yeah, well, I had no choice." Ray put his head on his knees. "Hand me that shit you made me drink. I feel like I'm gonna pass out again."

I pushed the bottle into his hand. "Drink it all, then lie back and let it work. It's a blood substitute."

Ray spewed Bloodthirsty all over my bed.

"Hey, now I'm going to have to wash all my bedding!" I jumped up and grabbed more towels.

"Blood." Ray did a bob and weave and finally fell over. Lights out.

"That went well."

"You couldn't have kept your mouth shut just a little longer?"

"Nope." Valdez gave me a doggy grin. *"A man's got to have some fun."*

I started stripping sheets, rolling Ray over, gawking at his package and that twinkling diamond before throwing a fresh blanket over him. Hey, a woman's got to have some fun too.

By the time Ray came to, I was dressed and ready to go to the concert, but didn't see how he was ever going to make it.

"What time is it?" He sat up, surprisingly alert.

"Eight thirty."

"Shit! I've got to get out of here. I've got a concert . . ." He rubbed the top of his head, making his beautiful hair wild. "I'm supposed to be onstage in an hour and a half." He jumped up, staggered and held on to the wall until he finally made it to the living room. He saw his shorts and T-shirt and managed to get into them, then collapsed on the couch.

"I don't think you're in any shape to go anywhere."

"I don't miss concerts, woman, or vampire, or whatever the hell you are." Ray gave me a narrow-eyed look. "I don't believe in this vampire shit, but let's say I'm playing along. Give me some of that crap you drink and a phone. This drink, it's not made from, uh, human blood, is it?"

"No, of course not. It's a synthetic." Okay, I know this sounds wimpy, but I threw him my cell and hurried into the kitchen to grab a bottle of Bloodthirsty. I wanted him to do the concert. It was a sellout. He'd let down thousands of fans, not to mention Flo and me if he didn't do it. But if he thought he was just going to waltz right out of here . . .

"Nathan. Yeah, yeah, save the lecture. I'm okay. I hooked up with a new girl last night. I know. Stupid, but what can I say? I *know* we're cutting it close. She's gonna give you the address. Have a limo here as soon as you can get here and bring my stage clothes." He paused and nodded to me to take the cap off the Bloodthirsty. "Just hurry. We'll talk later." He passed the phone to me. "Give him your address and any directions he might need to get here from the Irwin Center."

I spouted off the necessary then shut the phone. Call me

crazy, but then I flipped it open again. Took a video of Ray drinking Bloodthirsty on my sofa in his shorts and T-shirt. Sat beside him and tried to get the two of us in a shot. I glanced at Valdez, but didn't think he could hold the phone with his mouth or a paw. Damn. Ray just drank, like he was used to crazy women wanting a picture with him. Of course he was.

"How long do you think it will take him to get here?"

"About ten minutes unless traffic's bad." I kept watching Ray. He didn't look much better. I was afraid the Bloodthirsty wasn't doing it for him.

"I'll wait downstairs. Can't say it was a pleasure, lady."

Valdez planted himself in front of the door. *"That's not the way this is going to work, Caine."*

"I don't talk to hallucinations." Ray turned to look at me. "Get your dog out of my way."

"Talk to *me*, then. You don't have a clue what you're in for, Ray. I know you don't want to accept what you are. We can discuss the details later. But you're not stepping a foot outside of this apartment without me." I put my hands on my hips, then figured there was no point in emphasizing my worst feature, so I dropped them and settled for a hard stare.

"I don't take orders from a mother f—"

"Stop right there, asshole!" Valdez showed every tooth in his head and then some. *"Show some respect. Gloriana is a lady and you will treat her as such, understand?"*

"What?" Ray turned to look at me. "You're a f— freakin' vampire, but I can't drop the F-bomb around you?"

I smiled, rather pleased by Valdez's standards. Hey, I come from an earlier time, and Blade has always respected me. It's kind of nice.

"You heard me." Valdez moved closer, to make no doubt in Ray's mind what he'd bite first if provoked.

"If you think—"

I'd heard enough. I moved in front of Ray and looked him in the eyes. I put him under the whammy and told him to sit on the couch until I could decide how to handle this concert. Good timing, because the door opened and Flo and Richard walked in just then.

"Glory, we must hurry if we are to get good seats!" She suddenly grabbed Richard's arm and tottered on her four-inch heels. "*Dio mio!* Ricardo, I told you that man on Congress Avenue had drunk too many Scotches. I am drunk. I am seeing my dream lover on our couch." She put her hand on Valdez's head. "Help me to my room, doggy. I need a quick lie down before the concert."

"It's him, Flo." I grinned and sat beside Ray. I put my hand on his thigh just because I could.

"No, impossible. I'm seeing the most delicious man in the world in his underpants in our living room." Flo sighed and reached out. When she actually touched Israel's knee, she shrieked and lost the battle of the four-inch heels. Richard caught her just before she hit the floor.

"Israel Caine here? In our little apartment?" Flo licked her lips. "How do I look? The wind was blowing, and I know my lipstick is gone."

"You look beautiful. But I thought *I* was your dream lover." Richard frowned.

"Don't be jealous, Ricardo." Flo stroked Ray's hair. "Israel Caine is all fantasy." She turned and slid her arms around Richard's waist. "You are my real lover."

"That's more like it." He nodded toward Ray. "Whammy?"

"Yes. Ray's had a rough twenty-four hours. He's one of us now, thanks to Lucky."

"Vampire? She turned him *vampire*?" Flo collapsed in a chair and began muttering invectives in Italian. "I don't know whether to laugh or cry. Ray will live forever, but he'll never see the sun again. Remember that video for 'Cry for You'?"

"God, yes. He was standing on the deck of his boat, the *Forever Yours*. He was so beautiful. The sun on his face. And the way he sang. It was almost like a prophecy." I sighed and Flo had tears on her cheeks. Richard and Valdez made gagging noises. "Oh, come on. It was amazing. You put on that video, Richard, then see what Flo does to you in bed. It's a total turn-on for a woman." Now that got the men thinking.

We heard a horn honk downstairs.

"That's got to be Ray's limo."

Richard pulled the drapes aside. "That's what it looks like."

"Okay, we've got to make him take us with him to the concert, and he's got to keep us with him and come home with us afterward, and before dawn. I'm not letting him fry. Lucky's made him my responsibility, and I'm taking it seriously." I sure didn't want him escaping and then ending up facing the sun somewhere. The very thought of Ray coming to such a horrible end made me feel weak.

"It's too soon for him to go through a strenuous concert on only a bottle of synthetic." Richard picked up the empty Bloodthirsty. "New brand?"

"Yes, a bribe from Will."

Flo got up and squeezed in on Ray's other side. "Oh, to be this close to him." She leaned in and sniffed. "I don't think Lucky made him."

"Actually Etienne did it. He's signed on with Lucky and even promised Glory he'd steer Lucky right." Valdez snorted. *"You see what that means to him."* Valdez prowled in front of the door. *"You know they're not going to let me into the Irwin Center. If you're really going to the concert, take Richard and Flo with you."*

"Of course we're all going, but Caine's going to have to feed first." Richard looked from Flo to me. "Glory, tell him what you want him to do, including feed from you, then snap him out of it. Only aged vampire blood will make him strong enough to get through tonight."

So I told Ray that he would introduce me as his new girl-friend. That he would do his concert as planned and that he would come back to the apartment with me before sunrise. Then I told him to snap out of it.

The horn honked downstairs as Ray rubbed his eyes and looked around. "Well, who's this?"

"I'm Florence da Vinci, a huge fan, Ray." Flo put her hand on his chest, practically drooling. "And Glory's roommate."

"You're not . . ."

"Vampire?" Flo smiled, showing the fangs she was so proud of. "Of course, darling." She waved her hand toward Richard. "All of us here are except Valdez, of course. He's something else special." She blew my dog a kiss. "Welcome."

"Yeah, right. I still say this is all bullshit." Ray looked at Valdez. "Or am I allowed to say that?"

"I'll let you know when you screw up, man."

The horn honked again. "I've got to go." Ray tried to stand, but fell back again. "What the hell's wrong with me?"

"You're weak. You need to feed. The synthetic you had can't give you enough energy to make it through the concert tonight." I smiled slightly. "Flo and I really are huge fans. We've watched your videos and seen how you sing, dance and move all over the stage. You have to be in top form. There's only one thing that can give you the boost you need to give that kind of performance."

"So what is it? Give it to me. Quit wasting time. I'm running late." Ray tried to get up again. No go. "Hurry. I've never canceled a gig yet and I'm not going to tonight."

"You have to drink from another vampire. Here." I pushed back my hair and offered my neck. No way was I going to set-tle for an impersonal wrist. Ray's lips on my skin, his fangs sinking into my jugular. I shivered just thinking about it.

"Wait. I'm older than you are, Glory. My blood is much richer." Flo grabbed Ray's arm and wrenched him toward her. She tossed back her long black hair and offered her own ivory neck.

"Excuse me? Who found him in her bed tonight?" I gave Flo a cold look. She might be my best friend, but best friends don't poach.

"I know every word on his *Reunion* album and you know that was the one that didn't even go platinum."

"Cat fight. Richard, you want to put a bag of popcorn in the microwave?" Valdez settled in front of the couch. *"Think they'll start ripping each other's clothes off?"*

"We can only hope."

Flo and I glared at the men, then at each other.

"Lucky gave him to *me*."

"How do you know?"

"She left me a letter."

"Let me see."

"You always said you couldn't read."

"I lied."

"Ladies, I can't do this."

I pried Flo's nails out of my right wrist. Ouch. "Listen, Ray, if you're worried you can't perform, I'll be glad to show you how."

Flo snarled. "You insult his manhood? Israel will never drink from you now." She gave him a high-voltage, full-fang smile. "Don't worry, Israel. Your instincts will take over. Come closer. Breathe in the scent of my very old, very rich blood. You will *want* to drink from me. Your fangs will descend and you will *need* to taste me. It's a natural thing, you'll see."

Richard made a low rumbling sound, and I wondered if it was just going to be Flo and me in this fight.

"No, seriously. I can't do it. No way. No how."

We both stared at Ray.

"Why can't you drink from us?" I noticed Ray had gotten even paler and seemed on the verge of passing out again.

"I'm a vegetarian."

Fifteen

"This is ridiculous." Richard pulled back the coffee table and sat on it, facing Israel. He grabbed Ray's chin. "Look at me, Caine." Bright blue eyes stared into bright blue eyes. Richard put his wrist up to Ray's lips. "Drink."

Ray opened his mouth, his pretty new fangs descended and he latched on.

"Isn't he amazing?" Flo's eyelashes fluttered, and I figured she'd talked Lucky out of some of her tear-proof mascara.

"Israel?" I looked at him swallowing as fast as he could. There went the commitment to avoiding all things from animals.

"No, my darling Richard." She reached out to run her fingers through his white blond hair. "My man."

He gave her a hungry look. "And don't you forget it."

Downstairs all hell was breaking loose. Pounding on the front door, yelling and now sirens coming down Sixth Street.

"That should do it; we've got to go." I could see Ray's cheeks were pink. I hated to admit it, but Richard obviously

had a lot more power than I did. "Give him his marching orders, Richard, and let's get out of here."

Richard grabbed Ray's face again. "Caine. You're done.
Now we go downstairs. You're going with your new girlfriend and her friends. You'll perform your concert as usual,
then come back to Glory's place. Understand?"

"Yes. Glory?"

"I'm right here, Ray." I reached out and pulled Ray to his
feet. Bare feet. Silk boxers. T-shirt. This would be fun. We had
to go downstairs and open the door; by now his people and
probably a crowd had gathered outside. Hopefully the paparazzi hadn't gotten wind of the fact that Israel Caine was
in the building. And the sirens had pulled to a stop right in
front, if the strobe lights flashing around the edges of the
drapes were any indication.

"Just go, Glory. And be careful. I'll be here when you get back."
Valdez was obviously peeved that he'd be left out of the action, but there was no way to get him into a rock concert inside the Irwin Center on the University of Texas campus.

So we all trooped down the stairs. And stopped to take a
steadying breath. Israel was now lucid and cursing everything from stubbing his toe to freaks who thought they
were vampires. He wasn't exactly acting like my lover. But
that would have to change once the door opened.

"Calm down, Ray. Work with us here."

"Okay. I get it. Now get this. Here's how we handle
things. Glory, you're my new flavor of the month." He shook
his head at the look on my face. "Sorry, babe, but that's what
the tabloids call them. I don't. I just play along. I don't have
time to explain now. Just stay close to me backstage. Don't
get in the way. All of you keep your cell phones off or you'll
have hell to pay. Nathan Burke's my right-hand man and
my best friend. Obey him." He turned to Flo and Richard.
"What are your names?"

"Florence da Vinci and Richard Mainwaring." Flo was
hanging on to Richard, still torn between rock-star lust and

vampire lust. Right now Richard was winning, but I had a feeling once Ray started to sing, the pendulum would swing the other way.

"Da Vinci." Ray managed a smile. "Cool stage name. You a singer?"

"No, an artist." Flo eased up on Richard's arm.

"Can you quit flirting long enough to remember there's danger out there and we're backup for Gloriana and for you, Caine? Until you understand your new life, we're sticking with you. Got it?" Richard gave Ray another intense look.

"Yeah, sure. But I have my own security force. We know how to handle rabid fans, threats, you name it."

"If Richard named it, we'd be here all night. Right now I'm afraid your security force is getting ready to pull out a battering ram. We can't stall any longer. Brace yourself." I punched in the code and threw open the door.

"Ray! What the hell's going on with you, man? You realize how close we're cutting it? Are you all right?" A black man who looked like he'd stepped out of the pages of *Maxim* ran into the foyer and grabbed Ray's shoulders. "How'd you end up here? And what the hell happened to your clothes?"

"Long story, Nate. We'll make it. We always do. Am I right?" Ray reached around his friend and slammed the door in the faces of several people, including at least one cop, who were trying to see inside. "You bring me something to wear?"

"Sure, it's in the limo." Nathan looked us over with what was obviously a strained smile. "These your new friends?"

"Yeah. Sorry to disappear on you, buddy. My cell phone didn't make it with me when we decided to come to Glory's place. And then I was pretty busy if you know what I mean." Ray threw his arm around me and squeezed. "This is Glory St. Clair, my new lady. I want her close backstage during the concert. Let her friends, Florence and Richard hang out too. Arrange passes for them."

It said something for Ray's love life that Nathan didn't even blink, just pulled out his phone.

"Buster out there?"

"Sure."

"Call him first and have him bring me a pair of jeans. I'm not going out in that crowd in my shorts."

Nathan grinned. "Wouldn't be the first time." Then he was talking on his cell.

In less than two minutes, there were three short knocks, and I punched in the code so Nathan could open the door again and grab a pair of jeans. Ray stepped into them then looked at me. It was obvious from the noise that quite a crowd had gathered around the limo.

"Okay, Glory, you ever been hounded by paparazzi before?"

"Can't say I have." Or wanted to be. But to have my picture taken with Israel Caine? Flo and I made a silent bet. First one to giggle bought the other a pair of D&G sandals from the Nordstrom's spring catalog. I would *not* giggle. But I felt giddy as a teenager.

"The secret is to keep smiling and keep moving. If you try to hide, you'll look stupid. My guys are used to this and will run interference for us, like a flying wedge in football. Just stay by my side and, before you know it, we'll be inside the limo and on our way. Whatever you do, don't stop. We're already late."

He turned to Flo and Richard. "If you want to see the concert, stay right behind us and ride in the limo." He glanced at Nathan. "If we get separated, Nathan will have backstage passes waiting for you at the ticket booth. Hit the code, Glory."

Then before I had time to pat my hair to see if it felt presentable, Ray hustled me out and into a noisy and pushy crowd that seemed composed mainly of photographers with flash cameras. I kept a smile on my face, playing my role as Israel Caine's girlfriend.

I'd dressed like the rock-star groupies I'd seen in the tabloids. My denim miniskirt was short, my blue sweater low cut and my navy leather jacket had some sparkles on the fringe. High-heeled boots of course. I felt cute enough to stand inspection. I'd studied pictures of Ray's many previous girlfriends. You had to admire a guy who didn't always demand six-foot-tall models in a size zero. His girls came in all sizes, shapes and colors, but had one thing in common—they looked at him adoringly. Well I could fake that without a whole lot of effort. I couldn't wait to buy every copy of every sleazy tabloid that thought I was newsworthy. What a rush!

"Israel! Israel!" A pair of pink panties hit him on the shoulder, and the crowd went wild. Ray picked them up and grinned. I played my part, snatching them from him and tossing them back.

Next came a black thong. I managed to snag it before it could reach Ray to a chorus of boos. I just smiled and calmly dropped it on the ground and stomped on it. By this time we were at the shiny black stretch limo.

"Well played, Glory." Nathan helped me climb in. "I bet you catching that thong is the money shot."

I fell back on cool leather seats, Ray right beside me. He grabbed a bottle of cold water from the bar in front of us and gulped it down.

"Uh, Ray, that might not be a good idea." I looked around. "Where's Flo and Richard?"

"Here we are." Flo jumped in. "What fun! I hope they send us copies. Richard, we never get our picture taken. I think we make a cute couple."

"They don't know who the hell we are, Florence. And I'm not going to tell them either." Richard sat on the jump seat across from us. "How did they know Caine was even here?"

"The Internet. There's an Israel Caine message board that tracks his movements." Nathan pulled a bottle of champagne out of a cooler and began filling glasses. "His fans know all and tell all."

Flo and I exchanged grins. We knew the message board

well. Had even posted a sighting ourselves once, though it had been wishful thinking and not Ray but a look-alike.

Nathan shoved a cold glass into my hand. "A toast. To another sellout. Ray's had one in every venue he's played since 1998."

"That's incredible. No surprise to me though." I held my glass like I was going to drink from it. I sent a mental message to Richard and Flo to play along. The two men who'd held back the crowd jumped into the front seat next to the driver. The tinted dividing window was up and we couldn't be heard or seen from up there. Flo and Richard took glasses.

By the time Ray and Nathan were served, the three veteran vampires in the car had figured out what to do. I looked into Nathan's eyes and put him under the whammy, then gently took his glass.

"What the hell are you doing?" Ray raised his glass to his lips.

"Stop. You can't drink, Ray."

"Why the hell not? I know my limits. I'm not an alcoholic no matter what that reporter said in *Undercover Magazine*."

"I didn't say you had a drinking problem." Though his defensiveness had a familiar ring to it. Kind of like how I used to act when anybody tried to talk to me about my gambling. "Some vampires are born from other vampires, but you're a 'made' vampire, Ray. That means someone, Lucky and her bodyguard in your case, turned you into a vampire. Flo, Richard and I were made by another vampire too. 'Made' vampires can't eat or drink, not alcohol anyway. It will make you sick. Really, really sick. Trust me, not worth it. You drink that champagne and you'll be in no shape to sing tonight. Even that water you drank earlier might upset your stomach."

"Well, hell. This just keeps getting better and better." Ray dumped his champagne in the ice bucket where the bottle rested. "What did you do to my buddy Nathan? He looks stupid."

"I put him in a kind of trance. He can't see or hear us unless I address him directly. I can plant a suggestion and he'll have to obey me. Right now I'm going to tell him that he saw us all enjoy the champagne." I waited while Flo and Richard dumped out their wine too. "Watch me. You'll have to learn this."

"Wait." Ray frowned. "Nathan's my best friend. I don't like seeing you manipulate him."

"Would you rather try to explain what happened to you last night? Right before you're scheduled to sing?" I felt the car slowing and looked through the tinted windows. We were nearing the Irwin Center and swinging around to the back entrance.

"You think you can do that to his satisfaction in the next two minutes?" And if it was up to me, his good buddy Nathan would *never* find out the truth.

Ray ran an impatient hand through his hair. "Okay, okay, do it. But I don't like it. The whole concept sucks."

Yeah, and Ray would hate the fact that we'd done it to him to get him here. Minutes later we were inside the center and going through more security to get to the dressing room. I sat on a couch while Ray talked to Nathan about concert details. Members of the band came in and out and got introduced to me in an offhand way that made it clear there'd been many women here before me.

Didn't matter. I'd watched all these guys perform for years, seen those videos over and over again with Flo. Ray had surrounded himself with talent, and the men each had their own brand of charisma that left me speechless for a change and more than a little starstruck.

At some point between the drummer and the bass player Ray showered and dressed in a black-leather vest, no shirt and black jeans that hugged his butt perfectly. I licked my lips remembering just how his butt looked under there. Umm.

Nathan had insisted Flo and Richard leave the dressing

room, so they were in the backstage area doing reconnaissance, checking for suspicious characters. As soon as they
saw Nathan leave to check the front, they came back inside.

Flo threw open the dressing room door. "Look who we
found lurking around the stage practicing her whammy on
Ray's band."

"Get that bitch out of here." Ray gestured, and his two
bodyguards, who I now knew as Buster and Sam, moved forward.

Lucky and Etienne grinned and put the whammy to
work so that poor Buster and Sam were soon bookends who
couldn't have moved if a hurricane had ripped through the
room.

"Now, Ray. Is that any way to treat your first love?"

"Haven't you done enough to him, Lucky?" I pushed in
front of her. "There's something really pathetic about a
woman who won't let go."

"Don't cop an attitude with me, Glory. I figured you'd be
grateful to have Israel Caine dumped in your bed. You think
I didn't notice the shrine you and Florence have set up in
that dinky little apartment? All those DVDs and CDs of
his?"

Flo gasped. "It's not a shrine! It's a collection. Ray is a
very talented musician. We appreciate his music."

So what if we also had a photo album, a framed poster
and a collector's edition of Ray's unauthorized biography on
a special shelf next to the CD player. Oh, and a piece of
denim we bought on eBay certified to have come from a pair
of jeans ripped by a woman who'd stalked him in Atlantic
City during his "Coming-of-Age" tour in 2000. Hmm.

"He wouldn't be famous if it wasn't for me. This bastard
just used me. Told me he loved me one night and disappeared the next." Lucky began crying noisy tears into Etienne's white shirt. He patted her back and sent lethal looks
at Ray.

Nathan burst through the door. "Five minutes, Ray."

"Not now, Nate. Seriously." Ray tried to keep Nathan from coming in.

"What the hell's going on? What's wrong with Buster and Sam? Ray, you should be centering yourself. This kind of disturbance right before you perform isn't good for you."

"Let me." I got in Nathan's face and put him out, then gently moved him out of the way next to Buster, three bookends. "Now you." I grabbed Lucky's arm and hustled her toward the door. "Lucky, get the hell out of here. I think you've done enough. Etienne, why don't you explain to Lucky why you didn't stop her from getting that tattoo at the Tatt-ler the other night? You're ancient. You *had* to know what would happen later."

Lucky's head snapped up. "Why *didn't* you stop me? When I started screaming—"

"Darling, you were so desperate for the experience. How could I deny you? And it was such a beautiful dragon. For one night, at least, you had the most perfect bottom I have ever seen." Etienne glanced at my butt and frowned.

"One lousy night. Not enough. Not when it hurt so damned bad." Lucky stomped her foot, narrowly missing Etienne's right boot.

"But wait until you see, my darling. I have a special surprise for you. I took your picture. With my camera phone, when you weren't looking."

"You took a picture of my *ass*?" Lucky's screech made my eyes water.

"Gee, Etienne, can I have a copy? Maybe get one blown up for my bedroom? I'd love to know what a perfect ass looks like." I smiled sweetly.

Etienne pulled Lucky out of the room, whispering Italian nonsense in her ear while sending visual daggers in my direction.

Richard pulled Buster and Sam out of their poses and suggested they follow Lucky and Etienne to make sure they didn't come back.

"We'll see you after the concert." Flo smiled shyly at Ray. "Break a leg, Ray." She giggled. "Saw that on TV. We'll be watching from the wings."

I grinned and said, "I win, Flo."

"Oh, shit." She pushed Richard out of the room. "Now I have to buy Glory new sandals."

Ray collapsed on the couch. "Glory, if you can keep that bitch away from me, I'll love you forever. Now would you please get Nate out of that trance you put him in?"

Love? Yeah, right. Just rock-star rhetoric. But I hurried to rescue Nathan, giving him the suggestion that he'd come into a room full of my weirdo friends but they'd all cleared out now.

Nathan looked at me and shook his head. "Glad those friends of yours are gone, Glory. Ray needs some quiet time before he goes on."

"Lucky's not my friend, just a deranged fan who won't be back. Flo's my roommate. Richard's her boyfriend. They understood. Sorry if we messed up your routine, Ray." I sat beside Ray and put my hand on his thigh. I could feel the tension humming through him.

"Do I have a routine, Nate?" Ray grinned and looked longingly at the bar setup across the room.

"We usually have more time." Nathan paced in front of us. "But things look good out there. You'll be fine. No worries."

"Try to relax, Ray. How many concerts like this have you done? Austin loves you. Tickets sold out here in ten minutes."

"Glory's right." Nathan gave me an approving smile. "The opening act says it's a great crowd tonight. Singing along. Dancing. Hell, you could do this one in your sleep."

Actually with my vamp senses, I felt the building shaking with the fans clamoring for Ray to come onstage. His band was warming up, already playing the intro to one of his hits. Could Ray feel it too? His hand dropped down to cover mine, and I figured he probably could. Close up he looked tired and every one of his thirty-seven years.

Ray put his head back and closed his eyes. "Shouldn't have drunk that water. May have to throw up."

"That's nuts, man." Nathan pulled an icy bottle out of the minifridge. "Here's another one. Or do you need something stronger? To settle your nerves. I've got some Jack right here."

Ray swallowed and sat up. "No, that's okay. I'm okay. Let's do it." He squeezed my hand and pulled me up beside him. I watched him literally pull something from inside himself. Then he smiled, nodded and headed for the door.

I trailed in his wake. He *should* have a shrine, and I'd seen a really nice life-sized poster on eBay . . .

Sixteen

I have no idea how he did it. Thousands of screaming fans were still begging for more after six encores. Ray had tossed his leather vest to the crowd a half hour ago, his body gleaming with sweat under the hot lights. Finally he sang a slow love song that had me weeping guilty tears and wishing for Blade at the end of it. The building went completely dark for several long moments. When the lights came back up again, the stage was empty.

I jumped a foot when I realized Ray was behind me. Just goes to show how involved in the music I was, because I should have smelled him. He'd put a lot into the performance. The first thing he did when he got to his dressing room was jump in the shower again. I sat on the couch and closed my eyes, still soaring from that last sexy song. God, but the man could sing.

"You really shouldn't let down your guard like this, my dear."

I flinched when I realized a stake touched my sweater

above my heart. I turned my head to see Simon Destiny, his weasel face much too close for comfort.

"Back off, Simon. You know you promised you wouldn't hurt me or my friends. You swore on your demon's honor." Apparently even morally bankrupt slimeballs have some oaths they won't break, thank God.

Simon dropped the stake. "I've been trying to find a loophole. You need to die."

"So do you. But sometimes we have to live with disappointment."

"I hear you've made a new vampire, a Carvarelli."

Why did that interest Simon? "So?"

"The Energy Vampires are always interested in business. Making loans to paranormals could be a lucrative sideline. I would like to talk to Ms. Carvarelli. Perhaps recruit her if she has enough knowledge to be of interest."

"Now this is amusing. You come to me to discuss recruitment?" I wanted to laugh in his face. But, actually, hooking him up with Lucky could solve some problems for me. One, he could keep her away from Ray. Two, he would be so busy with Lucky, maybe he would forget about his son for a while. I really hated the idea of Freddy getting entangled in the EV world.

I tried to work up some qualms about throwing Lucky and Simon together, but what she'd done to Ray had pretty well snuffed any protective instincts I'd had toward her. So far she hadn't told me anything Ray had done that deserved the punishment she'd devised for him.

"I believe you would like to know who attacked Ms. Carvarelli in your alley. Am I right?" Simon toyed with the stake, pricking his own finger with it, then licking away the blood droplet in a kind of sick game that made me want to throw up or join in. Yeah, yeah, but we're vampires, remember?

Wait, did he say he knew who'd attacked Lucky? "Yes, I'd like to know who attacked her. Do you know?"

"I might. Or I might not. Introduce me to Ms.—I believe she goes by Carver now—and I'll tell you what I know. I understand there might be a reward. I expect a healthy percentage if my information leads to a successful conclusion."

Okay, how many people did I have in line for a payoff now? Seems like I was down to about 10 percent for myself. Still, 10 percent of a million was a nice chunk of change.

"Wait a minute. You came into my shop and assaulted my clerk. News flash—that clerk *is* my friend."

"I must tell you that that's no way to run a business, Gloriana." He gave me a pitying look. "I would never count one of *my* employees as a friend. Next thing you know, they'll ask for favors. Like time off, sick leave. Surely you can see that was an honest mistake." Simon poked himself again, and I tried to snatch the stake. No go. "Am I getting on your nerves? Delightful."

"Stuff it, Simon. If you want an intro to Lucky, you have to give me something. Back off my employees. We call a total and immediate truce." I threw up a block, but I figure a man as powerful as Simon could probably bulldoze his way right over it and read my every thought. It frustrated the hell out of me that I couldn't read *his* mind. But I didn't doubt he had a mother lode of info in there. Including what I needed to know. I could practically see my cash-flow problem solved. And a truce with Simon would be a tremendous weight off my shoulders.

"Oh, all right. Though hassling you is such fun. But since my son asked for the same favor, I guess I'd better grant it. He seems to think you walk on water for some reason." Simon chuckled, though the effect was like seeing Darth Vadar laugh. Yeah, creepy.

"Then we have a deal. What do you know?"

"The person who actually attacked her isn't on your list of debtors."

"How do you know about the list?" Had he talked to Greg?

"Your friend Greg Kaplan was fool enough to think he could use my headquarters as a base of operations for his own pathetic attempt to earn a commission from the Carvarellis." Simon smiled, and I figured Greg had paid a stiff penalty for getting caught. "He's taking a time-out. Don't expect to see your friend Gregory anytime soon. Or to get his help. So you're dealing with me, Gloriana."

I winced, then tried to cover it with a shrug. "Okay, then. Deal." Poor Greg. I hated him, but an EV time-out had to be pretty grim, something a little more extreme than being sent to his room without his supper.

"Don't waste your pity on Greg, Gloriana. Concentrate on the problem at hand. Ms. Carvarelli's hit man was hired by someone who is on the debtor list. Both the hit man and the debtor are still in town. Which demonstrates how incredibly stupid or incredibly arrogant they both are."

"How do you know this?" I thought this made sense though. But, wait. If the debtor owed the Carvarellis, where'd he or she get the money for a hit man?

Simon had been busy reading my mind. "The person came into some money and, as the weak willed so often do, instead of paying his or her creditors, hurried out to the EV headquarters for a little R & R." Translation: a Vampire Viagra binge. "Of course the Carvarellis still wanted to be paid. But this person thought he would rather get rid of Ms. Carvarelli. Obviously a miscalculation, but you know a vampire who will take a hit doesn't care if the person doing the hiring is making a wise decision or not. He or she will take the money and do the job."

"Guess so." Actually the soulless vamps who are hired guns are a mystery to me. Yeah, Valdez is a shifter who works as hired muscle, but I hope he'd stop short of murder.

"The person who hired the hit left the EV compound but not the area. The hit man is still around too. Seems both are dissatisfied with the outcome. Until Ms. . . . Carver is terminated, the contract isn't fulfilled, so there is no payment in full. Problem is, the window of opportunity for the person who hired the hit has passed. The hirer could pretend he had paid his debt. That the money was stolen when poor Ms. Carvarelli was killed. Now that story won't work. He will want to cancel his contract. But these kinds of deals don't *get* canceled."

I shook my head. "You've lost me, Simon. The world of hits and contracts is way out of my league, thank God. So you think the hit man will still try to kill Lucky and collect on the original contract?"

Simon smiled his evil little weasel smile. Yes, he's a vampire too. Born vampire, like his handsome son. Obviously Freddy takes after his beautiful mother CiCi. Lucky for Freddy.

"Charming, innocent Gloriana. Your hit man will probably wait to see what will gain him the biggest paycheck. If your Lucky lives up to her name?" Simon chuckled. "Well, her family has money. It would benefit them to get to him first and pay him off."

"I thought she was still in danger. But now she's surrounded by her daddy's goons. She'll be hard to get to." But if I could find out who the hit man was, that info might be worth the reward by itself. An interesting thought.

"I'm sure you're right. I suggest you look for someone who came into a large sum of money recently. That should lead you to the right person."

"Wait a minute." I jumped up and faced him. "You know who did it. Who hired the hit, don't you?" I wanted to skewer that creep into oblivion. He was *toying* with me.

"I might." He put his stake behind him, and I sure wasn't going to wrestle him for it.

"Then why don't you just go to Mr. Carvarelli yourself, collect the reward and be done with it?" And, yeah, wasn't I nice to lay it all out for him?

"I've lived a long, long time, Gloriana. Little amuses me these days. Watching a simple vampire such as yourself play detective . . ." He was suddenly facing me, way too close, and he flicked a finger across my cheek. I backed up until I hit the door. "Well, I am suddenly entertained again." His smile sent the creepy crawlies right up my spine, all the way to the ends of my carefully curled hair.

"Let's make this even more fun. Why don't you e-mail me the list of guests you had out there when you think this transaction took place?" I offered him a "Let's be partners" smile when I wanted nothing more than to run screaming from the room. God, this guy creeped me out. But this was a real break. I guess it was too much to hope he'd put a star next to the name I needed.

"Hmm. Let me think about that. Wouldn't want it to be too easy for you."

"Think fast. I figure this out on my own, and I keep all that reward for myself. Surely money still amuses you too." I could feel Simon's eyes on me as I strolled around the room, straightening a bottle here, a towel there. Oh, yeah, I knew he was eyeing my butt. I whipped around to face him. "Well?"

"You'll have that list when you get home tonight."

"Excellent." I walked to the door. "You want to meet Lucky? She's probably out in the hall, waiting to pounce on Ray, unless she's been thrown out of the building. Of course she wouldn't *stay* out. She and Ray have some kind of bad blood between them." I shut my mouth. That's the kind of information Simon loves to gather and use to his advantage.

"Anyway, come on. I'll make sure she knows you're a man with the kind of power she admires. Hey, you'll be a valuable connection for her in Austin." And if she ended up an EV minion or dessert for their goddess some night? Well, I'm sure the Carvarellis could afford to buy her out of that kind of trouble. Lucky wasn't that amusing, and money still talked with Simon. Speaking of . . .

"You got a cell phone, Simon?"

"Of course. Do you need to make a call?" He handed me

an old model, not even a camera phone. "I rarely use it." He tapped his forehead. "Energy Vampires are into nonverbal communication."

"Never mind. Let's go."

"Lead the way, Gloriana." Simon was suddenly very close. Too close.

"And, Simon, I'll say this one more time. Leave my employees—friends—whatever, alone. That were-cat you attacked has a mother who's hell on wheels. You even so much as cause a hangnail for one of my staff, and I'll make sure the were-kitty nation will be using the EV compound for a litter box." I wasn't backing away.

"You really shouldn't threaten me, Gloriana." Simon ran his stake down my throat, toying with the fringe on my blue leather jacket.

"Glory, have you seen my duffel?"

Simon and I both turned to see Ray step into the room wearing his second best look, a skimpy towel.

"Who the hell are you? Glory?" Ray fisted his hands and stepped closer, like he was going to defend me.

Simon grinned and nodded. He sent Ray flying to land on his butt against the wall, the towel a few feet away. Simon wrinkled his pointy nose.

"Oh, my. Israel Caine is a new vampire? I wonder what the tabloids would pay for that tidbit?"

Ray struggled to get up. "Why can't I move?"

"Ray, this is Simon Destiny, King of the Energy Vampires." I glanced at Simon, who was cleaning his nails with his stake. "He has you pinned, another form of the whammy. I could try to release you, but he'd just pin you again."

Simon smiled and nodded. "You bet his exquisitely sweet ass I would."

"What the hell is an Energy Vampire?"

"I'll tell you later, Ray." I turned to Simon. "Listen, you're not telling the tabloids anything. You've already got the Austin vampires, including your own son, ready to run you out of town, which can't be good for business. I suggest you concentrate on one project at a time. You want to meet Lucky or not?"

Simon strolled over to where Ray was still testing his strength futilely against the hold Simon had over him. "Listen, rock star. Energy Vampires, known affectionately as EVs, specialize in many excellent drugs. Come see us. Glory knows how to find our beautiful headquarters. First sample is free." Simon picked up the towel and tossed it to Ray. "Nice bling." He grinned and walked to the door.

"Come along, Gloriana. We have business to conduct."

"Glory, wait!" Ray finally managed to struggle to his feet. "What are you doing with a creep like that?" He ignored his duffel bag and his towel.

I just looked away. This was not the time to get distracted by his package, front or back view.

"Let's get something straight, Ray. This is *my* world. I've been a vampire for centuries. You've been one for less than twenty-four hours. So you're just going to have to follow my lead in all things paranormal. Got it?"

"No, I—"

"No is not an option. Get dressed. Wait for me here." I slammed the door and ran right into Simon.

"Oh, my, aren't you Miss Hot Stuff." Simon grabbed my arm and pulled me to him. "I like my women assertive. Come see me sometime without your boy toy and bring your whip."

I tried for a snappy comeback but gagged instead. Since he could read my mind, I just kept it blank and pulled away. Thankfully he let me go without a struggle and I walked off to track down Lucky with a mantra, "I hate Simon," to keep me from tearing an innocent bystander's throat open.

During my search, I discovered Lucky had managed to put Buster and Sam in a closet while Flo and Richard had been watching the concert. That reminded me. I hoped we didn't run into my roommate and her boyfriend backstage.

They had a really bad history with the leader of the Energy
Vampires. Or maybe I hoped we *did* run into Flo and Richard.
Right now three against one sounded like pretty good odds,
especially with this fury I had boiling inside me.

Etienne saw me coming with Simon and tried to steer
Lucky away. Well, of course. He was another enemy of the
EVs, but I guess he didn't feel up to a confrontation.

Simon apparently had no qualms and wasn't going to let
such a connection go to waste. He rushed forward, leaving
me in his dust.

"Etienne, surely you were going to say hello to me." Simon smiled at the woman clinging to Etienne's side. "Introduce me to your lovely companion." It was clearly an order.

I hurried up before Etienne did something stupid like
start a paranormal turf war in full view of about fifty mortals
who were breaking down sound equipment and packing it
away. This had been the last stop on a long tour for Ray.

"Simon, let *me* introduce you to Lucky Carver. Lucky, this
is Simon Destiny, a very powerful man who should be able
to help you find some of those"—I looked around—"um,
debtors, you're searching for."

Lucky smiled and held out her hand. Obviously she'd
forgotten Etienne's story of the whole sunlight room fiasco.
Then her smile widened. "I know who you are! The king of
that group that makes"—she leaned closer and whispered—
"Vampire Viagra. You didn't bring along a free sample, did
you?"

Simon glanced at me and flicked his wrist. I got the message. My work here was done. I couldn't get away fast
enough so I could wash off Simon's stench and slime. As I
headed back to the dressing room, I stole a look at Etienne's
face. He was not pleased, but not about to tell his meal
ticket to shut up either. Simon handed Lucky a packet of
pills. Uh-oh. That got the crew of mortals excited.

"Hey, that guy's dealin'."

"You take Visa?"

"Move over, I've got cash."

"I got to know what he's sellin'. I got hold of some bad shit in Houston. I'm still peein' purple."

"That's not from dope, fool. That's from that beet salad your mama made. I saw it on *Oprah*."

"Outta the way. I heard there's hash back here."

"No, man. It's X."

"Forget that. Make mine—"

I was grinning as I walked into Ray's dressing room.

"What's so funny? Oh, yeah. I guess it was a hoot watching me hit the wall like that. Or maybe you got a chuckle out of finding Buster and Sam in a closet." Ray was throwing stuff into a duffel bag.

"That was Lucky's work. No, none of that was funny, Ray." And none of it was anything I wanted to get into now. Not with Ray in a snit. "Are we ready to leave?"

"Guess so. I told Nathan to meet us in the limo." Ray zipped up the bag. "That Simon a vampire too?"

"Oh, yeah. Not all vampires are nice like me, Flo, Richard."

"I guess not. What about in New York? I really need to get back there. That's where my life is."

"Your old life is over, Ray." I hated to say it. Hated the look on his face as he sank down on the couch. No, it really hadn't hit him yet. Probably wouldn't for a while. He still couldn't quit staring at the bottles of Jack Daniels on the bar. Like I'd stared at the poker tables when I'd still been in Vegas.

"Look. I know this is hell. But I need for you to work with me for a while. Until I've clued you in to what you need to survive."

"And it has to be here? In Austin?" He got up again and actually walked over to the bar, fondling the Jack bottle like he could get some kind of pleasure from it. Yeah, right. And solitaire would do it for me. Uh-huh.

"There's a lot you don't know, Ray. Your life depends on learning what you need to know to survive as a vampire." I tried to put my hand on his arm, but he stepped back.

"I don't suppose you could come back to New York with me." He said it grudgingly. Of course he really didn't want me along, but I wasn't giving him any other options.

"No. I've got a business to run." I hated myself that this next one took effort. "And a boyfriend."

"Then I guess I stay for a while. I get that you're doing me a favor." He gave up on the bottle, picked up the duffel and finally looked at me. "Like you say. My survival depends on you."

Well, gee, he didn't have to sound so grim. I tried to think of something to cheer him up. "You're immortal now, you know."

He stopped, stared at me for a heartbeat or six, then dropped the bag and pressed his fingertips to his eyes. "This can not be happening." Finally he dropped his hands and picked up the bag again. "Immortal. Well, shit." He opened the door.

Seventeen

I walked by his side, dodging fans and photographers until we were back in the limo, where Nathan waited for us. The bubble of happiness at playing the role of Israel Caine's girl-friend had burst for real this time. I just wasn't feeling it. But I kept my fake smile on. We were halfway to Sixth Street before I finally tuned in to the conversation between Ray and Nathan.

"Ray, you really should come back to the hotel. We're supposed to fly back to New York tomorrow. Start work on the new album." Nathan was working his cell phone and his BlackBerry. He'd been very pleased with the concert and had been rattling off numbers like gate receipts and percentages. You see why I'd tuned him out?

"Cancel my flight. I'm staying in Austin for a while." Ray hugged me close, like I was the reason for the change. Good acting. I wondered why he hadn't tried Hollywood.

"You sure?" Nathan poured himself a large Scotch, then looked at us. We both shook our heads. "We've got the stu-dio all booked, Ray, you know that. It'll cost a fortune to reschedule. Besides, the band's psyched, that new song's being scored—"

"Cancel it all, Nate. Maybe I'll look for a studio here. Austin's a great music city. I like the vibe here." Ray actually kissed the top of my head. "I'm not saying it's a done deal, but I'm keeping my options open."

Nate drank half his scotch before he spoke. "Sorry, man, but I don't see it. You can get pussy—"

He was wearing the rest of his drink and Ray had Nathan's shirt in his fist before he could finish his sentence. "Respect the lady, Nathan, or you can get the hell out of the car and walk."

"Hey, ease up, man. I'm sorry. You caught me off guard or I never would have gone off like that. Glory, excuse me." Nathan's face was flushed. "I'm *really* sorry."

Ray released him. "You should be. You don't like my choices, you pull me aside later. We don't do this in front of the women. Ever."

"Yeah, Ray. Right. Out of line. Totally." Nathan answered his phone, sliding as far away to the other side of the limo as he could get to talk.

Ray looked at me. "I believe that's what Valdez wanted. Right?"

"Yeah, but he's not here. And I won't tell on you, Ray." I'd hoped it was what Ray *felt*, but I guess that had been too much to expect. He obviously didn't figure a vampire could *be* a lady. He really was a hell of an actor. Nathan had bought every word.

"We're here." Nathan snapped his phone shut. "Can I call you in the morning, Ray?"

"No." Ray started to open the door.

"Man, don't let this ruin our friendship. I said I'm sorry. I guess I'm tired. It's been a long road trip and there've been lots of . . ." Nathan didn't say it but his meaning was clear. Women. "Anyway, I had no idea you were getting serious so fast. But if you're happy, bud, I'm happy."

"No, Nate, it's not that. I mean, I'm happy, sure. But—" Ray stopped and ran a hand over his eyes. "Call me after sunset. We're both tired. Maybe we're getting old." He poked Nathan on the arm. "We'll touch base tomorrow night. After I sleep all day. You know we'll always be tight. What do we say? Sorry, Glory, but women come and go, friends are forever."

I smiled at Nate. Little did he know that Ray really would be forever while he . . . I'd lost more mortal friends than I could count. It came with the territory, but that doesn't mean it didn't hurt. Poor, clueless Nate just smiled back.

"Gee, Glory, you're taking this really well, most women shoot me the finger when Ray says stuff like that."

"What can I say? I'm a lady?" Then I stepped out of the car. Every swear word I'd ever heard in every language I'd never learned came to mind. The paparazzi had camped on my doorstep, and a million flashes went off in our faces.

Women screamed Ray's name and I braced myself for a rain of undies again. Cheapskates. I knew discount-store bikinis when I caught them. They'd bought these in the bargain pack. And the sizes! One look at this crowd and I could tell there wasn't one butt that could squeeze into the tiny panties being launched like missiles at Ray's head.

He just laughed and batted them away like pesky mosquitoes. When he accidentally caught one, the crowd moaned in ecstasy. Poor Buster and Sam did their best to keep the crowd back. Sam took a hard hit from a black satin bustier that could have fit a cross-dressing linebacker. It was all he could do to stay on his feet. Then a really nice black lace thong hit Ray's left ear. I tucked that one in my purse. Hey, it'll wash.

I did what Ray had told me to do, holding on to his arm and smiling like I didn't have a care in the world. At the door, while I punched in the code, he surprised me by turning to field a few questions.

"Who's the babe, Ray?"

"Glory St. Clair." He spelled it for them.

Everyone wrote it down.

"Ms. St. Clair, are you the owner of this store here?"

Okay, business first. It looked like someone had been doing homework.

"Yes, Vintage Vamp's Emporium. I sell vintage clothing, antiques and collectibles." Another big smile while I held the door ajar. A red bikini hit the door and I kicked it in. I'd check the label later.

"You planning to stay in Austin awhile, Ray?"

Ray took the door and looked down at me. Close up, I could see he wasn't exactly thrilled, but reconciled to the near future. "Yeah, I figure I'm here at least until New Year's Eve."

"Give your lady a kiss, Ray. Something for the cover."

I didn't know whether to be grateful or furious. But Ray is media savvy and tabloid covers must be near and dear to his heart. Before I could dash inside, he leaned down and planted a big wet one on my open mouth. Oh. And oh. And um. And ah. Just when I'd decided the cover would have to be X-rated, he eased us both inside the building and slammed the door shut.

I was still dazed when I noticed him scrubbing his mouth on the bottom of his T-shirt.

"What?"

"I can't believe I did that."

"What?" My vocabulary was now one word.

"Kissed a freakin' vampire. I swear to God I could feel your fangs."

"I didn't ask you to stick your tongue in my mouth, Ray." I stomped ahead of him up the stairs, fighting tears and pretending that the star of my fantasies since he'd first sung "My Own True Love" hadn't just shaken me to my toes.

"Reflex." Ray stomped right behind me. "God, I hate how I just went off on my best friend. Hell, I hate the whole friggin' thing. We're freaks, lady. You, me. Freaks with fangs. And now I can't even wash the taste of you out of my mouth with a decent drink."

I stopped at my door and turned to face him. "All right, listen. I guess I should be honored, you being the legendary Israel Caine and all. But, honey, *you* kissed *me*. Not only that, but judging by the bulge pushing against your zipper, you didn't exactly hate it."

Ray looked down. "Get real. That's just another reflex. Happens with any woman who's got the necessary equipment."

"Nice, Ray. Real nice." I fumbled in my purse for my keys, then unlocked the door. Valdez took one look at my face and growled at Ray.

"What the hell did you do to her?"

"Just told her the truth."

"Which is?"

"I don't want to be a freakin' vampire. You hear me?" Ray slammed out of the room. I heard him open the refrigerator, a stream of profanity chronicling his realization that there was only one choice he could make in there. He came back with a bottle of my old Fangtastic. Like at least that was a different brand from the one I'd given him. He sat on a chair, so I couldn't get close to him, I guess, and opened the bottle. Then he just stared into it.

"How was the concert?"

We both shrugged.

"Come on, now, Glory. An Israel Caine concert? Surely there's something to talk about. I've been stuck here all night with nothing to do but lick my—"

"Simon showed up."

"The hell you say."

Israel finally took a sip of his drink and made a gagging noise. Valdez and I ignored him.

"He wants to hook up with Lucky. Figures the EVs could get into loan sharking. Seems like a good fit to me."

Valdez chuffed. *"Those two probably deserve each other."*

"He said he was a drug dealer. Nice friends you got there, Glory." Ah. Israel decides to enter the conversation.

"He's *not* my friend. But I told him I'd hook him up with Lucky, Valdez. He's going to help me find her killer. It's a win-win." I finally looked at Israel. He'd conquered his revulsion and was drinking the Fangtastic now. "I know you don't care about this, but Lucky's father is offering a reward if we can find out who attacked her. I could use that money."

Ray tipped his bottle at me. "Good luck. I wish to hell you'd left her to bleed out. Then maybe my life wouldn't be in the crapper."

"Glory was a hero that night. You shoulda been there. We didn't know we was savin' a psycho." Valdez lay at my feet in a show of solidarity. I pulled off my boots, then rubbed his head with my toes.

"Thanks, puppy. But I guess I understand your attitude, Ray. You want to tell us about your history with Lucky? Or did you really just dump her because you were an immature jerk and deserve all this payback?"

Ray took a swallow and set his bottle on the coffee table. "You want to know what really happened? It's not a pretty story. I wouldn't want to offend a lady."

"I'm a freakin' vampire first, Ray. Lady second. I can handle an ugly story." I sat back.

"Yeah, right. You'll probably get off to this."

That earned him one of Valdez's growls.

"Sorry. Where's my respect?"

I hid my hurt behind a careless smile. I'd be damned if I'd teach Ray mind reading anytime soon, but I could see that this story had left really deep scars. He *never* shared it.

"I'm listening, Ray. Go ahead."

"Fine. I was eighteen. On my own in New York City. I'd wanted to be a musician since I started playing the piano when I was six. My dad took me on tour with him before I could hold a guitar." Ray got a faraway look in his eyes. "I loved it. The music, the people. Still do."

I had a hard time holding on to my hurt when Ray was like this. Sure, he loved music and it showed in every song he sang. "So you headed to New York looking for your big break."

"And I gót it. I started singing in small clubs. That's where I met Lucky. She was beautiful, full of life, and she knew everybody." Ray frowned. "Found out later it was because a lot of them owed her family money."

"So they don't just loan money to paranormals."

"Hell, no. They'll loan to anyone, anytime. But people soon found out they'd better pay the family back along with their exorbitant interest or else." Ray rubbed his neck and yawned. "I'm beat. What time is it?"

"You've got about an hour until dawn." Yeah, I was still hurt, but I felt an obligation to Ray. He hadn't asked for this, and I felt indirectly responsible. So I would clue him in. I saw his eyes closing. I reached out and shook him awake.

"Okay, Ray. Listen carefully. When the sun rises, wherever you are, you're going to crash. I mean, seriously, lights out. And if the sun hits you, you're a goner." I should have told him this stuff already. "The sun will kill you, Ray. So you have to be in a room with black-out drapes, like those in this apartment." I walked over and made sure they were closed tight.

"Valdez watches over me during the day because that's when a vampire is most vulnerable. We're utterly defenseless. Anyone can kill us then." Boy, did I know that. I'd spent way too many years worrying about where I could safely spend my days.

"That's the pits." Ray yawned again.

"Yes, it is. Let me give you an example. We had a fire here not long ago. If Valdez hadn't pulled all the vampires in the building to safety, we would've died in our beds. We can't wake up."

"This is bogus. It can't be happening."

"It can. It has. It can't be reversed. You're vampire. Forever. You'll just have to deal with it."

"How else can we die?" Ray drank his Fangtastic and got up to look at the drapes with their thick layers.

"A wooden stake through the heart or if someone cuts off your head. No cure for that." I glanced at Valdez. "But I want to hear about Lucky. Finish the story."

"This isn't a story. This is the truth. I fell in love with her. I was young, remember? She was inventive in bed and I was hooked. I wanted to marry her, was saving up to buy her a ring. You don't give a woman like Lucky a little diamond." He looked at Valdez.

"Hell, no. She'd want something from Tiffany." Valdez was obviously bonding here, guy to guy. I just waited for the punch line.

"That's where I made a critical mistake. I thought maybe I could get a loan. I had my first record coming out and the buzz was good. So I went to her father. Told him why I wanted the money." Ray was restless, wandering around the living room. He picked up the unauthorized biography.

"This is crap. My dad *never* hit my mother, even though they yelled a lot, still do if they're ever in the same room for more than two minutes." He took the book to the kitchen, and I heard him dump it into the trash can. I'd get it out later. I wondered if I could whammy Ray into autographing it. Would that be cheating?

"Sit down, Ray. About Lucky's father. Did you ask for her hand? Lucky says he's old-school Italian. I bet he expected it." It was way too late, but I'd always thought that old-fashioned courtesy the height of the romantic gesture. Blade on bended knee? Nope, couldn't imagine it.

"No, didn't think of it. But it wouldn't have made a difference. Next thing I know I get a visit from some of her father's goons." Ray finally sat on the couch again.

"Why does he always call them that?" Valdez just had to say something. *"They're hired hands. Enforcers. Show some respect."*

"Hey, you guys are all about respect, aren't you?" Ray laughed, but it was a bitter sound. "You're in the wrong line of work if that's what you're after. Anyway, that's what Carvarelli calls them and I'll be damned if I'll respect those goons after what they did to me." Ray picked up the Fangtastic again and seemed disappointed that the bottle was empty.

"Okay, what did they do?"

"You saw me naked, right?" He looked from me to Valdez.

Well, no use denying it. We both nodded. And, yeah, my cheeks were hot.

"That piercing? On my cock?"

"*Man, that had to have hurt.*"

"You have no idea."

"*Then why do it? I've heard it can enhance pleasure. But is it worth it?*" Valdez leaned forward, like he really wanted to know for himself. Just the thought made me shudder.

"I didn't have a choice. Carvarelli's goons grabbed me one night. Stripped me and chained me to a wooden table."

I met Ray's gaze and looked into his mind. Saw his terror when he'd been naked and laid out while three men laughed and stood over him. One held a chain saw, playing with it like he was trying to decide what body part to take off first. Ray cried, begged, then one of them grabbed his cock. I looked away, unable to bear watching what came next.

"Christ, Ray." I thought I was going to be sick.

He sneered. "Too ugly for you, Glory?"

"Just finish it, Ray." I looked at Valdez. "We don't want to cross Carvarelli, V. I can tell you that."

"*What the hell—*"

Ray touched his crotch. "They pierced me, Valdez. With a hammer. Nailed me right to the table. As a warning. Said if I ever saw or spoke to Lucky again, the whole cock was coming off, balls and all."

Eighteen

Valdez swore, using some of those words he forbid anyone to use around me. Then he laid his head on my knee and took a steadying breath. *"That's harsh, man."*

"Harsh? Naw. They figured they'd let me off easy. They unchained me and tossed me the hammer. So I could pry the nail out of the table and walk home. Even left me my clothes. Those guys were real sweethearts."

I tried to block out the picture of Ray staggering home, bleeding, with a hole in his penis. I put a fist in my mouth to keep from sobbing out loud. And he'd only been eighteen. That night should have made him an instant adult.

"Obviously Lucky has no idea that's why you dumped her."

"No, that was part of the deal. I couldn't explain. No contact with her ever again." Ray rubbed his crotch, and I had a feeling it was an old habit. Apparently respecting me didn't include forgoing that.

"A nail. That couldn't have healed well."

"No shit. But I didn't have time to worry about it." Ray

got up and went into the kitchen for another bottle of Fangtastic. He leaned against the doorway and twisted off the
cap. "The opening act for the Stones lost its lead singer to
rehab and I was offered the job. I jumped at it and left town
to go on tour. Hell, this was the break I'd been dreaming
about."

"My dad showed up in Philadelphia where I had a fever
and almost fell off the stage. Yeah, I got infected. Nails'll
do that to ya. Dad took me to the emergency room." Ray
walked over and sat again. He looked at me, then Valdez.
"Nobody else has ever heard this story. Just my dad, now
you two. It doesn't leave this room. I came out all right. Forget you ever heard it."

Forget it, yeah right. Like it wasn't now burned into my
brain, and trust me, I've seen some pretty horrific stuff over
the years. I nodded and so did Valdez. For once my dog was
speechless, only the twitch in his tail showing how much
this story had disturbed him.

"Sounds like you and your dad were really close."

"You could say that." Ray smiled. "Still are. Shit. He'll
be waiting for me in New York. I'll have to call him tomorrow night."

Ray took another gulp of Fangtastic. "It's got to be near
dawn. I feel like I'm dying here."

I glanced at the clock. "Yep, about five minutes. I wonder if Flo and Richard are coming back. We just took off
without them."

*"Message on the answering machine. She says she's staying at
Richard's. Ray can take her bed."*

"Good." Ray stood and walked toward the hall. "I assume it's down this hall."

"Wait. I have a question." My bruised ego would have
loved a minor skirmish with Valdez trying to keep Ray out
of my bed. Yeah, like that was going to happen.

"Hurry, I'm about to pass out." Ray pulled his T-shirt off
over his head.

I tried to look away. I did. But I've been a Ray fan-atic too long to go cold turkey. And a fine male body is a fine male body.

"Uh. Oh, yeah. Why do you still have a piercing? Obviously you finally healed. Why not just forget the whole horrible experience?"

"I decided it would be stupid to forget one of the most valuable lessons I ever learned. That piercing is there to remind me that love is for idiots and green-ass kids. I've had my eyes opened, babe. I hook up, but I don't get hooked, know what I mean?" And with that Ray staggered down the hall to Flo's bedroom. The door slammed shut, and Valdez and I just looked at each other.

"Ray's really been through some stuff. I guess I shouldn't take any of that personally." I yawned, just about as ready for bed as Ray was and I had about two minutes to get there.

Valdez chuffed. *"You knew he wasn't for you anyway, Glory. Blade's your guy."*

I grinned as I headed to my bedroom. "Oh, right. How could I forget? Especially with you around to remind me."

I checked my computer as soon as I got up the next night. Simon had actually come through. But, except for Etienne, there wasn't a single name I recognized on the list of visitors at the EV compound. Where had all these paranormals come from?

I stalled by taking a shower and getting dressed before I checked my cell phone for messages. For an hour I managed to put blackmail on the back burner. Relatively easy to do with Israel Caine sacked out in the bedroom down the hall.

"Come on, Blondie. You've fiddled with your makeup long enough. See if we've got a text waiting for us." Valdez stood over my fabulous purse like he was actually thinking of dragging it to me by the handle.

"Us? Like you're going to kick in on the payoff? Where

do you keep your savings? In with the kibble?" I was in a rotten mood just thinking about what that text might say. What had we been thinking, taunting a blackmailer with a dollar bill? "And if I find a tooth mark on this strap, I'm going to actually buy kibble. *Comprende?*"

"*Gee. Take a chill pill and open the phone already.*" Valdez sat in front of me, all innocent doggy. "*I'm just as nervous as you are. What if this yahoo actually gets the video on TV? Now you're Israel Caine's main squeeze. There would be a shit storm of publicity.*"

"Thanks for reminding me." I sank down on the couch, picked up my second Bloodthirsty of the night and took a couple of swallows. "Yep, there's a message. Hey, maybe it's an 'Okay, you win' message."

"*Just read it already. Caine should be up at any time.*" As if on cue, we heard a door slam, then the shower go on. "*There you go. Wonder if he takes long showers.*"

"According to the unauthorized biography—"

"*Glory!*"

"Okay! I'm reading the text. Oh, crap. Look."

"HA. HA. PAY UP OR UL B THE NEXT BIG THING ON YOUTUBE. 5 THOUSAND BUCKS. 24 HRS. SAME PLACE OR ELSE."

I sighed. "Might as well be five million. And if that video shows up on YouTube, we'll have every vamp wannabe in the world wanting to come check us out."

"*So? As long as you can keep your fangs under control, you can deny, deny, deny. Might even be good for business.*" Valdez scratched his ears. "*Come to think of it, you can say this Caine thing bringing you into the spotlight made you realize the potential of using the media to advertise the shop. What the hey. It's worth a try.*"

"Aren't you Mr. Cool?" I stared at him. "Where's this change of attitude coming from? Five minutes ago you were just as freaked out as I was." I ran the video again. Because, of course, it was included with the message, lest I forget why I should bankrupt myself. Oh, those fangs, that blood, the width of those hips!

"This deal with Caine has really got me thinkin'. The guy's in the tabloids almost daily. He shrugs it off. 'Cause most of it's lies. I say let the blackmailin' dude put it out there. Look at you, Glory. No way would anyone take you for a vampire."

I looked down. Okay, my blue dress and high heels would fit in at any bar on Sixth Street on a date night. Especially if I were going on a third date. Did I mention the dress is low cut and easy on, easy off?

"You're right. Now if I went in for the Goth look, I'd be in trouble, but—"

"But you're too smart for that, always have been."

"Thanks, Valdez." I shut the phone decisively. Really, what choice did I have? Chances of catching our blackmailer picking up a payoff were slim to none, and the demands for money would only keep coming, especially if I managed to come into some reward money for finding out who'd attacked Lucky.

I squared my shoulders. "Okay. I'll write another note and include another dollar with it, and we'll leave it in the park. I'll say, 'Bring it on.'"

"Bring what on?" Flo flung open the hall door.

"I thought I heard a crowd out in the hall," I said and smiled when I saw Richard right behind her.

"You did. Look who we found downstairs, outside the building, guarding our door." Flo pulled Sam inside, followed closely by Buster.

"Oh, hi, guys." Now this was a complication I hadn't anticipated. Of course Ray's bodyguards would expect to stay with him.

"Good evening, Ms. St. Clair. Ray around?" Sam was the talker of the pair. Buster just settled next to the door, a silent statue ready to strong-arm anyone who tried to get to his boss.

"Here I am, Sam." Ray walked into the room with a towel around his waist and nothing else. Obviously he'd just stepped out of the shower.

Sam sniffed the air. "No coffee? Want me to run downstairs to that little shop and get you some, boss? They've got some good-lookin' muffins too. Nate said you were sleepin' all day."

Ray smiled and shook his head. "No coffee, but you boys head on down and set up there. This building's as secure as a vault. I'll call down if I decide to go out." He glanced at me. "Right now we've got no plans. Right, babe?"

I was lost in a little experiment with mind control. Vampires can make things move with their minds, and I just about had the knot on Ray's towel undone. Flo saw where I was looking and grinned. Unfortunately Ray felt the towel falling and grabbed it before Flo got to see his diamond ring. Hey, I was trying to do her a favor.

Ray's cell phone rang and he picked it up from the coffee table. "Yeah. You're downstairs in the limo?" Ray looked around. "Give me five minutes, then I'll send someone down to let you up." He shut the phone.

"Glory, tell Sam and Buster the code so they can get out downstairs."

"Sorry, Ray." I looked at Richard. "You want to walk them down, Richard?"

"Sure, come on, boys." Richard made it clear they had no choice. The men looked at Ray, who was obviously pissed, but he merely nodded and the three men headed out.

As soon as the door closed, Ray turned to me. "No? You tell me no?" He was furious. Valdez got between us. "Why the hell can't my bodyguards have the freakin' code?"

"Because they're mortals, Ray. This building is for paranormals. I can give the code to anyone who is a paranormal I know and trust. But I won't give it to you unless you promise to respect that. Right now, I don't think you're ready to know the code."

"Shit." Ray stomped out of the room, losing his towel halfway to the door.

"*Dio mio.*" Flo was clearly impressed by the back view.

"You should see the front." I sat on the couch and picked up the bottle of Bloodthirsty again. There was a knock on the door and Flo hurried to answer it.

"Richard, you don't have to knock."

"Not Richard." Blade stood there with an armload of newspapers. "Thought you'd like to see these, Gloriana." He strode forward and dumped them none too gently on the couch beside me.

Richard eased in behind him. He had a newspaper too, this one I could see was the Austin daily. "Sorry, Florence, but Ray and Glory beat us out for the photo op."

Flo snatched it out of his hand and looked at the page Richard had folded it to. "Well, Ray certainly is showing the world that he has a new, how you say it, main squeeze."

I'd grabbed a tabloid that had given us a full color spread. Of course they would use a wide-angle lens. My butt looked *enormous*. I was never wearing a miniskirt that length again. It hit my thighs at their widest part.

"I'm reading your mind, Gloriana. Instead of focusing on your thighs, which are fine, by the way, look at your lover's open mouth on yours, clearly giving you a taste of his tongue. And the way his hand is touching your left breast." Jerry could have been an announcer for a golf tournament.

Gee, be technical, why don't you? Yes, ladies and gentlemen, two inches to the left and he would have touched nipple!

"Then there's your own hand, which is clutching his waist like you're trying to find his zipper."

"We were acting, Jerry. For the camera. It meant nothing. Ray loathes me. As soon as the door closed, he told me so, very clearly." And damn if I didn't tear up like a complete and utter wimp.

"She's right. I guess you're the boyfriend she told me about. Another vampire." Ray had pulled on his jeans and was stepping into the black loafers he'd worn the night before. He held a dark blue sweater in his hand. "I had no idea there were so many of you running around."

"Israel Caine. Jeremy Blade," I said. Jerry didn't offer his hand and of course Ray wouldn't, what with his anti-vampire stance. The men just seemed to assess each other. "You had no idea there are so many of us, Ray, because that's the way we like it. The fewer people who know about us, the better."

"Well, I'm telling Nathan. And I can't keep living here. It's too small. I have an entourage. Not just Sam and Buster either. Some of them are still in New York, including my father. He was planning to stay with me for a few weeks. At least until after Hanukkah." Ray looked around. He didn't say it, though why he held back when he'd been brutally honest about everything else, I don't know. Maybe he'd figured out that if he insulted anything Gloriana related, Jerry would knock his new fangs down his throat.

But Ray was like Lucky, used to finer things. Me, my first priority has always been safety. I felt safe here. Or at least I usually did. The recent fire had shook me up more than a bit, but, hey, we'd survived. Which proves that top-of-the-line security combined with Valdez is pretty fail-safe.

"Lucky could leave because she had Etienne, another vampire, to guide her." Flo looked at Richard. "I suppose . . ."

"No, absolutely not. Ray is *Glory's* responsibility. Let her handle him. He can endure his reduced circumstances for a few days while he learns the ropes." Richard had read Ray loud and clear. And Flo. He knew Flo way too well and had spent enough hours with her listening to Ray's music to know about her crush on him. And Flo's history with men told its own tale. Richard had already lasted longer than most of her lovers. He wasn't about to throw her together with another handsome man on a daily basis.

Blade had been busy reading Ray too. Unfortunately, he realized Ray had zero interest in hooking up with me. And I'm sure Valdez had also reassured him on that point. Ain't it swell being so . . . desirable?

"Let's bring your friend up here. We can help you decide how and what to tell him." Jerry was actually being cordial, which threw Ray way off his stride.

So Ray and Jerry headed downstairs. Flo picked up one of the tabloids.

"Here's a cute picture of you, Glory, catching panties." Then she gasped and stuck the newspaper under a cushion.

"What?" I made a grab for it.

"No, forget it, girlfriend. Tell me about Israel kissing you. Was it totally hot?" Flo's cheeks were pink and she was signaling Richard.

I jumped up. "Flo, what was in that paper?"

"*Stupido!* Or maybe my reading is not so good. Throw it away, Richard." Flo tried to wad it up and toss it to him, but I snatched it out of the air.

I walked over to the breakfast room and smoothed out the paper. My picture was in full color and I was snatching the panties from a grinning Ray. Of course he never took a bad picture. He looked . . . amazing. Then I read the caption.

"Israel Caine's New Flavor of the Month, Gloriana St. Clair. Check Out those Supersized Blueberries. But Lay Off the Marshmallow Crème to Last the Full Thirty Days." I felt Flo's arm around my shoulders and Valdez's cold nose on my wrist.

"*They spelled your name right.*" Valdez chuffed.

"You know what pisses me off?"

"What, honey?" Flo patted my back.

"They didn't mention the shop! You know what this kind of free publicity is worth?"

By the time Jerry and Ray returned with Nathan, Flo and I had picked our favorite stories and had piled up a few destined for the shredder downstairs. Richard had discovered that someone had already set up a "Defend the Blueberries" MySpace page for me on the Internet.

Nathan was clearly confused by the shabby apartment

and by the group of people who wouldn't leave him alone
with his friend, even when he threw out not-so-subtle hints
that they had business to discuss. Even Valdez seemed to
bother him. Of course my dog *would* stare at him, probably
reading his mind to see if he was the trustworthy sort.

Clearly Ray thought the world of the guy and a few minutes clued us in to the fact that the two had grown up together in an affluent Chicago suburb where Ray's mother
had settled with her second husband, a wealthy American
manufacturer.

"Don't listen to Nate if he ever tries to go all ghetto,
homeboy on you. The only hood he knew growing up was
the hood of his dad's Jag in their five-car garage."

"Now, Ray. I was going to run my act by Glory later."
Nathan grinned and winked. He'd already congratulated
me on the tabloid cover shot. Apparently good media cover-
age made up for a lot, even the inconvenience of staying in
Austin. I'd read his mind though, and he was planning to
get Ray alone and talk him into going back to New York,
even if they had to drag me along with them.

"Nate's got a Harvard MBA. That's why I trust him with
my business. That and the fact that he's like a brother to me.
That's why you people have to understand. I'm going to tell
him the truth." Ray looked around the room. He was in
one chair. Flo, Jerry and I were on the couch. Richard leaned
against the door not far from Valdez. One by one we all
nodded.

"Truth? What truth, bud?" Nate sat in the only other
chair. He put both elbows on his knees and leaned forward
until he was looking Ray dead in the eyes. "You're scaring
me, Ray. Are you sick? Buster and Sam said you're not eating or drinking. What's up with that?"

Ray took a deep breath, reached out and gripped Nate's
hands. "I had an accident, Nate. A bad one."

"Oh, shit. Is this about a DUI? They're not so cool
about that in Texas. I mean, if they'll burn the president's

daughter . . ." Ray must have squeezed hard, because Nate looked down and yelped.

"Hey, watch it, brother. I'll get you a good lawyer. We'll get this straightened out. Unless, oh, shit, man, there's not a dead body somewhere is there?"

"No, no DUI. No, dead body. Except mine." Ray tried to laugh, but it came out more like a sob. "Sorry if I hurt your hand, Nate. I guess I'm stronger than I used to be." Ray glanced at me and I nodded. He let go of Nate and wiped his eyes. "I can't do it. Tell him for me, Glory."

"Tell me what?" Nate jumped up and put a hand on Ray's back. "Shit, man, are you crying? We haven't cried since the Bulls lost Jordan."

"Hell, no. I don't cry."

But Ray *was* crying. I sniffled, and Flo broke down beside me.

"Nathan, listen to me. Just listen." That came out of me kind of shaky, but it was all I had.

Ray shook his head and stood up. "No, I should do it. It's on me." He took a deep breath, put his hand on Nate's shoulders and looked into his eyes. "Nathan, I'm a vampire."

Nineteen

Nathan looked around the room. We all just stared back, solemn as if we were at a wake. Suddenly he burst into laughter, slapping Ray on the back, then collapsing into his chair.

"Oh, man, you really had me then. You and your practical jokes. This is even better than the time you made Dave think he'd swallowed his contact lens with his Jack Daniels and that he'd have to have it surgically removed."

"No joke. Show him." Ray concentrated, then forced a smile, his fangs glinting in the overhead light. One by one, we all gave Nathan toothy grins, though it was definitely an effort on my part.

Nate just laughed harder. "Oh, stop! I can't stand it! Where'd you get them? Some costume shop? They're the best I've ever seen. Got to have some for next Halloween."

Ray pulled Nate to his feet and grabbed his hand. "Feel them. They're the real deal. They don't come out." He took a shaky breath. "Aw, hell, I can smell your blood, Nate, hear it pumping through your veins." He looked at me. "It's making me . . . thirsty, Glory." His eyes filled again. "This is sick."

"No, Ray, it's normal. But go get a bottle of Bloodthirsty, it'll help." I could see he wasn't in any shape to walk to the kitchen so I just passed him my open bottle. He released Nathan and took a deep swallow.

His friend still couldn't buy any of this. It was like he was watching a play, waiting for act two. He wasn't about to put his hand in his friend's mouth, but he did look curiously at the bottle Ray was swigging from.

"That tomato juice or something stronger? Sorry about that crack earlier about rehab, buddy. You know I don't think you have a problem. It's just that the tabloids have made a big deal—"

"Screw the tabloids." Ray handed me the bottle. "I'm serious about this. I have to get you to believe me because what happened to me changes everything. For me, for you. Forever." He grabbed Nate's finger and dragged it into his mouth.

"Ow! Son of a bitch! What the hell was that?" Nate stared at the blood welling from his index finger.

"Look at my teeth again, brother." Ray snarled.

"Aw, no. What the hell is wrong? You can't sing like that." Nathan glared at me. "I don't know what kind of freaky scene you people are into, but Ray's a straight-up guy. Come on, Ray. A good dentist will fix you right up. I'm taking you out of here. A little rehab, corrective dentistry and you'll be back to normal in no time."

Ray just shook his head.

Nathan grabbed Ray's arm and tried to pull him toward the door. "Come on, I said. I'd like to see these people try to stop us. Let's go before I start knocking some of these fake pointy canines loose."

"No, Nate. Nothing here's fake. This isn't a cult and I'm not in line for an intervention. I wish it was that easy." Ray looked down to where Nate jerked on his arm, clearly surprised that he now had the strength to resist a man who so obviously worked out more than he did. "Buddy, sit down. Listen to me for a minute, okay?"

"No. You're freaking me out. I've got to get us out of here. You can tell me all about this game these people are playing in the limo on the way to the airport." Nathan was really upset now that he realized this wasn't some kind of twisted joke. "I don't want to hear any more of this vampire shit." He glanced at Jerry and Richard, who seemed compelled to show off their enormous fangs. "Stop it!"

Of course I thought those fangs were impressive and very sexy. Nathan on the other hand was trembling, the whites of his eyes startling in his dark face. He looked like he was either going to start swinging or pass out where he stood.

"We're not going anywhere until I explain what happened to me the other night. You remember me telling you about that woman trouble I had in New York? The year you went to Harvard and I went to the big city to try my luck in the music business."

Nathan jumped when Valdez strolled over and sat near him. I sent my dog a mental message that if he said *one word*, he was going to be Randolph's date to the Winter Solstice Ball. He clamped his mouth shut and came to sit beside me, gazing at me with a false adoration that made me want to twist his ear.

"Ray, I don't think Glory wants to hear about some woman from your past. But, yeah, sure, I remember you tellin' me about New York. You were never the same about women after that." Nathan happened to catch Flo's eye, and she gave him a fang-filled grin. He moaned and closed his eyes.

"That's 'cause I learned a hard lesson. And Glory knows all about that woman. She was Lucky Carver, the deranged fan you saw in my dressing room last night before the concert."

"Yeah, yeah, concert. Big hit. Did you see the review in

the paper? They loved you. Already talking about having you headline Austin City Limits next year. That's huge, man. Bob Dylan got that gig last year." Nathan seemed desperate to steer the conversation back to something he understood, like business. He looked down at his BlackBerry, which had miraculously appeared in his hand.

"I guess you guys know it's a big-deal music festival here. Draws over a hundred thousand fans from all over. Held in Zilker Park. Outdoors. October. I'm already clearing Ray's schedule." He checked out Ray's reaction. "Assuming you still want to come back to the area by then. Maybe it's not such a good idea." He cut his eyes toward me. "Come on, Ray. You sure you're not ready to leave now?"

"Nate, this isn't going to work." Ray snatched the Black-Berry and tossed it to the floor. "Face it. I'm a vampire. A blood-sucking, 'never going to eat real food again, see day-light or, oh hell, any of the other things normal people do' vampire."

Nathan leaned forward and put his hand on Ray's knee. "Look, Ray, I know a place. Very discreet. We can get you help. No one needs to know." He gave me a hard look like he thought I was the ringleader of this demonic cult. "What the hell did you people give him? I'm calling a doctor. And then I'm calling the police. Let the tabloids print the story. We've ridden out storms before. I don't care what the f—" Nathan screeched when Valdez clamped down on his foot.

"Valdez, cool it." I grabbed his collar and tried to jerk him back.

"All I've got is shoe, no foot at all. I can't just sit here and lis-ten to him accuse you of drugging Ray. And I'm sure as hell not let-ting him call the cops."

"Valdez, you know we're not going to let this get that far. Release him." Jerry's word is law to the pup. So Valdez backed off.

Now Nathan was shaking like a vibrator on high. Ray squatted down in front of him. "Look at me, bud. This is an alternate reality. Shit happens like talking dogs and people with fangs who drink blood and live forever. Stuff we never knew even existed outside of comic books and movies."

"R-r-ray. I—I—I don't know what's happening. You heard him too? That dog? He didn't move his lips. But he said something. Inside my head." Nathan grabbed Ray's hands. "Remember when we played Dracula for Halloween? We put those fake fangs in our mouths. But they were wax. Tasted like shit. Your mom made us black satin capes and we ran around scaring the girls."

"Good times, buddy." Ray stood and walked over to stand next to me. "But these are bad times. That woman in New York was Lucky Carver, like I said. I dumped her or her father would have had me castrated. He wouldn't allow me to tell her why either. I had to just walk away with a souvenir hole in my cock."

"No way." Nathan stood too, like he didn't know what else to do.

Richard and Jerry exchanged horrified looks, Flo was obviously eager for details and Valdez nodded, like he'd be happy to fill in the rest of the gang after this was over, his word to Ray or not. I just kept quiet. I knew better than to offer sympathy. Ray had made it clear what he thought of me and anything I had to offer.

"Yes. And when she saw me in the hotel the other night, she decided to pay me back for dumping her all those years ago. So, Glory, why don't you tell Nate what Lucky had to do to turn me vampire?" And with that Ray sat again.

Well, nothing like dropping the ball firmly in my court. I cleared my throat. Actually I guess Ray really didn't know what Lucky had done to him.

"Okay. Here's what I guess must have happened." I hadn't had the time or the inclination to pump Lucky for details. "Lucky's a vampire, and she had another vampire with her. I figure Etienne helped her get past Ray's security in his hotel suite."

"How?" Nathan paced around the living room, stopping to pick up his BlackBerry. "Those guys are aces. They're especially careful about strange women. No way would they have let her in."

"Vampires have a special ability, Nathan. I call it the whammy. We can sort of mesmerize you, so that you're unable to move or disobey a direct order. Then we can walk right past you and you can't stop us. Afterward, we can make you forget we were ever there. Sort of like amnesia."

"I don't believe you." Nathan frowned. "You swallowed this bull, Ray?"

"Last night in the limo. We all toasted to my success, you remember that?" Ray crossed one leg over his knee and picked up my Bloodthirsty again.

"Sure, to your sellout."

"Never happened." Ray smiled sadly.

"Of course it did." Nathan nodded at Flo, then Richard. "You two can back me up. We all drank."

"Sorry, signor, no one but you drank champagne. Our kind of vampire does not do well with alcohol." Flo smiled at Ray. "I'm afraid Israel Caine is now—how do they say it?—on the wagon, permanently."

"You sure?" Nathan shook his head. "And that happened to the security guards that night?"

"I'm betting they were put under and stood there while Lucky and Etienne walked into Ray's suite." I turned to Ray. "Were you alone in that bed, Ray?"

He sat up and frowned. "No. Lindsey and Max. God. Lucky didn't kill them, did she?"

"Assuming Max is female . . ." I waited for Ray's "Hell, yes." "Well, then, before Lucky and Etienne got down to business, they apparently pushed the girls out of bed and sent them on their way with no memory of the night." I smiled at Ray. The rock-star lifestyle was apparently just as sleazy as the tabloids made it out to be.

Good for him, a little disappointing to this adoring fan.

"According to Lucky's note, killing Ray would have been 'too easy.' I'm not sure whether it was Etienne or Lucky who proceeded to rip open Ray's throat to drain him dry, but that was just step one."

Nathan gasped, Flo moaned and Ray closed his eyes. Naturally Jerry and Richard were stoic. This was standard operating procedure. For Flo too, but this was her idol we were talking about. I had to take a steadying breath myself. Horrific is horrific, and if I stopped and actually pictured the scene, the bloody sheets, etc., well . . .

"Now here's where Ray caught a break, if you can wrap your mind around this new reality as a break. Lucky could have left him for dead. In fact, he *was* dead." I stopped when Nathan sobbed. "Yeah, pretty rough, I admit. I personally would like to see Lucky Carver six feet under. Unfortunately I made the mistake of making sure *that* won't happen. She's got eternity to wreak her particular brand of havoc on the world."

Flo jumped up and ran into the kitchen. She came back with a paper towel and handed it to Nathan. He used it to wipe his eyes. "You poor man. This is horrible, isn't it?" She squeezed next to him in the chair and put her arm around him. "But, you see, there's a happy ending. Lucky obviously decided Ray should live forever. She is too new to do this herself." Flo looked at me. "I think Etienne made him vampire."

"Yeah. Lucky thought this would be a great punishment for Ray because he loves the sun so much." I swiped at my own suddenly watery eyes. "Now he'll never get to see it again except on TV or in the movies."

Nathan turned to stare at Ray. "For real?"

Ray was still processing this. Oh, I'd told him, but the reality would obviously take a while to sink in. His tan, his videos, the very fact that he owned his own island complete with yacht said it all. He was a sun worshiper. Former sun worshiper. Oh, hell. I was going to fall into a full-blown crying jag if I didn't pull it together.

"Ray?" Nathan extricated himself from Flo's grasp. "Is what this woman's saying true? You can't ever go out in the sun again?"

"Guess not." Ray's careless shrug was more like a jerk, as if he was spasming and trying not to break down. Nathan grabbed hold of him and pulled him to his feet. They just stood there, holding on to each other in a display of male affection that made Richard and Jerry look away and Flo and me tear up again. Ray and Nathan suddenly realized they had an audience and in typical macho form, stepped back and hit each other on the shoulder.

"Hey, it'll be okay. We'll figure things out. But I couldn't lie to you. Or keep doing this whammy thing to you. It wasn't fair." Ray rubbed his shoulder like Nathan had really hit him a good one.

Nathan seemed more than ready to change the subject and gestured at Valdez. "What's with the talking dog?"

"I'm a shape-shifter."

"No shit. What other things can you be? Show me."

Valdez glanced at Jerry. *"No can do. I'm under contract to Mr. Blade here. As bodyguard to Gloriana. Until I finish, I can't shift. But I'm a man just like you are, a little lighter maybe, when I'm not in dog body."*

Nathan shook his head. "This is surreal. Way more interesting than those comics we used to read."

"Vampires can shape-shift too. We'll teach Ray how to do that eventually." Flo smiled and stood to smooth out her skirt. "Maybe I'll take on that part of your training. Glory's not too keen on shifting. Makes her nervous."

"Why, Glory?" Now that Nathan had decided to believe us, he was really interested. Easy to see the intelligence that had gotten him into Harvard.

"I freak out. I turned into this really giant creature once. But it was exhausting flying around like that. When it came time to shift back, I didn't think I had the energy. And I'd hate to be stuck as something other than my female form."

"Yeah, that'd be a damn shame." Nate grinned and winked, obviously as much a bad boy in his button-down collar and Gucci suit as Ray was. "But, wait. You said Ray could learn to do that?" Nate turned to his friend, then sighed.

"Sorry, buddy. You're obviously really upset. I get it. No sun. No food. And those fangs." Nate looked at Jerry and Richard. "Don't mean to insult anybody, but they're really honkin' big things, aren't they?"

"Oh, yeah, that's not insulting the dudes, Nate. See how proud they are of them? I figure the bigger the better. It's a guy thing. Am I right?"

Jerry and Richard just grinned.

Ray frowned. "Aw, man. Mine don't seem very big. Florence? Should I be worried?"

Flo rushed to his side. "Of course not, Ray. They're perfect. And they'll get larger as you mature as a vampire." She had her hand on his arm when Richard snagged her around the waist and hauled her back to his side. "Hmm. Like my caveman here. You see his are . . . enormous." She patted his cheek, apparently pleased by his possessiveness.

Ray suddenly quit smiling. "Listen, Nate, now you see why I've got to stick around here for a while. Maybe we could rent a house. For a few months. I'm not saying move here permanently, but I've already figured out that I've got to stay near these other vampires until I learn what I need to survive. This isn't the movies. It's way more complicated than rolling out a coffin at dawn."

Nathan frowned. "Yeah, yeah, I get that. But, hell, we've got a corporation. Obligations. If I cut the band loose, they'll be hell to get back together again when we're ready for them. And I promised the label execs that we'd make that album in the next two months. We've got contracts, commitments and payrolls to meet. People who depend on us."

"There are good studios in Austin. Bring them all here. Set them up in a hotel or rent a couple of houses. But I need to be in my own place. Separate from the, uh, mortals. Because of my weird hours and stuff." Ray jumped when his cell phone rang. He picked it up from the coffee table. "It's Dad. I'm going to tell him to fly out here. I'm not sure how I'm going to tell him about this, but it's got to be done."

"Jeez, Ray, this will kill him."

Ray just waved his hand as he answered the phone. The conversation was short and basically involved telling his father to catch the next plane to Austin. I was used as a convenient excuse. Jerry frowned when he heard that, but since he'd seen me with Ray, he knew it really was all just an act. Ray had barely hung up the phone when it rang again.

"My mother this time. You know, I think she's got some kind of telepathy or a wire tap. If I talk to Dad, she always calls a few minutes later." Ray answered the phone. This conversation was held in a foreign language.

I looked at Nathan with a question in my eyes.

"Hebrew. His mom's strictly Orthodox Jew. So's his step-dad. Ever notice that Ray doesn't do concerts on Saturday nights? That's to respect his mother's beliefs. Ray's too, I guess. Ray's dad is more easygoing. I swear it's a miracle Ray's as balanced as he is considering the way his parents play tug-of-war with him. Rosh Hashanah with Mom, Hanukkah with Dad every year."

"He's a little old to be playing by their rules, isn't he?" We were whispering, but Ray had gone into the hall to talk anyway. Of course I already knew a lot of this from the tabloids and that unauthorized biography. Now Ray came back in.

"Okay, Nathan, been griping about my folks again?"

"Sure. Your no Saturday concert deal has cost both of us a ton of money over the years."

"Well if you had to listen to my mother complain about lapsed Jews, you'd make the same choice, so cool it, buddy. Besides, who flew forty-eight hours from Bangkok to sit down to Christmas dinner at his mother's table?"

"Yeah, yeah, but you've tasted her turkey and dressing." Nathan sat down hard. "Oh, man, the things you'll miss."

"I can't dwell on that stuff or I'll fall on a stake myself." Ray took a steadying breath. "I say we concentrate on the cool new stuff I can do." Ray winked at Flo and I thought she'd swoon. "Shape-shifting? Can I turn into anything I want? How does it work?"

"It's good defense, Caine, not a game we play." Richard, as usual, was Mr. Serious, but his hand was still firmly anchored around Flo's waist.

"Oh, come on, Richard. Didn't you and a group of other vampires do the bat thing over to Devil's Hole last month? A race. And who won?" Flo grinned because obviously this was a side of Richard he didn't usually advertise.

"You were in on that race? Damian told me there were a dozen vampires involved. He said some serious money changed hands and that the winning time was impressive. You set a new record." Jerry got up. "What's to drink in there, Gloriana? I don't like that Bloodthirsty you're so hooked on. I don't feel like it's doing it for me."

"There's some Fangtastic left." I didn't tell him that Will had sent me that Bloodthirsty. Jerry would just start in on a gripe about how Will needed to be saving his money to pay his debts. I frowned down at my Bloodthirsty. Not doing it? Maybe it wasn't giving me a real energy rush, but it was so delicious. It was fairly expensive, but I kept getting e-mails with money-saving coupons. I was definitely ordering more.

"You really turn into bats? Like they do in those horror movies we used to watch all the time?" Nate was practically jumping up and down. "Teach Ray to do that. I'd pay money to see that."

"I don't want to be a bat." Ray grinned at Valdez. "I want to be a black cat. A huge black cat. So big I'll scare the shit out of this bad boy."

"Good luck with that. You'll have to be too big to fit into this

apartment." Valdez sat and scratched behind his ear. *"And I could still whip your ass."*

"Wanna bet?" Ray grinned.

Flo clapped. "I have a hundred dollars that says Ray can make Valdez run out of the room first."

Oh, did I want to get in on this. But I'd already bet on one thing recently. I'd won a pair of sandals from Flo and still felt guilty. Was I on a slippery slope to getting hooked on gambling again? I started to open my mouth, then shut it. Jerry was backing Valdez. Richard and Nathan had decided the two were probably about evenly matched, but wanted to see the form Ray would take, if he could do it at all.

"Okay, Ray, since Flo doesn't think I can do it, let me try to teach you to shape-shift. As Richard said and even Jerry has told me a few hundred times, it's good defense." I smiled at my lover.

"She actually listened to me."

"Of course. I always listen when it's not issued as an order. Now, Ray, if a vampire hunter—" I saw Nathan's eyes widen. "Yes, Nathan, there are people out there who know about us and are determined to drive us into extinction." I sighed. "Anyway, if one of those hunters comes after you with a wooden stake, you'll want to escape. So you can shift into another form that flies or is small enough for you to hide quickly."

"Cool." Ray looked down at his sweater. "Do I need to undress or stay like this?"

"Get naked, of course." Flo grinned at Richard.

"No, Ray, you can stay dressed." I poked Flo. "It's weird, but you can shift, fly to Devil's Hole, shift back, and you'll still be wearing whatever you had on when you left, right down to your Gucci loafers."

"That *is* weird, especially if you start out in Nikes." Ray grinned at Flo. "Nice try, Florence. Better luck next time. Okay, what's first?"

"First get a clear picture in your mind of what you want to be. See it in your mind. I mean, *really* see it. Feel it in your body. If you want to be a giant black cat, feel the fur, your claws, stretch out your legs and arch your back." I stepped back and so did every other vampire in the room. I'd made a mistake by not having Ray move to an empty spot to start this. Of course in my small living room, an empty spot was about two feet by two feet.

We all gawked at what took shape in front of us. The chairs flipped over backward and even Valdez moved out of the way. Obviously Ray had changed his mind about what to become. Nathan ran to the kitchen, peeking around the doorway at his best friend. Jerry and Richard lounged next to the door, their admiring gazes making it clear that they'd never expected a novice to pull off such a stunning shift. Flo clapped her hands and danced around, moving some of our breakables out of the way, including the Israel Caine crystal egg on stand with the likeness of his face etched on the side that we'd ordered from the Franklin Mint. I pulled back the couch and shoved the coffee table to the wall.

"Ray, is *this* what you wanted to be?"

Twenty

Ray's answer was a roar that made the hair on the back of my neck stand on end. Claws at least four inches long reached out to lift strands of my blond hair. I forced myself to stand for it, but it wasn't easy. Brown fur drifted down to settle on the carpet.

"You're shedding all over everything. Somehow I have a feeling you and Nathan are *Star Wars* fans." I turned in time to see Valdez creep toward the hall doorway. "Where are you going, pup? This is one of the good guys."

"You sure?"

Just then there was another roar and Ray beat his chest and stomped his way toward Valdez, playing up his character. Since obviously Ray wasn't attacking *me*, my dog apparently felt like he could leave the scene and did with all speed.

"You sniveling coward! Don't you know—what's his name, Glory?" Jerry paid Flo with a hundred-dollar bill.

"Chewbacca."

"Right. Chewbacca. I say you could have taken him."

I grinned. "I think Valdez was just surprised. Now, Ray, here comes the fun part. You're going to have to shift back to yourself." I really hated this part but didn't say it out loud. Other vampires shifted all the time without my hang-ups.

Nathan still stood in the kitchen doorway, armed with a knife and fork. I wanted to make a joke, something along the lines of did he plan to chew on Chewbacca, but pity won. Poor Nathan. I'm sure he felt like he'd fallen down the rabbit hole. Maybe it would be kinder to whammy him and make him forget he'd ever seen any of this. I'd have to ask Ray about that later.

Ray obviously wasn't ready to change back. He'd followed Valdez down the hall and was making threatening gestures in my bedroom. Valdez had taken refuge behind the long skirts in my closet.

"Enough. You get that brown fur all over my velvet skirts and I'll send you the dry cleaning bill." I whacked Ray with a book, and he decided Nathan needed to see him up close and personal. He chased his friend from the kitchen, still making those unique sounds Chewbacca makes, more a loud moan than a roar, I guess. Finally Nathan locked himself in the bathroom.

"Ray, get a grip. Come here. You've got to imagine yourself back in your own body. Just like you always are. Israel Caine, rock star. Got it?"

And Ray was there again. With the magic of shapeshifting, Israel Caine was in my living room, the only remnants of Chewbacca a drift of brown fur on my area rug, couch and my dress, damn it.

Valdez emerged from the closet, hanging his head. *"Okay, I'm ashamed. I just didn't expect that. Once I'm out of this dog deal, I'm definitely expanding my repertoire."*

Jerry shook his head. "You *should* be ashamed. You'd better not cut and run like that when Glory is in real danger."

"No fair, Jerry, you know Valdez has taken arrows meant for me. He knew we were just playing." I patted his head.

"But you really should have kept him away from my velvets, Valdez. That fur!"

"*I know, Glory. Bad dog!*" Valdez shook himself. "*That stuff itches too.*"

"Not from where I was standing. That was totally cool. Maybe not everything vampire is going to be horrible." Ray looked around. "I guess I'd better go drag Nathan out of the bathroom."

"Wait. Are you sure we shouldn't just whammy him and save his sanity? This has been an awful lot for Nathan to take in tonight, Ray." I glanced at Jerry. "We probably should have put off the shape-shifting for another night."

"He'll be okay, he's strong and pretty open-minded. Obviously." Ray grinned. "Hey, he's been my manager for ten years. Vampires? What's the big deal?"

Flo and I exchanged looks. Chapter twelve in the unauthorized biography *Life on the Road*. Yes, maybe Nathan was used to some pretty off-the-wall things, but wild parties and tour bus drag races were nothing compared to shape-shifting and fangs.

"Think about it, Ray."

"Forget it. He's my best friend. He's got to know everything. But I do need to spend more time with him. I'm going back to the hotel. I'll be okay with Buster and Sam."

It was clear that Ray still didn't have a clue what dangers he faced in his new life. "Get real, Ray. Lucky's staying in that hotel too. No, you won't be okay there. You sure weren't before." I glanced at Jerry and he nodded. "Jerry and I will leave and you can visit with Nathan here."

"We're leaving too. You can have the entire apartment to yourselves." Richard silenced Flo with a look when she seemed inclined to protest.

Knowing my roommate, she'd make him pay for that macho order later. As it was, she made a big deal out of polishing the crystal egg and placing it just so on its stand in the middle of our, okay, Israel Caine shrine.

"There you go, then. Sleep in my room tomorrow. Nathan can stay in the hotel by himself or sleep in Flo's bed, but he's used to mortal hours. I'm sure he'll need to take care of some of your business then anyway. From now on you're going to be strictly asleep all day, awake all night. I'll go home with Jerry. If that's okay with you, Jerry?"

"Of course it is. But something will have to be worked out for Ray eventually. He's right that this apartment is too small. He'll want his own place. Perhaps we can find him a paranormal bodyguard. Like you have Valdez. I even have someone in mind."

"Sounds like a plan." Ray shook hands with Jerry. "Thanks. I know that picture in the tabloids had to have been aggravating, but I'm sure Glory told you there is absolutely nothing between us."

"Thank you, Ray, for clarifying that." Yes, indeed, let's put up a billboard. Israel Caine does not want Gloriana St. Clair. I just held on to Jerry's arm and smiled like I could care less what Ray thought. Ah, I'm sorry they didn't have the Oscars when I was on the stage.

Nathan had come out of the bathroom. "You know, I've been wanting to ask you about that. If Lucky Carver is the one who made you a vampire, Ray, how come Glory here seems to be taking all the responsibility for you?"

"Good question." Ray said it, but Jerry, Flo and Richard also looked interested in my answer.

"Lucky dumped him on me. Had him tossed naked in my bed in the middle of the freakin' day."

Flo sighed and Richard gave her a stern look. "What? It's romantic." Now it was Jerry's turn to look stern. "Oh, get over it. You'd both like to wake up with the present of a beautiful"—she winked at Ray—"naked woman in your bed. Admit it."

"She has a point." Richard grinned at Jerry. "You send me a blonde for Christmas, and I'll send you a brunette."

Jerry laughed and held out his hand. "Done."

"Yeah, yeah. You're both hilarious." I felt Valdez press against me. "Valdez can tell you we were both in shock. Israel Caine, now vampire." My eyes filled, and I turned to Nathan. "It's a horrible crime and Lucky had written a note *bragging* about it."

"I get that." Nathan said it, but I doubted he really and truly did. "But why'd she pick you to drop Ray on?"

"I'd turned her vampire in the first place. To save her life. And I'd made a big deal out of feeling responsible for her, wanting to mentor her, to put it in business terms." Nathan nodded.

I really didn't feel like going through the whole story again so I gave Nathan a short version. "So you see, Nathan, I unleashed Lucky on the world. She figured if I was so hot to mentor someone, here was my chance. And Israel Caine! I mean, I've always loved Ray's music, his singing. And he was naked! Helpless." I looked at him and got teary again.

Flo nodded and clutched that crystal egg to her breast again. I had a feeling she was about to burst into the chorus of "My One True Love" so I rushed on. "Jerry, quit glowering at me. It's like that thing you had for Marilyn Monroe back in the day."

"I did not." He glanced at Richard. "Well, what man didn't, I ask you." Male nods all around.

"So you see I couldn't leave Ray to fend for himself. He wouldn't have lasted past his first sunrise." I felt a hand on my shoulder. Ray stood close and, for the first time since I'd found him in my bed, I saw a genuine smile on his handsome face.

"I guess I owe you thanks, don't I?"

"Some people might say so." I wasn't about to make this easy for him.

"Gloriana is a kind-hearted person, Caine. She'd do as much for any stray." Jerry maneuvered me away from Ray toward the door. On the way he snagged my purse and my black shawl from the breakfast table in the kitchen.

"I guess we're going now." I smiled as Jerry opened the door.

"We're leaving Valdez here. He can supervise the cleanup." Jerry made it clear that this would be on Ray and his friend.

I glanced at Valdez. Since we'd been given twenty-four hours, I figured we could wait another night to leave our next blackmail payment. It wouldn't hurt to have a look around the drop zone though. "Someone needs to walk Valdez."

"No kidding. How about it, Flo?" Valdez picked up his leash and dropped it at her feet. *"What say we take a quick trip to that park across the street? You can hit the swings while I do my thing."*

"Sure, doggy. Richard, you can push me. I like to go high." Florence made a face. "No swinging when I was a little girl. We wore these stiff dresses, long and . . . Well, forget that. I never tell my age." She picked up the leash and clipped it on Valdez's collar.

Jerry looked at Richard. "I'll call you later, Richard. Lucky Carver has got to be brought under control or escorted out of the city."

Then we were out in the hall. I sighed as we passed Lacy's silent apartment and wondered how Will and his knockers were getting along.

"I paid Will's debt." Jerry had obviously read my mind.

"Jerry!" I threw my arms around him and kissed him, a long, very enthusiastic thank-you kiss. I pulled back and just stared up at him. "Why?"

"For you, Gloriana. He'll have to work it off, of course. I think a good place to start is to help with Caine, show him the ropes. You can get Ray out of your apartment, and I think Will could benefit from a change of scene. William will also have to join that Gamblers Anonymous group and attend meetings. Perhaps you could sponsor him."

My face was hot at the thought that Jerry knew so much about it. "He's got to be ready for help. You can't coerce him."

"I spoke to him after two days with his clown demons. I

think he's more than ready to change his life." Jerry frowned.
"I never understood that it's a compulsion, but seeing what
Will went through made that clear to me." He ran his hands
down my back to pull me snug against him. "I wish you'd
come to me for help when you needed it."

"It was something I had to do on my own." I leaned against
him and just rested there while I picked bits of brown fur
from my dress. Let me explain why I'd been so concerned
about Chewbacca fur flying. I'd worn a dress today that I probably shouldn't have, but when it had come into the shop last
week, I'd fallen in love.

Imagine navy blue velvet. Lacy said the color made my
eyes sparkle. It was a wrap dress. Okay, so since I'm full figured, wrap dresses aren't always successful on me. There's
more of me than there is of the wrap. It had been a close call
if I could even get it to tie at the waist. But I'd managed. So
I showed a good bit of cleavage. And a good bit of the hot
pink plunging bra I'd worn under it. I had on the matching
tap pants underneath, which made it a bit breezy in winter,
but with the vampire imperviousness to cold, I was okay
with that.

I'd had the satisfaction of walking out and watching male
eyes pop, and then every time I'd crossed my legs, there'd been
the suspense factor about what I might or might not have
on under there. Don't you love how predictable men are? I'd
also predicted this next move. Jerry reached for the side tie
that I'd triple knotted.

"Wait. If you undo that, I'm next to naked."

"Words to warm a man's heart." He grinned. "And else-
where. I've been staring at you in this dress all evening. Did
you wear it for me or him?"

"How can you ask that?" I kept my hand on his and
waited until his eyes met mine. "Ray's a fantasy man. You're
the real deal, Jerry. My lifetime lover."

Jerry kissed me again. When I came up for air of course
he untied that dress and it hit the floor.

"Now look what you've done. Flo and Richard could come out at any moment."

"And Richard could get his ass kicked for looking at my woman."

"What? Is the caveman attitude contagious?" But I couldn't mind a little of it.

"Glory, Glory, Glory. I don't think I could ever get tired of just looking at you, lass."

I grinned and tucked that compliment close to my heart. I started to kiss him, then froze. "Do you hear what I hear?" Inside my apartment, furniture scraped across the floor, then there was a noise that sounded suspiciously like a bull elephant trumpeting a challenge. When there was an answering call, I picked up my dress and tied a desperation knot.

"Those had better be the miniature variety. Come on, Jerry. Let's get out of here. If I lose my security deposit, that crew in there is paying."

"Every one of them can afford it." Jerry grabbed my hand and pulled me toward the stairs. We were laughing and were about to step into the cold night air when I stopped.

"Wait!" I could hear whispers right outside the door and eased it shut again. "Paparazzi." I wound my shawl around my hair and across the bottom of my face. "Think they'll recognize me now?" My voice was muffled.

"Let's go." Jerry tucked some of my hair under the shawl. "If they do take a picture, I'll handle it."

I shuddered to think what that meant. We stepped outside, endured the scrutiny of a few photographers who quickly lost interest, then headed down the sidewalk. As soon as we were out of earshot, I pulled the shawl away from my mouth and grinned up at Jerry.

"If they only knew what a photo op they just missed. Two vampires out for an evening."

"I'd rather not see myself on the cover of a tabloid. Let's leave that to Caine, shall we?" Jerry pulled my hand to his lips. "Let's get out of here."

"Can we take my car? I know it's not as pretty as the Mercedes, but I'm afraid the battery's going to go dead if it just sits there much longer." I pulled Jerry toward the alley. "Besides, it has an enormous cargo area. The backseat folds away and I have blankets in the back. We could have a veritable orgy in my Suburban."

"You don't have to ask me twice."

Jerry stopped at the entrance to the alley. We were always cautious back here, the scene of more than just Lucky's attack. At least the lights were working, but there was a group gathered near the back door to my shop. More paparazzi? Nope. Only my shop and Mugs and Muffins had doors into the alley. And it was Monday night. Shop closed. So there was no reason for anyone to be back here unless they had a car parked here. All I saw was my Suburban. This group had no business being back here. Jerry was putting me behind him and reaching for a knife when I heard a familiar laugh.

Lucky.

Twenty-one

"**What** on earth is *she* doing back here?"

"I'd say she's found herself some followers. Keep your eyes open, Gloriana. There are quite a few mortals here and not all of them are harmless."

"Thanks." I stepped away from Jerry to give us both room to maneuver. "Lucky, oh, and Etienne." I didn't think we had any reason to fear them, but I wasn't about to let my guard down. "What brings you to my alley? And who is this with you?" There were several black-clad Goths gazing at Lucky admiringly. Their spiky hair matched her wig. She'd opted for bright red stripes in hers. But Lucky couldn't bring herself to go for the dead white makeup and black lipstick. She'd already gotten tired of the all black wardrobe. Her only other concession to Goth was the thigh-high boots decorated with chains. She was showing off her fangs though.

"I have groupies, Glory. Don't you love it?" She waved at the five people clustered around her. "Etienne, show Glory and Blade your tattoos."

Jerry nodded at Etienne. "Tattoos?"

"I do a penance. To prove my, uh, love." Etienne rolled up his sleeve. "This is the one I'll show you. I had to get two. The other one is for Lucky's eyes only. Hurt like hell. Which made my woman very happy." Etienne glanced at Lucky.

"Payback's a bitch, isn't it, Etienne?" Lucky was sniffing one of her Goths' wrists. "Was this one the A?"

"Yes, my dear."

I checked out Etienne's bicep. " 'I heart Lucky.' Not very original, but I guess it's the thought that counts." I kept my eyes on the mortals. Glassy eyes, and there was still a joint being passed from hand to hand.

"Etienne, I want to try something more exotic this time." Lucky smiled at me. "I've had A and B from this one and that one." She pointed to a man and a woman with a long nail that had been painted a sparkling black. "Go higher in the alphabet. Is there something in a P or a Q?"

"Doesn't work that way." I inhaled and put my hand on a young man's shoulder. "This guy's high-octane because he's been drinking tequila shots along with his weed. You want to experiment, take a sip of that." I hated that she wanted to drink from mortals, but if I tried to stop her, she'd just move her action to another location. Maybe a few bad drinks would cure her of the urge. This guy's juice should give her the mother of all headaches.

"What the hell are you doing?" Jerry grabbed Lucky when she proceeded to pull the man to her and sink her teeth into his neck right there in front of everyone.

She didn't answer, just kept taking gulps until Jerry forced her to let go without ripping the poor man's throat open.

"Christ, Etienne, didn't you teach her any discretion?" Jerry looked into the victim's eyes and put him under the whammy.

"I tried. Lucky doesn't take orders." Etienne turned and began taking care of the other mortals until all of them were statues. "Now, Lucky, you can take your time, drink from whoever you wish. But you must be sure none of them panic and decide to escape and tell the police what you are doing."

"And take it somewhere a little more private." I glanced at my Suburban. "Like where you're not blocking in my car. And away from this light behind my shop." I grabbed Lucky's arm, and she wobbled. Ho. Tequila and weed. How did she like that combo?

"What di-difference does it make? They won't me-rember." Lucky leaned against my bumper, which was filthy. I had the pleasure of seeing a smudge on her leopard-print trench coat.

"But anyone could walk past. Stop and call for help. Like on their cell phone?" I know I wanted that reward, but at the moment, I almost hoped the hit man would finish her off. This was damned dangerous for all of us, but especially for me. Again, behind my freakin' shop, next to my freakin' car and, yes, I was freakin' out.

"Calm down, Gloriana. I'll take care of this." Etienne started to lead Lucky toward the shadows at the far end of the alley.

"Wait." She jerked away from Etienne. "I have to show Glory something. How I finally figured out the makeup thing." Lucky dug in her purse, another Birkin bag, this one black. Daddy must have sent her a new one. "See? I use this digital camera every time I do something. I take a pic quick." She giggled. "I mean a quick pic. Anyway, then I can see what I'm doing. It's just like using a mirror." She slung her purse over her shoulder again, staggering under the weight.

"You're just a genius, aren't you, Lucky?" Actually, it *was* pretty clever. And I'd use my own camera phone in an emergency from now on. "Now get out of my alley before I throw you out."

"I'm sorry, Glory. Sometimes I forget you saved my life. I don't want to get you in trouble." She teared up. "You ever need anything, *anything*, you come to the Carvarellis. Don't you forget it." She peered into the darkness, stumbling in her high-heeled boots. "Etienne, where the hell are you?"

He'd led the group, who had followed him like sheep, to a dark area at the end of the alley. "Coming, love bunny." He took her arm and looked back at us. "She makes me call her that." Lucky glared at him. "Which is *très bien*, of course."

I waited until they were out of sight. "Can you believe that woman and her Goth groupies?" I stomped over to the car and unlocked the door. "You'd better drive, Jerry. I might accidentally run over something or some*one*, I'm so mad."

Jerry put his hand on my shoulder and turned me to face him. "Relax. I have a little surprise for you in the hills. Would you like that?"

"A surprise?" Jerry always did know how to lift my mood. And my skirt. He unwrapped my dress so that he could see my pink bra again. He *really* liked it. It plunged so low it was hardly a bra at all. Don't you love Victoria's Secret catalogs?

"Hop in and we'll be there in fifteen minutes. Can you wait that long?"

I rubbed against him. As usual, his body reacted with enthusiasm. "Can *you*?"

"If you'll just sit there in the other seat and let me see you in nothing but those lacy things, I could enjoy the wait."

So of course I shucked the dress, threw the shawl down on the cold leather seat and played with the seat belt so it wouldn't spoil his view while he started what proved to be a reluctant engine.

"Where are we going?" I'd managed to stay quiet exactly, I glanced at the dashboard clock, seven minutes. Almost a record for me but I had a lot on my mind.

"You'll see. I hope you like it." The car lurched as we swung off the highway onto a gravel road. No, my car doesn't have four-wheel drive. I'm not exactly into off-roading. The Suburban is ages old and I'd bought it used because it was cheap and could hold a lot of stuff and pull a trailer. You know vampires have to move on every few decades when we don't show normal signs of aging. It's not as often as it used to be thanks to the excuses of miracle creams and plastic surgery.

More quiet time. I felt like I had to prove to Jerry that I could be a restful companion. Not always a chatterbox. Hey, I watch *Dr. Phil* and shows like that. I guess our relationship lasts because we've taken frequent breaks. Some of them have lasted decades.

"Any news on Lily?" You knew I couldn't just be quiet. Or smart. But this whole secret-baby thing was a big deal. Jerry was Mr. Responsibility—I was proof of that. He was bound to be hell-bent on finding out the truth about this "daughter."

"I think I may have a lead. And I'll definitely be getting our DNA tested once I find her. I'll not take Mara's word on this. Does that make you feel better?"

"It should make *you* feel better." High road. Oh, yes. Thank you whichever show I'd learned *that* one from. And I'm not such a selfish bitch that I didn't want Jerry to have a child of his own. "Where do you think she is?"

"Last news is from Europe. I hope to talk to Igor at the Winter Solstice Ball. He knows everyone over there. She may be staying with some of his many relatives."

"Good. And speaking of the ball." Oh, great, Gloriana. Jump from serious life-altering-event talk to trivia. "I mean, we might as well enjoy our last night before you take off to search for your daughter."

"You know I wouldn't leave you if I didn't have to, don't you, Gloriana?"

"Yes, yes. You *have* to go. This could be huge."

"I'm glad you understand. Now what about this ball? What do you have in mind? I suppose we have to wear costumes." Jerry took his hand off the wheel to caress my upper thigh. "If other men wouldn't be there to gawk, I'd like to see you as Eve or maybe Lady Godiva without the bother of the horse."

I shivered as his hand became bolder. "But other men *will* be there. Maybe we could do something that shows we're a couple." So we can stick it to Mara, of course. Oh, and Mother Campbell. She'd love to see that Jerry and I were bonding. Bratty Gloriana is on a roll here.

"*Star Wars.* I'd like to see you as that princess. I'll be Luke Sky-something." Jerry grinned at me.

"You are so not with it, Jerry. News bulletin. Princess Leia and Luke Skywalker were brother and sister."

"Can't do that then, can we?" Jerry's grin was anything but brotherly, and his hand had found the edge of my panties.

"I'll be the princess." I wasn't about to admit I always secretly lusted after Han Solo. What is it with women and bad boys anyway? "Forget the couple thing. There's only one costume I love seeing you wear, Jerry."

"Can't go naked, Gloriana. Try not to flash my mum more than once a century." He winked, and I hit him on the knee.

"I meant your plaid, Jerry. You know seeing you in your Campbell plaid always makes me"—I wiggled in my seat—"melt."

"Then by all means. And my mother will love it."

I made a face. "Wear it anyway. I guess we'll just have to demonstrate we're a couple in other ways."

"I can shag you on the dance floor if that will help." Jerry stopped the car and leaned over to trace the edge of my bra, then popped open the front clasp. "I'm always willing to demonstrate we're a couple, anytime, anyplace. Now out of the car." Jerry reached across me to open the door.

"Where are we?" I ignored the cold night air as I stepped out in only my tap pants. I'd kicked off my black suede pumps in the car. Then I looked out and gasped. We were on a hilltop with the most fabulous view of Austin I'd ever seen. The city lights stretched out in the distance. Below us was one of the several lakes in the Austin area. The closest house seemed miles away. In the distance I could see a bridge with cars moving across it and lights from the towers that served the city with power or satellite or whatever.

"I bought this property recently. I'm thinking of building here. What do you think?"

"A home?" He'd been renting from Damian since he'd moved here. He knew I intended to stay awhile, with my business actually close to becoming successful and all. I blocked my thoughts. That is if my freaking blackmailer didn't ruin everything for me. YouTube. And you can bet anything posted about vampires would get about a bazillion hits. The other Austin vampires wouldn't like the publicity. Damn it. I could see my cozy life in Austin blowing apart in my face. I couldn't let that happen.

"Yes, I like Austin and have several reasons to stay." He stood behind me and reached around to cup my breasts.

I leaned back against him, pushing my worries away for now. For just a moment, despite the way he held me, this was strangely nonsexual. I finally felt like we were partners. Equals. We'd shared more of our thoughts and feelings with each other recently than we had in centuries. It made me hope that we could finally have a stable relationship. I turned in his arms and pushed my hands under his sweater. He was smooth and warm and solid.

"I love this place you've picked. It has an amazingly good vibe to it." I pulled his head down to kiss him, then danced away. "There are an awful lot of rocks here. Ouch, ouch, ouch."

"Did you say there are blankets in the back of the car?"

"Yes. And I think I see a smooth spot over here with an excellent view of the city." I picked my way across a clearing, imagining a living room with windows that would have those great automatic shades that close during the day. But at night they would open and we could see the lights. Was I actually thinking about living here with Jerry? He hadn't asked, but why else bring me here? It was a long commute to my shop. Which I wasn't giving up without a fight.

I was standing on the edge of a cliff, looking down at a small creek that roamed aimlessly through a tumble of rocks when everything blurred. I grabbed for something to hold on to, but couldn't find anything. My feet slipped and I heard pebbles rattle and splash into the water below. "Jerry!"

"Gloriana?" He caught me just before I fell. "What happened? Did you step on a stone? Lose your footing?" He peered over. "God, it's a forty-foot drop."

Okay. So a vampire could probably survive that kind of fall as long as I didn't impale myself on a branch at just the wrong spot. But I can't say I wouldn't have done some serious damage, broken some bones. Vampires *do* feel pain. So I was shaking as I held on to Jerry.

"I don't know what happened. I felt dizzy. Which never happens." Jerry held me while he threw a blanket on the ground and settled me in the middle of it.

"I swear there's something off with that Bloodthirsty you've been drinking, Gloriana. I told you it's not doing it for me. If I didn't have Fangtastic or"—he looked at me apologetically—"I know you don't like to hear it, but I do drink from the occasional mortal, then I don't think I'd be strong enough to function as I should."

"The Bloodthirsty is all I've been drinking since Will sent it to me. I love the taste and it's a reputable company. Diana Marchand says Prince Igor himself owns it."

"It's put out by his company?"

"That's what she says. I guess she did research when she invited him to the Winter Solstice Ball."

"Invited him? Nay, Gloriana. I know he's coming to the ball, but Igor doesn't go anywhere unless there's a large donation made to his favorite charity. This month it's the Home for Orphaned Were-Kittens in Budapest. Diana can pretend he's just accepted her invitation and he'll go along with the charade, but it's really more of a business transaction."

"Really? I wonder where Diana got the money to pay him. I guess Damian is footing the bill." I felt another wave of dizziness and nausea. I put my head between my knees. What a pretty sight I must make, wearing nothing but hot pink tap pants and a pea green face.

"Glory, come here." Jerry dragged me to his lap. "Let me feed you." He pulled my lips to his neck. He'd shucked his sweater and jeans. Oh, well, I guess he figured I'd be so rejuvenated by feeding from him that I'd jump his bones afterward. He was probably right.

I felt the glide of my fangs and wrapped my arms around him to hold him close. My breasts scraped against his chest and the erotic pressure made me moan.

"I told ya they was vampires. Lookee there, she's a bitin' him right on the neck."

"Neck? Hell's bells, Leroy. Who cares about his neck? Look at them titties!"

"Focus, Earl. We're here to kill them vampires. Not watch porn."

"Speak fer yerself, Leroy."

Jerry reached for his jeans and the knife he had hidden there. *"Careful, Glory. I know you hear them."*

We spoke in our minds. I took a last gulp and immediately felt stronger. I licked the punctures closed and eased away from Jerry, though I hated to leave that wonderful taste and his warmth.

"How many?" I wished I could cover my "titties" but wasn't above using them as a distraction.

"I sense only two. Play along. Here comes the holy water."

Sure enough, two buckets of icy cold water hit us full force.

"Oh, the pain!" Jerry rolled away, taking his jeans with him. "I think I'm dying!"

"Oh, please. Have mercy!" I threw up my arms and

shook my titties, letting them speak for themselves. I covered my eyes, but peeked through my fingers to see the two men who'd been lurking around my shop recently. Leroy and Earl. One of them had the daughter with the Goth boyfriend. Tonight they were dressed in camouflage from caps to boot covers. And they were armed with spears they must have whittled out of canoe oars. Okay, now I was taking them seriously. I really hoped they didn't decide to throw those things.

"They didn't melt, Earl. Told you to spring for the water blessed by the Pope. You always got to pinch pennies."

"Damn it, she's *your* daughter. Why am I paying for the dang water anyway?"

I breathed easier when they laid down their spears to dig into their camo fanny packs. Suddenly I was pelted by garlic pods.

"Oh! Ow! Help me! What can I do to make you stop?" This time I grabbed my breasts and held them out like an offering. Jaws dropped, and I think Leroy and Earl forgot Blade even existed. He crept around the Suburban and moved up behind the two men.

"Now this one is your fault, Leroy. Shoulda bought the kind of garlic already peeled and crushed. Didn't you even read that book you got off the Internet?" Despite being the first to notice my titties, Earl was obviously the least susceptible of the two. He turned to pick up his spear and came face-to-face with Blade. Thank God for the whammy.

Leroy didn't notice. "This'll do it. I *did* read chapter eleven." He'd pulled out a giant electroplated gold cross and cautiously approached me. Apparently he figured if he actually touched one of those titties with it, he'd kill a vampire for sure. When he got close enough, I snatched the cross and kissed it.

"Oh, thank you, thank you, sir!" I knelt down and began to sob loudly. "You have no idea how long I've waited to be saved from that evil vampire." I sniffled and faked a grateful smile, even manufactured a tear. Applause anyone? Okay, I know I was laying it on thick, but this wasn't exactly a selective audience. Leroy had never looked north of my breasts. "Did you see what that horrible vampire made me do? Why he made me his sex slave."

Leroy's mouth hung open, but I could see his mind working. His friend Earl was a distant memory. Leroy was trying to figure out how to bring home his own sex slave without his wife finding out about it.

Jerry was laughing silently when he finally decided I'd had enough fun. He stepped in front of Leroy and whammied him into submission.

"Gloriana, you are incorrigible. It almost seems a shame to erase this man's memory."

"Oh, I have some suggestions for him." I got in Leroy's face. "Leroy, you will respect your daughter's choices. You will be a faithful and loving husband to your wife. You don't believe in vampires and you won't ever drive on Sixth Street in Austin again because it makes your stomach cramp and you have to run to the bathroom."

I glanced at Jerry, who was choking on his laughter. "Hey, he was trying to figure out how to take me home as a souvenir. The very least he deserves is a little gas."

"Don't mind me, Gloriana. Carry on." Jerry leaned against the Suburban, arms folded across his chest.

I got up in Earl's face. "Earl, you need to find a better friend than Leroy. He takes advantage of your good nature by making you chase after his daughter and her boyfriend. He owes you money for nonsense he made you order off the Internet. You're going to hound him until he pays you every dime. If you have a wife, you will tell her every day how beautiful she is. You will be faithful and true to her."

I turned to Jerry. "Now you can do all the regular stuff and send them on their way. I'm just going to sit here and look at this incredible view. Then after they drive off, we're going to have a little christening party for the house."

"House?"

"Oh, yeah. You've got to build it here." I dipped a finger into an imaginary pool and slid it between my breasts, then sat on the blanket with a sigh.

"Ah, the temperature's just perfect. Can you see the steam rising from the water? And just look at the lights in the distance. I'll always remember our first night in our hot tub with Leroy and Earl as our towel boys."

Jerry laughed. "Let's leave the boys out of this, why don't we? Don't move, Gloriana. I like this scenario very much." He walked off into the darkness to deal with Leroy and Earl. I lay back and looked at the stars. Well, what do you know? I was happy. Then I saw the stakes the men had brought but hadn't gotten around to using cast aside in the dirt. Yes, I could freak out, melt down or dwell on all the danger out there, but what was the point? By the time Jerry came back, I had a nice romantic fire going.

Twenty-two

I took one look at Jerry and knew things were going to get even more interesting. He had on a camo cap and nothing else. He'd also pulled out the old boom box I kept in the back of the Suburban and set it on a rock nearby.

"I'm going to demonstrate my complete confidence where you're concerned, Gloriana." He punched a button and I recognized the intro instantly. Israel Caine began to sing of love. Jerry held out his hand and pulled me to my feet.

"Still dizzy?"

"No more than usual around you, lover." I wrapped my arms around him as we danced to a song that always made me melt. Jerry had obviously found the CD in my car too, one of a stack I kept in there. Sharp stones bit into the soles of my feet, but I figured the pain was worth it.

Jerry slipped his hands inside my panties, caressing my bottom as he moved us to the music. I closed my eyes and put my head on his shoulder, letting the music, the man and the night carry me away to dreams of a permanent home here. Security. Something I'd never allowed myself to have before.

Why? Fear, I suppose. That Jerry would tire of me. That I'd disappoint him because some part of me had always believed his mother when she'd declared me his inferior. The song ended and a throbbing bass beat began. One of Ray's faster, hard rock hits.

"I hope you don't expect me to dance to that." Jerry smiled down at me.

"And break the spell? Turn it off." I pushed back and walked over to the blanket. On the way, I stepped out of my panties, twirling them on my fingers before I tossed them aside. "Would you check out that view?"

Jerry switched off the boom box. The sudden silence was almost startling. "Oh, yeah. I'm checking out the view. What are you doing, Gloriana?"

I looked back over my shoulder. "Hmm?"

"Strutting around naked like that. Do you want something from me?"

"Don't I *always* want something from you?" I turned and snatched the cap from his head. "Going hunting, Mister?"

He grabbed me around the waist and swung me up into his arms. "I already caught what I was looking for."

I smiled and waited for whatever he decided to do next. What happened absolutely stunned me.

"Jeremiah Campbell, what's this?" I looked down at my hand.

"Your ring. The one you lost in Las Vegas. You didn't think Valdez wouldn't tell me about it, did you?"

I couldn't look at him. Shame clogged my throat, and I kept my head down, trying to focus on the lovely ruby and diamond ring I'd had to hock during the worst of my gambling days. Back then, I'd convinced myself that I could get it back, no problem. But it *had* been a problem. And by the time I'd scraped together enough to make a payment on it, it had been sold. I'd wept bitter tears and that had been a turning point for me, the day I'd finally forced myself to walk into a Gamblers Anonymous meeting.

"I don't deserve it."

Jerry put me on my feet, then walked over to stare at the city lights. "I admit that for a long time I was so angry that I would have agreed with you."

I bit my lip. Did I dare touch him? Of course I did. He'd given me the ring back. I walked over and put my trembling hand on his back.

"I'm sorry, Jeremiah. Truly. I was sick. Out of my mind. Though there's no excuse, really. I guess I had to reach bottom before I would get the help I needed."

"Like Will has done." Jerry turned around. "When you finally felt you could trust me enough to tell me about that part of your life, I realized I wasn't angry anymore. Happy Christmas, Gloriana."

"You're a little early, Jerry." I sniffled and tried to lighten the mood before I bawled like a baby. "You'll have to wait for your gift unless you'll settle for"—I twined my arms around his neck—"a free pass." I wiggled a little. There was nothing like being skin to skin with my guy.

"Oh? And just what is this pass good for?"

"A ride on the Glory train, of course. Kind of like a Eurail Pass. You can go anywhere you want as many times as you'd like. Unlimited access." I jumped up, throwing my legs around his waist. "All aboard."

Jerry laughed and backed me toward the blanket. "I hope there are no more unscheduled stops on this trip."

I looked around and shivered. The darkness outside the clearing with its flickering firelight was pretty complete. Of course Leroy and Earl had managed to sneak up on us earlier, and they weren't exactly seasoned vampire hunters.

"Maybe we should get in the car and lock ourselves in."

"Now I've spooked you." Jerry kissed my chin, then laid

me gently on the blanket. "But you're right. We're very un-
protected here. I'll not let another interruption spoil my
first trip." He smiled down at me and my heart turned over.

"All righty then." I jumped up, grabbed my panties and
headed for the car. "Let's try out the back of the Suburban.
I'll grab the boom box if you'll put out the fire and get the
blanket."

I lay back and watched Jerry toss his clothes in the driver's seat, then close the door and lock us in. He crawled in
beside me.

"Now where were we? Ah, yes. My itinerary." He used
a fingertip to draw a path from one of my nipples down to
the valley between and up to the other nipple. "The twin
peaks of pleasure." He leaned down and followed the same
line with his tongue. "Definitely worth another look." He
pulled one into his mouth while his hand slid down my body.

"Mmm, Jerry, I think there are some special events
planned." I walked my fingers up his spine and buried my
hand in his hair. "Would you like to hear about our highlights tour?"

He finally looked up. "You think I need a guide? I've
traveled these paths before."

"If there's nothing new, why bother?" I wiggled under
him until I felt the tip of his length just where I wanted it.

"Oh, it's no bother, old girl." He eased inside, just an inch.

"I am that. Old. Ever think—" Suddenly I had Jerry's
mouth on mine, his cock deep inside me, hard and fast. Yes,
sometimes it's better just to shut up and go with the flow.
Then, when I could gather more than one thought together,
I decided I was letting Jerry distract me. I caught him by
surprise, rolling him under me.

"Now you didn't think I was going to let you take the ex-
press, did you?" I slid down him until my mouth hovered
above his cock. "Sometimes we need to revisit the familiar
to really appreciate it. Now just look at this stout fellow." I
dragged a fang down him, and Jerry moaned and arched his

back. "Hmm. I'd say that no matter how many times I've seen him, he's still . . ." I put Jerry out of his misery, pulling him deep into my mouth as he groaned my name and dug his fingers into my hair.

By the time Jerry and I had explored all our favorite scenic areas, I had a new respect for the cargo capacity of the mighty Suburban and figured I definitely needed new shocks. Jerry lay beside me, more absolutely relaxed than I'd seen him in a long time.

"I may have to go to Europe if Igor says Lily's there, Gloriana."

"Way to spoil a mood, Jerry." I sat up and studied him in the dim moonlight coming in through the back window.

"I just thought you should be prepared. I know my mother and Mara will be sure to tell you when you see them later."

"Oh, at your house." Usually staying over at Jerry's is a treat. He's got a fabulous master bath, with a Jacuzzi tub built for two, not to mention a steam shower bigger than my closet. "I guess a hotel tonight is out of the question."

"Too complicated."

"It's getting late. I guess we'd better go then." Too much to hope that the ladies had barricaded themselves in their rooms. I crawled over the seat, which led to a little slap and tickle, which would have led to more except it *was* late and we had to beat the sun home.

By the time the Suburban chugged into Jerry's driveway we had only about a half hour to make small talk with the ladies before we could climb the stairs to Jerry's bedroom. Just as well. Mara and Mag, with Randolph as their mirror, were trying on costumes in the den.

"Oh, good, Jeremiah. How do we look?" Mag paraded past us in an Elizabethan gown that could have graced court. Fortunately for traditionally minded Mag, there had been several costume drama movies out lately. Don't ask how she got the gown to Austin, Texas. The woman has her ways.

"Very elegant, Ma. Gloriana and I will keep ours as a surprise." Jerry stared at Mara. "Interesting choice, Mara."

"Do you like?" She struck a pose.

"How could I not?" Jerry grinned at me. "What do you think, Gloriana?"

"I think Mara's been reading your diary." Can you guess? Of course Mara was Marilyn Monroe right down to her beauty mark. She'd put on the blond wig and the cinched shirtwaist, which I swear she'd found at my shop, damn it. Had she pilfered or paid? You can be sure I was checking my receipts when I got a chance. Of course she'd unbuttoned the dress low enough so that cleavage spilled out like dough that had risen a bit too long. Hello, ladies.

And who was I going to be? A princess in pants! Oh, fine. But I'd just spent the evening entertaining Jerry with some of my acrobatic moves while poor frustrated Mara had been playing dress up with his mother. And now I was about to go upstairs and see if I could squeeze in another round so I could make the downstairs chandelier shake in the dining room. Ha!

Jerry strolled over to examine the beading on his mother's skirt, and Randolph jumped to the table next to me. He hissed in my ear.

"Gloriana, block your thoughts, you skanky little bitch. Want to bet Mara gets him to the altar before you do? Or would you like some advice?"

I turned to check him out. He wore a diamond collar with "Save the Kittens" spelled out in rubies.

"Nice costume, Randy. I never knew you had such a tender heart." Now he looked like a rat with bling.

"Of course, Gloriana. That's why I'm willing to help you."

Help? This was new, but I wasn't about to ignore him. "All right, Randy. Lay it on me."

"Your charm to Jeremiah has always been that you've played hard to get. Don't stop now, chickadee. Clingy women are tiresome."

"Randolph! Are you speaking to Gloriana?" Mag had noticed.

"Yes, Mother, she wanted to know if I could get her a costume." Randolph laughed, which sounded more like a meow with a vibrato. "I think she should shape-shift and come as Jeremiah's pet. Remember his lambkin, dear one?"

"Oh, yes. Jeremiah always did have a soft spot for the orphaned lambs. He raised that one by hand." Mag smiled and showed fang. "It made a tasty Twelfth Night supper."

"Come on, Gloriana. Obviously my mother is not fit for company tonight." Jerry held out his hand. "Good night, Mara."

I shuddered at thoughts of Jerry's lambkin in a stew pot. Since neither Mara nor Mag had bothered to speak to me, I didn't bother to say good night to them.

It was a miracle Jerry had turned out to be such a kind and decent man. Of course I did want to keep him interested. Maybe Randolph had a point. Men like the chase. Wait. Was I listening to *Randolph*, whose agenda was clearly Mag's agenda? But then again, Jerry had called me "old girl" in the car. He'd been steadfast for centuries, but I'd be damned if I'd let him take me for granted.

Of course that didn't mean I still didn't want to rattle that chandelier to get on Mara's last nerve, and to help Jerry forget about poor lambkin of course. A girl's got to do what a girl's got to do.

The next evening, Valdez and I nipped across the street to drop off my sack for the kidnapper, but this time the paparazzi caught me.

"Glory! Glory! Tell us about Israel Caine. Is it true you're pregnant?"

"When's the wedding?"

"Does the dog sleep with you two?"

"Give us the scoop. Is his drinking affecting Ray's performance in bed?"

I'd ignored all of them, but that last question stopped me in my tracks.

"Excuse me?" I put my hand on Valdez's head. He'd practically jerked my arm out of its socket at the notion of a threesome with Ray and me. I was just grateful he hadn't decided to speak up. I turned to face the pack of photographers.

"First, I don't discuss what goes on in my bedroom. Second, I'm not pregnant. And third, I know for a fact that Ray has quit drinking. Make that your headline." Flashes went off until all I could see were spots and dots. At least that announcement sent the group running for the nearest place to send in their photos and news.

"I hope Ray wanted that leaked to the press." Valdez watched as I slipped the bag under the trash can.

"It's good news, V."

"I guess. Better than thinking you and Ray are kinky enough to need a dog, even an exceptionally handsome one like moi, *in your bed."*

I sighed. How on earth was such a public figure going to function as a vampire? And if I ended up on YouTube, I would be under the same microscope—no, worse. People would be watching and waiting for me to do something incriminating. Like now, when I caught myself using vamp speed to get back across the street. Oh, this was stupid. I had the whammy if I needed it. And if things went the way I was afraid they would, I was going to be whammying every waking moment just to keep from being staked.

A business owner's got to keep her business going, especially during the Christmas rush. I needed to work most nights, and my blackmailer was quiet for a few days. I took a break to go with Will to his first GA meeting, and what an emotional deal that had been. Will and I both had to come clean that we have an illness. Gamblers Anonymous doesn't put up with the "I'm cured" crap.

I had my ring back from Jerry as a very concrete reminder of just how sick I'd been in Vegas too. It made it a
little easier to tell Flo not to buy me those sandals I'd won
with our bet. Of course she wouldn't listen. She was already
studying the Nordstrom's catalog that had come in the mail
just yesterday to tempt us both.

Will was having a harder time. Buster and Sam were
sports freaks and betting just seemed to be part of that
scene. As his sponsor, I urged Will to tell Nathan and Ray
about his problem. But Will was afraid it would make him
sound weak, not the macho bodyguard image they'd signed
him up for. I could see his point. Tough situation. I understood. I still hadn't told Flo either. So Will and I were on the
phone a lot.

I was staying at Jerry's, but Valdez met me in the shop
each night with an update on the Ray and company situation. Of course, Will had the code to the building, but we'd
had to give it to Nathan too since he had to go in and out
during the day. Nate had made good use of his time, and it
looked like lodgings for the crew were just about worked
out. A studio had even been booked, and the band and various technical experts were supposed to arrive right after the
holidays.

Now it was really late and Valdez and I were alone in the
shop. I was sifting through receipts looking for that shirtwaist Mara had been wearing for her Marilyn Monroe impersonation. Suddenly a credit-card receipt stopped me in my
tracks.

"Oh, my gosh! Derek sold CiCi's ermine muff last week
before he left for Paris."

*"Yeah, you didn't notice it was gone? It was locked in that glass
case with CiCi's breakables over there against the wall."*

"I guess I've been too busy to notice." I rarely got into
that case. Jerry's mother had been about the only customer
with the kind of taste and cash to appreciate CiCi's high-end
collectibles. "Even my little percentage represents a nice

profit." I looked at the billing information. D. L. March. Now why did that . . . "This name is on Lucky's hot list! One of the debtors she's looking for." And I was pretty sure it was on Simon's list too. I'd pored over that one until I just about had it memorized.

"No kidding." Valdez came to look over my shoulder. *"D. L. March. Doesn't ring a bell. But I'd say this is our somebody who just came into a wad of cash. We've got us a suspect!"*

"I'm calling Derek right now. You know we all use different names. Maybe he can give us a description." I hit the speed dial on my cell phone then glanced at my watch. "Oh, great. Voice mail. It's probably already daylight in Paris. Hi, Derek, it's Glory. You sold CiCi's ermine muff last week to a D. L. March. I need to know all you've got on this person, what they looked like, if you would recognize him or her again. Even better, if they were with someone we know. I'll explain everything when I talk to you. Call me as soon as you get this message and you think we might both be awake. Love to all of you. Bye." I closed the phone. "You know, this could be a Christmas present for someone else. But they've got to be paranormal to be on Lucky's list. Oh, this is going to drive me crazy."

"Wow. A breakthrough." Valdez paced by the front door. *"Took us long enough. I was sure one of the others would beat us to the cash."*

"Us. You figuring you're in on the reward?"

"Well, sure. I'm Tonto to your Lone Ranger. Right, kemo sabe*?"*

"I'm sure you butchered that, but, yeah, I could toss a few bucks your way."

"What would you do with a million? Retire from this place?"

"I sure as hell wouldn't give it all to a freaking blackmailer. I wonder why we haven't heard anything yet?"

Valdez shrugged. *"Who knows? Maybe he was bluffing. Just be glad, and forget him. What* would *you do with a million bucks?"*

"I've got forever to plan for. It would just finally give me a nice fat emergency fund. After I bought a new car first, of course. I'm thinking a snappy new hybrid. Austin is all about living green. I love that concept."

"Yeah, especially since we plan to be on this planet a long, long, long time." Valdez settled by the door. "When I'm out of this dog body, I'd like a Corvette. Yellow. Walking on all fours for almost five years has given me a real craving for some four-wheeled speed. I know it's not necessarily energy efficient, but it's a guy thing."

I grinned and shook my head. "I have to admit, you've stuck to that contract. Must be a big bonus at the end for you to be so determined not to shape-shift before then."

"Yep. Enough that I can open my own casino." He glanced at me. "Well, maybe I've changed my views on that since seeing what that kind of business can do to people like you and Will. Now I'm thinking a restaurant. Or even a hotel. Yeah, I'd like to own a hotel for freaks like us. Look what happened to Ray when he happened to stay where a vampire was hanging out. Bad news."

"Good idea, puppy. Just the other night Jerry and I would have loved a place to stay instead of going home to Mom, Mara and Randolph." I made a face. "You can imagine."

Valdez shook himself. "Yeah, thanks for leaving me at the apartment. But you'd better be prepared to come back home. Ray's probably coming by tonight to turn in his keys. Maybe you'll get to meet his dad."

"Did Ray tell his father the truth? About being vampire?" I was now busy stitching a Princess Leia costume out of harem pants and a sequined halter top. You didn't think I was going to go as Frumpy Leia, did you?

"Yeah." Valdez yawned and stretched. "That's why I'm so tired. The man took it really hard. I was up practically all day, listening to him carrying on about it."

"Well, yeah, it would be a major melt-down moment. Ray's his only child." Thank you, unauthorized biography. "How'd Ray do it?"

"It was rough. I don't know about you, but my dad never gave a damn about me. Shifters, we're not like were-wolves or the cats. It's *like you procreate and forget about it."* Valdez chuffed. *"Sometimes we make mortals, sometimes not. Basically we're freaks of nature."*

I rubbed his ears. "I'm sorry, puppy." I hadn't had such great parental units myself, but not as bad as that.

"Hey, how'd I get off on that shit? Anyway, Ray's dad . . . He's something else. I never saw a man so heartbroken. The two of them sat and talked for a long time. Then Des, that's his dad's name, Desmond. Des gets on the Internet, wonders if there's a cure, like that." Valdez chuckled. *"Got to like the guy. Once he got past the first shock and denial, he was all over the security thing. Really concerned about the daylight. Really happy Ray had quit drinking too. Tabloids ran with that one."*

"Which just shows what a problem Ray had." I hadn't seen him since my confrontation with the paparazzi. Of course I'd picked up copies of the papers after that. No unflattering pictures of me. Instead they'd run old photos of Ray obviously under the influence, with headlines like "Caine Drying Out" and "Rehab or We're Done Says New Caine Cutie." I liked that Cutie label, but Ray was shown slumped in the back of a limo, stoned out of his mind.

"Yeah, more than once I caught his dad just sitting by Ray's bed while he slept, staring at him. You have no idea how you guys look during the day. Dead. It's pretty freaky."

I wiped my eyes. "Wow. You have to feel sorry for the family. I wonder if Ray will tell his mother."

"I don't think so. Ray and his dad seem convinced she couldn't handle it." Valdez lifted his head. *"We've got company."*

The bells on the front door tinkled.

"Glory." Brittany smiled tentatively. "Rafe." She looked around and even sniffed the air.

"Hi, Brittany. I hope this doesn't mean Lucky is on the way. She's not welcome here." I glanced at Valdez. I hadn't told him about Lucky's drink-a-thon in our alley.

"Hey, Beth." Valdez stood and walked closer to her. *"Are you okay?"*

"No, I'm not okay. I don't know where Lucky is and I don't care. I quit." Brittany glanced at the chair next to the counter. "Can I sit down?"

"Sure. You quit the Carvarellis?" I pulled out the stool we kept behind the counter and sat. Cute boots are not good work boots. "What happened?"

"I couldn't take it anymore. Lucky's always been a grade-A bitch, but becoming a vampire just made her worse. Now she's got Etienne to protect her in bed and out. I just got in the way."

"What do you think about Etienne?" I glanced at Valdez.

"I don't trust him, but then what do I know?" Brittany's eyes sparkled with unshed tears. "I think Mr. Carvarelli's still suspicious of me. He wants me to go back to work as a clown demon." She turned to Valdez. "I can't do it, Rafe. You remember what that's like. 'Knock knock' until you want to kill yourself or your poor victim. I'll starve first."

Valdez growled. *"You won't have to starve, baby."* He showed some teeth. *"Damn me if I ever sign another contract. Glory, help me out here. Can't you find Beth something?"*

"Brittany, Rafe. All my ID says I'm Brittany Raines now." She smiled at me. "I know I screwed up that night here in the shop, but I'm a fast learner, Glory. If you still need help . . ."

"Brittany, I think—"

The bells over the door tinkled again. Will, Ray and an older silver-haired version of Ray walked in.

"Glory, I want you to meet my father." Ray was his usual dazzling self in snug denim and a leather blazer. He led the older man toward me.

I jumped up from my stool and held out my hand but was enveloped in a warm bear hug that would have knocked the breath out of me if I'd been a mortal female.

"Gloriana St. Clair. How can I ever thank you for all you've done for my boy, Ray?" Desmond Caine held me away from him and smiled, his eyes wet. "Oh, but you're a pretty one.

Too bad you're already taken or I'd make a run at you myself."

"Let her go, Dad." Ray grinned and shook his head.
"Dad's not kidding." He looked down when Valdez bumped
his leg. "What's up, Valdez?"

*"Meet Brittany Raines. She's a shape-shifter and one of the best
bodyguards in the business. I think she's just who you need for daytime duty, Ray."* He looked at Ray's father. *"Des, Brittany is
perfect for backup during the day now that you're moving out. She
can sniff out predators while Will's asleep."*

"I'll never get used to a talking dog." Des smiled at Brittany. "But another pretty lady. What's not to like? Are you
vouching for her then, Valdez?" This was obviously a man
who let nothing slip past him.

"Yes, sir."

Will eased into the circle and put his arm around me.
"Isn't this the bodyguard who disappeared when Lucky Carvarelli was attacked?"

Valdez sent him a look that should have flattened Will. I
stepped between them. All eyes were now on me. Brittany's
were begging me to help her. In my gut, I didn't think she
could have conspired to kill Lucky. Now that I knew her ex-
boss, I figured Brittany would never have left the scene without making damned sure Lucky had truly breathed her last.

"It was one mistake, Will. You ever make one?" I looked
him in the eye, then turned to Ray and Des. "I'm convinced
a vampire whammied her then attacked Lucky. That's why
you need two paranormal guards you can trust. Daytime,
you'll usually be locked up in your house with electronic security and Buster and Sam. But none of that will stop a
paranormal. Brittany will sense that kind of threat, wake up
and deal with it. Like Valdez can do for me."

"Exactly. She does get it." Valdez was very pleased with
me. *"Brittany, show Ray and Des your golden retriever."*

"Rafe, I mean Valdez, I'd like to save the shape-shifting

for emergencies." Brittany smiled at Ray. "Love your music, Mr. Caine. It would be an honor to work for you." She turned her baby blues on his father. "His safety would be my number one priority twenty-four seven."

I smiled at Brittany. "There you go, Ray. Can't ask for more than that. When you're out at night, you should always have a paranormal tag team watching your back."

"Sounds right, son." Des hadn't taken his eyes off Brittany. I didn't blame him. The blond commando Barbie was pretty mesmerizing in black jeans and a leather jacket. And he hadn't even seen her kick butt yet.

"Yep, Will and Brit for the paranormal threats, and Buster and Sam get panty patrol." I grinned.

"Can we switch?" Will said, and everyone laughed. The doorbells tinkled and two women pushed inside.

"Oh, my God! Israel Caine! I told you, Lisa! And there's that blueberry he's been dating! *The Nosy News* said she owns this shop. Quick, take a picture!"

Ray grinned and slung an arm around me. "Ladies, please. Glory and I are just friends. How'd you like a picture with *me*? My bodyguard will take it for us."

"Oh, my God! Oh, my God!" The two women were hopping around like bunnies at Easter.

Will took the camera phone and had a good time posing them all in front of the mural. Then he led them over to the T-shirts.

"Buy something and I bet I can talk Ray into autographing it for you."

Squeals of joy. Ray just grinned and gestured for me to follow him to the back room.

"I haven't seen much of you lately."

"No, you've been busy; I've been busy." Actually, I'd only gone up to change clothes, then run down here. We weren't exactly avoiding each other, but Will had assured me that he was being careful to teach Ray what he needed to know

about being a good vampire. One thing he'd done was order
a different brand of synthetic. We'd decided there was definitely something lacking in the Bloodthirsty. I was drinking Fangtastic at Blade's.

"I'm packed and we're moving into our new place tonight. You can have your apartment back."

"Great." I looked away from his eyes, so blue, so intense.
"I mean, that was fast."

"Yeah, Nathan knows how to get a job done. He leased
a fantastic house on top of a cliff on Lake Travis, fully fur-
nished. He arranged the blackout drapes for the master bedroom today. It even has a boat dock with an elevator that
goes from the house down to the water. I figure I can still
enjoy the water at night."

"Yeah, sure." I hated the wistful look in his eyes. He had
a lot of adjusting to do that I had never experienced. Out-
door sports in the 1600s? Walking to the privy and back in
winter.

"You still going to stay at Blade's?"

"No, I like having my own place. And his mother's there.
Until after the ball."

"Oh, yeah. I'm going to that winter solstice thing. Nathan
and Dad too."

"You're kidding." Hard to imagine. But I guess Ray
might as well start mixing and mingling with the local
vampire crowd.

"Damian, Flo's brother, invited us." Ray shook his head.
"What a character he is."

"Yep. I think he has a panty collection to rival yours."

Ray laughed. "I don't keep them. Well, not all of them,
just the really unusual. You ever want a pair made out of
beer bottle caps, call me."

"Ouch. Maybe you can open a panty museum some day,
one of those 'believe it or not' things."

"My whole life's turned into a believe it or not thing.
Damian says this party's a benefit for orphaned were-kittens?"

"Yes, Ray, isn't that sad?" I knew Ray was waiting for an explanation of were-kittens, but it was fun to make him wonder.

"I don't know what the hell they are, but orphaned anything is sad. So I told Damian I'd sing and help raise some money. I've written a new song." Ray glanced out at the two women who'd been joined by three more. "Oops, I think I'd better sign some things and get out of here before you have a riot on your hands at four in the morning."

"That's nice, Ray."

"What? That I'm sparing you a riot?"

"That you care about orphans."

"Well, sure. I had two loving parents." He watched Des putting the moves on Brittany. "Sometimes too loving. But I've always had the security of knowing I've got a home to go to. Two homes. I'll see you at the ball. I want you to hear my new song, Glory. I wrote it for you."

And then he just walked over to those giggling fans and signed T-shirts and skirts, refused to sign bras and breasts, and left. Leaving me hanging. A song for me. Israel Caine. Oh.

Twenty-three

"Glory, I thought you'd never get here!" Lacy met me at the shop door. She held it open and practically shoved Valdez inside.

"I'm only five minutes late." Okay, closer to ten, but to give Lucky credit, the camera thing for checking makeup is genius. I'd spent some time with my camera phone trying out an eye-shadow technique I'd seen on the Home Shopping Network. I'd also left another message for Derek and one for Greg. I needed help if I had even a whiff at the reward for finding Lucky's attacker. If just one of them could describe D. L. March for me, I might actually have a chance at figuring out who had hired the hit on Lucky. Then I had checked my computer and YouTube.

A quick search for vampires had taken me straight to my video. Yep, there I was. Fangs out, kneeling over Lucky. And the hits! Forty-eight thousand and climbing. I was a regular media star. Thank God I'd had a brainstorm about how to handle the fallout.

"Sorry, Lacy. Have you been swamped? By weirdos looking

for a vampire?" I tensed while I waited for her answer. The video had been handily tagged with the name of my shop and the address. My blackmailer obviously played hardball. There were a few customers in the place, but none of them rushed up to me, begging to see my choppers.

"No. But that guy came back. The one who was asking questions about you before. The first one. I was right. He was from Mr. Carvarelli. He gave me a wad of cash to stay late so you could take a meeting with Mr. C." Lacy looked out the front window. "They'll be back any minute. They came in a huge black stretch limo."

"Lacy, calm down." I felt as jumpy as she looked. Lucky's father here. A mob boss who had the power to make me rich or put a stake through my heart. There were four customers in the shop in various stages of decision making. One was actually on her way to the register. I gestured to Valdez to follow me to the back room and closed the door.

"You know he's not going to let me get into the limo with you, don't you?" I collapsed in a chair.

"*Then don't go, Blondie. You can bet he's going to have his bodyguards with him.*"

"No, I'll make that a condition. We meet one-on-one."

"*Like he'll let you set terms.*"

"I saved his precious daughter's life. He's grateful."

"*Now that we know his precious daughter, maybe he wishes we'd let her bleed out.*" Valdez paced restlessly. "*I don't like it. You should call Blade. You think Carvarelli's people found out who attacked Lucky?*"

"That would be a good thing." Even if it cost me money. Let the Carvarellis handle their own enemies. I pulled my cell phone out of my purse and stuck the purse in a drawer. No text from my blackmailer. I thought he might have wanted a farewell swipe at me. No message from Derek either. Too bad. If I could deliver a name to Lucky's father that might actually pan out, then maybe he'd hand me a check.

There was a voice mail from Jerry confirming what time

he'd pick me up for the ball tomorrow night. He was meeting with the architect about the new house tonight. That message made me smile. A few naughty words about our hot tub on the hilltop. Yeah, I'm easily distracted. I snapped the cell phone shut and slipped it into my pocket.

"*You gonna call him back?*" Of course Valdez had listened in.

"No, I'll handle this meeting. But don't do anything crazy, Valdez. I've got a shop full of customers. And I noticed Mugs and Muffins is busy too. Remember, you're just a dog. Nothing extra as far as they're concerned." I threw open the door.

"Woof." Valdez almost knocked me over on his way to the front door.

"Glory, this is, um, Mr., well, he wants to talk to you." Lacy was in the middle of writing out a sales receipt and gestured at a tall man in a neat black business suit.

He didn't look like a gangster. She'd described him before as a fairly harmless type. But she must not have stared into his cool gray eyes. They weren't missing a single detail as they scraped over me. I suddenly wanted to run back upstairs and wipe off some of that taupe eye shadow I'd gone so nuts over.

"I'm Glory St. Clair." I smiled but didn't offer my hand. Instead, I scanned the shop to make sure a customer didn't need me. I wanted this guy to know my priorities.

"Ms. St. Clair, Mr. Carvarelli hopes that you'll join him in the car outside for a brief discussion. If you wish, you may bring your escort." He nodded at Valdez. "And we'll not move from in front of the store."

Lacy finished her sale, then rushed back to help a woman who was trying to carry two long evening gowns into a dressing room without dragging them across the floor.

"We're kind of busy now. This really isn't a convenient time." I took a stack of vintage books from a woman and began to write up a sales receipt. "*Nancy Drew!*" I gave her a smile. "A classic."

"I'm buying them for my granddaughter. I read them all when I was a kid."

"I'm sure she'll love them."

Black Suit eased behind the counter next to me. "Mr. C. will only be in town tonight. If you wish, I'll stay here and assist your clerk." He manufactured a smile. "Not handle your money, of course." He slid the books into a bag. "But do whatever else I can. I assure you, Mr. C. will be brief. He knows your time is valuable." He handed the bag to the customer. "My daughter is eight. Maybe I should get her one of these. Not violent, are they?"

I kept a straight face while I counted out change. And tried to talk myself into getting into that car. Ridiculous. I'm a badass, blood-sucking vampire. Lucky's father was an old man who was even allowing me to bring Valdez with me. What was the worst that could happen? I found out when another black-suited man who obviously worked out more than Black Suit number one opened the limo door.

Lucky was with her father. A pouting, tear-stained, angry Lucky slouched in one corner of the leather seat and seemed to dare me to say more than hi and bye to her father.

Yes, he was old, but still had some good years left I'd say. He exuded power like some vampires exude evil. In fact he reminded me of a mortal Simon Destiny. Except Mr. Carvarelli was deeply tanned with the furrows of a man who'd spent a lot of time squinting into the sun, probably deep-sea fishing while he visited his laundered money in the Caymans. Hey, I watch *The Sopranos*.

I wouldn't want to cross Old Man Carvarelli and thanked the gods once again that I'd never heard of his loan company when I'd been deep in the throes of my addiction in Vegas.

"Miss Gloriana." He smiled. "I knew I had to meet the woman who saved my little girl's life."

"Papa—"

He held up his hand and Lucky's mouth snapped shut.

"You did a remarkable thing. Remarkable. Will you tell me how you found her that night?"

"*Glory*—"

This time I held up *my* hand.

Valdez snapped his yap. I wasn't about to be upstaged by my bodyguard, even if I did feel like I was in a bad off-Broadway production of *The Godfather*.

"I'm afraid the details would distress you, sir. But it was obvious to me that a vampire had ripped open Lucky's throat and left her for dead. When I came upon her body, she was about to breathe her last." Oh, jeez. Breathe her last? I was so far off Broadway, I was in Peoria.

"It happened right here, in the alley behind my shop." As if on cue, we all turned our heads to look at my pride and joy. Now, decorated for Christmas with colored lights and with a bustling crowd in front of it, the shop was way too cheery for it to seem possible that a grisly death scene had happened right behind it. I shuddered and turned back to face Lucky's father.

"Such a coincidence. The timing of your arrival." Mr. Carvarelli reached out and took Lucky's hand. "I have sent a large donation to the Church. A very large donation. Said many prayers. Have a whole convent in Vermont praying several times a day for you, Gloriana. It's truly a miracle that you found my daughter."

I was embarrassed at the thought of legions of nuns on their knees on my behalf, but I forged ahead. "Well, I wasn't exactly the right vampire for the job. I'd never turned anyone before. I was scared and really didn't want to make any new vampires." I narrowed my eyes on Lucky. "I don't think it's right to do that. But this, well, this was an emergency."

"So you went against your personal beliefs to save my Luciana." I saw Lucky wince and looked down. Mr. C. had dropped her hand.

"I couldn't just let her die. I got someone on my cell who told me what to do. Then I carried her upstairs and took care of her."

Mr. Carvarelli sighed. "You are a good person, Gloriana. And how does my daughter repay you? She leaves another vampire in your bed. A famous man who she felt betrayed her."

Lucky burst into a spate of Italian. That earned her a slap and a few sharp words.

Valdez and I just sat there, afraid to move.

"My daughter also thinks being a vampire is 'cool.' She has a new vampire bodyguard who is also her lover. She dresses like one of those silly people who *pretend* to drink blood and she is seen around town near your store with her followers, actually biting them where anyone can see her. Even returning to where she is almost killed. *Stupido!*" He turned to Lucky and said a few more choice words in Italian, then he mopped his flushed face with a handkerchief.

"Excuse me, Gloriana. I should not let you witness my family problems. But I say these things to let you know I am aware that all of these actions by my daughter may be causing difficulties for you. Yes?"

"Yes." I was really warming up to Mr. C., though any man who slaps a woman is bad news in my book. Obviously Lucky has reasons for the way she acts.

"I think we will find out who arranged this attack on Luciana very soon. If you are the first to give me the name, the reward is yours. But I will also grant you a boon. I will put my daughter's future in your hands." He looked at her, then at me.

"It seems Luciana likes Austin. She wishes to stay here and take the southwest region for her papa's business. But I wonder if that will suit you, Gloriana."

I gave that a full one second's thought. Lucky in Austin? No way in hell. I wouldn't look at her and threw up a block because I knew she'd be trying to send me all kinds of mental messages from promises to threats if I'd go along with her on this.

"I tell you something, Mr. C., if I may call you that." He

nodded. "Well, Mr. C., your daughter is smart and has a lot of potential. If she would listen to people with experience like her bodyguard Etienne, she might even turn out to be a vampire I could be proud to have made. But right now?" I shook my head. "You'd be doing me a huge favor if you sent her as far away from Austin as possible."

Mr. Carvarelli chuckled. "Very wise of you, my dear." He picked up my hand and kissed it, his lips cool and dry. Then he turned and pinned Lucky with a hard look when she made a noise that sounded suspiciously like a snarl. "It will be taken care of. Now, if you'd like to get out of the car, Gloriana, I know you're anxious to get back to your business." He tapped his ear, and I realized that what I'd thought was a hearing aid was actually a Bluetooth phone receiver.

"My associate tells me you have many very excited customers in your shop." He looked at Lucky again with narrowed eyes. "I wonder why they would be asking to meet the vampire."

"Papa, I don't—"

He lifted his hand, and Lucky shut her mouth again.

"Yes, well, I'd better get in there. Good-bye." Valdez and I jumped out as soon as the door opened.

"Ms. St. Clair, here are Mr. Carvarelli's private numbers." The gray-eyed man pressed a card into my hand. He surveyed the area in front of my shop, which was positively teeming with people. I pulled my coat up to cover my face. "Be careful. I'm not speaking out of turn when I say any involvement with the Carvarellis can change your fortunes." He gave me a slight smile. "Forever." The front door of the idling limo opened. "If you ever need anything, anywhere in the world, use those numbers. Mr. Carvarelli never forgets a debt. And that goes both ways."

He jumped into the limo, and it sped off. I looked at Valdez, both of us bursting to discuss the last few minutes. But we were surrounded by the early evening holiday crowd and more Goths than anything else. I steeled myself for what was to come and pushed inside. Lacy obviously needed help and Jasmine hadn't arrived yet to back us up.

The Saturday night before Christmas. With any luck, some of these curiosity seekers might actually buy something. Now that I knew Lucky was leaving town, I could really look forward to the ball tomorrow night. I gave Valdez a look and pushed inside the shop.

"Oh, my God! There she is! The vampire!"

"Ha! Ha! Is that why you're here?" I grabbed a box I'd hidden behind the counter. "You must have seen the video on YouTube."

"Yeah. Cool video. Let's see those fangs. Glory. Right?" A man held up his camera and began snapping pictures.

I refused to inhale, even though there were some pretty delicious blood types circulating near me. I opened a plastic-wrapped package, then tossed one to Lacy.

"Give me a minute." I bent down and slipped the fake fangs into my mouth. They'd been popular sellers before Halloween. I'd remembered them after we'd told Nathan about Ray being turned vampire. Lacy grinned at me, her fake fangs glinting in the light.

"How do I look, boss?"

"Great. All we need is the fake blood, and we could do another death scene right now."

"Oh, man. Told ya." One couple headed for the door just as my least favorite TV personality came in.

"Forget vampires. This is a cute shop, and I see a dress I want to try on." A woman dragged the man with the camera over to a dress rack.

"Donna Mitchell, Channel Six News. Gloriana St. Clair, are those fangs in your mouth?" The news reporter for the local TV station signaled to her cameraman to start shooting, and the camera's record light came on.

I slipped out the fakes and dropped them on the counter. "Sorry to disappoint you, Donna, but I'm just taking advantage of some guerrilla marketing to boost sales during the holidays. I assume you saw my YouTube stunt. That *is* why you're here again." I turned to Lacy. "Lacy, grab that bucket of pig's blood out of the back. We'll do a reenactment. Where would you like to shoot, Donna? In front of the mural again? We're thinking of putting in a flat screen on that wall over there. Run the video all the time; make some others. We'd love to have one of yours."

The reporter frowned and poked the fakes with a gloved fingertip. "Damn. No way am I giving this dinky shop any more free publicity. Cut, Lyle. We're out of here. There's a cat up a tree near the capitol building."

"Waste of time."

"Did that dog just say something?" Donna stopped and stared down at Valdez.

I laughed. "Been hitting the eggnog at the office party, Donna? Go chase your kitty story. Sorry to disappoint you, but the only vampire here is the one painted on the wall. Oh, and Merry Christmas."

"Whatever." The reporter stomped out of the door, pushing Goths out of her way as she went.

I tossed the fangs back in the box.

"Hey, what about that video?"

"You need another victim? Bite *me*, Glory."

There was some pushing and shoving, and Valdez moved in front of me. I winked at the crowd. "Maybe next time, fellas. For now, this is strictly a no-bite zone." I put on my shopkeeper's smile and began ringing up sales.

The night of the Winter Solstice Ball was cold and clear and perfect. I threw a black velvet cloak around my shoulders as Jerry helped me out of the Mercedes in front of Damian's castle on the hill. Leave it to Damian to find a perfect replica of a castle, though with all the modern amenities and without the drafts, in central Austin. He had an excellent security force, one of whom was parking our car while we strolled up to the well-lit terrace. Valdez trotted by our sides until we got there, when Jerry told him to stay alert but to only come if one of us called him. Obviously my dog was already on the lookout for Brittany.

Heaters were placed strategically around the open area, and guests were encouraged to keep the party circulating indoors and out. A band played next to the flagstone terrace, and several couples swayed to the music under the starlit sky.

"Very romantic." I smiled at Jerry. He'd worn his plaid as I'd suggested and looked a treat. Security had required a hurried discussion on headsets about his broadsword, but Damian's okay had allowed it in.

Jerry reached down and pulled open my cloak. "Now *this* is romantic. I admit I know next to nothing about any of those space movies, but this princess was obviously hot stuff."

I grinned and did an undulation to show off my harem outfit. "She was held prisoner in this."

"Obviously the man had designs on her body." Jerry pulled me to the dance floor, depositing my wrap on a table on the way. "Let me keep you warm, Gloriana." He fitted me to him, one hand low on my hips. "Warm enough?" He smoothly guided us across the floor.

"Perfect. Have you been taking dance lessons?"

He smiled and executed another neat little move. "I may have. Someone told me a man these days should be able to do more than shuffle his feet."

"Jeremiah Campbell!" I leaned back and looked up at him. "I told you that very thing decades ago."

"Well, perhaps I finally listened."

I wasn't going to ask. I threw up a block. Had Mara been giving him dancing lessons in his living room? I'd been so busy in the shop I hadn't seen him for three nights in a row. Oh, we'd talked on the phone, but briefly and not even naughty fun stuff, like what are you wearing.

"Why are you frowning? Am I doing it wrong?" Damn if he didn't try to dip me.

"No, Jerry, you're doing wonderfully. I'm thirsty. Knowing Damian, he's found some exotic new synthetic for us to try. And I want to find Prince Igor and give him a donation for his charity."

Jerry smiled. "Not necessary, Glory. I made a donation in both our names already."

I stopped on the edge of the dance floor. "I can afford to donate to an orphanage, Jerry. Thanks just the same."

"I didn't mean—"

"I've had a good holiday season." And my YouTube groupies had actually turned out to be big spenders once they'd gotten over their initial disappointment. "I know my pitiful little donation won't matter much, but allow me some pride, okay?" I walked over to the silver fountain in the living room and sniffed. A nice quality B negative. I filled a crystal cup and took a sip. Was I being too sensitive? I felt Jerry's warm hand on my shoulder. When would I quit thinking it necessary to dress like I had to be Miss Sex Pot and settle for warm and cozy? I smiled wryly. Yeah, yeah, I know myself. Probably never when there's a good-looking man around.

"I'm sorry, Glory. I just thought—"

I turned and put my hand on his chest. Nice warm wool plaid. And I'd suggested it.

"Forget it, Jerry. It was nice of you to add my name to *your* donation. Would you bring me my cloak? I'm feeling a little chilled." Not that I was freezing, but when you've made your own costume and you're not that great a seamstress . . . Well, let's just say I had issues with the top. I'd been smart enough to put on supersturdy straps. Those suckers could hold up watermelons. But, for the top itself, I'd underestimated when sewing the shiny gold fabric. Too many deep breaths or a little slippage and I was going to be showing nipple. 'Nuff said. I had shit for brains.

"Of course."

"Trouble in paradise?" Randolph rubbed against my leg with a purr. "I really am on your side, you know. Jeremiah is a habit, Glory. Look around. There are dozens of men here you could snag if you put your mind to it. Ah, here comes one now." He slunk off as Damian approached.

"Good evening, Glory! Love the costume. Let me guess. Was there a harem in *Troy*?" He grinned. "Or maybe Johnny Depp has taken his pirate ship to Istanbul."

"She's Princess Leia from *Star Wars*, Elvis." Jerry dropped my cloak over my shoulders. "Tell me you're not going to sing for us later."

"Sorry, but there are earplugs in the powder room. Feel free to avail yourself." Damian smiled and nodded toward the band. I noticed a chrome and white electric guitar on a stand nearby and a crew rolling out a gleaming ebony baby grand piano.

Jerry grinned. "Which way is that powder room?"

"Hush, Jerry. I can't wait. I had no idea you could sing, Damian." Though he certainly looked the part in vintage *Viva Las Vegas* style. "Cute sideburns." I took another sip of my drink. Now *this* had an energy boost.

"Thanks. My sister promised a large donation to Igor's charity if I'd do my Elvis impersonation tonight." Damian grinned. "I've been told I'm not too awful." He picked up my hand and kissed it. "Promise you'll clap for me, Glory."

"Of course. I'm sure you'll be wonderful. Where is Prince Igor? I'd like to meet him. I've heard about him and his many charities for years."

"He and Lady Campbell are holding court in the library." Damian smiled at Jerry. "Your mother and Igor are very old friends. When my sister gets here, ask them about the scandal they caused in Venice. Your father almost divorced your mother over that one."

Jerry looked startled. "I heard it was the other way around.

That Ma almost divorced Da over an incident in Prague with a certain countess after the Russian Revolution."

"Then I guess they're even." Did I really want to go within a hundred feet of Jerry's mom? And wouldn't she have a laugh over my pitiful little donation to his orphanage? "Damian, do you have a basket or something where we can drop our donations?"

"Of course, Gloriana. Right over there next to the mantel." Damian gestured at the massive marble-fronted fireplace. "And there's a nice fire. Instead of wearing your cloak, you can get warm while I talk to Blade about a certain security matter. Nothing to worry your pretty little head about, my dear."

"Now see, Jerry. This is why I needed to bring a laser gun. Then I could drop our host where he stands for being a Neanderthal throwback."

"Just pulling your chain, Glory. You should have seen your face." Damian grinned and clapped Jerry on the back. "Actually I want to find out how Blade managed to steal that prime piece of hilltop property out from under my nose last week."

I left them talking points and interest rates and wandered over to the roaring fire flanked by stone lions. Sure enough, there was a silver basket on a stand piled with a dozen or so linen envelopes. I pulled my discount-store envelope from the pocket of my cloak and tucked it with the check inside under the stack. I figured every little bit helped. The fire was so hot I couldn't bear to keep the cloak on and dropped it on a chair.

"Glory."

I turned and saw Israel. Alone.

"Where's your entourage?"

"I think I'm safe enough in Damian's living room. Brittany and Will are around here somewhere. Nathan is with our hostess, Diana, hanging on to every word that Prince Igor has to say in the library. The prince is an interesting character. Dad's hitting on a woman who's actually his age for a change and not young enough to be his daughter." Ray nodded, and I saw his father talking to a woman I recognized instantly.

"Uh, well, on the surface, you're right. That's Richard's mother. You know, Richard's Flo's boyfriend. I'd say she looks about fifty."

"There you go. And good-looking too."

She was. Richard's mom has the same silvery blond hair as her son along with a slim figure and a wealth that bought her the best of everything. She was also a vampire who'd been made during the Crusades.

"Want to learn something new? Or has Will taught you to read minds yet?"

"No, Will never let on. He's probably reading me all the time, of course. The guy never misses a trick. Fun to have around though." Ray winked. "You're not kidding? You mean I can look at you and tell what you're thinking, not just guess?" Ray's grin was all hopeful, like it would be in the kind of naughty, get-me-into-bed thoughts women usually have about the legendary Israel Caine.

"Maybe this isn't a good idea."

"Oh, no, you started this, you've got to finish it." Ray steered me to a couch where we could see the dance floor. "Tell me what to do."

"Okay. I think you should know a little about the woman your dad is so hotly pursuing out there." I nodded to where Des was dipping Sarah Mainwaring and she was laughing and pretending she didn't want to just sink her teeth into his neck right there and then.

Sarah was as slinky a Catwoman as I'd seen. Des had gone for a Zorro cape and black satin shirt he'd bought in my shop the night he'd hired Brittany to work for Ray. He'd left the shirt open to show off a nice chest. Obviously he kept a gym membership and used it.

"Catwoman's not really a cat, is she?"

"No, but she's not just a regular mortal either."

"Leave it to Dad. Okay, fill me in." Ray leaned forward. He'd shown up in Han Solo garb, complete with laser gun. Maybe he had a little latent mind-reading skill anyway.

"All right. Here's the deal with mind reading. I don't like to do it on a regular basis. I can read mortals easily. Usually it's too much information, if you know what I mean."

Ray grinned. "I figure some of the druggies I've been around don't have much going on upstairs at all."

"Exactly. Like some of my customers. 'Oh, gosh, is this lipstick too orange or too pink? Maybe I should change to the gloss. But then I'd have to change my nail polish too.' A giant yawn."

"I've dated those woman." Ray glanced at the dance floor and grimaced. "The old man would break out those moves." The band had switched to the disco era, and Des was trying out his John Travolta impersonation. Sarah was all over it but got tangled in Zorro's cape.

"He's cute and Sarah's really into him. So you'd better be ready for what I'm about to tell you." I faced him and opened my mind. "Now look into my eyes. I'm going to show you what I know about Sarah Mainwaring. Just look and try to read what you see there. It should come clear to you. Like a phone call, direct message from my brain to yours. Sometimes it comes complete with pictures, like a TV show, but usually just the sound."

I told him that Sarah was an ancient vampire who'd become one after finding out that her son, a former priest, had been turned during a Crusade to the Holy Land. That she was a devoted mother, a successful investor who supported her son while he chased and eliminated dangerous rogue vampires all over the world. That she attended church and belonged to book clubs and investment clubs and would probably drink blood from his father, but definitely wouldn't kill him. As for sex . . . Well, vampires were known for strong libidos, and if he hadn't discovered that for himself yet, too bad.

Ray took a deep breath. "Well, that was a trip. I'm glad I didn't get pictures that time." He sat back and pulled out his laser gun. "I don't know whether to wish this thing was real or not. Then there's the dilemma of who to use it on— Dad, the woman, or myself. Of course there's always Lucky, but everyone on that list but dear old dad would heal, wouldn't they?"

I patted him on the knee. "Now, Ray. Dad's a grown man, but, yeah, I think you at least need to take him aside and warn him what he's getting into."

"This mind-reading thing. Of course it goes two ways. So you can read mine. Go for it." He looked into my eyes, mind wide open.

I held up my hand, the glimpse of desire there so unexpected that it literally knocked me back in my seat. No way. Not Israel Caine. Not after the start we'd had.

"Stop. Let me tell you something about this. You can block your thoughts. Try to read my mind now." I threw up a block. Then saw Ray concentrate. He wrinkled his brow.

"Okay, this time all I'm getting is snow. Like when the cable's out."

"Exactly. That's because I'm blocking you. You can consciously do it. And if you try to read minds at this party, you'll find that most paranormals block as a matter of course. It's a privacy issue. And it's considered rude to just go around trying to read people's minds. I personally hate it when someone pokes into mine without permission." I rubbed my forehead. Blocking always gives me a headache. Sure, my friends claim it doesn't bother them, but I guess I'm the one in a thousand who never gets used to it.

"All right, how do I do that?" Ray didn't mention the blast of lust he'd sent my way a few moments ago. Which was totally a good thing.

"Put up a mental wall. Like a brick wall. Or a metal one. Anything you want that you feel is impenetrable. Then when people try to read your thoughts, their probes will just bounce off. Like a blocked e-mail does."

"Okay, see if you can read me now."

I tried and still got an image of Ray and me on black satin sheets. His thoughts or mine?

"Nothing, Ray, good job." Was that disappointment I saw on his face? I wasn't sticking around to find out. I jumped up and grabbed my cloak when I felt my top sliding down. "You'd better get outside before Sarah drags your dad into the trees to taste him. He may want a little vampire experience, but I'd hate for him to be taken by surprise."

Ray got up too but took my arm. "Wait. I want to ask you something. You've been with Blade a long time, according to Valdez."

"Yes. Off and on. Since 1604." I smiled. "Boggles the mind, doesn't it? Look around, Ray. There are vampires, weres and shifters even older than I am here tonight. It's a whole new world you've landed in. Fascinating stuff, if you decide to explore it and talk to some of these people."

"Yeah, I get it. And I plan to stick around and do just that." Ray slid his hand down my arm to grip my hand. "But in the four hundred odd years that you and Blade have been on and off, he's asked you to marry him, hasn't he?"

"Oh, sure." I felt a flush heat my cheeks. How pathetic would I be if he hadn't? "More times than I can remember."

"Why didn't you ever do it, Glory? Why didn't you ever tie the knot? Even I can see the guy's crazy about you."

Now wasn't that the burning question of this and every previous century. I managed a casual shrug that sent my cloak to the floor.

"I don't know, Ray. Sometimes the timing wasn't right. Famine, flood, pestilence. We've been through some pretty harrowing times. This century is amazing. Very different from when we started out. Certainly for women."

Ray nodded. "I get that. I'd think you would've jumped

at his protection in the early days. But you didn't. That's pretty amazing."

"Well, thank you." Now my cheeks were really hot. Maybe Damian's minions had put too many logs on that fire. "But I guess I've always been something of an independent woman. And when you're going to live forever, tying yourself to one man seems fairly shortsighted, don't you think?"

Ray grinned. "Now that sounds like a rock star talking. Live for the day. You don't strike me as a love 'em and leave 'em type."

"You never know, Ray. You never know." I bent to collect my cloak, flashing a fair amount of cleavage Ray's way before I said anything really dumb or burst into tears. What was Ray doing questioning my life choices? And why was I suddenly doing the same?

"By the way. You ever find out about were-kittens?" I flung the cloak over my shoulders.

Ray grinned. "Oh, yeah. Your neighbor, Lacy, is here. With her mother, brothers, sisters, they're all from the same . . ." He wrinkled his brow. "Seems derogatory to say *litter*."

I smiled, very glad to have changed subjects. "No, I wouldn't go there. So Sheila Lyons is here too. I'm sure this cause is close to her heart."

"Definitely. She decided to give me a private demonstration of how a woman becomes a were-cat."

I couldn't believe it. The very experienced Israel Caine actually flushed. "I guess cats *do* get naked to shape-shift."

Ray laughed. "Well, I didn't know that when I went out to Damian's side terrace with her." Ray reached out to straighten the stand-up collar on my cloak. "It's really a fascinating world I've landed in, Glory. Wouldn't have believed it, if I hadn't seen it for myself." He ran a fingertip down my cheek. "Thanks for not turning your back on me that night. I owe you my new life."

"Mr. Caine, we've got the piano ready. You want to check the setup?"

Gerry Bartlett

Ray smiled and nodded to the man who'd appeared just inside the door leading out to the terrace. "Be right there. See you later, Glory. Hope you like the song."

The song. I'd meant to ask about it. But somehow actually being in Ray's presence turned me into part blithering fan-girl every time. I watched Ray bend over the piano in his Han Solo pants, then remembered to look for Blade. He was obviously enjoying a discussion with a group of wealthy vampires. Business, no doubt. Had he even noticed me with Ray? If he had, he was *confident* where I was concerned. That was a good thing. Right?

I snagged another glass of synthetic brew and gulped it down. Surely I had better things to do than watch hunky men go about their business. Right. I'd brave the gang in the library. I wanted to meet the prince, damn it, and I wasn't letting Mag scare me away from it.

Twenty-four

"Glory, come sit here. Prince Igor was just about to tell us about his home in Transylvania." Nathan jumped up and hurried to my side. He was a to-die-for gladiator in skimpy body armor that showed off his buff bod.

"Glory. Is this then Jeremiah Campbell's friend Gloriana?" A handsome man apparently in his early thirties stood and came to greet me. He'd been sitting on a yellow damask sofa between Mag and Diana. He'd probably been glad for an excuse to escape from Mag's Elizabethan beads and Diana's *Gone With the Wind* lace hoop skirt.

I managed a credible curtsy (stage training, you know). "Your Excellency, it's a pleasure to finally meet you. I've heard so much about your wonderful charitable work." I smiled up at him. Tall, dark and obviously aristocratic down to his toes. By all accounts he was almost a thousand years old. He'd worn a traditional tux and reminded me of George Clooney about to rob a casino as he scanned my gold top. I was glad I'd hiked it up before I'd entered the room.

"Gloriana, aren't you chilled in that costume? Close your cape." Mag issued that order.

"Now, Magdalena, you know that would be a shame." Igor sat beside her again and made a point to notice her own décolleté. "I enjoy seeing a beautiful woman showing her figure to advantage."

Mag laughed. "Don't be naughty, Igor." She glanced at me. "Or exaggerate."

I deposited my cloak in a far corner of the room and decided I'd flash nipple at the world before I put it on again. I glanced around the crowd, hoping to spot the ermine muff.

"Glory, you should have left your wrap with one of the maids. We've turned a closet and a powder room by the front door into a cloak room. I plan to collect my cape when it's time for the concert." Diana rose and patted the seat beside the prince. "Come sit beside Igor. He's been telling some great stories. I have hostess duties." She winked at me. "We'll all bundle up and go outside when it's time for the show. Damian as Elvis and Israel Caine! I can't wait."

"It's a wonderful party, Diana." I clasped her hand and meant every word. Diana's had a hard life, and she was glowing with this success. I was still a little surprised that she and Damian were trying to make it as a couple again. But he did have his charm, just no inclination to be monogamous.

"It's the kind of thing I always dreamed of hosting. I put the squeeze on Damian to provide the house, but the rest is all on me." Diana pulled me toward the door. "You know my dear gentleman friend Kenneth Collins was quite wealthy when he came to an, ahem, unfortunate end not long ago. Not everyone may have approved of how Kenny got his money, but it was his to dispose of as he wished. And he wished to leave his entire fortune to me."

"Diana, I'm glad for you." Kenny had inherited his money and just passed it on. Vampire to vampire.

"Now I finally have enough money to do some of the

things I always wanted. I grew up poor in the South before the war, you know the one." Diana looked down at her Scarlett O'Hara dress. "I know this is silly, but back then I would have killed to have a plantation. Now I just put a deposit on a penthouse apartment not far from here." She grabbed my arm. "Just wait till you see it. I can shape-shift and fly right off the balcony!"

"Cool!" I patted her hand. Not so sure I wanted to hear this. Sudden windfall. Diana Marchand. Could she be . . . ? Well, this was her big night. Without more proof, I wasn't about to start asking ugly questions and spoil it. But starting tomorrow night, she was going to have to tell me if she knew anything about the Carvarellis.

"Okay, I know, you don't shift. There's an elevator, of course." Diana grinned. "Go talk to Prince Igor. It will drive Lady Campbell insane. Oh, and Mara is here somewhere. I saw her not five minutes ago." Diana looked around the large room filled with about two dozen people. "Don't worry. If I see her anywhere near Jerry, I'll put her to work counting donations."

"Thanks, Diana." Oh, God, I hoped Diana didn't have a dark side that would actually make her order a hit on someone. I was blocking my thoughts like crazy and had the headache to prove it.

"Nathan, why don't you come with me? You know how Israel likes things set up, don't you? It's almost time for the entertainment." Diana winked at me and leaned close. "I think Nathan would like to be a vampire. Not that I'll do that. No way. But a little vampire lovemaking? The man will never know what hit him."

Okay, so Diana definitely had an edginess to her. I watched Nathan charge after her.

"Nathan!"

"Yes, Glory? Hurry, Diana needs me." He looked after her longingly, already hooked and eager to be reeled in.

"Be careful around Diana. She's a vampire. If things, well, she'll want to bite you, drink from you. It's, uh . . . " I shut up. Crap. I'd almost told him how erotic it was. That would have really sent him flying to her bed. "Just be careful. Remember what happened to Ray."

"Thanks, Glory." Nathan kissed my cheek. "I'm a big boy. I can take care of myself." Then he took off, his fake sword bumping against his knees. At least Diana should be too busy to try her tricks on him until after the performance. Maybe I could get to Ray and we could kidnap Nathan and chain him somewhere until the urge to get with Diana passed. And maybe I could mind my own business.

I smiled and sat beside Igor, fended off a few discreet passes and tolerated Mag's not so subtle digs for the next half hour. Somehow this party had lost its zip.

"So you see, Gloriana, something simply must be done about these vampires who are refusing to be discreet. There's a real movement in Eastern Europe that's attracting young radicals."

"There are always a few like that in America too, Igor." He had given me permission to call him that. "But it sounds like your part of the world is in crisis." I stifled a yawn. Yes, even vampire politics can turn into a bore. And I could hear the music from the terrace calling me.

"In crisis. Very well put, my dear." Igor picked up my hand, ignoring Mag's sound of disapproval. "These renegades endanger us all, of course. Vampires such as you, working hard to make a living with your little shop and trying to stay undetected." Igor smiled. "I shudder to remember the days of vampire hunters with their torches and stakes."

"Igor, really, this is a party, is it not?" Mag rose and shook out her skirts. "I want to dance."

"Of course, my dear. I'm being a dead bore. You're right to chastise me." Igor held on to my hand and helped me to my feet. "Shall we all go out to where the band is playing? I wouldn't mind dancing myself."

I couldn't believe Mag had come to my rescue. I'd be damned if I'd smile at her though. I looked longingly to where I'd tossed my cloak. It was gone. A maid had silently collected it a half hour before. I guess I was going to have to keep an eye on my sliding and slithering top. Certainly Igor was.

We all trooped down the hall just as a maid began hitting a little gold xylophone to chime a warning that the entertainment was going to begin in ten minutes. We could hear the band before we got there. Someone had requested a Glenn Miller medley. World War II jitterbug. Obviously those immortals who'd been around back then were out on the floor working it. Including . . . Jerry and Mara.

I stood next to Mag and felt her claws sink into my arm when I started to step forward.

"Aren't they a handsome couple?" Mag turned to Igor. "Mara's been giving Jeremiah dance lessons. He's just a natural, isn't he?"

"Do you know this dance, Gloriana?" Igor smiled down at me. "I learned from the American nurses in England during the war. I had an interesting time then."

"I'll just bet you did." I took his arm, wrenching my other arm free from Mag. "I'd love to dance." Thank God for my part in a fifties revue in Vegas. Of course Mara's dress was perfect for the jitterbug, while I looked like *I Dream of Jeannie* on speed. That wasn't about to stop me though.

Igor could have taken the trophy on *Dancing With the Stars*. We soon left Blade, who, sorry, was *not* a natural on the dance floor, and Mara, who'd worn one too many petticoats, in our dust. The fact that every man in the audience was waiting to see if my top could contain my bouncing boobs obviously helped our popularity. Igor threw me over his shoulders, through his legs and finally we shimmied off into the night when I was afraid I'd tested my bra straps to the max. I hurriedly jerked up my top. Yep, the girls were showing but hopefully I'd moved fast enough to make them a blur.

We laughed and collapsed into each others arms as the band segued into a slower big band number.

"That was fun!" I took the handkerchief Igor handed me and carefully blotted my makeup. "I hope I didn't embarrass you. You're a terrific dancer! You could have given Fred Astaire lessons!"

"I did!" Igor was grinning while he led us around the back of the crowd to the silver drinks fountain in the living room. He handed me a cup of synthetic. "Drink. You look like you could use it. You were great. But if you want a few private lessons . . ."

"Thanks. You know, for a while I was hooked on your Bloodthirsty." I sipped the B negative, then sat on a chair nearby. I looked around for Jerry and saw him in deep discussion with his mother and Mara. "I hate to tell you this, but there was something wrong with it. It just didn't do it for me. Energywise." I took another sip. "This is much better. I'll have to ask Damian the brand. Sorry, Igor, but I'm switching again."

Jerry strolled up. "She's right, Igor. What's wrong with your quality control? After a week or so of your stuff, she was so weak she almost fell off a cliff." He took a cup and filled it. "This is more like it."

"This is Bloodthirsty too, Gloriana, Jeremiah." Igor ran a hand through his dark hair, looked around and gestured toward the front door. "Please. Will you come with me for a moment? Both of you?"

"What?" I looked at Jerry, but we followed Igor, who shooed a startled maid out of the small powder room that had been turned into an auxiliary cloak room and shut us inside.

I leaned against a sable stole and wished I had it in my shop to sell. It was worth big bucks.

"Okay, Igor, what's the big mystery?" Jerry didn't appreciate being wedged between a toilet and a black marble pedestal sink.

Igor shook his head. "I have done a terrible thing, a terrible thing."

"What have you done, Igor?" Jerry tried to adjust his sword and the toilet flushed.

"Obviously you know that I own the company that makes Bloodthirsty, Jeremiah." Igor was almost chest to chest with me, his hand planted in sable next to my head. "I own many companies, I support many charities. This is what I do. I'm always looking for ways to help the helpless. And I hate those who take advantage . . ." He looked away.

"The point, Igor?" Jerry wasn't bothering to be tactful. Maybe it was the fact that Igor's chest had just brushed mine that made him testy. I was okay with that.

"A man came to me. He wanted to give me a lot of money to have access to my computer records in one of my companies. And I'd just found out about those poor were-kittens! They needed so much!" Igor made eye contact with me. "So I listened to him. He wanted to know when you, Gloriana, ordered a blood substitute from me. You never had, so he sent you a coupon and made sure a friend of yours got one too." Igor sighed. "I'm sorry, Gloriana, but I had no reason to care what happened to you. Magdalena has complained about you for years. She says you are a, excuse me, slut, who wants Jeremiah's money and his status. Claims you are lower class—"

"That's enough, Igor." Jerry's face was red, his sword rattled and the toilet flushed again. "What the hell did you do?"

"This man, this Westwood—"

"Westwood, Brent Westwood?" I knew I looked as astonished as Jerry did. "He's the man who gave you money?"

"Yes, he sent the Bloodthirsty you got. I hope," Igor shuddered. "I hope it wasn't poisoned."

"No. But it could have been. Brent Westwood is a big-game hunter, Igor. He thinks vampires are a trophy. He collects fangs and has a necklace made out of them. Even MacTavish's." I looked at Jerry and saw his pain. "He's tried to take Jerry and me out more than once and has a real hate on for me because I made a fool out of him. Right here, actually. At Damian's Halloween party."

"I didn't know. Please understand, Gloriana. Mag had convinced me you were evil. A bad influence on her son. I thought I was helping a good friend."

"My mother simply refuses to see Glory as she really is." Jerry managed to take my hand. "I'm sorry, Gloriana. I'll talk to her—"

"Don't bother, Jerry. Tell us more, Igor. What else did Westwood do?"

"I don't know. You've been drinking the Bloodthirsty he sent you and nothing happened?" Igor looked sick.

I thought about it for a moment. "Nothing. Including none of the energy I need to survive. Killing me long distance wouldn't give Westwood much satisfaction. I guess he wanted me weak. He likes to hunt with a special bow and arrow. He was probably planning to come back and stalk me again. This time I wouldn't be able to fight back."

"Son of a bitch." Jerry looked like he wanted to punch Igor out. Unfortunately the close quarters didn't leave room for much more than a head butt.

"I'm sorry, so sorry." Igor thrust out his chin, like he was willing to give Jerry a shot.

"Wait. Let's think about this. How to use this information to our advantage. Jerry, when you head over to Europe to look for Lily, maybe you can launch a surprise attack." I admit I hated to see Jerry go, especially with Mara by his side, but if they could rid the world of the bastard Westwood . . .

"Igor, don't let Westwood know you're on to him yet. Okay?"

"Yes, I can help you with that, Jeremiah. I am renting this Westwood a villa near my factory in Transylvania."

"By God, Igor. Next you'll tell me you've arranged security for him."

"Well . . ."

I wedged myself between the two men when I heard a clang and a flush. Oh, great. Jerry was going for the broadsword. "Cool it, Jerry. Igor couldn't know our history with Westwood. Blame your mother. She's the one who made him think I'm the money-grubbing slut of all time."

"Now that I've met you, Gloriana, I see Magdalena is so wrong. You're charming. Not at all as she's painted you." Igor backed up until he must have been way too cozy with the door knob, and I figured Jerry had managed to show his sword. "Truth be told, I never met this man Westwood. We communicated through e-mail, phone and intermediaries."

Jerry growled. "I'll bet. Pretty tight with your own security, aren't you? You just didn't give a damn what happened to Glory."

"What's done is done, Jerry. At least now we know where Westwood is hiding out. I'm sure you'll be able to finally get to him there and take him out permanently." More sword rattling.

"And I'll help you, Jeremiah. Any way I can. Also I have to make this up to you, Gloriana." Igor looked thoughtful. "I'll send you free Bloodthirsty. Any type you want. Just not the type Westwood's been sending you. Then you'll know it's safe, full strength. I'm so sorry, Gloriana."

"Hey, that's a nice start, Igor. Thanks." I wasn't about to turn that down.

"Free synthetic is not nearly enough, Igor." Jerry obviously had a lot more to say. "You're damned lucky Glory wasn't seriously injured. You realize that if I let other vampires know what you've done, your business is finished; don't you?"

"Jeremiah, please. I'll make this right. I swear it. We'll talk. Once we're in my country, I can be a huge asset for you. Let me help you bring him down."

There was a knock on the door. Then more chimes. The lights were being turned way down in the powder room and I assumed in the rest of the house, and the music was changing outside.

"People need their wraps." Igor threw open the door, and a crowd hurried toward us, intent on getting ready for the entertainment. "I'll bring your cloak, Gloriana." Igor hurried toward the closet next door.

Jerry took my arm and escorted me outside.

"Jerry, talk to me."

"What can I say? I've let you down again, Gloriana."

"You? How could you have known any of this?"

"I'm supposed to take care of you, as your maker. And I didn't even notice that you were getting weaker until you almost fell off a damned cliff." He stopped at the edge of the terrace and held out a wrought-iron chair.

I shook my head. "Nope, I don't think I'll sit on cold iron until my cloak gets here. And no, I don't expect you to take care of me."

"But you expected to show Lucky what to do and you feel responsible for Caine. Now think about that and tell me why I shouldn't have the same kinds of feelings for you." Jerry put his arms around me as a spotlight suddenly singled out Damian in his Elvis garb.

"Good evening, ladies and gentlemen. I hope you're enjoying yourselves tonight." Loud applause and whistles. "Well, all that's over." Howls. "My sister has promised a large donation if I'll sing 'Are You Lonesome Tonight?' in my best Elvis voice. Please feel free to shift on out of here during the performance, but come back right afterward for a performance by our special guest, Israel Caine." Wild applause and meows.

"There are silver bowls placed throughout the castle, even in the bedrooms. Donations to Prince Igor of Transylvania's Home for Abandoned Were-Kittens may be made in those bowls as the spirit moves you. If you are having an especially good time"—Damian grinned and winked—"throw an extra hundred in the pot for the kitties." More meows and howls.

The music started as Damian strapped on the chrome and silver guitar. It's always been one of my favorite songs. Igor handed Jerry my velvet cloak then melted into the crowd. Jerry wrapped me in the warmth, his arms around me.

Are you lonesome tonight? I looked around the crowd. Some paranormals were in couples, some were in groups. Lacy was surrounded by what had to be her brothers and sisters, the family resemblance strong. All of them were tall, good-looking with auburn hair. Mom-cat was missing in action. I wondered if she was shape-shifting for Ray again and tried not to feel jealous. Because I didn't see Ray in the crowd. Maybe he was centering himself like he was supposed to before a performance.

Mag and Mara now flanked Igor, and there was a lot of whispering going on. That man finally turned on his heel and marched over to join another group of ladies on the far side of the terrace. Well, seems he'd tired of Mag's I hate Glory campaign. I swayed to the music as Damian really got into it. He had a good voice. Not Elvis, of course, but strong and romantic.

I looked toward the darkness surrounding us. Lonesome? I had been. Vampires usually are to some extent. Damian's castle was surrounded by an iron fence that was electrified but never turned on because he'd found out that neighborhood kids dared each other to climb it to get a closer look at the castle. So he had armed guards patrolling the grounds day and night. Which was fine if you were a rich vampire.

I blinked and could have sworn that I saw my black labradoodle and a golden retriever scamper off into the darkness. I smiled and decided I had plenty of security around me for now. Including Jerry's strong arms. Valdez deserved a break and if he'd persuaded Brittany to go canine for him he must be a hell of a lover.

Are you lonesome tonight? I snuggled up against Jerry, and he tightened his arms and kissed my neck. No, I wasn't. But then I saw a flash of white ermine in the center of the crowd. A red velvet cape covered the lace Scarlett O'Hara dress and the white ermine muff with the black tips was the perfect accessory. Diana grinned up at Nathan and whispered something in his ear that had him sliding his hand under her cape and around her waist.

So Diana Marchand was D. L. March. Not a stretch. Probably one of her many aliases. We all had them. She'd obviously hung on to an old credit card and used it at my shop. Why the hell hadn't she paid the Carvarellis? Was she really so stupid that she would hire a hit man rather than take care of an old debt and think it would all just go away?

Damn, talk about a mood killer. Jerry pulled me back into the darkness. Well, I had to go. I let him kiss me, even developed a little enthusiasm for the project. By the time Damian finished his song, I was able to put the Diana dilemma on my tomorrow night to-do list. But I finally had to push Jerry away.

"Israel's next. He wrote a song for me, Jerry. Come on." I pulled Jerry's hand out of my top and fixed my straps, then slipped my lipstick out of my cleavage and carefully traced my lips, wiped off my teeth, and I was good to go.

"Guess that's all I'm getting for now then, isn't it?"

I grinned and patted his cheek. "Patience, my man. Your time will come." I took his hand and hurried back to the terrace.

"You've got to understand. Flo and I— Wait a minute, where *is* Flo? I haven't seen her, even when Damian sang."

"I wasn't supposed to say anything." Jerry looked sheepish. "Well, here she is, finally. Let her tell you herself."

"Glory, my best friend always. I did it." Flo's eyes were sparkling, she held on to Richard like she was never letting go and she kept glancing at him and blinking madly.

"Did what? You missed Damian. He sang 'Are You Lonesome Tonight?' Said you promised a big donation to Igor's charity if he'd do it."

"Yes, yes, of course, no problem." Flo suddenly thrust her left hand under my nose. "*Mira.* Look."

I looked. She had on a platinum—because, knowing Flo, it sure wasn't merely sterling or even white gold—band set with a row of baguette diamonds. "Is that—" I couldn't say it.

"A wedding ring. Richard and me. We are married!"

"Oh, my God!" I grabbed her and hugged her so she couldn't see the absolute disbelief in my eyes. This was a woman who had never in hundreds, and I do mean hundreds, of years committed to one man. She *always* moved on. Usually after mere weeks. She'd *married* Richard?

"I am so happy."

"Richard Bartholomew Mainwaring!"

"Mother! Did you hear our news?" Richard turned, his arm around Florence. I wasn't sure who was holding up whom. "Florence and I just got back from Rome. An old friend of mine from the Vatican married us there."

"In the *church*?" Sarah Mainwaring might as well have said in hell. She'd never approved of Flo, whose history with artists and all other creative types of men was no secret. For her son the former priest to sanctify this union . . . Well, with such a crowd watching, thank God, she was speechless.

"This calls for a toast." Igor came forward with a cup and kissed Flo on the cheek. "To the happy couple."

Everyone raised glasses while Ray's dad, who didn't have a clue what was going on, tried to steer a stunned Sarah over to the punch bowl. She snarled when he tried to hand her a glass, and I was afraid that romance was over.

Damian rushed forward to clap Richard on the back and convince all and sundry that this was a match made in Heaven. "Now I forgive you for missing my performance, Florence. At least I didn't have to follow that announcement. But I'm sure our guest is up to the task." Damian, ever the showman, held up his hands.

"Ladies and gentlemen. We are very lucky tonight. No, I will not say *lucky*." He winked at me. "We are very blessed tonight to have a new vampire with us." There were a few gasps, so not everyone knew about Israel's recent conversion. "Of course, if that news goes beyond these walls, I will have to hunt down the source and kill him or her." Damian's smile was all fang and all serious. There was a nervous titter from the crowd.

"If you have never heard of Israel Caine, then you have been living in a cave somewhere. Oh, that's you, eh, Rudolph?" More relaxed laughter this time. "Ray has entertained all over the world, for kings and queens, and now for our own Prince Igor and his wonderful charity." Loud applause and meows. "Ray, I have to assure you there will be no panties thrown at you tonight. Most of the ladies here tonight don't even bother to wear them." Howls and male laughter.

"Ladies and gentlemen. The incomparable Israel Caine."

The lights went off except for a spotlight on the ebony piano. Israel sat on the bench, his white costume a dramatic counterpoint. Obviously he didn't need a microphone. Damian certainly hadn't.

"Tonight's a special night for me. I'm coming out as a vampire. This gig is new to me. I'm still learning about this world. I had no idea the Winter Solstice Ball would be such a big deal. But it makes sense. The longest night of the year. Got to love it." He played a short burst of a haunting melody.

"But I'll always be part of my old world. Tonight, in one

of those eerie coincidences that happens more often than not, is the first night of Hanukkah. It's a tradition of my beliefs that we give a gift on each of the eight nights of the celebration. So I wrote this song tonight for a special lady. Here's your first gift, Gloriana St. Clair."

Twenty-five

Ray's fingers stroked the keys of the piano, coaxing that haunting melody from it again. He built the tune until finally he began to sing. The music wound its way around me slowly, erotically until I could feel it inside, tugging at me the way Ray's songs always did. I swayed and felt the end coming, building to some kind of climax. Ray looked across the empty dance floor and our eyes met.

> Now we lie so close, so close
> That I can see forever in your eyes.
> 'Cause these will be my glory years,
> My glory years.
> My. Glory. Years.

It was so quiet I could hear the rustle of Diana's lace skirt as the last pure notes faded away. I didn't realize I was crying until Jerry handed me a handkerchief.

The applause was deafening. Meows and howls of appreciation broke the solemn notes of the song, and soon every-

one was moving forward to talk to Ray. I blotted my cheeks
and pulled myself together before anyone thought to look
my way.

"Well, that was quite a gift." Jerry took his handkerchief
and tucked it into his sporran. That's a Scotsman's purse. I
happened to know he also had our cell phones in there.

"I had no idea. I guess he really is grateful I didn't kick
him to the curb after Lucky dumped him on me." I looked
at Jerry. "I should go thank him."

Jerry put his hand on my arm. "Seems there was a hint of
something extra in that song."

"Extra?"

"Sounded like a love song to me."

"Oh, come on, Jerry. Israel Caine? He writes for the public. He was probably trying to make it commercial by taking the idea of my name and putting it to music. I thought
it was pretty clever to get in the whole night thing and mortals won't have a clue what he really means."

"Oh, yes, the man's very clever. Made mention of your
skin, he did. Like he'd been touching you."

Okay, now I was pissed. "What are you insinuating, Jerry?
That Ray and I have been up to something behind your
back?" I dropped my cloak on a chair. "Like dance lessons?
Oh, wait. That's you and Mara. And it wasn't me flashing ass
during the jitterbutt, I mean bug." I scanned the crowd.
Where was Jerry's partner in crime anyway? "Would it kill
you to wear underwear?"

Jerry crossed his arms over his chest. "A true Scotsman
doesna' bind himself under his plaid. And I'd not be
casting stones if I were you. Every man here was hoping
your straps would give way when Igor threw you over his
shoulder." He winced and dug into his sporran. "And
would you answer your phone or turn the damned thing
off? It's been vibratin' me privates every few minutes since
we got here."

I looked down at said privates. "Ooo. That can't have

been—" I gasped when he jerked me against him. "Well, maybe you didn't mind it so much."

Jerry and I locked eyes until we both grinned.

"Did I really show my ass?"

"And a fine ass it is, my love." I kissed his cheek, then flipped open my phone. Hmm. Every call was from one of my so-called partners in the reward for Lucky's killer. I'd made the mistake of giving them a deadline. Tonight actually. With Lucky sure to be headed out of town, I'd hoped to wrap up this reward thing, then never hear the name Carvarelli ever again. Unfortunately they'd all be disappointed. My story was going to be that Mr. C. had taken care of it himself and we'd been cut out of the action. I just hoped I could work things out with Diana. Obviously I was never going to have that emergency fund I'd always dreamed of.

"Glory, lass, everything all right?" Jerry rubbed my back.

"It will be." I turned off the phone. "There. No more vibrating to jiggle your joystick, big guy. Here comes Nathan." I slipped my phone into the sporran.

Nathan was grinning as he rushed up to us. "Great song, wasn't it, Glory? I think it should go on the new album. I don't know how Ray does it."

"He's brilliant." I smiled. "I should go over and thank him. Tell me about Hanukkah, Nate. How many nights does he give gifts?"

Nathan grinned. "Eight. The last night Ray gives gold. It's great being on Ray's gift list, let me tell you. Then I spring for one Christmas present in return. Not fair, but there you go."

"Jerry, you want to come with us?" I held out my hand.

"No, go ahead. My mother is waving at me. She plans to leave for Paris tomorrow, so I can spare her some time tonight." He smiled, obviously over his jealousy. "Tell Caine the song is fine."

Nathan shook his head. "More than fine. It has top ten written all over it. Wait till Ray gets it in the studio." The crowd around Ray was clamoring for an encore.

Nathan scowled. "Not sure about that, folks. Night air's not good for Ray's vocal chords."

"Ray's vocal chords will be golden forever now, Nate. But don't sing, Ray, unless you feel like it." I put my hand on his shoulder. "Thanks for the song. That was the most amazing gift I've ever received."

"You're welcome." Ray grinned at me. "I just heard my girl Flo got married. So I'll take a request. Flo, get over here and tell me a song you and the lucky groom would like me to sing. Something you two can dance to for your first dance."

"*Dio mio.*" Flo leaped across the piano. Yes, completely over it. Ray's mouth dropped open. "I'll teach you that little trick, Israel. Oh, please sing 'My One True Love.' My Ricardo and I can dance to that." She held out her hand to Richard. "*Sì*, Ricardo?"

"Whatever you want, Florence." Richard was clearly in way over his head.

Ray grinned and sat at the piano. "You sure you don't want 'Hurt me'?" He pounded out the chorus of one of his hard rock hits. The look on Richard's face was priceless. "Relax, Rich. I'll slow it down. The rest of you let the happy couple take a few spins, then feel free to join them on the dance floor." Ray winked at me. "Glory, why don't you sit here next to me. You can sing backup if you want."

"No, Ray. Trust me, you don't want me singing. But I want to hear you." I sat while Ray sang and dozens of couples swayed to one of the most romantic songs I've ever heard. I could feel Ray's body close to mine while I went over the words to that song he'd written for me in my mind. What did they mean? A love song? Ridiculous.

Then Ray nodded to a piece of paper on the piano. The

words. He'd signed the paper at the bottom. "Always yours, Ray." I folded the paper and tucked it into my bra. This was definitely going in the Israel Caine shrine right after I copied it so I could study it. But that was the future. This was now. I swayed to the music and savored the moment. Ray had just come to the end of the song when I felt a presence at my elbow.

"Oh, great. There he is, Israel Caine, with Glory by his side. Way to mentor a new vampire, Glory."

I jumped up when the piano suddenly slid away from us. Ray jumped in front of me.

"Lucky. What the hell are you doing here?" I put Ray behind *me* this time. "Stay," I hissed. "Let me handle this."

"I came to bring a donation. For the poor little werekitties." Lucky held on to Etienne. "And to say good-bye to all the wonderful people of Austin, of course."

"A donation?" Igor stepped forward. "Thank you. I am Prince Igor of Transylvania. The orphanage in Budapest is in great need of donations." He took in Lucky's costume, one of her more outrageous Goth getups. This one had a ragged hemline with a low-cut top that emphasized her abundant cleavage. Igor was obviously a boob man. He probably didn't even notice her spiky multicolored wig and overdone black eyeliner. If he did, he probably thought she'd come as a character in a slasher movie.

"Transylvania? That's in my new territory. I'm going to be my father's representative in Eastern Europe starting in the new year." Lucky gave me a fang-filled smile. "Thanks to my friend and maker, Gloriana."

"What kind of business does your father conduct? Perhaps we will be in touch." Igor was nothing if not a businessman. He led Lucky to the punch bowl and gestured to the band to start the music. A welcome diversion. Ray and I hustled out of the way, and the band broke into a medley of Ray's greatest hits.

"Loans, Prince. Are you in need of one?"

"Not at all, my dear." Igor looked around for help and gestured for Diana, who was hurrying in the opposite direction. She pretended not to see him. "Damian, will you help Miss, um . . ."

"Carver. Lucky Carver."

I decided Diana had the right idea and pursued her down the hall. I managed to catch up to her in a small study next to the library.

"Diana, can I talk to you for a minute?"

She turned and smiled. "Oh, sure, Glory. Wasn't that a fantastic surprise? I assume you didn't know what Ray was planning."

"No, not at all. A song dedicated to me. That was the most amazingly cool thing." I patted my chest. "I have a copy of the original right here." I noticed she'd already put up her cloak and muff. "Didn't I see you with the ermine muff outside?"

"Yes, I got it at your shop. I just love it. I thought it was perfect with my costume." She flushed and stepped inside the study. "Can we sit down a minute? My feet are killing me. I had to fill in at Mugs and Muffins for a few minutes before this shindig started because my help was late. Can you believe it?"

"Oh, yeah. Happens to me too." I stepped inside and shut the door. "I need to ask you some questions." I turned the lock, and Diana's eyes widened.

"What's this about?"

"D. L. March."

"Oh, my credit card? Diana Lynn March. One of my previous identities. No big deal. The card's good." She made a face and slipped off her high heels and began to rub her feet. "I admit I had some credit-card trouble a few years back. Had to take a loan out to keep my business afloat. But Kenny's money was a godsend."

"Did you spend some time out at the EV headquarters lately? For a little R & R?" I stretched, like I was tired too.

Fat chance. I was totally revved up, like I was on the verge of a major breakthrough. "I know I've said I wasn't into it, but maybe that Vampire Viagra, under the right circumstances . . ."

"Okay, okay, you've got me. I went out there." Diana giggled. "They've got whatever you want. Not only the VV, but some hot young studs who will do whatever you want to go along with it." She pulled out a lace-trimmed fan and used it on her face like a Southern belle. "I tell you, honey, I was as relaxed as you get by the time those fellas got through with me."

"Hmmm." I leaned forward. "Hate to break it to you, Di, but I happen to know that you might've done another kind of business out there. Like hire a hit man to take out Lucky Carver." I peered into her eyes and saw the answer before she had time to block her thoughts. "Damn it, Diana. Why couldn't you just pay your debts with your inheritance?"

Her eyes filled, and now a lace hanky came out of her reticule. "Do you know what it's like to be poor?" She dabbed at her eyes. "Oh, of course you do. Sorry, Glory, I'll save the sob story. Damn it, for the first time in my life I had real money of my own. Not some man to support me, not a business that barely made enough to pay expenses with a little left over for me at the end of the month if I worked twenty shifts myself." She kicked one shoe across the room. "No! I had real money. The Carvarellis didn't need my money. It would represent spit to them."

"But you borrowed it, you pay it back. That's the way it works." I knew how she felt. Unfortunately. But a hit man. That was way beyond drastic. "Come on, Diana. Wouldn't being debt free be enough for you?"

"You obviously don't get it, Glory. The interest rate is humongous. By the time I paid all I owed, I'd be right back at square one. Nothing left but my business. One bad month and I'd have to borrow again." Diana sniffed. "But then I met this guy out there. He made it clear he'd do anything for money, even take out Lucky." She grimaced. "Yeah, sounds cold saying it like that. Anyway, at the time, it seemed like the right idea. This guy would take care of Lucky, and I'd tell the Carvarellis that my payment must have been stolen when she was killed."

Yeah, this was really logical. In hell, maybe. I wouldn't let myself glance at the door I'd locked. *Really smart, Glory.* I wasn't about to let Diana see that she'd just scared the be-jesus out of me. I strolled around the room and idly picked up a nice antique letter opener that could work as a weapon in a pinch. Hey, hanging out with Blade had taught me a few tricks. I also put a chair between us.

"Listen, Di, whoever you hired screwed up. First, he didn't finish the job and second, he should have taken Lucky's purse or at least her BlackBerry because she keeps records of all her appointments and payments in that thing. Her father could have checked to see if she'd collected from you earlier that night."

"Well, you can be sure I didn't pay that screwup another cent." Diana studied me closely, but I was blocking my thoughts big-time. "What are you going to do with this information?"

"First, don't even think about killing me, Diana. I've made sure to put what I know in several safe places where it will be found if something happens to me. And you know Blade. He'd make sure you didn't live past sunrise." I actually kept a straight face through those lies. "Second, I need the name of your hit man."

"Why?" She slipped on her shoes.

"I'll tell you, but first give me his name."

"Oh, what the hell. I don't owe him discretion. He's Etienne, Lucky's bodyguard. Funny, isn't it?"

"Oh, a laugh riot. And I kind of suspected it anyway." I had. I mean, look at the timing of his appearance in my shop. "Now here's what I need for you to do. Pay back the Carvarellis. Every cent you owe them."

"No way in hell."

"Diana, it's only a matter of time before they track you down anyway. Come forward and pay before the interest doubles again. I met with Mr. C. myself last night. He's not a nice man. Don't mess with him. No more hits. Just forget penthouses and pay off your debt. Mugs and Muffins is a nice business. You had a great party. Move on before Mr. C. shows you what an efficient hit man can do."

Diana bit her lip. "And I had an incredible weekend out at the EV compound. Okay, I hate worrying about that debt. And the penthouse is not as convenient to the coffee shop as my old apartment."

I knew rationalization when I heard it, but I let it go.

"What about Etienne, Glory?"

"From now on, I own the hit. I need to have that power. Tell him that you've transferred it to me. If I need him to take Lucky out, I'll pay the freight. How much is the balance due?" When Diana told me, I blinked but didn't say a word. Obviously murder doesn't come cheap.

"So we're clear now?" I eased around the chair and moved to the door.

Diana sighed and stuck her other shoe on her foot. "Oh, yeah. I go back to being a regular vampire with a coffee shop. The high life was nice while it lasted." She grinned. "Igor was cute, but actually these high society things would end up boring after a while. Unless Israel Caine dropped in at all of them and brought his cute friend Nathan. I think I'll console myself with a little gladiator action."

I started to warn her off, then decided that would be pushing my luck. So I unlocked the door, and we headed our separate ways. I was sorry to find out a woman I'd called friend had such a dark side, but then even I think I would be willing to use Etienne if I had to.

I ended up in the living room, where Lucky was handing Igor a check. Etienne was close to her, swigging Bloodthirsty like there was no tomorrow and looking around nervously. Ray was still surrounded by adoring fans but broke away when he saw me coming.

"Glory, everything all right?" He glanced at Lucky.

"Sure, why wouldn't it be?" I walked up to Lucky. "Did you want to see me, Lucky?"

"I sure as hell did. Listen to me, Gloriana. I have this one last night in Austin, thanks to you. I'll never forgive you for telling Daddy to send me away. Do you hear me? Never." Then she turned to Ray. "And you. I know your secret. Remember that. You keep looking over your shoulder, rock star, because I could drop the fact that you're a vampire to the tabloids anytime I choose. When it will give me the most pleasure. Got it?"

I grabbed Lucky by the arm.

"Glory, let her go." Etienne played the bodyguard and tried to step between us.

I gave him a hard look and let him glimpse into my mind. I let him see that I knew he'd blown the hit and that I now *owned* him. I could turn him over to Mr. C. or pull the trigger on the hit. Either way, he needed to cooperate. He quietly moved aside.

"Etienne, rip out her throat."

"Go quietly, Luciana. Glory won't hurt you. She just needs to tell you something." Etienne turned back to the punch bowl.

Lucky struggled against me, but the older you get, the stronger you are in the vampire world. Especially if you've been drinking right. I was pretty pumped by the high-octane Bloodthirsty I'd had tonight. That and what Jerry had slipped me recently from his own personal pump station.

When Ray and Igor looked inclined to follow me, I shook my head. "I can handle this." I pulled her past Jerry. He stepped forward.

"No, Jerry, Lucky and I need to do this in private." He

seemed inclined to disagree, but obviously read my determination and just nodded. I kept going until Lucky and I were beyond the lights and surrounded by darkness. Then I got close to Lucky. She looked startled and tried to jerk away. No go.

"Do you remember who made you vampire, Lucky?" I hissed, making sure my fangs were mere inches from her face.

"Yes. You, of course."

"That gives me special powers over you. Did Etienne tell you that?"

"No, he didn't. What kind of powers?" She tried to jerk free again.

"Of course I can read your mind. And yelling will gain you nothing. The people here tonight are my friends and they don't like the things you've been doing in Austin. You've been making trouble for all of us, drawing attention to yourself and stirring up things, making people think that there might be vampires and other paranormals living in these hills."

"Well, you've made sure I won't be around to do that anymore." Lucky sobbed and tried the old go-limp trick. I just let her collapse on the grass, but still didn't release her arm.

"I'll not allow you to ruin Ray's life any more than you already have. I want you to know that I've found out who ordered the hit on you. I now own that hit." I gave her a moment to process that.

"Tell my father! He'll reward you and make sure that vampire is staked out at dawn." Lucky looked like this concept really turned her on. I stifled the urge to kick her.

"No, I *like* owning the hit. I may need to use it." I pulled her to her feet again. I needed to look into her eyes. "Because if I ever get a mental message from you that you're even *thinking* of going public with Ray's conversion to vampire, then I'll pull the trigger. The hit will happen. And, poof, Lucky Carver will be no more."

"I don't believe you. Daddy will—"

I stared into her eyes. Saw her fear and just let it simmer for a minute. "Right now you're remembering the alley where you were attacked. You were afraid that night. You knew you shouldn't have gone to an alley that late and Brittany was tired because you'd kept her up late the night before partying in New York." I smiled. "You really are a selfish bitch, aren't you? Then, while you slept on the plane, Brittany had to guard you. No wonder a vampire could whammy her and take you out."

Lucky put her free hand to her face. "You saw all those memories? I didn't . . ."

No, but Brittany had told me the story herself while Ray and Des had shopped for costumes in my store. "You're lucky that the vampire who attacked you was tired from an ordeal he'd gone through recently himself. It made his work sloppy. If he'd been in top form, we wouldn't be having this conversation."

"So even if I'm all the way over in Transylvania . . ."

"I'll know if you try to betray Ray's secret, Lucky. And I'll call in the hit." I grabbed her chin and stared into her eyes. "You'll be dead before the next sunrise. Guaranteed. Do you believe me?"

"Y-y-yes."

"Now get out of here and take Etienne with you." I released her and she fell on her butt. "And Lucky?" I stared down at her.

"W-w-what?"

"Don't even think of trying to harm me. If your maker dies, you die." I smiled into the darkness. I loved that little twist. I'd have to be sure to give Etienne a heads-up on that one.

"Well, shit." She actually tried to shoot me the finger, but her hand shook so hard it looked more like a good-bye wave.

"Thought you'd like that." I sauntered off, using my cloak like a matador's cape after taking out a bull. Olé.

I stopped next to Etienne, glad that the band was loud enough to keep a quiet conversation from being overheard. "You took that video in the alley, didn't you?"

He carefully set his cup of Bloodthirsty on a table. "What?"

"Don't play innocent with me, Etienne. You blew the hit, then hung around and took a video of me." I leaned close, gesturing to where Jerry was talking to his mother. Oh, big frowns there. "I didn't tell Jerry about this. How do you think he'd feel about the man who caused me so much grief?"

"I didn't take you for a woman who lets a man handle her problems." Etienne flashed one of his patented smiles.

I would have smacked him but didn't want to attract a crowd. As it was, Valdez noticed my body language and strolled over.

"What's going on here?"

"Seems like I've finally found our blackmailer. Your old friend was the one who blew the hit, then stuck around to take a video."

"No shit." Valdez seemed to swell before my eyes.

"Don't you dare shift and screw up your bonus. This creep is so not worth it. And I've got it all worked out. Trust me."

"I need to do this, Glory. I practically vouched for him."

"No. I forbid it. Now listen to me, Etienne. I expect to be paid back every dime of hush money with interest. And I want some nice presents from Europe. Some pretty little things I can sell in my shop."

"Yeah, right." Etienne tried to turn his back on me and walk away.

I stopped him with a vamp move that put me in front of him again. "Don't be stupid, Etienne. Jerry will be in Europe too. Transylvania. Ring a bell? I believe that's Lucky's territory. You owe me five hundred bucks, plus at least another five hundred for the aggravation you caused me. You think you're a badass vampire, but I could also drop a word in old man Carvarelli's ear too, you know."

"Listen to you. Next you'll be texting threats like a pro." Etienne moved closer, like maybe he thought his charm could work on me. Valdez growled and threw himself between us.

"*Back off, asshole.*"

I put out a hand. "Full cooperation, Etienne, or I spill the beans to anyone who might want a piece of you." I smiled.

"You've got no proof that I—"

"*Au contraire, mon ami.*" I was proud of that French touch. Proud too of the way I whipped the phone out of a special little pocket I'd sewn into my pants, and showed it to him. "I took this video earlier. Not as colorful as the one you made in the alley, but it works for me." I held the tiny phone against my breast for a minute. It wasn't mine, but one I'd borrowed from Lacy just for tonight. It had been a trick slipping it out and taking the video I needed without being caught, but I'd managed it. "And don't even think about trying to snatch it. I already sent a copy of the video to my computer at home. For insurance purposes." I opened the phone and hit play.

Yep, there was Diana confessing that she'd hired Etienne to do the hit on Lucky.

He paled and looked like he was ready to shift right out of there. Then he took a steadying breath and muttered something in French that I was sure was rude. Valdez thought so too. The two squared off and, judging by their expressions, there was some serious mental messaging going on.

I patted Etienne's cheek as Lucky walked up. "Thanks for advertising the shop on the Net, by the way. Business is booming."

Lucky grabbed his arm and jerked him toward the door. "Is that why you used my computer? To help *her*?"

"She saved your life, Lucky. I thought—" Etienne winced when Lucky tugged on him.

"I don't pay you to think. Let's get the hell out of here."
I watched them leave, then breathed a sigh of relief.

"Steve has really changed. He used to be a stand-up guy." Valdez
sat, staring at the door.

"I guess he thought he had to do those things to survive.
We've probably all done things we're not proud of when our
backs were against the wall." Don't ask. My life in Austin is
positively cushy compared to some of my earlier days. "Not
that I'm condoning anything Etienne did. He's getting off
way too easy."

"He's stuck with Lucky. That won't be easy. I sent Steve a men-
tal message that if he tries to quit her, I'll let Mr. C. know he's the
one who blew the hit." Valdez gave a doggy chuckle. *"Ah, re-*
venge is sweet."

"I can't believe my darling dog has such a dark side." I
rubbed the top of his head. "I like it. Now I think it's party
time." Since most of us can't drink alcohol, the wild aspects
came from purely high spirits, but there were plenty of those
to go around.

I dropped my cloak on a chair, grabbed Jerry from Mag's
side and spun him onto the dance floor. He could always
handle a rock song, and we ended up laughing and having a
good time. At one point I saw Mara dancing with a real stud
muffin dressed like Johnny Depp in a *Pirates* movie. When
I saw the bracelet on his wrist, I almost swallowed my tongue.
"Save the kittens" in diamonds and rubies. Randy? I didn't
dare point him out to Jerry.

The music slowed and Jerry held me close.

"Your mother's about to stroke out about something,
Blade." Ray appeared at Jerry's elbow. "I just met the lady,
but I'd say you'd do us all a favor if you'd handle the situation."

"The hell you say." Jerry eyed Ray suspiciously but he
couldn't ignore Mag's frantic wave from near the band.

"You'd better go, Jerry." I slipped out of his arms. "Maybe

Randy's made a bolt for freedom." Or a shift for something else.

Jerry plucked my cloak from a nearby chair and wrapped it around me. "Hopefully this won't take long." He gave me a proprietary kiss on the lips before he strode toward his mother.

Ray put his hand on my elbow and steered me farther off the dance floor. "I'm not sure about the song I wrote for you. Some of the words don't seem quite right." He hummed a few bars. "I think the chorus needs work."

"Oh, no. I thought it was perfect." Hmm. Now we were so far from the terrace we were near the fence line. "Ray? Where are we going?"

"Here." He stopped at a small white gazebo. A heater had been set up on one side with at least a dozen candles in sconces hung on lattice supports. Thick rugs covered the floor and the benches that lined the octagonal building.

"Are you kidding me? How did you manage this?"

"Casanova did it. But when his date fell through, he said I could take advantage." Ray pulled me up the steps.

"With *me*?" This was so not happening. It was like a fantasy come true, except . . . Fantasies shouldn't. I love Jerry. Not Ray. Sure, he's hot and when he sings something inside me goes all gooey, but . . .

"Just relax, Glory. Sit." Ray managed to get us both on the same bench. "Man, I'll never get used to this not eating or drinking thing. This is where I'd be pouring the champagne, pulling out the chocolate truffles or the caviar." He laughed. "You want to bite me?"

"Now who needs to relax?" I sighed and kicked off my gold sandals. "This is nice, Ray. But I hope you don't think—"

"Look at me, Glory. Then you'll know exactly what I'm thinking." Ray put his fingers on my chin.

I wasn't going to do it. This was probably all about gratitude. The song. Now the fake romantic moves.

"Stop, Ray. I've got a guy. Jeremy Blade. He'd tear your head off if he thought you were trying to move in on his woman." I finally looked at Ray.

"I don't believe for one minute that you 'belong' to any man, Gloriana St. Clair." Ray grinned, his teeth white, his eyes brilliant in the candlelight. "Are you afraid of me?"

"Excuse me?" I knew he was trying to manipulate me. Knew it. But . . .

"If I kiss you, are you afraid you'll want more? Afraid you'll forget Blade and want to crawl into my bed? Vampire sex, Glory. I haven't had it yet." He leaned closer and touched the vein throbbing in my neck. "I've been waiting for *you*."

"Don't." I sighed the word as his lips replaced his finger-tip. Oh, but I could smell him, his rich blood, what I'd always considered ordinary, O positive, but somehow it called to me like the most exotic of brews. "You kissed me once, then scrubbed your mouth because . . ." I couldn't remember what the hell I was trying to say because Ray's mouth moved up to the corner of mine.

"I was an ass. In shock about the vampire thing. Let me try again. Please." He covered my lips with his, tasting me, offering me a chance to taste him. He pulled me against him until we were breathing together, one hand in my hair, the other suddenly busy with my bra strap.

Sanity whispered that this had gone far enough. I actually listened and gently pushed Ray away.

"I've got to get back. To Jerry." I slipped on my sandals, then stood and wrapped my cloak around me.

"I'm not giving up, Glory." Ray blew out the candles, one by one, until we were in total darkness except for the glow of the small heater.

I put my hand on his arm as he helped me down the steps and onto the brick path that led back to the terrace. "Jerry and I are pretty solid, Ray. Don't save your vampire virginity for me."

He slid his arms around me and held me for a minute, his chin on my hair. He hummed my song, like he thought his music might work on me when his words hadn't. I felt him pressing against me and knew he wasn't going to wait long before he took care of the whole virginity issue. I was flattered, flustered and more tempted than I wanted to be. And I was not turning around.

"Good night, Ray." I slipped out of his arms and hurried back to the party.

Twenty-six

Valdez joined me at the edge of the dance floor.

"I was about to form a search party." He sniffed. *"You been up to something with Caine?"*

"Don't start. He made a move, and I told him no. You happy?" I looked around and spotted human Randy stuffing a hundred-dollar bill into a silver donation bowl. "Oh, this is choice. Follow me. You're going to love this." I strolled over to Randy.

"Have a good time upstairs?"

Randolph froze, then turned around and smiled. "A gentleman never tells."

Valdez sniffed, then growled. *"If it isn't rat cat. Does the mistress know you're out tonight?"*

Randolph looked at me. "And does your mistress know how you and your girlfriend—"

"Shut your mouth—"

"Enough!" I stepped between them. Several people had turned to look at us. "Randy, I have a feeling Mag's been looking for you. And Mara. Are we allies now?" I smiled and waited for his reluctant nod. "I'm glad we understand each other. You get some information I need, you'll pass it on. Right?" Another nod. Oh, but I loved the power. "And Randy? Your secret's safe with me, no matter what. You ever need another job, come see me. Can't be easy as Mag's whatever." I put my hand on Valdez's head when he seemed inclined to put in an opinion. We both watched Randy disappear into the darkness to no doubt change back into kitty form.

"*Now if that isn't a kick in the pants.*" Valdez sat and scratched on his ear. "*Randy and Mara? What would Blade say about that?*"

"He will never know." I looked Valdez dead in the eye. "Now about Brittany."

"*So? We had us a moment. Won't happen again. Look at me.*" He slumped down on the tile floor. "*Look where she hangs out. With Will, Caine, God knows how many other hot guys. Hell, I'd be lucky to get play from a stray Chihuahua lookin' like this.*"

I rubbed his ears. "I'm sorry, puppy." And I was. "I'd like to be alone with Jerry. At my place. What if I ask Ray if you can stay at his house tonight?" I leaned closer. "And if you shift during the day while the vamps are asleep? Who's to know?"

"*I'll know, Glory. I gave my word. I'll keep it.*" Valdez sat up, his tail thumping. "*But I'll take the time with Brit. Here they come.*"

Sure enough, the entire Israel Caine contingent was headed for the door. Even Nathan, whose pale face meant Diana had probably had her way with him.

"Ray, could Valdez go home with you guys tonight?" I smiled, hoping no one was going to ask why. Especially after what Ray and I had gone through earlier.

Ray looked down at Valdez. "The old lady kicking you out?"

"*I was hoping you'd take me for a boat ride, Ray. Brittany says you go out on the lake every night.*" Valdez looked at his lady, his tail quivering. Which he'd hate if he knew he was doing it.

"Come on, then. We've got a couple of hours before dawn." Ray smiled at me. "Some night I'll take you out, Glory. Nothing like night water skiing, or we could take out the Jet Skis."

"You're going to break your damned neck, boy." Desmond Caine slapped his son on the shoulder.

"Guess it would heal. What do you think, Will?"

"One way to find out." Will grinned. "Nate, you don't look so good. What did Diana do to you?"

"What didn't she do to me?" Nate's grin was lopsided. "I think I need a rare steak, some red wine and a vitamin."

"Now you're being mean." Ray was supporting his friend as they headed out the door. "Dad can cook you all breakfast after I'm out for the day. Vampire sex really hot, is it?" He glanced back at me and winked.

I watched them go, Valdez close to Brittany. Jerry walked up behind me.

"You let Valdez go home with them?"

"Yep. I thought we needed some alone time. Your mother okay?"

"She thought she'd lost Randolph. Was sure one of the were-wolves had taken him down. Then Mara had disappeared. But they both showed up. Mara had been counting donations and Randolph doing his usual spying. Had some gossip about a European countess Ma hates." Jerry hugged me. "I'm glad you're not that devious."

I didn't comment. "Then, come on, old man. Take me home." I glanced at one of Damian's antique clocks. "Did Lucky and Etienne take off yet?"

"To everyone's relief. I think there are at least half a dozen people here who owe her family money. She claims there will be another collector arriving shortly to take over where she left off." Jerry smiled as he settled my cloak over my shoulders. "You don't owe them anything, do you?"

"No, but thanks for asking." I looked around the room. I could see at least a dozen costumes that had come from my little shop, including a Spiderman that was about a size too small. That guy never should have been showing off the goods like that.

"We need to say good-bye to Damian and Diana."

"Diana is dancing with Igor. I don't think she wants to be interrupted. They're taking the tango to a whole new level. Not easy in a hoop skirt." Jerry chuckled. "And I'm not the only one here who doesn't bother with underwear. I could hardly tear myself away."

I slapped Jerry on the arm. "Where's Damian?"

"Here I am, my darling." Damian had changed out of the Elvis costume and was now a cowboy. "I'm Russell Crowe in that last western he did. Do I look dangerous?"

"Always." I reached up to kiss his cheek. "Great party. How do you feel about your sister's marriage?"

"I'm amazed. And pleased. Richard is a good man. Not an artist. Florence is coming to her senses." Damian turned and laughed. "Here comes the bride! But you didn't let me give you away! Did she wear white, Richard?"

Richard was wise enough to keep his mouth shut. Florence hurried forward. She *was* wearing white, a beautiful white satin slip dress beaded and embroidered from the plunging neckline to the short hem. Her dark hair fell to her shoulders, and she'd pinned a white orchid in her hair. Her shoes were perfect, of course, strappy high heels of pearlescent ostrich. She was glowing and very beautiful.

"Damian, you're not going to make me mad. I'm too happy. My roomie, you're not leaving so soon?"

"We got here a long time ago, Flo. You were late with your grand entrance." I hugged her and felt tears sting my eyes. "And you can't call me roomie anymore. You're going to have to move out."

"Richard, is this so? I have to move?"

"I've heard that's the way it usually works, Florence. But

I know better than to tell you what to do." He grinned at me but had his arm around her waist and wasn't about to let Flo go.

"This is your honeymoon time." Jerry dug in his sporran and came out with a set of keys. "I have a little cottage in Marble Falls about twenty miles from here. I rented it as a surprise for Glory, but you two take it for a week. Directions are here." He produced a piece of paper. "Consider it a wedding present." He turned to me. "Hope you don't mind. I was hoping we could use it to get away from"—he nodded toward his mother and Mara, who were steaming toward us—"but now obviously Richard and Flo will be gone, so I say we head for your place."

"I like the way you think." I tucked my arm through his.

"Thank you!" Flo grinned and kissed Jerry's cheek. "A honeymoon. I never had an official one."

Richard held out his hand and pumped Jerry's. "We won't ask about the unofficial ones. Thanks, Blade. I owe you." He glanced at the map, then at Flo. "You need to pack a bag or can we shift right out of here?"

"My darling husband." Flo looked at me and giggled. "Oh, that word! Yes, no, no bag. Let's go! Bye, Glory, Jeremiah!" She kissed us both and pulled Richard out into the night.

Damian turned to look behind him. Mag and Mara were headed our way.

"Run, Jerry!" I grabbed Jerry's hand and headed for the front door. No way was I waiting for Mag and Mara and whatever gloom and doom they were prepared to spread.

We ended up stalled at the valet parking when the two ladies and Randolph, back in his carrier as a cat, caught up with us.

"Are you going to give us a ride home, Jeremiah?"

"No, Ma, I'll arrange a taxi for you. Glory and I are going to her place." Jerry kept his hand on my shoulder while we waited.

"Here's my car. Good night, ladies." Jerry pressed a large bill into the valet's hand. "Would you see that these ladies get a taxi to take them home?"

"Certainly, sir."

I settled back in the leather seat with a sigh. "You were rather abrupt with them, Jerry."

"If I'd stayed, my mother would start in on me again about going with them to Paris."

"You're not considering it, are you?"

"I wasn't." Jerry shifted gears as we wound our way down Castle Hill Road. "Then Israel Caine sang that song and you looked like you wanted to crawl right into his pants."

"I did not! And I certainly didn't ask him to sing it. It was a surprise. The guy is a world-famous rock star. You realize how totally cool that was? Come on, Jerry. Who wouldn't be blown away? The Glory years. I was a freakin' inspiration." Jerry had reached the bottom of the hill, and we headed toward my shop.

And, yes, I'd always had a crush on Israel Caine. The guy was hot. I was a woman with urges. Naturally—

"You'd better block your thoughts, Gloriana. Your lust is showing."

I slid my straps down my arms and wiggled out of my top. "And what's showing now, Jeremiah?" I leaned closer and slung my leg across his.

He stomped the brake just as a light turned red. Fortunately it was so late we were the only car on the block. He looked down and growled.

"Oh, dear, I've become predictable." I stuffed my breasts back in my top. "Green light, Jerry."

"Shut up." He dragged me across the console and kissed me until I yelped because the gear shift was becoming intimate with my backside. I pushed him back.

"So, are you still mad at me?"

"If it makes you throw yourself at me, hell, yes." He put me back in my seat and shifted into first. "Funny about Flo and Richard. He'd told me what they intended a few days ago and swore me to secrecy. He doubted she'd really go through with it."

"Yeah, I can't believe it. After all these centuries."

"Think you'll ever take the plunge?" Jerry pulled into the parking lot behind my shop. The lights were working, so we weren't in total darkness. The alley was empty and we sat there a moment, my old Suburban a reminder of a lusty time on a hilltop.

"Don't know."

"Please don't tell me it's because the right man's not come along."

I could see his knuckles white on the gear shift. "No, I'd never say that." I cupped his cheek and kissed his firm lips. "I've known the right man for a long time. Guess I just need to be ready. Keep asking, Jeremiah. Maybe someday, when the planets are aligned, I'll say yes." He shut me up with a kiss. Jerry can be a very wise man.

Ray's Song for Glory

I always played it fast and loose.
Played it hard and played it hot.
Played in sunshine all day long.
I played it, babe, and then moved on.
But what's the use of stayin' 'round,
When nothin' lasts and just comes down.

Yeah, I was a shootin' star,
Burnin' hot and goin' far,
Risin' high and fallin' fast,
Always knew it couldn't last.
So I played the game my way.
Lived it full and for the day.
Loved the sun hot in my face.
That was how I ran my race.

Then one night my time ran out.
I thought I died or maybe not.
The world so cold, the world so black.
I reached for me, found someone else.
Where's the sun? Where's the heat?
Where's the man I used to be?

But then she came, soft in her voice,
Moon in her hair, ease in her touch,
And then she said, "Feel my warm skin,
See this world through my eyes,
There are things you couldn't dream.
Hold me and I will show you.
Hold me and I will take you
To the man that you are now."

So now I play it slow and tight.
Now I play it soft and cool.
Now I play long in the night.
Now I play it for a while.
'Cause staying 'round makes sense to me.
Yeah, you'll see me here again.

I wish to God I'd never died.
Wish I'd never told those lies.
Wish I'd never made you cry.
Now we lie so close, so close
That I see forever in your eyes.
'Cause these will be my glory years,
My glory years.
My. Glory. Years.

Read on for a special preview of
Gerry Bartlett's next novel

Real Vampires Don't Diet

Available in January 2009 from Berkley Books!

"Of course I understand. No problem. Have a nice trip." I snapped the phone closed and thought about throwing it against the wall. But at the moment, I loved my state-of-the-art cell a lot more than I loved Angus Jeremiah Campbell III, who in recent centuries has called himself Jeremy Blade. The phone rang. I knew who it was, and if I didn't answer, he'd just keep trying.

"Yes?"

"Are you angry? You hung up on me."

"Oh? Ya think?" I glanced at the three dresses I'd laid out trying to decide what to wear tonight. New Year's Eve. Yep, he'd broken our date for New Year's frickin' Eve. No biggie.

"I explained, Gloriana. I have to go."

"I get that. I said, 'Have a nice trip.' Oh, and be careful. Don't let a hunter shoot you down." My erstwhile boyfriend shape-shifted into a hawk to do his traveling. Me, I prefer first-class service or, better yet, the comfort of my own car—I frowned—when it was running.

"You're mad. But I promise I'll make it up to you when I get back. Drive the Mercedes while I'm gone. I left it in the alley for you."

Okay, that made me feel a little better. "But you don't know when you'll be back. Right?"

"No. Lily could be anywhere. All I know is that she's running with a pack of dangerous radicals. She's got a boyfriend who's set himself up as leader of the group. I've got to find her before she gets herself staked."

Jerry had just found out he may have a daughter, Lily. I personally think it's a hoax created by a woman hot to have him for herself. But until he can track Lily down and do the DNA thing, he's gone all protective father. Which is typical Jerry. He made me vampire back in the day, the early 1600s actually, and has been protecting me, not to mention playing the passionate lover whenever I let him, ever since.

"All right. Go. And happy birthday. I'll give you your present when you get back." I blinked back sudden tears. I do love Jerry, and I hated the fact that he was going to have to cross the Atlantic and land in the middle of a bunch of vampires who thought stirring up mortals against us was good, clean fun. I hoped this "daughter" was worth it.

"You got me a present?"

I didn't blame Jerry for sounding skeptical. My funds were always pretty limited. But I'd had a fairly decent Christmas season in my shop, Vintage Vamp's Emporium.

"Yes. And not just me naked on satin sheets either." Though he never seemed to mind that gift.

Jerry groaned. "Now you're making me want to come over there and—"

"If you're going to beat the sun, you'd better hit the skies, Jerry." I sighed and looked down as I felt a warm, furry body press against my legs. My bodyguard, Valdez, a shape-shifter with a little something extra. "Take care. Seriously. Call me every night."

"I will. I love you, Gloriana."

Now how could I stay mad when a reticent Scotsman busts out a declaration like that? "I love you too, Jerry. Happy New Year." This time I closed the phone gently. I looked down at Valdez. "What? No snort? We were getting pretty mushy there."

"Sounded right to me. Blade's your guy and don't you forget it, no matter who else makes a move on you while he's gone." Valdez trotted into the living room. *"Since we're obviously staying in tonight, how about a movie? Something with action."*

"Might as well. That's obviously all the action either of us is going to get." I scooped up the dresses, the best my vintage-clothing shop had had to offer in a size twelve, and hung them back in the closet. I took a moment to rub my cheek on the midnight blue velvet, which matched my eyes. Nice low-cut bodice. I figured Jerry would have had it off of me long before midnight. The red was made for dancing: swingy skirt, another low neckline. I've got the goods and know how to use them. As for the black . . . I liked the way it slimmed my hips, enough said.

Action. I thought about putting on my flannel jammies and really vegging out, but my roommate might drop in. Not that she was really living here anymore, but she and her new—I couldn't believe it—husband still had a closetful of shoes to pick up. I was sorting through my DVD collection and threatening Valdez with *The Devil Wears Prada* when the phone rang.

"Hello." I hadn't even glanced at the caller ID. That's how depressed I was.

"Glory, I think you need to get over here. Right now."

"Brittany?" I felt Valdez practically hanging over my shoulder. He had a thing for the shape-shifter who served as bodyguard for another vamp in Austin, a rock star who was turned recently in a pretty nasty trick. I'd taken on the role of mentor because I'd felt kind of responsible for his condition. Long story. "What's going on?"

"A party. Typical rock-star blowout apparently. And guess who's getting drunk off his ass?"

"Will?" This could be a problem. Will Kilpatrick is a vamp I'd recommended to serve as another bodyguard for Israel Caine. Caine is routinely hounded by paparazzi and girl groupies.

"Of course Will, but worse than that. Ray's drinking too."

"God, no." Ray—Israel—is a made vampire. Like me. Turned by another vampire. We can't eat or drink anything but blood. Alcohol can make us really, really sick.

"God, yes. He went on a rant about how he was tired of watching everyone else have a good time and how it was New Year's freakin' Eve, then he started hitting the Jack Daniel's. The mortals thought he was just falling off the wagon." Brittany sighed and I could hear yelling in the background. "Now they're all drunk and talking about going out on the lake."

"Keep them there in the house. Valdez and I will be right over." I turned off the phone and jumped up. Mercedes keys. I kept my spare set in a kitchen drawer. Valdez already had his leash in his mouth and was sitting by the door when I grabbed my coat and purse.

I wished I could change clothes. Put on one of those sexy dresses. But my snug black jeans and the low-cut blue sweater that matched my eyes weren't too bad. Not exactly New Year's Eve glitz, but when I threw a sparkly silver knit scarf around my throat, I felt slightly less pathetic. Besides, I was on a mission here.

"This is bad, Valdez. That idiot could actually succeed in killing himself, and he's supposed to be immortal." For the second time that night, I felt tears fill my eyes. For a badass vampire, I was turning into a real wuss.

"Aw, Ray'll be all right, Blondie. Probably have the mother of all hangovers; that's all. Let's go. This will be a hell of a lot better than spending New Year's Eve watching one of your chick-flick DVDs."

"You would say that. You'll get to be with your honey." I opened the door, and we headed down the stairs. As usual, Valdez checked out the alley before we ran to the car and jumped in. I felt a real urgency. I liked Ray and hated to think he'd end up breaking his damned neck on the lake. Vampires can heal from a lot of things, but a broken neck . . . Not sure. I'd hate to put it to the test.

I drove through the Austin hills to the area where Ray rented a house on top of a cliff, complete with elevator down to a boat dock. I pulled up to a circular driveway filled with cars. Bad sign. Since Ray didn't hang out with other vampires, this meant he was surrounded by his band buddies, rockers who were used to his hard drinking.

Brittany met us at the door. "I kept them here, but it wasn't easy. Hurry. They're in the den downstairs."

The den was a massive room down a curved staircase. A two-story wall of windows framed a view of Lake Travis, the twinkling lights of houses outlining the water. The men and women lounging on the leather furniture scattered around the room didn't spare the breathtaking view a glance. Music pounded from large speakers, and a drummer used his sticks on a black lacquered coffee table. Three couples danced across the tile floor until one of them broke off and headed for the stairs, brushing past me with barely a nod. They were clearly into each other and looking for a bedroom.

I turned to say something to Valdez, but he and Brittany were still by the front door, whispering. Well, hell. I guess I was on my own. I spotted Ray standing on the balcony. I took a moment to just look at him. The sexy heartthrob whose poster had stopped me dead in the middle of an Austin mall one night was not a happy camper if the way he was tossing back the Jack straight from the bottle was any indication.

I stepped off the stairs and headed for him when a hand shot out and grabbed me around the waist.

"Dance with me, darlin'." Will swung me around. He was clearly drunk.

Damn born vampire. He wouldn't even have a hangover. "Out of my way, Kilpatrick." I pushed him and he staggered. "Fine bodyguard you are. Ray's out there on the balcony presenting a target for whoever feels like taking a shot, and you're in here getting drunk off your ass." I gave him another shove, and he landed on a couch.

The idiot just grinned and grabbed the woman sitting next to him. She didn't seem to mind, and I turned on my heel in disgust.

I dropped my coat and purse on a chair, then stepped out into the cold night air. I closed the French doors and stood beside Ray.

"Rough night?"

"Not at all." He smiled his famous guaranteed-to-seduce-you smile and winked. "In fact, it just got even better. Looking good, Glory." He took another swig from the bottle. "You here to kiss me at midnight?"

Would you believe it? I felt myself flush like a grade-school groupie. "No, I'm here to keep you from doing something stupid." I gestured at the bottle. "That working for you, Ray?"

"Hell, no." He held up the bottle. "It tastes the same, but I'm not even feeling a buzz. What's that about?"

Ray might not be feeling a buzz, but I sure was. Inside, someone had put on one of Ray's songs. There were some groans, but then the lights dimmed and I could see people pairing off, slow dancing to the seductive tune. Ray sang with the kind of passion that made a woman turn to liquid right where it counts. The last time we'd been alone together, Ray had even made some moves toward me. If I weren't involved with Jerry . . . Well, Israel Caine was and *is* temptation wrapped in a delicious package.

I deliberately blocked out all sexy sounds—thoughts—whatever, and focused on the problem at hand. Ray was still